THE
WORLD'S
LAST
NIGHT

BOOKS BY WILLIAM JOVANOVICH

Now, Barabbas

Madmen Must

The Money Trail

The World's Last Night

THE
WORLD'S
LAST
NIGHT

WILLIAM
JOVANOVICH

Harcourt Brace Jovanovich, Publishers

SAN DIEGO   NEW YORK   LONDON

HBJ

Requests for permission to make copies of
any part of the work should be mailed to:
Permissions Department,
Harcourt Brace Jovanovich, Publishers,
Orlando, Florida 32887.

Library of Congress Cataloging-in-Publication Data
Jovanovich, William.
The world's last night / by William Jovanovich.
p.   cm.
I. Title.
PS3560.084W6   1990
813'.54—dc20   89-15635

Designed by Michael Farmer
Printed in the United States of America
First edition
A B C D E

What if this present were the worlds last night?

—John Donne, HOLY SONNETS, XIII

THE
WORLD'S
LAST
NIGHT

1

Beginning the second day after his discharge from the United States Navy on Pine Street in March of 1946, John Sirovich made the rounds of book publishing houses in Manhattan bearing a stiff red folder with a black tie string which he had pinched from the supply base in Norfolk. He wore his navy raincoat over a Brooks Brothers suit he'd bought for sixty-four dollars. It needed alteration but he wore it as was—he was in a hurry. Inside the folder were three letters and three poems, all "prewar" in origin. Two of the letters were from professors at the University of Colorado attesting his having been a junior-year Phi Beta Kappa, editor-in-chief of the yearbook, and honors scholar in history and comparative literature. The other letter, from the registrar at Yale, was proof that still awaiting him was a two-year graduate fellowship in English literature—won on his graduation from Boulder in 1941. As for the poems, one titled "Steeraged" seemed to interest the editor who interviewed him at the New World Press, a small house that specialized in political books. A stanza from the poem went:

Drawn from home, not native, Conrad
Sailed away to pacific listless places
Where men, devolving days, go mad
From muddling desires and losing faces.

This editor offered him piecework at thirty cents a page copy editing manuscripts, which is to say, correcting spelling, improving syntax, querying an author on inconsistencies, and, finally, marking the copy for the printer. This could be learned, apparently, by a diligent use of *The Chicago Manual of Style*. Before deciding, John returned to Macmillan on lower Fifth Avenue to talk a second time with a college textbook sales manager who had earlier offered him a sales job—eight states from Salt Lake City to Seattle and Salem to Bismarck—that was daunting even for a Westerner like Sirovich.

"It's a lot of ground," the manager had commented, "but manageable for a bachelor."

Not really so for John. He was a bachelor but one who might turn out to have a lady in tow. Nancy Tuck Bowen was willing to join him but, as she had declared angrily when they parted in Mobile, not as a sailor's girl following him from port to port— or, in this case, from one railway station to another through the Dakotas and the Northwest.

At the corner of Madison Avenue and Thirty-Ninth Street he was suddenly, shockingly overtaken by a recognition: for the first time in his adult life he could see future's end, when possibility might not play, when luck might become inessential. It was three o'clock in the afternoon and he had no place to go, no one to face, no one to expect him. He stared at the people walking briskly by, passing each other, turning corners, jumping the streetlights. He wanted, all at once, to run fast. Instead he stopped.

At the age of sixteen, in 1936, John Sirovich alarmed his mother as she pondered his pallor and boniness—collarbones, sternum, and ribs showed each time he undressed. He was six feet tall, destined to grow taller, like his father and many of the Serbian men who were boarders in the Sirović house, yet he weighed but 120 pounds. She blamed Ilija Sirović that John should look impoverished like the peasants Jadwiga grew up with in Poland or some of the girls who had worked alongside her in the weaving mills of New Jersey. She began to feed John double suppers, the first consisting of boiled sausages and dark rye bread which he ate alone on coming home from Manual Training High School at three o'clock. When John failed to gain a pound, she reproached her husband that their only living child was born in a coal camp where the wet winter winds of northern Colorado pierced the miners' shacks and only canned food was available. Between them there was no peace, only a constant attrition of feeling.

Conditions were better when they escaped the mines to Denver and Ilija Sirović took a pick-and-shovel job at twenty cents an hour. Without her boarders, they would starve, his mother said again and again in Serbian, his father's language, even when he became foreman of a street gang of four laborers. They dug the residential streets and lawns of houses to install "natural gas" just now accessible from wells in Oklahoma. For Jadwiga his promotion was hardly notable because Iliya still wielded a pick and shovel. It was not until after her death that John realized his father had accepted as a given that Jadwiga was right about most things. She saw circumstance plain, without fatefulness; and if she had hopes she never obscured her immediate view with expectation.

When John proudly announced to Tata—"Dad" in Serbian—that he had obtained working papers having attained age sixteen, and found a summer job in the Benjamin Moore paint factory near the Broadway Viaduct, Ilija was quick to realize that his son was not up to filling and pulling four-hundred-pound vats across concrete floors. Accordingly, he summoned Bogdan Perović.

Bogdan, who was a regular summertime boarder at the Sirović house, worked the mines on the eastern slopes of the Rockies. So that he could take advantage of the weather on days when he hunted and fished, he started the fall in Butte and moved southward a bit ahead of the winter, with the result that by spring he was in Raton, New Mexico. Fresh from Raton, he appeared on the Sirović porch one June morning wearing leather leggings and high-top shoes with knobs over the toes.

"What's wrong here? Jovan, you weigh less than a lamb and stand like a dead tree!"

Two days later, entrusted to Bogdan's care, John arrived in Thermopolis, Wyoming, a small town that was a workingman's spa, its two-story hotels holding tin tubs that drew sufferers of arthritis and rheumatism and lay the smell of sulfur across the town day and night. John had once before come to this town when his father had testified, improbable though it seemed, as a character witness in a murder trial. A Montenegrin named Slavko Kekić had exchanged curses with a man in a bar, left quietly to obtain from his room a pistol, and returned to shoot the man four times in the head. On the stand in the county court Ilija, speaking in his heavily accented English, had ventured to make a legal distinction that amused and perhaps influenced the judge.

"It's true he was insulted, and nobody should be insulted, but he did kill a man. So he should go to jail—but only for a short time. You see, Judge, he didn't hurt anyone because the dead man was a bachelor and left no children."

Four years later Slavko Kekić showed up in Denver and according to his friends looked as distracted and dangerous as before. Ilija deduced that justice, unlike revenge, had little effect after the event.

Bogdan and John stayed only briefly in Thermopolis. Beyond the town, northward, lay the ranges of the Big Horns. This was high country scented by pine resin and mountain mint and the peppery seeds of needlegrass—the right prescription for a boy of sixteen apparently on the verge of consumption. No doctor had made this prescription. It was Ilija's conviction that Serbs—both Serbians from Serbia like himself and Montenegrins like Bogdan—if they survived the repeated wars of the Balkans, tended to die of assaults on the body's bulk, of clogged lungs and stopped hearts.

They spent the night in the coal town of Gebo in a boardinghouse owned by Stevo Radulović, a man of forty-five who had emigrated from Montenegro with Bogdan in 1914, a year that began with no war. On the earlier visit with his father, John had been introduced to the ceremonial deference shown to men in Montenegrin families. Only thirteen years old, he had waited for the women, the married ones dressed wholly in black, to be seated at supper. But they remained standing until John's father pulled him down, whispering, "You must sit! They are honoring your manhood." Yet now he could see that this was no mindless subservience. The women spoke freely and with both humor and passion. A younger one had teased him: Did he enjoy good dreams? He wasn't sure. Well, it was a useful thing because dreams were the only vacations Serbs could afford. When the talk turned to the Old Country, the older women would speak with a measured fierceness about the enemies, all the vassals of the Ottoman Empire who from 1389 until 1912 had invaded and occupied Serb lands. But they spoke as bitterly of new enemies, people of the same race and language as themselves, the Catholic Croats, who two years earlier had assassinated King Alexander of Yugoslavia. John had never failed to sense his mother's disapproval of the sort of political declamation he'd heard in Gebo. Years later, after her death, he realized that Jadwiga, a peasant girl who had never spent a day in a schoolhouse and had never been able to read throughout her short life, had grasped the capitalist idea unerringly on arriving on America's shore at age thirteen. She had been thrilled to learn how to operate a machine in the Botany mills, then *two* machines on opposite sides of an aisle. She perceived early that money ought not be saved against bad luck or, worse, spent on ceremony or adornment; rather, it was best spent in favor of itself—as in, renting a larger roominghouse while subletting the smaller one you left. At bottom it was work she sought to make constant, not merely money.

As Stevo, Bogdan, and John stood next to the Ford Model A outside the boardinghouse door, Stevo's mother came out, stepped up to John, kissed his heart over his shirt and said, "*Bog ti bio u pomoć: neka samo Bog sačuva mušku čeljad!* God will give you aid. May God also keep the Serbian men safe."

As they pulled away, John was shaken and tearful. Fatefulness seeps through Serb idioms like blood through a bandage.

Bogdan had not intended to use the money Ilija pressed on him in Denver and so asked Stevo to drop them off at Ten Sleep at a lumbermill. If he cut timber for three weeks, he figured he'd earn enough to pay their keep in the mill boardinghouse and buy provisions for four or five weeks of fishing.

The mill foreman offered him a rugged section of the forest traversed with outcroppings of basalt edged like knives. This caused Bogdan to tell John in Serbian, "I may hand the *čuar* his head to carry home like a cabbage for his slut of a wife."

Years ago, when Serbs and Croats first came to America, they saw for the first time men chewing tobacco. In retaliation for being called "Bohunks" they began calling English and Welsh Americans in the mines the "chewers," hence *čuari*. Still, Bogdan admitted that chewing was clever because it allowed a man wielding a pick or shovel or ax to savor his nicotine without slowing.

Bogdan would pick out a white bark pine or a lodgepole, ax out a V-shaped notch, and commence sawing inside its crevice, pausing only to place wedges to keep the cut from closing on the blade. Felling the tree was not the most arduous part. He and John lopped branches, then cut the trunk into fourteen-foot logs that were skinned down the mountainside by a mill mule team. Whenever he grasped one end of the crosscut saw, John felt like a galley slave forced to a punishing pace; and at night in the boardinghouse he'd start awake from palsied arms.

At last, on the Fourth of July as the loggers slept, they took up their packs and began a looping trek to rise four thousand feet above Ten Sleep onto the rim of the Big Horn Basin. The great meadows below were bright with yellow daubs of gentians and larkspurs and the blue of columbines. Clumps of iridescent violets on rotted logs stood out from a mile away. As John paused several times just to gaze, he noticed Bogdan's impatience.

Finally they pitched tents, set a circle of stones for a cooking fire, and built a lean-to covered by branches to keep their flour, sugar, salt, and coffee dry—all done in a couple of hours. Then they began to fish. Each day they caught the legal limit of twenty rainbow trout from the fast-descending streams and Loch Levens from the lakes. They were alone except for a ranger who came by every five days or so and who reported that a CCC camp, in its third year of operation under the New Deal, was about twelve miles away. On the glacial Lake De Sneit, a huge sheet of chill water large enough for boating, there wasn't a single cabin or lodge.

It struck Perović that the boy was altogether inconsistent. He was physically strong despite his leanness, yet was uninterested in the ordinary tests of prowess, such as leaping over rivulets or stretching for high branches. He was obviously well-read but apparently uninterested in politics—despite his obvious pride in *Srbstvo*, their common heritage. As for himself, Bogdan deemed politics a necessary undertaking for his own reasons.

"A man," he told John, "can trust a friend and, just as easily, an enemy, but he needs to be wary of bosses. It's why we Montenegrins try not to salute."

Bogdan rarely spoke as they walked or fished, but after supper he'd roll a cigarette and choose a topic. Inevitably he would reveal a deep misanthropy. He admonished John that history was so full of misery that "in the mouth of a clever man" it could be proved that earth was fit really only for animals, because they were spared the curse of memory.

In Bogdan's village, Tuzi, a river named "Gun Barrel" ran inside a deep crevice it had cut into the soft white karst over centuries. "The *Cijevna* drops like tears and is lost from sight. Above it crops are uneven and few houses stand. If you don't starve you die of the wind. Here"—he waved with his cigarette—"the land is rich, but if a man settled here, he'd kill all the animals and then another man over what little was left."

"That's terrible! Why should human beings be made to seem so different? Man is part of nature, isn't he? He's probably punished and rewarded in much the same way as other animals."

"Listen, Jovan, calling something normal doesn't make it right. Nature impresses you because it's all around. But a mistake was made in the beginning. It's why religious people like Zorka, Stevo's mother, try to give God nice jobs to do—like take pity on us all. *Ali mi ne pripadamo ovamo.* But we don't belong here."

It was just before Labor Day when Bogdan lifted John to the top step of the coach car in Thermopolis. He grunted to acknowledge that the boy was heavier. John saluted Bogdan as the train pulled away. Months later he would recall the meadow floors, so densely covered by sage and sedges and unmarked by human trails. There was space, still, and time.

That same summer of 1936, Nancy Tuck Bowen arrived with her parents, Harold and Willa Ellen, in New York City to board a liner to France. They left Mobile on the LandN, stopping in Washington because Judge Bowen, a prominent Alabama Democrat, was involved in the reelection of Franklin Delano Roosevelt to a second term that fall. Nancy Tuck was eleven years old. Afterward a myth persisted in the family that her brother James was too young to take the trip, although in fact he was only a year younger than his sister. The truth was, James got along much better with their brother Blaine than with Nancy and had begged off without telling their mother that he had no stomach for arguments over where to go sightseeing, or when to leave once they arrived. He accepted that his sister was his father's favorite and guessed, accurately, that he'd lose disputes of that sort. As for Blaine, now fifteen, there was no myth. His grades in prep school in Mobile had been so low in tenth grade that he was obliged to endure summer make-up classes. His father could get him into Princeton, but his grade average had to be at least a B-minus—lower than that and the admissions office could decline even a family of Princeton men. While James spent most of the summer up-country on the Alabama River fishing and roughhousing with his cousins, Blaine was in the large house on Beaulieu Street alone except for the servants. There he discovered the sweet uses of privacy by inviting agreeable girls to the shaded lawns and rooms during the long afternoons.

Two days in Washington served to impress on Nancy that her father was influential beyond Mobile. His being a United States district judge was of course noteworthy to an eleven-year-old; and she knew that an earlier Bowen had been a congressman. Wealth played no part in her impression because the subject of money was never raised in the household, even though the Bowens had been landowners and timber shippers for generations and the Tucks were once among the largest cotton growers on the Alabama River. The second morning of their visit Harold Bowen called on the President, and that evening at their hotel, the Hay-Adams, he entertained William Brockman Bankhead, who had just that week become Speaker of the House. Nancy liked Speaker Bankhead, who patted her head several times and called her mother "Miss Willa Ellen" and seemed not merely conventionally congenial. Their single evening in New York they saw the Speaker's daughter Tallulah in a play on Broadway and were invited backstage to greet her. She was hardly taller than Nancy and held both her head and cigarette holder high, tossing her hair whenever she laughed. Nancy later recalled that her voice was hoarse and the holder black and incised with silver and green gemstones.

The Bowens sailed on the *Paris*. On the dock at Le Havre, Harold picked flowers, calling them by their French names, and not only that, his good French enabled him to outwit a porter who had claimed too much fare. Willa Ellen was set to pondering over Harold's fluency. Had he learned his proficiency from French girls while serving in Pershing's Expeditionary Forces in 1918 and 1919? He said he'd twice been in Paris on long leaves from General MacArthur's Forty-Second Division, which drew "occupation duty" after the war. Her sister Jane had said that a foreign language was best learned from a lover—she had said, actually, "live-in beau." How was it Jane knew such things? In any event, while Willa Ellen had been a virgin when she married Harold, she'd not expected him to be so. That her husband had never been in love before, she was certain: their early affection was awkward but genuine, and it had never failed to be refreshed without their resorting to nostalgia. Willa Ellen, who was not a confidante of her husband's thoughts, was a sure student of his feelings.

On the boat train to England Willa Ellen was unnerved by the presence of life preservers in their sleeping car, and perhaps for that reason failed to warn Nancy Tuck against overeating at dinner an hour out of Paris. She fell sick from indigestion—too many quenelles—but it was Harold's efficiency that avoided a crisis. He brought an English doctor from another car, an elderly man who peered into Nancy's throat and palpated her belly. He used the term "palpate" in explaining, after pressing her abdomen with his hands, her condition as not serious. Nancy was to treasure the word like a memento of her tour. She used it only once. One night in her sorority house at the University of Alabama when she was eighteen, she was obliged to fend off a senior football hero who was feeling her up. Finally she whispered, "You're palpating!" He had at once jumped up and examined his white twill pants anxiously—and for him the moment was lost.

Judge Bowen's reason for undertaking a long and expensive overseas tour was mainly a desire to revisit the scenes of his soldiering days. He also hoped his daughter would accrue a measure of sophistication from the many tours of France, Bavaria, Italy, and Switzerland. How much you learned and how much you revealed was always a nice balance in a society where pretense was common. Some friends of his own age—R. J. Fredericks came to mind—were better informed than they admitted, fearing that knowledge somehow aroused distrust. Others were ignorant but considered themselves exempted from any sort of test by their fortunes or their genealogy. Nancy Tuck, he knew, regarded him as the brightest and best-read man in Alabama—or the world.

Harold Bowen was able, he thought, to avoid having to pretend to either more or less than he actually knew of affairs. Over the years he had developed and refined two styles of communication. In District Court Judge Bowen wrote learnedly and even elegantly; outside, he had made himself a reliable and largely uncritical listener. Officials and party bosses regarded the judge as "sound," a man of discretion who could confirm what was happening because he was "in touch." Moreover, Harold Bowen recognized that his not wanting to leave the bench, which for him was a haven, was regarded as a working self-sacrifice by those congressmen and senators whose positions he did not threaten. None of this could ever be said to his children, least of all Nancy, because she saw him as—exactly what? Perdurably right? Constantly and faithfully informed?

Standing in Green Park he watched with pride as his wife and daughter made their way to gaze at the guards and gates of Buckingham Palace. Willa Ellen eased the elastic on her child's puff sleeves and declared, "You can see, Nancy Tuck, there are people everywhere who have never heard of Mobile."

Harold laughed. His wife had chosen a most insular place to make her point.

CHAPTER

2

In early June of 1945 John Sirovich was, at twenty-five, in full form, six feet three and two hundred pounds. He sat on a Louisville and Nashville train on his way from Norfolk to Mobile wearing a naval uniform bearing the two and one-half stripes of a lieutenant commander and the oak leaf cluster insignia of the Supply Corps. It was not unusual for an officer to travel alone— not part of any unit or group—from one stateside post to another. He'd done so going from Denver to the air station in San Diego and later to Galveston, and then after sea duty from Boston to Norfolk. Now he chose, eccentrically, to make of his solitude a typicality. In general he believed that the things that happened to a man were like the man himself. People who drown are the sort of people who fall off docks. He had first formulated this principle of sorts the summer of 1941 in San Diego, while working at the Hotel del Coronado, when he told it to a girl who had fallen in love with him while married to an unfaithful man. It was a terrible irony, he realized later, that after he left the city he'd never seen her again or even written her.

Fancifully he wondered, as he sat in the Pullman and stared out the dirty window, if solitude, *his* solitude, could become a destination and not merely a temporary condition. He might arrive in Mobile to find the city of seventy-five thousand wholly deserted—all the men, women, and children fled as if from a plague or a rumor. A moment later Sirovich's bizarre notion was confuted as the tracks ran alongside the broad Mobile River and on the far shore he could see the white numerals on the bows of navy ships with both sailors and civilians working on the main decks. Closer and below, a series of tar-papered shacks ran by, black children's faces visible at their doors and windows.

Sirovich stepped down from the train and inserted a five-dollar bill, like a playing card, in the white jacket pocket of the Pullman porter. Behind the station he could see an unused wharf with large lead-colored bollards. On the platform were baggage wagons whose hard rubber wheels were painted red for no sensible reason. The train tracks were like steel ribbons bordered by wood which separated the station from the downtown. Sirovich entered a telephone booth marked U.S. NAVY CALLS ONLY and asked for a ride, then waited, staring at the street. It was paved with six-by-six splintered and bleached planks that reached the doorways of shops and small warehouses opposite without the intervention of curbs or sidewalks. Mobile was a very old city.

Soon a navy jeep—his ride—came into view and Sirovich climbed aboard. Right off, however, he felt things had gone awry, as if he'd willed them so. He had unwisely chosen to wear blues—rejecting whites as too dressed up and khakis as too plain. The double-breasted uniform of serge cloth was winter wear, and even the motion of the jeep did little to relieve his sweating. Inside the navy main office, he found a yeoman of a breed known to every sailor, the scribe who can harass others with nothing heavier than a piece of paper. This one was also an actor. He lighted a cigarette as he flipped through the lieutenant commander's order packet and yawned when eight bells sounded, the end of his watch.

"Let me see. 'Sire-vits.'"

"It's *Seer-oh-vitch*."

"Whatever. Supply? We've got five supply officers at the station and none has orders to be replaced."

"Does Roan Island's navy office come under this command?"

"No."

"Roan Island is right there on my orders, isn't it?"

"Yes."

"Tell you what, Yeoman. Give me back my orders. Stand up. Put out the cigarette. Put on your cap and salute and say 'Sir,' which is closer to my name than your version."

The sailor rose in a half crouch, eyes kept warily on the big officer, and said reluctantly but slyly, "I don't keep a cap in the desk."

Sirovich was enraged, suddenly and thoroughly. He clamped the packet under his armpit, grasped the edge of the officer-of-the-day desk, and dumped it toward the yeoman, leaving him that way, forced to seize his side of the desk to protect his feet, arms strained, desk objects pooling in his lap, the butt stuck to his dry lower lip. Outside Sirovich didn't give him another thought—his rage had been blown out, as an explosion will extinguish its own flames. On the motor launch crossing the Mobile River, he recognized that nothing travels faster than bad news. The boatswain didn't speak and when Sirovich stepped onto the grid bottom of a gangway leading to a pier, he barely had time to catch up his bags before the boatswain gunned the launch away. On the opposite side of the pier a Liberty ship was being fitted. It rode high in the water because so much of its gear was in boxes on the pier, and its steel plates, unpainted, had oxidized into red streaks like sky fires. On the main deck women in coveralls flipped up their masks to stare at the officer who stood awkwardly in a blue uniform they had seen only in the movies. They watched him stride rapidly away as if he had a clear purpose. Two hundred yards from the end of the pier was a two-story building. On the steps a seaman told him he could report topside.

Nancy Tuck Bowen was waiting for him at the officer-of-the-day desk, having seen him approach from a second-floor window. He was a lieutenant commander, all right, but what identified him was his unseasonable uniform and the two bags he carried. Why did he arrive by crossing the river? The normal route to Roan was through the Bankhead Tunnel under the river onto the mainland and over the small bridges across Mohawk Island. It was the route Nancy took coming and going to work in the office station wagon. His mistake, if it was that, had piqued her curiosity. He was a day early: his orders called for him to arrive on Monday, June 4, another difference. Was he in a hurry? That particular question, one of timing, nowadays concerned her mother. Willa Ellen Bowen, who still chafed that she didn't really know why her daughter had left the university in February after the start of the second term, kept reminding Nancy that many of her junior year classmates had become engaged at Easter and no doubt would, as was traditional at Tuscaloosa, become wed following graduation the next year. But Willa Ellen was adept at a double standard. While she could talk of engagements to her daughter, she was glad that Blaine was safe from marrying "the first silly thing who comes along." In this he was indeed safe—aboard Admiral Halsey's flagship in the Pacific.

It was not as if Nancy lacked company in Mobile. Every evening she was asked out by a man; sometimes two or three requests were pending for the same night. There were officers all over town—at the naval station at Todd Shipyard (where Sirovich had gone), at the station behind the Alabama Dry Docks, at the army field, Brookley, and farther away, the naval air station in Pensacola. She was so good-looking the officers were always surprised she was not engaged or married and, further, that she was a working girl—this status suggesting to their fevered male minds a certain accessibility. Nancy was big by Southern standards, five feet eight with full breasts and strong legs that were "well turned"—this a phrase her brother Blaine used to apply to other girls he admired, as if calves and ankles were shaped on a lathe. She was "blessed," her Aunt Jane long ago commented, with a classic matching of auburn hair and green eyes, setting off a fair skin.

"You're twenty-seven hours early," she told the officer as he arrived upstairs and dropped his bags.

When he didn't reply, she continued, "And you've already been in a fight. A yeoman from the Todd Station called, asking for the OD. He said he was going to sick bay because you wounded him. You threw a desk at him. Is that true?"

"Yes. It was not a great moment. I didn't like the way the office was decorated."

"Then some woman is lucky you're not married."

"Did you read my mail?"

"You don't have any mail. Don't pout. I read your BuPers folder."

"Okay."

"Is it a secret, or what, that your father is your only next of kin? I've got so many kin no one is next. Where are your khakis? You did come from Norfolk? You *are* the angry man in the folder?"

"I am. I am! I'm the right one, twenty-five, just promoted to two and one-half stripes, unmarried, and hot as hell in this uniform."

"Right? Right for what?"

He realized the banter had turned sour. He was no good at teasing, either giving it out or taking it, but on any occasion he liked to end with a verbal rally—it made him feel he'd done his duty, for one thing, and for another he was never quite sure how to say good-bye crisply. At that moment he had no desire to say good-bye.

"Can I start again? Is this the supply office? Where do I stay? Why is it so quiet? Is the war over?"

"Hey, hold up! You aren't in the right place except to report in. Your office, such as it is, you can find in the BOQ—and I guess you'll live there, too. It's quiet because it's Sunday. You remember now, don't you? You're early. I'll log you in. Chester downstairs will drive you over to Mohawk."

He was looking at her legs and her impractical, expensive shoes, brightly colored cloth affixed to thin soles. She broke his attention by turning on one heel so abruptly her pleated skirt rose slightly like a parasol opening. She walked back into the office, grinning.

Within an hour he was on the telephone, pleading, "Listen, this is the desk-thrower. I'm sorry. Can I see you again? Where do you live?"

"Off Government Street. Everybody in Mobile lives off Government Street."

"Can I come calling some evening?"

"Whatever for?"

"Listen, I really wish you'd say yes. What can I tell you? I talk. I play bridge pretty well, poker better. I'm polite to kid brothers and grandparents. I don't dance very well."

She laughed then. "This is not an employment agency, Commander."

"I'm serious. Can I explain? Something strange happened to me, our being alone on a quiet morning in the middle of a war. I really would like to meet a family. I've missed seeing adults since I joined the navy."

It was, as her Uncle Charles Hobson would say, "too clever by half." And too quick. But then, the last few months she had become sick of listening to dates talk—when they were discouraged from groping her—only of things they could touch: cash money, scarce automobiles, PX liquor, and cigarette cartons denied civilians. She decided.

"You're on trial. Come to dinner Wednesday night. It's my mother's night for paying off dinner dates and she always needs the odd man. You qualify, I think. Seven o'clock. Ninety-one Beaulieu Street, pronounced hereabouts *bow-loo*. Are you John? You don't look like a Jack."

"John, yes. And you're Nancy Tuck Bowen."

"How did you know that?"

"Chester, the seaman, told me. What's the Tuck for?"

"For my mother. She's a Tuck. And *she's* your date, not me."

It was time to hang up. From the age of eleven or so, she'd been cautioned against saying the "overmuch" remark. Lingering in a conversation was like having no place to go. She hung up without saying good-bye.

The space provided for the supply office was no more than a converted bedroom—*cleared* might be a better term. It held two desks, two chairs, a typewriter, and a filing cabinet containing no papers of current activity, mostly Supply Corps bulletins issued by Washington. The office, it was obvious, caught no more from Roan Island than the din from its shops and docks. No visitors or messengers arrived on Monday or Tuesday. Sirovich called the Roan office to talk with the CO, a Captain Morse, but couldn't get past the exec, a full commander named Harding who amiably advised him to be patient, only that. On Tuesday morning a storekeeper, third class, arrived to report for duty. He said he was told at the naval station that the previous supply officer and his storekeeper had departed three weeks earlier after a duty of only four weeks. Before them there had been no supply personnel at all. The storekeeper's name was Roy Braddock. He was about thirty, overweight, and given to sweating and looking worried. As it turned out, Sirovich was motivated to take a course of action by what he heard in the BOQ rec room. Sirovich found the captain of an LST whose ship was taking on ammo downriver at Armstrong Point. He complained he couldn't requisition supplies from the station other than food.

John telephoned Nancy both days. On Monday, explaining his lack of work and repeating Harding's response, she said cryptically, "I don't think patience is a virtue. Good luck." On Tuesday she wouldn't talk because she was running for the station wagon on its three-thirty mail run to the city. It passed the BOQ and like all the cars and trucks left a nimbus of dust. On Mohawk the sand cover was so thin that when it rained the red clay showed through like sores.

In the rec room Sirovich also met officers whose ships were in dry dock and began to hear more talk of the coming peace than of the usual naming of past posts, seas, ships, stations. It was, after all, a few days from the anniversary of D Day, June 6 the year before. A two-striper from Chicago told him that after the war a lot of companies "will go public to raise capital" and he, already a lawyer, wanted to enter corporate practice. Sirovich had no idea, but nodded his head. He hated not knowing facts, as he'd once told John Winterfield, the elderly man who'd been his friend in California before the war. Winterfield had laughed and said that at least the problem was not incurable.

Jane Hobson was curious. Her sister had called to say that, for the first time, Nancy had invited to dinner some officer who worked at her office. It was a genuine piece of news, minor though the occasion might be. Mother and aunt had been waiting for a break in Nancy's mood; and this might be the thundercloud that brought a change in the weather. When the tall officer appeared at the Bowens' doorway on Wednesday evening, he was met by Nancy as well as Lucas, the butler, and he was momentarily confused: he ended up nodding at Lucas and handing his cap to Nancy. Well, he didn't look like the sort of man who would go door-to-door reading meters or selling encyclopedias. He stood straight, a bulky figure with coal-black hair, blue eyes, a light skin, and a prominent nose between high cheekbones. He didn't smile, but then neither did Nancy.

Jane observed him as he stood with Nancy and her father in front of the fireplace, next to the shiny brass fender in front of which Willa Ellen and she, growing up in this house, used to lie on rainy afternoons confiding in each other. The house had changed little over the years. When their parents fell ill at the same time, Willa Ellen had come down from Birmingham where Harold was then a district attorney. After their parents died the house stood empty, but the gardener was kept on, and Jane's maids walked over every week to wash the downstairs windows and air the rooms. Later, when Harold was elevated to district judge and he and Willa Ellen returned to Mobile, the house was again filled with sounds.

Willa Ellen introduced the lieutenant commander to her senior guests, the president of the First National Bank and the chief counsel for the Waterman Steamship Company and their wives. She left him with them knowing her daughter would rescue him, which Nancy did after about fifteen minutes by offering to show him some prints of old Mobile, a good excuse, since the judge owned a fine collection.

"Have you figured out that you're not needed as a supply officer?" she asked him when they had broken away.

It was provocative but not hostile, John decided, and replied, "I figured out my predecessor didn't work."

"I met him a couple of times, a real sport. Commander Collins said he spent his time chasing war widows and betting on cock-fights in Chickasaw."

"That's not for me. I want to work. I've joined the middle class."

She laughed—for him a lovely celebration—and asked, "Where on earth did you get *that?*"

"I enlisted in the middle class in college. It wasn't a big deal. I doubt if anyone but me noticed it."

"I've no idea what class we Bowens, or Tucks, are in. Probably we settled all that when we were baptized. What *are* you going to do?"

"I hope to see a lot of you. God, you're beautiful."

Pleased as she was, she didn't let go of the thread. "I mean about the captain."

"I've got a plan."

"He won't hear it. Practice up on cockfights. Hey! My father is beckoning. You better be spanking smart. I told him you were."

"Commander, are you from the East?" the judge asked, shaking Sirovich's hand and at the same time drawing Nancy to him with his left arm.

"No, sir. Colorado. But my father was. The Balkans."

The judge smiled. Did this young man possess insouciance or just bravado? Insouciance was a natural trait, but few were favored. Nancy Tuck possessed it, as did Blaine, but not James. Willa Ellen did, more or less, but not her sister or brother. As for himself, it wasn't his place to say anything incriminating.

"Daddy, John has nothing to do in his new post. It's worrying him."

"Well, things are slowing down all over. Up to six months ago the shipyards were on three shifts; now the dry docks are on one and Todd on two. It used to be so hectic here that out-of-town workers rented rooms for half a day—those places were called 'hot beds.' "

"And what happens when the war ends?" John asked. "I mean, in industry. Wars bring work. President Roosevelt had another depression on his hands when Hitler invaded Poland."

Harold looked at him closely. Was he so quickly contentious?

"No one wants killing just to create jobs. I'm sure you are not putting that kind of price on prosperity."

"There's always a price. The communists pay it every day."

"Are you interested in politics, then?"

"I don't think so. I didn't mean to get into this so far, Judge. I just happened to remember arguing with one of my father's friends who was a communist. It was ideas, really."

Nancy was by now scowling at him as if his fly were unzippered. Had he done it again—been serious at the wrong moment? When was it the right moment? He wasn't any good at small talk.

He was saved by a Negro maid opening the sliding doors and announcing dinner.

Jane Hobson, who sat on John's right, asked, "How long have you known Nancy Tuck?"

"About a quarter hour on Sunday and no more than a half hour on the telephone since."

"Old friends, I see. Do you mind if I ask whether you were born in this country?"

"Mrs. Hobson, I don't mind. No, there is one thing. People are always asking me, because of my long Slavic name, if I played football for Notre Dame. I didn't. Yes, I'm the first of my family to be born American."

"My sister, Nancy's mother, and my brother, who lives in Anniston, are the last of the long line of Tucks. I mean, the latest. I'm a Daughter of the American Revolution, not to speak of the Confederacy, which some people still do."

When igloos of meringue covered with fresh strawberries were placed before them, John waited for her to pick up either the fork or the spoon resting above her plate and almost nodded, relieved, when she took up both.

"My husband is in Birmingham tonight. He's a lawyer, too. I mean, he's in *front* of the bench, while my brother-in-law is behind it. They were in law school together, two classes apart."

"Has he ever wished he were a judge?"

To this tactless remark she replied quickly, "Heavens, no! He's not patient like Harold and he likes to win—or lose. He says Harold makes everything 'moot.' It sounds like shushing some-one, doesn't it?"

"It means something is not yet settled or doesn't count."

To this pedantic attempt to make the conversation less familiar after his tactlessness she replied gently, "You're the first officer from Roan Island Nancy Tuck has asked to dinner. That's not moot, is it?"

He found Jane winning in both manner and appearance. She

was small like her sister. They shared Nancy's fair skin and thick, rich hair.

Nancy waited in the living room, offering coffee. John couldn't get back to her for another half hour because he was made by Mrs. Bowen to sit on a sofa with the older ladies, who said among other things that it was a shame he'd missed the flush of azalea blooms that covered Mobile every spring.

When he was free he said to her, "Your mother and aunt are beautiful women. You're lucky."

"They're tiny. I favor my father."

"I noticed."

"What does *that* mean?"

She turned a quarter on her heel so as not to look at him directly.

"Hey! You're getting sore. It's going to be Sunday all over again."

She turned back, and he found himself regarding her figure Picasso-like: the long neck, strong calves, the breasts outlined by the thin dress larger than he had initially guessed.

"No, it's Wednesday," she said. "And you're upset about Captain Morse. There's a fight waiting for you, isn't there?"

"I'm more anxious about you than upset over him." He stepped closer until his stiff white tunic was almost touching her nipples. "Can we have another date? Jesus! I need to see you in private."

Mrs. Bowen once again intervened, leading John to a very thin man who was at least seventy, a bachelor and collector of antiques. He said that if you lived long enough, even the housewares of your youth became valuable.

"The other day I paid thirty dollars for a copper luster pitcher that I once saw in Woolworth's for ten cents. Things become rare with age, and valuable too—just as people do not."

"How do you know what to save as you go along—I mean, what will be valuable later?"

"You can't anticipate people's tastes. Married people find that."

John was uncertain what it meant. It sounded witty yet subtly devious. But he didn't have time to probe, however indirectly, because the Waterman attorney and his wife offered him a ride to close the evening. They were staying at their summer place in Point Clear and said it was not out of their way to drop him off at the BOQ. When he saw Nancy standing outside under the driveway portico, clasping her fingers against her palm in a mute mocking adieu, he felt victimized.

Among her family and friends it was still regarded as mysterious that Nancy Tuck had left college in midyear, but her aunt was an exception. Jane regarded the decision as predictable, however precipitate. Nancy wanted to get away, just that. The impulse reminded her of a few friends of her youth who so passionately wanted to leave, to get up and out. It always irritated her afterward that they should presume that she and others who stayed behind would in the interim remain unchanged. It gave the adventurers a certain smugness—a sense of not really having missed anything at home, however little they found abroad.

When Nancy came down in February Jane had said to her sister, "I wonder if it makes any *difference* if you ever get to China in your lifetime. And if you did, would acquaintances respect you for it?"

"What on earth! What have you been reading?"

"Willa Ellen, you don't have to read anything right off the press about China to imagine going there."

She was half-vexed, half-amused.

"What has it to do with Nancy?"

"Something. I'm not sure. Nancy wants strangers to admire her. But it's well known there are no strangers in Mobile. And probably not the right kind in Tuscaloosa."

Willa Ellen dismissed this odd exchange by noting that Jane was these days rather wistful. What was it? Even a sister as close as she couldn't demand of a middle-aged woman if she was happy without implying the opposite. In truth, she admitted, you couldn't actually ask yourself the question without feeling a certain doubtfulness, like a speck in the eye. Long ago Willa Ellen had decided with a doleful resignation that it was unavailing to examine too closely the truisms of marriage and parenthood. It amazed Willa Ellen how inaccurate, or maybe it was ineffective, conventional wisdom was. She'd been told that it was useful to stay in touch with those nice couples you met often while overseeing children of the same ages, yet years later, the shared commonality gone, you found most of them quite uninteresting. Or again, her mother had often said that once you outgrew the needs of your young children and aging parents, both liabilities of a kind, you could spend time with friends more often—but you found it was time alone with your husband that you wanted.

She did not tell Harold of Jane's speculation about Nancy because he had refused, by indirection always, to involve himself in the issue of her quitting college, despite her being an A student and immensely popular. He accepted her decision as if it were one of several good choices. Yet had Blaine quit college in such a way—or James, who was at present a sophomore at Princeton—then the judge would have inquired first, then inveighed against youthful inexperience. Then again, truth told, Harold had not raised their children; she had. He wanted his children's respect and admiration and so had more or less made a trade: he hoped his leniency in their youth would gain their adult friendship. But such barters, like truisms, did not work, Willa Ellen realized. Her father had done the same, yet she and Jane had remained close to their mother throughout their lives, and although she saw a lot of her father when he was old, never once did she discuss anything momentous or decisive with him. What Harold sought was tranquillity—it became the stuff of his profession—and in some ways he made his wife pay the price for it. When Nancy left Tuscaloosa, he had treated it as a matter to be defined by women in confidence—like menstruation. If Nancy had confided to him, he had not revealed it to his wife.

Nancy had the habit of talking to her father in his study or, some afternoons, stopping by his chambers downtown. That was something Willa Ellen herself would never do. Her reticence was of long standing. Willa Ellen Tuck had left home at eighteen to enter Randolph-Macon but left in 1919 during the middle of her second year to marry Harold Bowen. Blaine was born late in 1920 while her husband was in law school. Twenty-one years later she overheard Blaine admonished by his father for criticizing his mother for not knowing that Axis was the collective name for their country's enemies. Harold had told Blaine that it was not only unmannerly, but also foolish to underestimate his mother's native wit. Even so, she recalled catching in Harold's eyes the pain of confusion when he'd asked her opinion of the dedication in his first-published book—and had realized she had not got around to opening its binding.

"When I was young," Willa Ellen told Nancy when she took the job on Roan Island, "young women were made into spinsters by the selfishness of families—someone always needed a sister's or daughter's constant care."

"My god, Mother, I'm not a spinster!"

"Of course not. And you won't be one. I'm just saying there's no *need*. Is there anything I don't know?"

"I'm not pregnant."

"Nancy Tuck!"

"I'm sorry. What do you want me to tell you?"

"Would you like to go to New York with Jane? She'd love to see some plays. Go shopping. It's not as hard to travel these days as it was two years ago."

"Mother, please don't fret. The war will end soon enough. Blaine and James will be home and we'll all be together."

War's end. It was on everyone's mind these days—as in earlier days. As a child Nancy had kept in a cake tin among family souvenirs a brass matchbox bought by her father on Nassau Street in Princeton. It bore in raised letters BELGIUM MONTENEGRO RUSSIA JAPAN SERBIA FRANCE and, centered top and bottom, IMPERIUM

BRITANNICUM and CHRISTMAS, 1914. Her father once repeated a favorite admonition of *his* father's: "Mind, Hal, don't stomp on another man's shadow. Everyone walks with a past." In the Bowens' past were four generations at Princeton, that Ivy League college most congenial to Southerners. Harold's father, Thomas Blaine Bowen, liked to call Woodrow Wilson "the failed president," but his reference was not to the defeat of the League of Nations by the United States Senate but to Wilson's botched attempt to abolish the exclusive eating clubs at Princeton when he was the school's president. Harold himself arrived at Princeton Junction in 1913 on the last day of August—too early to register but with plenty of time to examine unhurriedly the buildings and streets and shops whose names he'd heard since boyhood. The next fall the war was on in Europe, and he brought home the brass matchbox over the holiday. Alongside it young Nancy had kept a deckle-edged menu of the graduation dinner of her grandfather's club in 1880, whose courses included "Molded Salmon" and "Vermont Turkey Stuffed with Oysters" and "Quail on Toast." Blaine, who routinely teased her, said of this menu, "Nancy, honey, yo' folks sho' do knows how to eats."

Once Blaine had graduated, in 1942, he took a commission in the navy. Then, one evening a few months later it was not a teasing but a solemn young man in starched whites who now and then caught his sister's eye when his family sat with him as he prepared to leave for San Diego to join a carrier. He appeared much too thin, and Willa Ellen, seeing his neck muscles strained, hoped it was merely his youth demanding too much of his body. She sat between him and James and patted their hands now and then to reassure herself. James at sixteen was a sophomore in high school. He looked at his brother wonderingly, enviously. That evening Harold had shocked his wife. He said it was ridiculous how marvelously war could enhance a man's memory—much as poetry did, or old songs.

"Harold, how can you! Blaine could be hurt!"

"I know, dear. I must make myself clearer. It's unreal in a way. I've written two books on civil law and dispensed judgment on the lives of my neighbors. That should be enough for any man, shouldn't it?" He asked this rhetorically of Willa Ellen and Blaine, as if to plaintiff and jury. "Yet probably, as I lie dying, my final recollection, after my family, will be my days in France."

"That's unkind." His wife had placed her hand to her face as if to ease a smarting.

"Willa Ellen, I'm not summarizing *our* life."

It seemed to Willa Ellen that soldiering was a much too praised and too regular event in her life history. Harold had gone off in 1917 and Blaine in 1942, and, going back, she could count Harold's uncle in the Philippines in 1899 and her own grandfather, who never returned from the last winter campaign in 1864. Awake on the pillow the night Blaine left, she wondered why in the Deep South everyone was so submissive to the summons of war and why they so regularly volunteered. Of course they were patriotic, but maybe also they were too embarrassed to beg off because the government was a stranger. You don't beg from strangers.

3

On the Thursday following the Bowen dinner John was on the telephone twice to Commander Harding. His persistence won him a summons from Captain Morse for the next day. Arriving early, he waited inside the cafeteria, which smelled of rancid meat and steamed greens. In pleasant contrast Morse's office was cool and relatively quiet. On the floor were fans with safety covers; and the windows facing the piers were double-paned. John's immediate reading of Captain Morse was hopeful; and this confused the dialogue that ensued. Morse, a heavy man but not out of condition, was attentive and brisk on greeting him.

"What is it you need, Pay?" he asked, using the common nickname for supply officers.

"Sir, on Mohawk I can't find any records of what was done by my predecessor."

On his part, the captain regarded the interview as unnecessary. But his exec, Harding, had insisted on it. Roan Island didn't need a supply officer—as he'd told the Eighth Naval District Command in New Orleans when the first one arrived about two months earlier. It certainly didn't need a replacement. Sirovich, he was told by Harding, was chafing every day over at the BOQ.

Why didn't Harding calm him down, then? It was more his line.

"He didn't do anything. The truth is, we don't need another officer. There must be an oversupply." It was not said as a pun. "The first man, and now you, were sent by mistake. Somebody disturbed your file probably, and you got transferred. It happens."

"Sir, there's no supply officer at the ammunition depot on Armstrong Point. And I found out that the station over at Todd refuses to handle disbursements and family allowance changes for those ships coming into port for tests."

"Is this the history of World War Two?"

"Can't we handle funds and emergency supplies for those ships?"

"Have you seen those ships? Hell, they come in here so full they're like geese at night."

In Sirovich's jacket pocket was a list of items commonly needed in small crises, such as extinguishers, flares, small-boat pumps, medic kits. He now spoke of these without withdrawing the list.

"Sit it out, Pay."

"What, sir? Sit out what?"

Morse coughed, and the effort infused his face. "Let things be. It's now a one-ocean war. This old port will soon go back to sleep."

It was not credible! John couldn't grasp this suggestion in any systematic way. Not acting was justifiable only as a phase—when you stood at battle stations or waited your turn on deck.

"Captain, I need orders."

"You've not been listening. Now, I'm busy."

"That's what I want to be."

"Don't you know when to give up?" Morse was suddenly angered by this brazen refusal to desist. He was an engineer by profession, and his instinct was to put machinery right. Nothing could interest him less than the logistics of keeping busy. That must come under the title of career guidance, for god's sake! "Listen, I've been reasonable, but now I'm tired. You are one stubborn bastard."

"Sir, I know my father. Obviously, I don't know you."

"Goddamn it, get out of my office!"

A transcript of what had occurred would strike any senior officer as trivial and embarrassing. It had been all too sudden for them both, and each was immediately chagrined, Sirovich that he could so blithely say something so rude to a superior officer, Morse that he could lose his temper over so minor a nuisance, a matter he could have decelerated and for the moment ended by simply telling Sirovich, "See what Harding can do for you." An apology by Sirovich was not enough; and an official punishment by Morse was too much. They were at a stand-off, one not contemplated in navy regs.

Of his journey along the road past the machine shops with stacks of supplies at varying heights, the main latrines, the security quarters, and the row of small buildings holding the time-card machines and the pay cashiers, John could recall nothing he saw. He arrived at the BOQ with a huge stain of perspiration like an hourglass on his shirt and pants, the belt pinching between. As Braddock stared, he went directly to the typewriter and punched out orders on a form.

Braddock read them and was nonplussed. "What do I do—I mean, exactly? Won't I run into trouble?"

"Yes, you might, but just show your orders and tell whoever it is to call me. Be sure to find out if *any* supply officer, anyone at all, outside New Orleans reports to the CO of the supply depot."

The orders read: "Storekeeper Third Class Roy T. Braddock will proceed on special duty without reassignment to the U.S. Naval Depot, Eighth Naval District, New Orleans, on June Eighth nineteen hundred and forty-five, and on completion of his duty will report by sixteen hundred hours on June thirteenth to the Port Supply Officer at Mobile, Alabama."

"Are you really the port supply officer?"

When Roy left, Sirovich asked the question of himself. Motion makes direction. It was true of physics, so why wasn't it also true of how you acted? He was on his way to becoming the port supply officer *because* he had acted. As for his motive, no matter how Captain Morse might read it, John didn't seek revenge for his humiliation in the office on Roan. He wouldn't forget it, yet it didn't impel him. No, it was simpler and more profound. He wanted work. From the first day he had entered Twenty-fourth Street School in Denver, barely speaking English, he had been enchanted. He had understood quickly that schooling was a form of work, and he'd been glad of the chance to begin.

Less than a half hour after Braddock left for the naval station to pack his gear, John decided not to wait on receiving his store-keeper's intelligence. He put through a call to the supply depot in New Orleans, hoping the admiral who was CO was not off fishing for the afternoon. A yeoman handed him off to a chief, who handed him off to a lieutenant, probably senior grade, and soon he was talking with Admiral James T. Priestley.

"Sir, I need funds, trucks, warehouses, men, supplies," he told the admiral, identifying himself only by name and rank and "Roan Island."

"Take a breath. You have them in the right order: money first, goods next." He coughed. "A lot must be happening in Mobile."

"No, sir, that's the point: nothing is happening. My commanding officer told me to sit out the rest of the war. I'm in trouble."

"I can see that. How long have you been in, Pay?"

"Since February of 1942. I worked on PBYs out of San Diego and Port Hueneme. I was on an AK in the Pacific, at Saipan."

"I don't know your CO. Do your Roan ships use the naval station for supply and disbursing?"

"Yes, sir, but that's not the problem as I see it. Ships coming in for ammo at Armstrong Point can't requisition small emergency gear either from the station at Todd or from the supply office at Alabama Dry Docks."

"And how did you find that out, Pay?"

"An officer at the BOQ told me."

"Well, I can see you're not much for paperwork. Are you sure?"

"Sir, it can't be right to sit it out. We haven't won the war."

It was his only shot, and as was confirmed later by Braddock, it was right on target. An old chief had told Braddock that Admiral Priestley was too old. He'd been passed over for sea duty and sat behind an empty desk at the depot. The chief had served with him on *Arizona* in the thirties.

"Come ahead, then. Bring your requisitions. And cut your own orders. If your CO fights them, Pay, you're on your own."

"Jesus, sir!"

"Don't promote me."

Without telling Nancy about the events earlier in the day, John asked for a date. She already had one. He pressed: could her mother help him find a room in town? His need was convincing to Nancy. Sitting without anything to do for eight or ten hours was bad enough, but over twenty-four hours it became incarceration. She promised to do what she could. How about Sunday for a date, then? She was busy, which he didn't doubt, but this time she explained that an officer was driving over from Pensacola to see her—and this he found discouraging because it was so contrivedly explicit. Then she relented by calling back late on Friday to say her mother had convinced a Mrs. Winston, a widow whose grown children were no longer at home, that a bachelor officer in the house would be companionable. She lived on French Court, a better address in Mobile than most.

On Saturday morning Nancy picked John up in town, which he reached by hitching a ride on a station wagon that was returning to the station at Todd. French Court was a cul-de-sac where two streets separated by a grass mall ended at a high wire fence overgrown with wisteria and laurel. Decorously, Nancy remained downstairs as Mrs. Winston showed John a room on the third floor. She knew that from that vantage he could see the antebellum buildings of the Mobile Infirmary. She and her brother James were born in that hospital; and her grandparents had died there. As a child at Old Shell Road Elementary School she had read how the Confederate wounded, there being so many, had lain on its lawns following the Union Army's assault from the east, which ended the war in Mobile.

"It will be hot as Hades up there," she warned as they drove away. "If you don't brush your white bucks every second day, they'll go green."

"I will, too, if you keep refusing to go out with me."

"You've got worse problems, sport. Betty Howard, Captain Morse's secretary, says that if it weren't for Commander Harding you'd be long gone. The captain was all set to send you back to sea duty. Close. Very close."

"Stop the car."

This command was so unexpected, so peremptory, that she obeyed at once. Moments passed. He stared through his half of the windshield.

"Are we waiting for dark? Or for The Word?"

"No. I don't want to wait. I want you to be my girl."

He put one arm hard across the top of her breasts and with the other brought her head about to face his own. He kissed her very softly as if held by some restraint. She was astonished: this force of arms and the merest caress. Then he opened the car door and stepped from the running board as from a high ledge and shoved the door so that it neatly clunked. For no deducible reason, he began walking in a direction away from town. Nancy, annoyed, wanted to call after him something sardonically trivial like, "Well, shucks," but he was already out of earshot. He had not been clever, nor quite childish either. What was it? A whim, a *serious* whim? He did not seem to have planned this short scene, but neither did it seem spontaneous. She didn't know him.

He moved into French Court the next day early, arriving in a taxi with his two bags and one of the office typewriters. Incarceration at the BOQ had reawakened in John Sirovich a desire to write, as he'd done before the war—not only poetry but also a novel. His only novel had been derivative of James Cain and Horace McCoy and was more like a screenplay than prose fiction, so dependent was it on dialogue. This he discarded and had submitted for publication only his poems.

Standing outside the house while Mrs. Winston was attending the Dauphin Way Methodist Church, driven there by her gardener who doubled as a chauffeur, he saw a family across the court just returning from Sunday services. A girl Nancy Tuck's age, wearing a gauzy hat and wrist-length white gloves, smiled at him and paused as her parents went inside.

"I'm John Sirovich," he told her, crossing over. "It's my first time here. Hello."

"I know about you. Mrs. Winston told my mother, and Nancy told me. Nothing stays fresh in Mobile longer than five minutes."

She laughed and, to his surprise, put her arm through his and led him down the street. They were going for a walk, it turned out. Within forty minutes he learned that Rosemary Roberts worked in the Federal Building for the Maritime Commission, that her father owned a company that sold creosote and coal oil and the new synthetic fuels, such as butane, to Todd and Alabama Dry Docks and lumber dealers. Within a half hour she learned he was quick and confident but also reflective, that he'd been aboard ship in the battles of Saipan and Leyte Gulf, that he was going to write a dissertation on Emerson as a graduate student at Yale once the war was over but had to contend with the fact that "the war has spoiled fine distinctions."

The next morning he intercepted Rosemary as she ran for the bus on Old Shell Road and as they rode downtown extracted from her the promise to dine Wednesday night at the Admiral Semmes Hotel before taking in a movie. He was on his way to

New Orleans, he said, but would take the late afternoon train that day. On his return he found Rosemary a delightful date. She was a born listener and lively; and although not as striking as Nancy, she was not bristling with prejudices, either. To John she seemed quite willing to be courted in a hurry.

Two nights later she invited him to dinner, and from her father he heard of a Mr. R. J. Fredericks, a lumber dealer who also owned some coal piers on the river that were now unused. He sat on the left of a well-dressed middle-aged woman who held his attention with a piteous story of the suicide of one of her kinfolk, only to reveal in passing that she had in fact never laid eyes on the victim. It was ludicrous. After all the guests had departed and they sat on the Turner porch swing, he recounted it to Rosemary.

"I never before heard a story like it. It was confidential but absolutely impersonal."

Rosemary laughed and assured him such stories were not unusual in her family circle. Many families known to her parents seemed to be burdened with the responsibility of a drunken uncle or, say, a recluse aunt who might be grossly overweight—or a violent relative once removed. Later, they kissed deeply, and he felt her breasts through her dress. It went on at such length that his groin still ached when they met on the bus the next morning. Rosemary watched him walk gingerly, and smirked.

In Bienville Square, inside the largest building there, four stories high, John called on R. J. Fredericks. He was a man of about fifty who reminded John of photographs of H. L. Mencken, round-faced, flat-eyed, imperturbable yet mindful. On his desk rested a large brass bowl holding cigar stumps of even-layered ash. The desk was dusky, almost obscured by papers that looked as if they should have been filed years before. Fredericks was alone except for his secretary, a thin girl who sat at one end of the room glancing furtively from the platen of her typewriter to a notebook on her table, as though cribbing on a test.

"Commander?" An ante.

"Mr. Fredericks, I'm John Sirovich." Paying in, then betting. "About your unused coal piers. What if the navy took one and patched the broken planking and crossbraced the pilings and caulked the walls and roofs on the warehouses?"

"The navy stopped looking at my piers a year ago. What's happened? Have we declared war on Russia?"

Sirovich laid down his hand. "I need about eight thousand square feet of office space in town. The Maritime Commission uses but half of a floor in the Federal Building. Now, if the commission were to rent three or four thousand feet here on the square and if I were to take the commission's whole floor, then the United States of America would save a lot of money."

"No doubt my friend Mr. Roberts told you I'm one of the maritime commissioners here, and no doubt you guessed that I own the building we're sitting in." He reached for his hat. "And how much rent will the navy pay?"

"That's one card too many, Mr. Fredericks. After all, you do keep the restoration improvements on the piers after the war."

"Damned little coal will be shipped out of this old town again," RJ said. "But no mind. What do you say we take a walk in this unholy heat? We might just pass the Fredericks Lumber Company."

Once again, as in California with John Winterfield and as with all the friends of his father and the boarders in the Sirović houses throughout his early years, John felt at ease with men older than he.

The negotiation was quickly concluded, which was fortuitous because Admiral Priestley proved to be prompt as well as profligate. Within a week ten seamen, six storekeepers, and two chiefs reported for duty, and within ten days over forty tons of supplies arrived by truck. The weather turned profligate, too. While they were setting up the warehouse and the office, the temperature was often above one hundred five degrees. Inside the warehouse the ceilings were stippled from humidity. John felt guilty every time he escaped to the office in the single building in town whose windows, each separately, were fitted with small air conditioners.

He hired a staff that for a time included Rosemary Roberts, who, like several other Maritime Commission people on civil service, had transferred to the navy without moving her desk. Although she worked for only three weeks, she became in that period part of John Sirovich's routine. When she left he missed her, in no small part because in the office she spared him the noisiness of certain Southern women whose greetings were like screams. It seemed to John afterward, when he'd left Mobile, that his days there were tolled by a series of familiar sounds. He would awaken in French Court to the small cries of wrens in the backyard pecan trees, and at the office the pace of work could be gauged from the familiar combination of typewriters clicking, file drawers rolling, and conversations overlapping at uneven distances until, when it was noon or quitting time, the talk tended to merge as people left the floor. And in the warehouses the forklifts would buzz like hornets; the metal straps snapped like popguns as boxes were opened.

When Rosemary quit, she informed John she meant "seriously" to become engaged. She had winked and parted her lips just a bit after pronouncing this. Since he'd not taken her out again after the memorable night on the porch swing—having since been seeing Nancy Tuck Bowen repeatedly—he appraised her anew, as if they had just met. She was blond, with striking gray eyes that in novels were usually called "smoky." On her last day he kissed her politely and perfunctorily on the cheek in front of the clerks in the office, but then, seized by the force of a sudden regret, he followed her into the corridor and grasped her waist and pressed, feeling her lips and breasts and thighs all at once. She broke away and walked to the elevator without looking back.

4

Nancy Tuck Bowen was puzzled by what she deemed to be his sudden actions. He had gone off to New Orleans on a mysterious mission—Betty Howard had seen copies of his travel chits—and he had called on R. J. Fredericks, this last reported by her father, a longtime friend of RJ. She called John the day after he returned from New Orleans to invite him to dinner at her father's club on Bienville Square—her home ground, so to speak.

John was dropped off by his storekeeper, Braddock, driving a shiny new red truck. In the soft evening he walked with Nancy down Government Street past the great old houses guarded by huge trees. She told him that Captain Morse was leaving that same evening on the LandN for Maine, taking his first real leave in nearly three years. Betty Howard said he'd be gone four, possibly five, weeks. John showed no relief on hearing this and left Nancy feeling in some small way betrayed, like a rooter for a player who offhandedly concedes a match. He seemed distracted, then eccentric. He spoke of Mrs. Winston's gardener.

"You know, he might read French. I saw a book by Daudet alongside a pair of drugstore eyeglasses on the tree bench. He'd been cutting the grass."

"How do you know it was his book? His glasses?"

"I don't. But then, Nancy, how would I find out? You can't ask Southerners direct questions. Everything here lurks, even facts lurk."

"Lurk? What a crazy word! What has it to do with Mrs. Winston's man?"

When they arrived at Harold Bowen's club, Nancy was scowling as she ran up the worn sandstone steps. When John reached the foyer she'd already gone into the dining room, so he waited for the steward to seat Nancy and then followed him to the table. She looked up with one arm hitched over the finial of the chair arm. She could not be insensible, he thought, that this gesture outlined her breast through the thin silk blouse.

"Do I sit down?"

"Sit down, John. I expect nothing much is settled between a man and a woman standing up."

"That sounds promising. Are you sore at me?"

"No. I'm wondering what you are up to. What happened in New Orleans?"

"I got the admiral at the supply depot to send me a lot of things: men, rates, chiefs, supplies, and an account number to draw money from your family's friendly bank, the First National."

"And you're going to put all that on one of RJ's piers? Except for the money which goes into the Federal Building when you get *that* arranged."

"I give up."

"Did you know that Rosemary Roberts and I were once 'pinned' to the same boy at Tuscaloosa—not at the same time, I mean."

"Lordy! Incest. I've been hearing gruesome tales of the Deep South from Rosemary."

"You're mean. I want to go home."

"I'm sorry. I am, really." He put his arm on hers gently. "Let's start over tomorrow night at the movies. Please don't tell me some hotshot pilot is coming over from Pensacola."

"He is—he was. I'll cancel him. There's a dance at the armory. Did you mean it that you can't dance?"

Before the dance Nancy's father engaged John in conversation as the officer waited in the sitting room. The judge had been told by Sirovich that he had small interest in politics, yet this seemed improbable for a bright young man. He sought to test it now. Nancy Tuck had told him of the scholarship at Boulder and the fellowship at Yale, and he'd already heard something of Sirovich's professional machinations from Henry Roberts and RJ, although their import was unclear. Perhaps, to round his own view of how things *should* turn out, Harold Bowen wanted him to be radical-minded and so, somehow, fulfill the inheritance of immigrant parents.

As they began to talk, Nancy came downstairs and listened uneasily. Her father was not being ungenerous, yet his questions clearly arose from the tentative opinion he'd expressed to her earlier that John, however "remarkable" he might be, was a show-off really.

"Are your people Democrats, Commander?"

"Neither one ever voted. They weren't citizens."

"But your father does have views?"

"Of course, Judge. He has opinions on what goes on in Yugoslavia, but a lot of the events are dated 1389 and 1914."

"And your mother? Oh, I'm sorry. I mean earlier."

"She believed in work, literally only work."

"Well, that's a political belief," the Judge said, smiling. "Ask any New Dealer."

"Did you know, sir, that Samuel Gompers was a Republican?"

"The founder of the AFL? Are you certain? It seems improbable."

"I think it's so. He said all he wanted of politicians was their support for unions and the encouragement of more jobs. More.

My mother understood that. More—it's like in *Oliver Twist*. I don't think 'more' is an ideology."

"And how does that fit your view of politics?"

What was the issue? Nancy had lost track, but the judge had not.

"Judge, I distrust politics because it turns ideas into faith. Maybe I arrived there by not believing in history. When I was sixteen I drove a friend of my father's all over the coal camps. He was a convinced communist and was recruiting men for the Republic in Spain. We argued over bumpy roads for four hundred miles. I ended up distrusting the notion that history proves or promotes anything."

"And what about this war?"

"I'm more American than seems possible." He smiled then. "I'm patriotic. That's political, I guess."

"Well, John, in the United States it's not because no one disputes it, but no mind."

At the armory, which they reached in the red shiny truck that Admiral Priestley had sent along with other equipment from the depot in New Orleans, the music was special: Louis Armstrong led a band with a few of his own people and some local pickup musicians. Nancy found out John danced eccentrically. He could turn left only, and when the pace picked up he often couldn't adjust. At the trestle tables on which drinks were set up, she accepted a rum and Coke and then two more. They sat outside under yellow bulbs that were designed to repel bugs.

"Do you think much about time?" she asked. "What happens next week or next year?"

"I think all the time."

"What will happen?"

"I'll be ordered out of town when Captain Morse comes back."

"Well, you'll go in any event. The war will end."

She paused and rested her head against one palm, her elbow braced on her knee.

"Daddy says a boy like you comes to town, changes some things, and then leaves without looking back."

"Was he passing sentence on me?"

"Goddamn it, John! Your conceit is something else. It must grow in the dark, like a mushroom. It hasn't got to do with you—he was thinking of *me*."

"I don't understand, Nancy. What keeps setting you off?"

"Listen, John, will you listen? When the war ends, girls like me will go back to Wednesday night dinners at the country club and Sunday night dates at 'nigra' places out of town. It'll be as if everything between didn't happen."

"Then leave, Nancy Tuck. All roads lead away from someone's hometown."

"That's not easy for Tucks and Bowens. We're planted. Daddy's brother is probably the only one who got away—he left Princeton straight for Italy." She tried to smile. "Of course he drank."

He reached over with a hand clasped lightly around her inclined neck and kissed her cheek.

"John, where do you go when you think so hard—when you scheme? Are you a schemer?"

"I go places I can't seem to find again."

"Nice ones?"

"Of course! I wouldn't think up nightmares."

"Who's in those places?"

"Nobody."

"You ought to put people there. Don't end up crazy, John."

At a stone bench in the Bowen garden that was secure from view of both the house and street—although never safe from mosquitoes—they paused, and then he sat while she remained standing. Without a signal, she unfastened her brassiere inside her high-necked blouse and stood motionless. He stared in amazement, then reached out and cradled her breasts through the thin silk. She sensed his surprise in the uneven pressure of his fingers and their hesitation before gently pinching her nipples. She felt no excitement—only the apprehension that she might not feel any. Then, when he kissed each breast against the cloth, she had the odd sensation that he was blessing a stole. Suddenly she felt betrayed: he seemed no more hungry than she. She backed away and ran into the house.

John walked to French Court through the silent streets, keen to the fragrance of crepe myrtle that laced the sour breath arising from the garden beds bordering the sidewalks. The night air was warm and, for Mobile, not as wet as usual. He paused on a street corner for a moment and felt bereft, fearful that he might miss the summers of his life. How did the opening line of Crane's "The Open Boat" go?—"No one knew the color of the sky." He decided, walking faster now, that he must allow himself openings. The fine proceedings of war had brought him to this city and this girl.

Seeing lights on in the house Nancy crept upstairs without stopping by her father's study to visit as she might on an evening when her mother was out playing bridge. Almost furtively she crept along to her room. Undressed, she sat combing her hair without counting the obligatory one hundred strokes, and in the freedom of this routine found her thoughts straying to Cassie Newhardt. It was six months since Cassie went away, ending up in New York, and she was no longer a regular target of gossip in Mobile. The inveterate Newhardt watchers had fallen into silence out of disappointment. No fresh news was forthcoming; and as Aunt Jane once told Nancy, it sets scandal on its ear when the wrong partner in a bad marriage commits the final treachery.

God knows, Austin Newhardt had been as unfaithful and brazenly careless as a man could be. Of those Nancy trusted, Jane's husband Charles Hobson knew the most of him but refused to gossip because he was counsel to one of the Newhardt lumber companies. One time, when pressed by Blaine, Uncle Charles had repeated the axiom "If you take the king's shilling, then you keep his secrets." Still, everyone knew that Austin drank and gambled and whored at places near Bayou L'Batrie, where he regularly paid the local police to bring him away from the companions he'd sought earlier in the night—when he was sober enough to name his pleasures and count his money. It was rumored he'd seduced his aunt, probably at the lodge on the Tombigbee River where it was said that the Newhardt men invited guests singly. Still, the Newhardts kept their position in Mobile society: each year they took prominent places in the Mardi Gras court and their philanthropies were reported in the *Mobile Press-Register*.

Cassie had been very pretty and never seemed tempted to wear vulgar shopgirl clothes and makeup, although it was widely believed that in her small town she'd not finished high school and had never traveled to a city larger than Mobile. Her parents were called "land poor," but in fact they were plain poor, a long-faded and impoverished gentry from upriver. No one seemed to know how Cassie had met Austin. In any event she had not complained publicly of his ways and had been gay-spirited, if not exactly carefree, right up to the day she left town. Nancy wondered as she stared into her mirror if Cassie had been drawn to strangeness—or if she'd run away from it. Had she exhausted the familiar? Perhaps sensation, a pressing passion rather than final frustration, had caused her to flee.

Nancy had no answers and was glad of it. Certainly she didn't want to flee like Cassie, even if she'd just an hour before offered her mouth and breasts to John Sirovich and by so doing promised more. It was possible she was giving herself the choice, even an obligation, to commence an affair, a way to declare herself foreign in exigent ways from her family and friends. Perhaps John had sensed an exigency; and that explained the hesitation in his fingers.

John struck her as being, in an obscure way, somewhat as she imagined Cassie, willing to accept everyone, high or low, without showing either respect or disdain. It could be that he was interested only in himself, and if he was tolerant of others it was because he was free of them. One clue, so it seemed to Nancy, was that he appeared not really conscious of his own good looks and made no attempt to show them off in ordinary ways. He wore boot-camp haircuts, starched-stiff shirts, ill-fitting trousers, and half-polished shoes.

She was not in love with John Sirovich and, come to judgment, not even sure if she consistently liked him. But she would keep on. As she undressed she wondered if her body would become the obedient ally of her present calculations. Looking it over, even as she appreciated the rightness of its proportions, from her narrow waist to her springy slender ankles, she was dismayed that her mind should proceed so far without waiting on her affections.

5

When John was in elementary school, the bodies of young girls amazed him even before their breasts filled and their buttocks spread. In the sixth grade he'd been infatuated by a girl with a graceful neck, a small nose and mouth, and short blond hair. She had appeared regularly in his dreams over the next few years after her family moved to Youngstown, Ohio—he remembered the city always, ranking it in importance ahead of Kansas City or Saint Louis. He had willed her to come back, imagining again and again how she would feel relief and gratitude on seeing him, on recognizing the proof of his constancy. In fact she *did* come back, enrolling at Boulder as a freshman during the fall of his second year at the University of Colorado. Under boughs bent by wet snow on the walks alongside the cold rushing waters in small ditches that irrigated the lawns of the campus, she passed him on the way to class. She seemed not to remember him. And he was too proud to block her way, to say right out, "I dreamt you back. You owe me. I was faithful."

At Colorado there were far more women than men in John's junior and senior classes in English literature, as if here, as in medieval times, the women kept the culture while the men were otherwise ignorantly occupied. These girls were earnest and, to his mind, much too genteel in their approach to art. Most of them questioned little and accepted obviously superficial criticism. They would no doubt attend more lectures in what he called their "afterlife"—when their children had left home and their husbands were financially secure. He took one of them to bed in the Pi Phi sorority house where he was head hasher, the waiter in charge of five other undergraduate men who worked for board. It had given him a momentary fright. He feared she was dying of asthma or some kind of shock, for afterward she lay still and seemingly comatose. Then she revived suddenly, looking up abashed, and he conceived the notion that for a woman sex was not a need to be satisfied, but a crisis to be endured. That she might have been a virgin, he had not considered.

John's recurrent if not constant ignorance of women partly attached to his aversion to marriage. It owed something to sharing a house with his mother and father. Not once had he seen his parents embrace—or even touch each other familiarly in passing. This coolness caused him to regard his mother as a figure almost without gender. At her funeral he was surprised to be told by several women how beautiful she had been. There were no photographs in the house of Jadwiga as a girl, and only one of her as a relatively young mother. It was as if his parents wanted no reminders of their past as they moved, a couple of blocks at a time, uptown from Larimer, the poorest street in Denver, to Arapahoe, then Champa, California, and finally to Glenarm Place, where his father now lived alone. By the time John was eight, he had been stricken with the realization that Ilija Sirović and Jadwiga Choparska were a wretched mismatch, their marriage an accident that had occurred to two otherwise talented persons. He knew by then that his father should have married a woman of less harsh conviction and less ambition, one given to eliciting and expressing feeling; and his mother, with her quick and clever mind that had had no formal training, should have remained resolutely single so she could work harder and still harder, unencumbered, until at last she owned property. Only later did he acknowledge that they themselves perceived all too clearly the mistake which for him was a painful daily remonstrance.

One fall afternoon in 1940 John had sat in Norlin Library watching the girls pass in pairs outside. On the table lay a book he'd checked out in search of a subject for a paper he was writing on Colorado history. As he turned the pages idly, he came upon photographs of the Great Coal Strike of 1913–14, which had made the little railroad junction town of Ludlow notorious—the only site of a massacre on the Great Plains not involving Indians. There were pictures of the tents where the miners' families stayed during the winter of the heavy snows, and over one photograph John paused, disbelieving, so startled that for a moment he thought he was hallucinating. It showed a funeral procession moving on a street with false storefronts. Two lines of men were strung behind a glass-sided hearse pulled by four horses bearing plumes. When he obtained a magnifying glass he had no doubt whatsoever that the third pair of mourners, their faces barely discernible, were his father and godfather, young and gaunt, wearing suits and hats but no neckties. Under the photograph the caption read: "The Funeral of Louis Tikaš, killed by the Colorado National Guard near Ludlow, Colorado, April 27, 1914. Commercial Street, Trinidad."

His father and godfather, like the horses whose forelegs were held stiffly high, seemed to float above the light snowcover on Commercial Street. It was a respite. That winter the Colorado Fuel and Iron Company had evicted the strikers from the company-owned houses—all the Poles and Italians and Greeks and Mexicans and "Servians" and "Montenegrans." John knew the story keenly, painfully. In 1933 he was the driver, his mother alongside in their Model T as they drove two hundred miles to Trinidad along the draws and breaks of the foothills of the Rockies, arriving in early afternoon to sit with the Cerwińskis and Olszewskis in a small frame house near the railroad tracks. Only the women were at home. Despite the Depression, their husbands and sons were fortunate in having work.

Anna Cerwińska's daughter was to be wed the next morning. Like her younger sisters as well as the Olszewski girls, she was blond, pink-skinned, and busty—and John wanted to touch them all. He spoke Polish like the rest and so didn't find it unusual that Anna and Maria called his mother Choparska, using her maiden name, or converted Serbian into Polish: Sirowiczka. Jadwiga had not seen Cerwińska in more than fifteen years; and only that afternoon did her friend correct her impression that as girls they had landed in New York. She explained it had been Baltimore. It was, John realized, another absurd result of his mother's being illiterate.

Jadwiga said, "When you and your husband, Anna, came to La Veta, it was the first we saw each other since working together in the Botany mill in Passaic. I was living in a house with one room and no water. That was before the CF&I chased us from the Big Four camp. It was October when we went into the tents. You remember, Maria." Then she said, "We slept in Ciotka Nowoset's house the first time we had to run from the tents because of the shooting. It was my husband's Easter."

Did Cerwińska and Olszewska understand that the known fact that the Orthodox—the Serbs and Russians among others—celebrate Easter later than Catholics, according to the "old calendar," was here introduced because her mother invariably interchanged personal and public misery? Such a conjunction would never occur to his father. One night on the porch at Glenarm Place John had sat listening to his father and Savo Lubradović as they related once again how they had timbered rooms three hundred feet below ground and drilled holes for black powder, using copper-pointed rods to keep the inserted charges from firing accidentally. As the talk went on, they were drawn back to the night when the strikers waited on the hogback in the mountains above Walsenburg and Ludlow. At dawn they'd been surprised to see soldiers of the Colorado National Guard just opposite, crouched behind a bluff.

"When the firing began," Savo said in Serbian, "we couldn't reach them with our shotguns, naturally. Even our rifles didn't reach—they were badly bored and the loads were undersized. After a while we stopped shooting. So did the guard. A guard lieutenant climbed out and paraded in front."

"It was a mistake," Ilija said. "A Hungarian with us had an English rifle, a forty-forty, like an elephant gun. He had only three cartridges and wouldn't fire them. Savo took the gun from him and balanced it on a forked stick. He killed the lieutenant through the chest at six hundred yards."

"Jadwiga," Maria said in Trinidad the day before the wedding, "it's only we waited too long. We hoped Louis Tikaš could talk to the soldiers and at least get the women out with their children. But my husband knew better. He said there was no chance. He was on the hogback with Ilija."

Jadwiga stood rigid, with her fists balled at her sides. Her five-foot-one-inch frame like a block of granite. She said, "They killed Louis Tikaš in the back. They set fire to the tents from all that shooting. *Bože moj!* My God! Putowska's children were in the hole under the stove!"

Her eyes had filled and John conceived the frightening notion that she was permanently blinded by tears. Olszewska went over to guide her to a chair and cradled her shoulders and said, soothing her, "Jadwiga, Jadwiga, stop thinking about your baby boy who died. Look here, you have a healthy boy. He is so big, so smart."

On the porch with Ilija, Savo said, "We came down the last day of April in the worst rainstorm I ever saw. The hogback was a waterfall. We walked in line to give up our guns to the U.S. Army that President Woodrow Wilson finally sent there. At least we didn't give up to that Walsenburg sheriff who was on the payroll of the CF&I. I piss in his beard to eternity."

As John looked out the library window in Boulder that fall and saw the girls passing in their sweaters and beads and skirts and saddleshoes on a high, dry day of Indian summer, he could not bring himself to believe it could ever be thought to be *their* fault—by making history a debt—that America before they were born had created its own Black Hole beneath the charred poles of Alcarita Pedregon's tent where the bodies of women and children lay suffocated, as did elsewhere Putowska's twins and his own brother, all of them dying in the din and dark. How could it, by any twisted logic, be called their fault? The communists, the Marxists, had it wrong about the historical succession of guilt. You don't inherit; and you don't owe the past—it is inhabited by the estranged.

At Trinidad, as he had sat watching his mother among those soft young blond girls, her eyes like blue beads and her head shaking, he realized what was so terrible: it was not that people will remember; it was that they cannot forget.

CHAPTER

6

The war lost stridency week by week, as became obvious in plain ways. Whole cartons of cigarettes now could be bought by civilians. Gas coupons were plentiful enough to cause the usual accidents at highway intersections. On the sidewalks men were wearing the badly designed veteran's pin that had already earned the sobriquet "the ruptured duck." A few discharged sailors came down to the pier to reminisce with the crew on duty, but it was awkward—they were out of it.

On the wall of the office on the pier, a warehouse chief had pinned the enemy identification chart he had brought back from the Battle of Leyte Gulf. On silhouettes of Japanese warships he had crossed out the enemy's losses in that battle: four aircraft carriers, three battleships, ten cruisers, nine destroyers. One might surmise that the invasion of Japan would result in fewer losses than the Normandy invasion, yet anyone who had seen action in the Pacific, like the chief and Sirovich, knew better. The sea lanes to the home islands of Japan had opened once Okinawa fell, true, but to invade the Japanese main islands of Honshu and Kyushu was another matter: American soldiers and marines would have to advance on beaches where Japanese soldiers would enfilade line after line, and once beyond the shoreline, the invaders would find lanes and paddies both defended and heavily booby-trapped so that they and the defenders would die together.

Sirovich believed there was a madness in the Japanese that was too easily ignored because scholars were inclined to speak of chrysanthemums and tea. This late in the war it was becoming known that they were exceptionally brutal to prisoners, as at Bataan, and fanatically ready to die so long as they could attach ritual to suicide, like the kamikazes after Leyte Gulf and especially at Okinawa.

That a million men might die and another million be wounded on Honshu and Kyushu was not a speculation to be found in the press—patriotic spirits must be kept high. But perhaps there was more to this evasion than a simple optimism. Sirovich, after all this time, could still not get a grasp on how Pearl Harbor had happened. The whole carrier fleet had been at sea while battle-ships rode unprotected at the dockside even as Secretary Hull was receiving threats from Japanese diplomats and the admiral and general in Hawaii remained unwarned. Sirovich had imbibed a large dose of isolationist cynicism at the University in Colorado and in late 1941 in California. He could not forget the fact that only a war in the Pacific could have overcome the opposition of Westerners to entry in the European war. After Pearl Harbor, all reluctance disappeared.

As its anniversary approached, John Sirovich thought often of the Battle of Saipan, June 15 the year before. He had stood with other officers on the bridge of USS *Zenith*, AK-183, just as dawn broke. It was the same time in Tokyo fifteen hundred miles to the north—0542 hours. Three hundred ships faced the shore while overhead the planes crossed, the F6F Hellcats making lateral sweeps, strafing the Jap machine gun redoubts, the TBM Avengers heading straight inland, whistling rockets at the low ridges behind the shore. At precisely 0800 hours, the LCI gunboats had churned toward shore leading the first assault wave to give fire support. For a moment they seemed to be stalled under the arc of the big shells fired from destroyers and cruisers and battleships. But soon they all started in, the LVTs and LCVPs carrying the marines. Everything appeared to be in order—at least as seen from *Zenith*, where the view was partially blocked by the fat hulls of the tank ships, the LSTs.

Then *Zenith* raised anchor to station herself alongside a number of amphibious water and ammo carriers about three thousand yards offshore. Thomas Nicolson, the skipper of AK-183, was the only support-ship captain to go ashore that day. He was an old hand who regularly addressed Admiral Turner, the commander, by his nickname, "Kelly." Tall, taciturn, over fifty years of age, he was a reserve officer in both world wars who never got around to telling his subordinates what he did between. At dusk on June 15, Day One, the officers and men gathered as he mounted the gangway. With his back to the shore the skipper said a requiem.

"God couldn't want it this way. It's out of hand. There are maybe twenty thousand marines of the Second and Fourth out there and more than a thousand dead and two or three thousand wounded. Our amtracs couldn't clear the Japs out of the ridges. Tomorrow."

These days fewer ships were coming into Armstrong Point for ammo and firing trials, but all were customers of the pier warehouse and the office in the Federal Building, especially as most, once they departed the bay, were headed directly for Guam and points east. Crews were relieved to be able to obtain cash pay and to attend to pay allowances for their families before sailing. The ships might be "full," as Captain Morse claimed, but a surprising number were by inadvertence short of emergency gear and medical supplies. The port supply officer, however he had been designated, represented for many of the ships and crews a last chance of sorts.

On Tuesday an LST captain showed up at Pier 1 to ask for T-beams and welding equipment. It was unusual that John's secretary, Carrie Brown, came in to him to plead the captain's case. On short acquaintance, she had become dear to Commander Sirovich, a gentle girl with a boyish figure who was easily moved to simple joy and plain regrets. On her urging he went down to the pier an hour later and there found Captain Larsen with one foot against a bollard, leaning as if to ease a cramp.

He was a couple of years older than Sirovich, a grade lower in rank but no less than master of a landing ship, LST-812, a vessel 320 feet in length, carrying seventy men and officers.

The 812, he said, was possibly the last warship to come down the Mississippi from the Great Lakes shipyards. At New Orleans she had been commissioned, fitted out, and sent in the Gulf for structural tests and firing. Then she had proceeded to the naval station before heading for the Panama Canal. At the station the main deck had been covered with forty large army cannon, "breech to barrel," Larsen complained bitterly, to be off-loaded at some Pacific staging area. His chiefs, not to speak of his officers, had argued with the station officers that the main deck would buckle under the weight of those guns once the LST hit rough water, but they were told to cast off. This young skipper had risked censure or loss of command by asking his help. LST 812 could miss the war! It was, after all, the second day of July. In the sea lanes north and east of Japan, more than a hundred LSTs were waiting to execute one more time the landing maneuvers the Americans had perfected.

Larsen, John realized, had but one chance. He must clear the bay faster than fate in the hope that once he was through the canal locks, he'd be ordered to off-load the artillery. He could then proceed, trim and seaworthy, to a place in the front line of ships. Behind him would ride the four lines of destroyers and carriers and the fifth, the battle line, cruisers and battleships. At that moment, looking at Larsen as he stared down the bay, John knew that Saipan hadn't been enough. He wished he could go, too. He wanted to see them go in.

Larsen, from then on, did the right thing: he didn't inquire about particulars or ask that his own men assist in the work. The pier crew braced the main deck from the tank deck with telephone poles that John bought with the immediate assistance of R. J. Fredericks. The poles were seated on six-by-six wooden platforms secured to the tank deck with welded angle irons; similar platforms above formed capitals. From a distance—say, from the viewpoint of a Japanese gunner on the shore—the tank deck would appear, once the bow doors opened onto the sand, like a forest of trees rising from huge lichen-colored boulders.

Larsen nodded as the gangway was winched up on Wednesday late afternoon. "See you around, Commander. Thanks."

Harding stood by Sirovich and said, "Do you think he'll make it?" The afternoon before, Harding had brought from Roan two civilian engineers and together they'd laid out the specs for placing the poles, factoring load and stress.

"I've been on this duty more than three years," he said as they watched the LST become smaller downstream, its masts lit by the late sun. "I've seen a hundred ships built or refitted. Two years ago we had our first sideways launching of a Victory Ship while a Mexican admiral was visiting the yard. When the chocks were knocked out from Number Five, that ship's hull hit the river with so big a splash I thought it would wash away the railway station on the far side. Then the ship bobbed up like an apple in a tub and the admiral, I remember, told me, 'You Americans, if you sink one ship, you just go ahead and build another one tomorrow because you can afford it.' But he was wrong. We have money but we make it work—money at ease isn't worth spit. Now the war's ending. Things change, John, and if that weren't a law of physics then Congress would pass it. Speaking of physics, you don't know a damn thing about it, John, but you did right to support the main deck with those telephone poles, even if they are a fire hazard. Wood gives."

He looked up. Carrie Brown was signaling hectically. What was it? She wanted him to pick up his telephone receiver. Her eyes were wide with excitement, and it was obvious she was tempted to keep her ear to the extension as Commander Sirovich responded to Captain Morse—who hadn't even bothered to ask Betty Howard to make his call.

"Sirovich? Who in hell gave you the right to commandeer an office and that old dock?"

"Captain? I got supplies and bank authorizations from Admiral Priestley at Eighth Naval Headquarters."

"All you have is a bureau account number. I can take custody any minute."

With his grip on the telephone so firm that his wrist tendons showed like ropes, John said nervously, "Captain, I'm holding eighty thousand dollars in the First National Bank."

"So?"

"Captain, I'd be careful over a matter of money—it's the business of the Supply Corps and the GAO and Congress."

"My God, a sea lawyer! I won't talk with the likes of you. I'm putting you on charges. Commander Harding will be over."

Harding showed up an hour later with two SPs, neither one older than twenty and both so eager that the exec had to order them to stand at ease in the corridor. Harding sat heavily in the chair next to John's desk and emitted a sigh that was hardly an indication of sympathy—more one of futility. The exec was by temperament more or less how he looked, trustworthy, a smiling man whose strong facial muscles and center-parted black hair seemed to assure others of his steady goodwill. Earlier, on an occasion before helping with Larsen, he had warned Sirovich that he didn't have to live by the nuances of bureaucratic behavior bred into career officers. Such officers left Annapolis for their first lowly posts, uprooting their families as they moved from station to station through the meager periods of peace, all the time living in fear of that day when they would either enter the elite or be passed over, and so lost to early retirement. For a reservist like him, no mistake could loom later in his career to ruin him—he was going back to civilian life. Regular officers like Morse knew navy regs like the minister knows the New Testament.

"You never gave him a chance. Couldn't you at least have written a report? You know, explaining your intentions?"

"I tried to tell him once. He wouldn't listen."

"John." Harding sighed again. "Why did you have to threaten him about the money? It's true that COs shy away from it, but *he* knows that. Why did you have to be right—about something so obvious?" He put on his cap. "He's calling you subversive. Jesus, he's using that word."

"Commander, don't let him fire all those civilians I hired here and on the piers."

"John, I'll try, but an inquiry will put an end to everything. It may be limited to an official charge like 'actions taken without the consent of a commanding officer,' and it doesn't seem to me like the captain would have a good case, but then"—he ran his hand over his face tiredly—"your admiral in New Orleans is an old Annapolis man like Morse. They'll not go up against each other over you."

After stopping off in French Court so Sirovich could pick up his shaving gear and changes of clothes—Harding told him to bring his whites, "just in case you're called up"—they rode in the navy station wagon through the Bankhead Tunnel to the BOQ. John sat with his hands held tensely under his thighs. His eyes and teeth ached as if from overuse. Not once in his life had he been accused of any misstep, not even at school.

Stepping away from the jeep at the BOQ, out of earshot of the two SPs, Harding said, "Let the captain make his own case. You talk too much. Don't help him make it. It's late. It's 1945."

7

Within the hour Nancy was on the telephone. "You're confined? You're in jail!"

"I'm back in the BOQ in my old office—only now there's nothing here but a bed."

"That's enough for a prisoner who's got a friend."

Would she really risk coming over? he wondered. In a town this tight, if a man sneezed at one end, someone blessed him at the other. That night on the stone bench had been no fluke. She had taken the lead in a contest where a man is said to be driven by the urgency of his nature and a woman held back by tradition. But she was no tease. Nancy was by no means like those heart-stoppingly beautiful girls in Boulder he'd known who wore fraternity pins as prizes, not as pledges, as many as three a year. Why would she come if not seriously? Her very appearance was compromising.

Driving through the tunnel she kept going over how she should present herself. It had to be right, else it might turn out tawdry or, worse, farcical. Just covering her tracks made her feel the melodrama. She had called Rosemary and made her promise to say she had spent the night with her. Luck was the best conspirator of all: the senior Robertses were spending the week at their summer place on Point Clear.

It was dusk when Nancy entered the BOQ. She pushed open Sirovich's door without knocking—that she had also planned—and while steadily facing him, she stood with her ankles braced against the outer rims of her spectator pumps. If he chose to be reminded of a Petty girl in *Esquire*, let it be. She had carried into the room a cake tin on which were balanced crystal plates, dessert forks, and linen napkins. As she stooped to put the tin on the floor and was straightening, John jumped up from the bed where he lay in his jockey shorts and clasped her low with both hands. He drew back, quizzically. She wore no underclothes. She plucked off one shoe and then the other, reaching behind her in that lovely motion only girls learn.

Undressed, she stood waiting. Driving over, she had convinced herself she must not in this moment act coy or rabbity. But now she realized it took brazenness to stand still and allow him at a distance to examine her purpled nipples and the nearly bare crease where she had scissored her pubic hair.

On the bed she lay tensed as he ran his hands over her skin lightly in what seemed a gesture of wonderment—as if he couldn't believe she was whole and present. They were at first too awkward. Then he slowed, waiting until she was breathing hard and until her lips, like a blind infant creature, strained forward. Soon they were contending for harmony, desiring equally but not unevenly, and finally came together.

"We're like strangers on a train," he said.

"We're not strangers. Think of something terrific to say—to a friend."

"You can't thank a lady. You can't compliment her, either."

"Why not?"

"It suggests she's experienced."

"You're not a virgin, John," she said sharply. "And neither am I. I'm wearing something. You didn't become a father tonight."

"Jesus! That sounds like the last entry in a log book!"

They were going to argue. She realized it wasn't true what girls said, that in bed disputes were put to rest.

"Nancy? Let's talk about it then."

"No, let's don't. About women, men don't mean 'experienced.' They mean 'damaged.'"

Her mouth was sour with regret. Tears hesitated on her cheeks. She wanted to turn away, but it would hardly seem to him to be a rejection. She was just as nicely rounded in back as in front.

"Well, sport. I'm damaged. You're my fourth." In the Kappa Delta sorority house she and her friends used to sit in the sunroom in nightly sessions wearing housecoats and woolly slippers, filing their nails in unison like fiddlers as they gossiped. Had the dean of women actually told a girl how to get it "fixed" after she was made pregnant by a Negro? When a girl was "swived"— as one of the sisters from Dothan kept calling it—did her nipples darken *permanently?* They would discuss sociology classes where they had heard how primitive peoples invented contraception and how Mexican girls of ten could become mothers—Mexico was always cited, as if sociologists were denied visas to other places. It was after such an evening, the talk disgusting her as childish for women of eighteen or twenty, that Nancy had decided to let some guy push on her bosom, work off her panties, and do it—zip, zip, zip, like having your tonsils out. Then, six months later at Anniston while staying with her cousin Catherine Ellen Tuck, she had attended a dinner dance at the country club. During a dance break, her date had got her down in the backseat of his Hudson. She was drunk. He'd plied her with heavy drinks and she let him. Back at home her cousin said admiringly that Nancy's date was a VMI man. Still feeling the drinks, Nancy misheard "FBI" and had thrown up in the toilet down the hall. As she leaned against the flowered wallpaper afterward, a conviction formed that she would be frigid forever.

"Two months before you came to Mobile," she told John, "I

met an officer in Gulfport who was on leave. That was the first real time before you. I know now because I had the same feeling, all in a rush. Afterward, when I went to dress in his mother's room—we were of course alone in the house—I stood in front of one of those full-length mirrors on a tilt stand. I didn't look dainty, so I decided from then on to cut my secret hair. That's it, John. No more, ever again. And I picked you tonight. You didn't decide. I did."

"Don't be proud, Nancy Tuck. Just be lucky."

In July, Mobile was intolerably hot but remediable for those who were fortunate enough to have time and excuses to escape. Almost to a man officers in the BOQ fled the coercive heat by seeking the fine ocean beaches at Gulf Shores at the opening of Mobile Bay. Other than the prisoner, the sole officer who remained in the building was an ensign asleep in a bathtub with a hunk of ice floating over his navel. A half-empty bottle of Old Grand-Dad rested on the floor nearby.

Commander Sirovich lay with his forearms wrapped in hand towels to keep from staining the poems of William Blake, one of the volumes Braddock had brought from the public library in town. He sought consolation, not justification; and he looked for assurances not wholly contingent on reason. His choice proved to be right. Blake was a magician who made real events epiphanous. He was to Coleridge what Melville was to Emerson, the dervish to the cleric, the sleight of hand to the laying on.

Morse had so far done nothing further, not said or written or delegated any motion against the prisoner whose only inkling that he was under charges was Morse's angry statement on the telephone. Even Harding, in escorting him to the BOQ, hadn't declared anything official. Exasperated by the lack of information, Sirovich tried to reach Harding by telephone and was told by his secretary that he was "down the bay with Captain Morse." Surely they weren't swimming at Gulf Shores! Not when so much was at stake! With some uneasiness Sirovich was forced to admit that Morse was a man with his own personality apart from his position. Why couldn't he go swimming on a hot day? He might be a fisherman or a sailboat enthusiast. He might grow roses in his backyard. Was he married with children at home? John fell asleep tolling such questions.

He was awakened twenty minutes later by shouts and the scream of tires on pavement. He jumped up and ran to the south window. At a half mile's distance there was a disturbance of some kind. He could see stick figures like puppets jerked into action. With his shoelaces flopping, his thumbs pushing brass buttons through the eyeholes of his starch-stiffened white tunic, he ran to the front of the BOQ and there found an army jeep parked with its engine running. Without hesitating he jumped in. The sergeant driver emerged to see his vehicle careening away toward the steel bridge and only narrowly missing pedestrians who seemed to be fleeing Roan Island.

John raced past the open-air shops where the machines hummed, power on but unattended, and pulled up at the main yard opposite the navy office. There were no uniformed sailors or officers in sight and it struck him bizarrely that he was late, as if to a ceremony.

All the windows in the Quonset hut marked "Payroll" were smashed, and through the door, hanging askew, he saw that the wooden shutters of the pay windows inside were splintered open. Behind a stack of steel plates workers were facing off against shipyard guards at a distance of thirty yards or more. A canister of tear gas sailed from the rear of a storage shed and was promptly picked up by a young man in Levi's who obviously had army training—he returned the canister with the stiff-arm motion, unnatural to baseball, used for grenades. John braked the jeep and now sat sweating, his arms held stiffly to the steering wheel.

Below the pier, to the right, about twenty Negroes, both men and women, clung to the pilings with only their heads and arms above the oily surface of the water. Others sat tensed on the edge of the dock, glancing backward at the knot of white men wielding hammers and two-foot wrenches who stood on the ramps leading to the piers. To the left, through a thicket of chairs and benches piled up against the windows of the cafeteria, eyes were peering. This officer's intrusion here was at once ambiguous and disturbing. His uniform and vehicle were symbols of authority, yet he sat alone, unmoving.

The sirens and Klaxons of police cars and fire engines drew closer, then the brakes of a police car sounded, pulling up next to the jeep. On the passenger side sat a man in a blue uniform on which a gold shield shone.

"It's okay now," he said, leaning out. "Everything's under control." Then he added, "It's a civilian yard."

"There are people hurt in the water."

"Did you see how it started?"

"It looks like a race riot. Maybe like the one in Detroit."

"Let's not be looking that far."

By the time John reached the BOQ a half hour later, pendants of rain were bounding off the jeep's hood—and off the cap of the army sergeant who came running out to claim his vehicle. There followed eleven hours of heavy rain. On the radio in the rec room he heard the Mobile sheriff declare that Providence had indeed intervened, and that "nobody goes completely crazy in the rain." A half hour later, the announcer said the yard was open and had resumed work, despite the weather. The needs, indeed the urgency, of wartime were mentioned. The demon of disorder had been caged. Soon the headlines would lose points of type and the broadcasts stop altogether. The police cars would cruise the streets passively, and at bus stops people would wait in their usual order.

8

Nancy arrived without warning at ten that night, carrying a small linen bag under her rain slicker. On entering she rattled her pumps against the closed door and undressed rapidly. In the bag were a negligée, slippers, a makeup kit, and three packs of Luckies for John. She had told her folks she was spending the night at Rosemary Roberts's, once again neatly retiring the only other girl John Sirovich had dated in Mobile. Excitedly she related events on the margin of the riot—fending his hands to get the whole account told—as found out from Betty Howard, who had the vantage of the captain's window, and from her father, who was afforded reports by both local and federal officials. The consensus was that a wildcat action had erupted among workers, black and white alike, outraged on hearing that their union officials had routinely agreed to a change of pay hours. They'd attacked the paymaster windows and then fought civilian guards; but how the whites came to chase and threaten the Negroes, worker against worker, no one seemed to know firsthand.

"Why did you go? Wasn't it dangerous?"

"No. I was a spectator, like Betty."

"Why are you so glum? You did nothing wrong."

"I didn't do anything."

In the dark he felt the whisper against his cheek, "It wasn't your fight."

The next morning Harding knocked at the door rather lightly, calling his name. John replied through the thin paneling that he'd meet him in the rec room; and as he kissed Nancy under the hood of her slicker he realized that the melodrama of lovemaking will out. Harding would have seen her car parked in front, recognizing it from those times she'd driven to work at the Roan office.

"You broke confinement," Harding said dryly, as if reminding someone he'd left on a Bunsen burner in the lab. "Captain Morse is willing to forget that."

"That's white of him. Jesus! What a word to use here: white!" He paused. "There won't be an inquiry?"

"John." Harding sighed, furrowing his hair straight back along the center part with his fingers. "You *are* a hard case. Of course it means that. He's forgetting your breaking confinement and all the rest."

"I appreciate your helping me, Commander."

"I didn't. You and Morse had it figured about the same. You risked going against the orders because it did help some ships at a time when the war's closing. He backed off for the same reasons."

Harding left dissatisfied. He wasn't used to speaking harshly. It had wearied him arguing the now-dead case first for Sirovich, then for Morse; and in the exchange he came to decide that he had less in common with either than they had with each other.

When John returned to French Court, Mrs. Winston pecked at his open door to declare her concern that he had been absent without any word for three nights. She offered to send the cook up with coffee, but John begged off by saying he badly needed sleep. He lay on the nubby coverlet with his hands pressed under one cheek as in prayer. Against the cinnamon screen of his closed eyelids he watched himself as a newly commissioned ensign standing next to Tata. Behind them, unsettled, almost escaped was the figure of his mother with her golden hair braided into a crown. Then he saw Government Street deserted of cars, as before a parade.

He awoke when summoned to the telephone. Going downstairs he heard Mrs. Winston exchange some courteous words with Judge Bowen, whom she called "Judge Harold."

Nancy's father was determined to make a fresh start with John Sirovich—to be fair. His judicial role gave him an opening. There need be no preliminaries, he was glad to note.

"Nancy told me yesterday that you were confined under some kind of charges. I'm glad you're back home. Is it no longer a case? Or can I be of any assistance here, John?"

Whether from sleepiness or because he was emerging from some other depth, Sirovich thought the judge was talking about the shipyard problem.

"Can you talk about it? Couldn't the case come before you on appeal?"

Harold noted that Sirovich was speaking somewhat indistinctly. "I don't hear navy cases, John."

"I mean the race riot, Judge. I was in the shipyard at the time."

"You weren't confined, then?"

"Yes. I broke a couple of rules. It's the riot I meant just now."

"Yes. Well. You can't have read the morning paper, I suppose. Twelve workers were charged. They appeared last night at Recorder's Court."

"What? The place where traffic tickets are handled?"

"It's the right place to hear misdemeanor cases. When you *do* read the paper, John, you might enjoy the district attorney's remarks. The fool talks of 'misdemeanors and felonies and treason,' an absurd set of choices. I must say I would like to hear— just once would be enough—a case of 'treasonable misdemeanor.'"

"What about the Negroes? Does it mean they don't have a case?"

Bowen hesitated as he lighted a cigarette. This was going to be difficult. He was sorry now that he'd called. He should not, for Nancy's sake or anyone else's, have attempted the role of Good Samaritan. After all, it was not his profession. Long ago, when he was a district attorney in Birmingham, an elderly U.S. circuit judge had paused in open court to admonish him and the defendant's counsel following a raucous exchange between them: "Gentlemen, there are times when, for the jury's and my own sake, I wish I could dispense mercy. But justice is the business of this court."

"I presume you're talking about the closing events of the incident, when some Negroes were threatened. Yes, they *could* argue that their rights were abridged. But it would come to nothing, I'm afraid, because the fact is that both white and black workers were breaking windows and fighting the shipyard guards, presumably allied in a common grievance. Now, one would have to identify those whites—let's call them 'the second whites'—who chased some black workers. Identify them first, then adduce their motives, then determine their actions and the consequences."

"That's it, then?"

"John, I don't know what you are searching for. Perhaps you think there's hypocrisy at work here. But *anywhere* in the United States, to make a case, you have to name a person and adduce a motive and describe an offense and apply it to a particular statute. Naming a color won't stand up in any indictment. Nor should it."

After a few more words the exchange ended. John sat looking down at the yard. The gardener was scissoring the hedges that boxed out the backyard from the alley and led to the wire fence next to the infirmary grounds, but he soon gave up as wet leaves clogged the cutting blades. Beyond, the alleyway glistened, the mica in the pavement made rich by the night's rain. It was frustrating—no, neutralizing, John decided—to hear something so momentous explained away by a generality. What was needed, the judge said, was detail. Yes, detail counted. It made a difference if you knew what was wanted; and particulars were crucial if you were in charge. It was said that Napoleon knew the first names of his sergeants. And John summoned to mind the picture by William Blake, who drew God in the morning, bent in a straddle with his left hand spread like a protractor to place man on Earth precisely.

9

Two hundred guests were invited to the Bowen house after the wedding service at Christ Episcopal Church, Saint Emmanuel Street, at eight o'clock in the evening on Saturday, August 2, 1945. Taylor Jackson Tuck did not, in asking his brother-in-law to act as host of the reception, have to admit that his purse had fallen a mite lower than his pride. The locale made sense in any event. The Tucks and their soon-to-be-wed daughter Catherine had far more friends in Mobile than in Anniston, to which they'd moved but four years before. Both Jane Hobson and Willa Ellen Bowen welcomed the busyness demanded by all the minute preparations, making things look fresh in the old house that everywhere held the preferences of several generations: picture frames of repoussé silver, oiled fruitwood chairs kept steady by dowels, porcelain boxes for diverse purposes or none, hurricane lamps with heavy pendants and translucent crystal shades. The house on Beaulieu shone from paste applied to silver, ammonia applied to crystal, wax to the walnut floors—the concentrated work of the five Bowen servants aided by two of the Hobsons'.

As they sat across from one another in the upstairs sewing room inscribing place cards by hand and telephoning florists and other vendors for the third or fourth time, Jane said to Willa Ellen once again that it was not unpredictable that her niece should have just resigned her job on Roan Island. After all, hadn't Rosemary Roberts openly announced her intention to wait for the right man to do his duty? Jane was dissembling for her sister's sake, however unsuccessfully. She didn't believe Nancy Tuck was looking to be married; and it struck her, little as she knew of him, that Nancy was not unlike John Sirovich in this respect. Both seemed to be defending a probably temporary independence. What renewed this discussion was not the wedding at hand, or Rosemary's too-public declaration, but Nancy's resignation from the navy office the day after the terrible disturbance at the Roan Island shipyard. That she quit her job was not as decisive for Willa Ellen as the conversation that followed, one she could not bring herself to confide to Jane—not yet at least.

"Are you in love with this boy?"

"He's not in love with me."

"I didn't ask you that."

"I know, Mother."

"Nancy, I must tell you. And it's not Rosemary's fault. Mrs. Winston talked with Mrs. Roberts. I can say—and no one is asking you to confirm it—that it's known you were with him over at the BOQ."

"Mother, this is impossible. We can't talk about it."

"No; it's difficult. Are you counting on him in some way?"

"Yes."

R. J. Fredericks called. "I hear you almost got shot. How was it?"

"I fell into the Void."

"That's bayou talk for the 'world.' Hell, I just called to say hello."

"You're not much of a Baptist, RJ. The Void is in the Bible. So is the Leviathan."

"You do know how to smarten up a chat. I'm asking you if

you want to come down Saturday to my place on Dauphin Island."

"I would imagine you were invited that day to the wedding of Catherine Ellen Tuck, Nancy's cousin."

"I was. But I'm asking you out, not her. You're not going?"

"No, I wasn't invited. Right now, there's no heavy traffic between French Court and Beaulieu. Yes, I'd like to come. But I can't promise to be interesting."

"Hell, I never promise principal—let alone interest."

On Saturday RJ drove into French Court behind a huge and silent Negro in a 1936 LaSalle with chrome chevrons on the fenders and big vents cut into the hood. After about an hour the LaSalle turned off the concrete highway and closely followed the western edge of the bay. Only a few boats were in view, stalled over the nearby oyster beds. Did Providence, the same Providence that had conveniently rained on the riot, make the large harbors the simplest? Mobile Bay opened from a broad swift river and ended thirty miles south at a narrow mouth. It was a marvel that no adventurer had so far canted or looped a bridge across this span. So John told RJ.

"You fancy, do you, grand and useless public works?"

John was piqued. He pointed out that the Golden Gate was built *before* towns lay north of it. In the old days, tracks were laid before there were towns.

"Myself, I never wanted to go to Grand Rapids. You know, people just can't let things be. Some friends of mine want me to invest in raising Admiral Farragut's ironclad *Tecumseh*. They want to exhibit it like those two-man subs the Japs sneaked into Pearl Harbor."

"Can it be done?" John was fascinated.

"Supposedly. It lies at forty-five feet, silted over, in swift water, tricky tides. Inside is the skeleton of Captain Craven. He reached the escape hatch in time but stood aside for the pilot, who lived to tell the tale."

As the car descended toward the causeway to Dauphin Island,

brushing marsh grass and pussywillows on the roadside, RJ resumed. "It's a caution anyone ever *wanted* Mobile. It's wind and water with tree roaches as big as coons. Hell, the British won the town in a war and didn't even know it—like a guy who comes back from the toilet to find he's left chips on a winning number." He paused to look out. "Captain Craven ought to be left to his dreams."

Unlike Jane, Willa Ellen was not inclined to underestimate their niece's feat in capturing a nice boy from Meridian, Mississippi, whose parents owned a hardware-brokering business and had enrolled two generations of their men at Ol' Miss. Marriage was the sine qua non for Willa Ellen. She recalled that their grandmother had cautioned the Tuck girls when Jane and she had made their debuts: "If you take good care of a husband, all else follows." This reasonable adage was not universally applicable, Willa Ellen had come to admit. For Jane, despite her loving care of Charles Hobson, not all else had followed.

Charles was a tall, thin man who despite the heat wore a vest and a boater. He looked like a man for the road, a traveling salesman who might well have a girl in every town or perhaps the manager of a semipro baseball team. Toward him, Jane was gentle and uncensorious and usually witty. Charles called her two or three times a day from his office in the course of corporate law practice. This habit was prompted more by his own need than his wife's. They were childless and, feeling that lack, both were lonely.

Dauphin Island was a triangle whose seaward side was given to a row of wood-frame houses with unpainted steps leading down onto the sand. In the distance pelicans folded their umbrella wings in that dive that always looks like a mistake. By the time John left the house to take a swim, the evening primroses were closing against the cold. He stood shivering as he examined the faint foundations of old Fort Gaines, which Admiral Farragut had burned in 1864 just before he damned the torpedoes and forced Fort Morgan, across the channel to the east, to strike its colors. Looking at the flickering white and red waters passing between, John had to concede that RJ was right. What connected these points was their distance.

The next morning, after another swim, he found RJ sitting on the porch protected from the western blaze by a bamboo shade. The older man greeted him with a disquisition.

"I saw you running. I doubt a man can make a dollar—or a woman for that matter—by running, don't you? Do you reckon many men die at the climax of love from too much exercise?"

"RJ, how on earth could anyone verify such a statistic?"

"That's the trouble. Coroners keep such things quiet, else some folks might think a wife demanded too much of her husband, or else asked so little that he died in a strange bed."

After lunch cooked by a fat black woman whom John guessed to be the chauffeur's wife, RJ took a nap on a wooden chaise. Clenched in his mouth was an unlit cigar raised like a gun barrel.

The morning after the wedding Willa Ellen sat with her husband at breakfast in the Battle House. For Harold it was unsettling, the first time they'd eaten alone in a hotel in Mobile—any meal, not to speak of breakfast. He overate and drank three cups of coffee as his wife waited patiently.

"Harold, if I told you that Blaine was going to bed with a girl, I expect you'd be annoyed but not surprised."

"What? That's hypothetical, Willa Ellen."

"Harold, we're not in court. Nancy is sleeping with John Sirovich."

The judge stirred his cup repeatedly, removing the spoon to inspect it like an alchemist who hopes the dross will turn to gold.

"Do you doubt what I say?" his wife pursued.

"I don't doubt you, Willa Ellen. I don't know what to say."

"You can begin by asking if John intends to marry her."

"I would much rather hope that Nancy would say no. He's not suitable, not suitable at all. He's too different from Nancy, from *us*, a man of another place and station."

"You don't like him."

"No, I don't. But I won't be rude about him. He's extremely intelligent and he's forceful—always ready, really. He'll take charge of something one day, but that doesn't bear here. He's possibly dangerous for Nancy. You agree, I'm sure."

"That's not the issue, Harold, dear. It's not the long run we are talking about."

"Isn't he bound to leave soon—to go to a ship or be discharged?"

"*That's* the issue, Harold. It's whether Nancy Tuck will go with him when he leaves."

At this the judge stared at her in alarm. "You must advise her!"

"I can't."

"You're her mother."

"Harold, dear, if I talk to her now, it will seem I'm accusing her. Afterward, my advice won't be worth an old dance card. Harold, what did Nancy tell you when she left college?"

"She said she came home because it was unreal going to classes in the midst of a war. I can understand that. I wouldn't have gone to law school had the war kept on."

Willa Ellen turned her head slightly away. He had dismissed her momentarily as he once more considered his choices as a young man. She had left Randolph-Macon to marry him, to stand by, to bear Blaine into life, to make a place for him as he studied at the law day and night.

"It's not quite the same thing as for you. *You* went to war. I think Nancy is wondering about after the war."

"Blaine and James will be home. We'll all be together again. Can't that prospect serve to settle things for now?"

"Maybe Nancy thinks her life will pass unnoticed. I don't know how to sort it out. And if you can't, then I can't."

As John and RJ made their way back to town about three o'clock, RJ became untypically talkative. The summer house had been built by his father, but the senior Fredericks rarely stayed in it because of his frequent traveling. He had bought and sold and exchanged property, timber lots mostly.

"My father was a born trader who now and then stopped working just to rest his suspicions. He always said that unlike the law or medicine, trading is quick but, thank God, not continuous."

"I never traded anything I can remember. It follows, I think, from not owning anything."

RJ caught the irony played against his homespun account and retaliated, "Well, don't fret about it. You don't need any lessons. You are a good businessman already."

"That's the first time anyone ever called me that."

"There are worse names. By the way, old horse, does everything happen to you for the *first* time?"

10

It was Sunday, August 3, when the LaSalle dropped John off at French Court. When he went to the Federal Building the next day he found a telegram instructing him to report to the depot in New Orleans, no more than ten words. He had Carrie cut his orders and pay chits and buy his ticket on the LandN. He was off by eleven o'clock. Braddock was once again looking anxious: he'd begun his career with the lieutenant commander by being sent on dubious orders to act as a scout, or spy, at a depot covering twenty or more acres and holding over two thousand men; he had watched a pier with a warehouse and a fancy office fill with supplies and staff, all the result, it was said by the two chiefs, of a telephone call to an admiral. Then in dismay he had glimpsed his man under charges being escorted out of the Federal Building and later had delivered books to him in his odd jail, their old office. Finally he had heard of the foray into the shipyard and, as if in reward for breaking confinement, Sirovich's release and apparent exoneration. He wasn't so sure that the lieutenant commander could pull another rabbit out of his cap—maybe the admiral had had enough of his tricks.

John didn't see Admiral Priestley. He reported to Priestley's aide, a full commander, on the morning of the fifth. The aide was pleasant enough, another Annapolis man, about thirty, who at war's end probably would return to a peacetime rank, two stripes instead of three, maybe one and one-half. Commander Fuller told him that there was a good chance Sirovich would be ordered to sea over the next month. What provision could he make to "wind up things in Mobile" in that event? When John explained that none of his subordinates was an officer, not even a warrant officer, Fuller was visibly disturbed—no operation that large in the Supply Corps could allow authority to fall all the way from two and one-half stripes to the three chevrons on a chief storekeeper's sleeve. He recovered, however, by deciding to assign two officers within the week, probably a senior grade lieutenant and an ensign. Sirovich should return first thing in the morning with a report on the current state of stock, funds, navy personnel, and civilian hires.

When John had checked into the Saint Charles Hotel downtown, carrying along with his bag a depot typewriter and stationery, he ordered room service and wrote, flat out, twenty-two pages with headings and even footnotes. It was a feat of memory not all that remarkable for a straight-A student who must be, by definition, a test-taker. That afternoon he walked in the French Quarter and, by appearing at Antoine's before it opened, he obtained a reservation so that at least it could not be said he had twice visited New Orleans and failed to eat oysters Rockefeller. The next morning Commander Fuller was busy; and not until eight-fifteen did they meet—for all of five minutes. Sirovich rode a jeep to the railway station. On finding he had just missed the train, he proceeded to rent a large sedan and make the 150-mile drive without stopping, a most pleasant tour through the coast towns, under leafy boughs and alongside sea walls.

When he reached French Court he found Mrs. Winston away and the telephone ringing.

"John? Where on earth have you been?"

"New Orleans. Didn't you ask Carrie?"

"Why didn't you telephone?"

"Wait a minute. What's happened? Are you all right?"

"Why would you say that? Nobody is."

"I don't know what you mean, Nancy."

"You didn't listen to a radio? How's that possible? President Truman said our country has dropped a bomb on a Japanese city—a bomb two thousand times larger than an ordinary one. An atomic bomb, a terrible new invention."

"Atomic," he repeated, drawing his breath.

"John? I'm sorry."

He lighted a cigarette and changed his shirt, then sat down for a moment to look out at the garden, lighting another cigarette from the butt of the first one. He didn't know what to think, having no facts, having heard no news that was comprehensible in ordinary terms. But it did not prevent him from wondering if God was so clever that he chose this day for a man to arrive in a rented room by rented automobile in a foreign city to hear a beautiful young woman inquire of him, "Where were you? Today was Armageddon."

They were seated in the living room. And it seemed somehow averse that it was daylight still and tomorrow would dawn on a workday.

Willa Ellen said, "Auntie Cora called, Nancy Tuck, to ask if you were safe. I must say it's the only sensible question I've heard all day."

Auntie Cora was the nanny, a gnarled old black woman of eighty who stood four feet ten inches and had wiry hair that always managed to tangle into ropes like deer antlers. She had been a housemaid in Nancy's grandmother's house and nanny to Jane and Willa Ellen before tending Nancy. Now she was retired to Toulmanville, outside Mobile.

When James had called from Princeton to ask if he should come home, his father dissuaded him. Certainly the war would end now; James's accelerated training for a BA would reach completion and he'd be back in Mobile without being called up.

"This terrible thing, this atomic bomb, is too large to be realized rightly. Maybe"—Harold Bowen looked at his wife now—"Auntie Cora puts it best by asking about those she loves. I've spent part of today hoping that if we *have* killed a million people, or a quarter or half million, we did not *choose* Orientals as victims."

Willa Ellen frowned. Why did her husband presume that introducing vastness, this talk of unknowable decisions, could help any of them? She had the sense he was speaking to Nancy, as if to persuade her that great events would be comprehended at home as well as away in supposedly sophisticated places.

"If we had need to, Daddy, we would have dropped it on the Germans."

"I wonder. It's hard to understand a single instance of anything. There was the shipyard riot that bothered John Sirovich so much. I understood his dilemma, but he didn't believe me."

Nancy was distressed that her father had introduced his misunderstanding with John. The shipyard was one thing. Hiroshima and the possible end of civilization were another. All day long on the radio announcers used the phrase "civilization as we know it," as if Martians and others did not know it as well.

Then her father made his point. "There is something awful in our own nature that we fear—something worse than the occasional reminder that one's own life will end, maybe suddenly. I think it is race—belonging to one race and fearing others."

"Daddy!"

Nancy was as much embarrassed as shocked. He'd started off by saying Auntie Cora was right—and now was apparently saying that even she, the shriveled and toothless black woman, was in some obscure way a person compromised by world events.

"You're not saying, Daddy, that we dropped the bomb out of fear of the yellow race!"

"No, I am not. If there is a legal case in this bomb's devastation,

I'd say there are millions of plaintiffs but no defendants. Maybe it's like the shipyard. There's an offense but no crime."

Willa Ellen sat unmoving. This occasion was for her not unlike the time when Harold's father died. They had, after the funeral, talked until daylight; and after the logs in the fireplace had fallen to ash, they'd moved to the warmth of the wood stove in the large kitchen. Harold had that night spoken of so many things, so variously and so remotely, that finally, feeling her own grief, she had clung to herself inside and hoped that in the end he would make everything connect, the hooks catching the right eyes, and so weave a safety net. What good was it to examine events that were bigger than yourself without a resolution?

On Saturday, on the port supply officer's floor in the Federal Building, work quit an hour early, at noon; and, at Carrie Brown's summoning, the chiefs and rates and seamen arrived from the piers. They stood with the secretaries and clerks eating breakfast buns carried over from the Greek's place across the street. The older of the chiefs, with knotted biceps and a paunch, his jacket rumpled top and bottom, stepped forward to present to Commander Sirovich a brass six-inch shell casing that had been sheared and beveled—no doubt originally someone's souvenir—into an ashtray that was in fact useful only as a spittoon. The ceremony was over quickly—it was Saturday, after all. People called out, "Good luck!" and a few waited to shake his hand.

Inside Sirovich's office, Carrie fell to crying. She searched for a handkerchief and, failing to find one, turned away as though she'd become unclean. He put his arms about her starched blouse, his hand on the back of her small collar which was loosely joined by a red rayon tie.

"I'm going home to Demopolis," she sobbed.

"Is it bad? That bad?"

"I feel blue, that's all." She looked at him. "Should a person wait for something?"

This most basic query caught him by surprise; and on impulse he took from his pocket a five-dollar gold piece given him on his seventeenth birthday by Savo Lubradović—a piece he had repeatedly risked paying out with ordinary silver change.

"Don't wait for anything, Carrie. Fall in love. Take a trip. Catch a man. Here, give this to your first son."

He bent to kiss the top of her neatly brushed walnut-brown hair, knowing he'd never see her again.

Two hours later he found Mrs. Bowen about to leave. She invited him to have coffee and was about to instruct the young Negro maid when he interrupted.

"Thanks, no, Mrs. Bowen. I'm leaving Mobile within a couple of hours. I got my orders last night."

Willa Ellen put her hand to her mouth.

Sirovich stood, clasping his cap in both hands. They heard Nancy's step on the staircase. Willa Ellen turned and left the room without a word.

Nancy stopped in the hallway before the pier mirror to comb the swirls in her thick hair, rearranging more than taming it. Her blouse was unbuttoned at the top and unevenly tucked into her white skirt. She wore pumps. Her legs were bare.

"Nancy, Nancy, sit down. Nancy . . ." He stopped.

"John, John, John. Hey! When I was seven Auntie Cora took me to a tent meeting where a 'nigra' preacher brought a miracle. He made her nephew talk after years of being dumb. Cora was real sore when he had nothing to say after he was cured. She kept saying, 'What wus yo doin *all that time?*' " She laughed. "Well, John, John, John."

"I'm leaving on an AKA in two hours."

Nancy stared at him.

"Like that! Just like that! For God's sake, it takes longer than a morning just to cut orders!" She stood, shaking. "Sure it does. I've typed orders. I'm an expert when it comes to sailors leaving. So Captain Morse got his revenge? He got me, not you!"

"Now, Nancy. It was probably his due. This is his last command."

She was infuriated by this remark. So it was a manly competition, no more. Wasn't she at stake?

"Who the hell cares about him? What about me? Goddamn it, John, I feel like a passenger in a car wreck." She sobbed, turned away, turned back. "I've not seen you since you had your way with me. Cheap, John, cheap!"

"I wasn't invited to the wedding. I know your family wants me to stay away. I had a feeling all of you were deciding what to do about me."

"Where are you going on this AKA?"

"The war's almost over. I may be assigned to a station near here. Who knows? Charleston, maybe."

"Swell, just swell! And what am I supposed to do? I get it. I'm the girlie who follows you from station to station, right?" Her eyes were wide from suspicion and fear. Her breasts rose and fell against the blouse.

"What can I say, Nancy? What do you want me to say? I've got no plans."

"Oh yes, you do. I'm one of your plans. You asked me to spend a week's leave away just two weeks ago. Then I didn't even hear from you. And you went alone to New Orleans. Was she good?"

"Nancy. You know better. I went to New Orleans on orders. Morse may have pulled the trigger, but the supply depot loaded the gun that's blown me onto an AKA."

"And what about next time? Am I supposed to come running to Charleston—or wherever?"

He stared at her in obvious pain. It was rare that he was speechless—as if stricken dumb like Cora's nephew. What *had* he been doing all this time?

Then, to her own surprise Nancy broke into a throaty parody, "Sailor, I'm going to sit around the house chewing gum and filing my nails until I hear from you. Okay? Okay?"

He clasped her low at the buttocks, as he had that day in the BOQ. She anticipated his astonishment, again.

"You don't have time." She said it in her own voice.

Roy Braddock drove him to the dock in Roan Island and offered to carry his gear up the gangway, but Sirovich knew better than to report to the officer of the deck accompanied by a valet. They shook hands twice. Roy asked for his home address, which was delivered with the certainty that it would never be used. Then Sirovich handed over the shell casing and asked that it be delivered to R. J. Fredericks with the message to hold it for him.

Braddock stood on the dock as USS *Orion*, AKA-136, headed for the channel between the two old forts. He got into the jeep wondering when he himself would be mustered out. What with the Bomb, the war was really over. Everyone said so. Then it struck him that as a civilian he'd have to decide where to work, where to live. Braddock hadn't made any such decisions in more than three years and it was unsettling now to face them.

11

The first letter arrived in Mobile September 3, postmarked Norfolk.

Orion emerged from the Windward Passage the day the war ended, the fifteenth. The next day we were ordered to Norfolk for decommissioning, and I spent my last two days at sea duty lying in the captain's bunk while the pilot took her up the James River. As the last officer aboard, I drew the short stick. *Orion* was anchored alongside about forty Liberty and Victory ships in a big cove. I handed over to an officer who walked aboard across gangways laid flat between the gunwales of a half dozen ships. I can't remember if we saluted each other out there on the river. Something should have been said. They deconsecrate churches, don't they? I'm ordered to Bush Terminal in New York, where British LSTs we lent during Lend Lease are being decommissioned. Has Blaine got his discharge? He has more "points" than I do. I dream about you. There's a novel with the ending: "Why can't people have what they want?"

A second letter arrived, dated September 12:

When I reported to the Third Naval District I was oddly disappointed by the building right in the heart of Wall Street. It didn't look the least imperial, only walleyed from white window shades! On the sixth floor I sat listening to the loudspeakers call, "Now hear this" every two minutes. It was like that over three years ago when I first reported in uniform to San Diego. I spent my first night in New York in the Midston House on 38th and Madison. Did I ever tell you about my first time to New York? I paid sailors in underwater crews cutting away the *Normandie*, which sank from water poured into her when she caught fire. I slept aboard *Seattle* and ate aboard *Camden*, old World War I cruisers no longer seaworthy. I kept close to my three ships—as if they'd sail without me. One night I tried out the New York City subway system and ended up on a sidewalk in Harlem. A Negro prostitute asked me, "What are *you* doing here?" She had a point. What am I doing here now, years later? But there are choices, I hope. There's the Yale fellowship. Then there's California—if Mr. Winterfield is still alive.

Nancy was bewildered when not furious. White window shades! *His* three ships! They were letters, she finally defined, of the kind writers kept copies of—for their memoirs. But he was struggling, not just in deciding what to do but also in what to say to her. There was some satisfaction in that because, perversely, for John Sirovich to admit uncertainty was a gesture of intimacy. She knew him *that* well.

Writing Nancy about Winterfield made Sirovich think of that fall in Los Angeles when he had worked at RKO. It was just before Pearl Harbor and he was staying in Winterfield's home on December 7th. The next day he left to enlist in Denver. In

Hollywood he had been hoping to write screenplays and was so reminded the first night in New York when he picked out of *PM* a movie house where two MGM pictures were playing, probably "block booked"—a term he had garnered in Hollywood. The movies were *Bewitched* and *Dangerous Partners*, both detective stories but each lacking the innate tension found in those stories by James M. Cain and Horace McCoy that he'd tried to emulate while working part-time at RKO as a scriptwriter. He had marveled at their tone. You felt a saddening enervation as you watched the death of witnesses. It had come to little for him back then in 1941. Nothing he wrote was used by RKO—not a single line of dialogue.

When he returned to Broad Street to pick up orders for duty at Bush Terminal, a yeoman told him his discharge points qualified him for discharge within a month. Then the CO at Bush decided it wasn't worth his starting a new duty that he would so soon leave unfinished. The same afternoon he went from desk to desk at the separation center on Pine Street and emerged into the four o'clock Wall Street traffic with a document that noted, "September 19, 1945, Separation, Honorable. Released to Inactive Duty." He was given one hundred dollars mustering-out pay. It was over.

12

On lower Fourth Avenue Sirovich bought secondhand copies of *The Chicago Manual of Style* and *Webster's International,* Second Edition. At Kresge's he bought candy bars and on Herald Square a box of blue pencils, paper clips, Scotch tape, typing paper, and a scratch pad of red paper—all in aid of working on the first manuscript he'd been assigned by New World Press, *Spoiling the Victory.* The author's intention was to urge the President and Congress to impose "social justice" on Germany and Italy before U.S. industrialists and the reviving bourgeoisie in those countries could establish "hegemonies." This absurd prescription was not Sirovich's concern—only the author's spelling, syntax, and citation of names, places, and dates. After a fifteen-hour sitting, he looked at the number (by now he had learned it was called the "folio") on the last page. It was 320. Thirty cents a page times 320 was ninety-six dollars. John Sirovich was at work. Like his mother, paid by the yard at the Botany Mills, he'd found himself piecework.

When Nancy came on the line he cracked open the accordion door of the public telephone booth to let in the sound of brakes and horns and the indistinct gabble of pedestrians' voices.

"That's New York, Nancy. And I'm a civilian who's just earned enough to pay your fare here."

"Is that a proposal?"

"Nancy, I *need* you."

"Well, we've both seen *that* need."

"Nancy, I need to have a serious talk with you. Will you come? I'm begging you to come."

"Then it's a serious proposal but not for marriage?"

"I'm running out of quarters. Tell me you'll come."

"A lot of days have passed, John."

"Yes or no? Nancy?"

"Yes."

"My God. I'm in luck."

"I'm bringing Aunt Jane."

"She's in luck, too. I'm at the Midston, Thirty-Eighth and Madison, Room Eight Twenty-Four."

She didn't call or wire him, to prevent his meeting them at Penn Station, where it would be awkward at best and might put John at an unnecessary disadvantage. He would not be their host, greeting and welcoming them to the big city that belonged to everyone and nobody. Arrived, they climbed the iron staircase of Pennsylvania Station into that vast gray space where Nancy half-expected to see her own breath, reminded as she was of the smoky vaults of Les Halles in Paris when she was eleven. She was wearing a dark suit with modish squared shoulders and carried in her gloved hands an expensive new leather cosmetics case. Jane Hobson, smaller in stature and less severely outfitted, would have struck an onlooker as also less purposeful. Once checked into the Waldorf, Nancy insisted they could visit Saks and Bonwit's or, if Jane preferred, Lord and Taylor's and Altman's and then, after a bit of rest, see a play. There was plenty of time to let John know of their arrival. They would be here for a whole week.

Jane found this casualness part and parcel of the anxiety Nancy had shown when she first approached her mother about the trip.

Her niece had packed too many clothes and had left much unexplained, yet she had repeatedly asserted that she didn't know John's plans. If Jane were a betting man—as Charles always introduced his shrewd speculations—she'd put money on Nancy's staying in New York without receiving a definite proposal. It might seem a shocking denouement, given that protocol concerning the conduct of young women was not all that different in 1945 from that of 1923, which year Jane Tuck had married Charles Hobson. But the cast of characters was different. She and Charles had not been looking to leave home. Nancy was on the verge of shocking herself. It put Jane's guardianship in a doubtful light and, to the Bowen family, might make her seem treacherous.

"You arrived *when?*" John asked from the hall telephone at the Midston House's eighth floor.

"Jane and I were amazed to find so many new fashions at Saks—it's just as if there'd been no war! And then we had the best time at Billy Rose's nightclub, the 'Horseshoe.' I thought *I* was too tall! Showgirls must be six feet. Jane's trying to get some musical tickets right now—well, I mean after she has lunch with an old college classmate who lives in Bronxville."

"Stop it, Nancy."

"What?"

"Stop making yourself trivial. I'm not your old college classmate."

"You're mean."

"The last time you said that was at your father's club. Now we're in New York."

"Lots of people are here."

"Nancy, meet me in an hour at the fountain in front of the Plaza."

He hung up without waiting for a reply. He wasn't sure she'd show up, but then, when you're down to your last five dollars, you ask for the last card.

John sat chain-smoking, seated on a bench across Fifty-Ninth Street, aware that Gatsby's Daisy had set up a meeting at the Plaza by crying out gaily, "I'll be the man smoking two cigarettes." He saw Nancy emerge from a taxi in front of the hotel. She stood under the portico, after nodding the doorman politely away, and then looked obliquely at the fountain—not committing herself to the possibility of being stood up in a public and exposed place. She looked fashionable in a green suit with gray gloves, hat, and leather pumps.

He came up behind her, saying, "Not quite sure of me, are you, Nancy Tuck? Let's cross over to the park. I know another bench."

They didn't kiss. She looked intently at him as if he'd aged or fallen ill since last she saw him. He took her gloved hand and urged her to run with the green light across Fifty-Ninth, then onto a pathway to a bench that faced a grass mall from which the lake bridge was just visible.

"This is *the* serious talk."

"Yes. I've rehearsed a million words, Nancy, and they've all come out wrong. I love you, Nancy. I've never been in love before. I told a girl I loved her in California and I worry that it ruined her life. That's not all. I'm afraid to ask you to marry me because marriage can freeze people before they know what they want—or, maybe, just what they are capable of. I watched my mother puzzled—cheated, really—by finding all her possibilities closed by marriage; and it killed her. My father's life hasn't been wasted because he has his men friends and his Old Country patriotism—and of course me—but he spent nineteen years of his marriage bearing the guilt of being the wrong partner. Good God! All that time, all those years she criticized him, he respected my mother's opinion."

Nancy's tears formed within seconds at the start of this astonishing account. They fell onto her clenched hands.

"John, it's awful. I'm sorry. I'm sorry that your mother and father suffered so. But I wasn't part of all that."

"No. I was. I can't forget it."

"Who was the girl?"

"She was nineteen. It was just before the war. She married a brutal man because she thought she was pregnant—but she wasn't. In the end he and I had a fight, and she ran away to her father, a navy chief in Honolulu. She loved me so much she wrote to free me—to say she didn't expect anything of us."

"What was her name?"

"Jean. Jean Fancher."

"How do you know you didn't love her?"

"I told her I did, but I just knew it wasn't true. I redirected her life, but then I took no part in her future."

"John, don't make it so bad! How long ago was it? Four years? You're sounding brave now, but fooling around with a married woman wasn't all that hard. I don't want to talk about her. I'm not Jean."

"I want you to stay with me but not marry me, not here, not yet."

"I guessed *that*. What is it you want to do? Write? Teach?"

"I don't know. That's the point, Nancy, because you don't know about yourself, either. You're very beautiful and you're bright. You need chances. In California a man named Zernbach once asked me what I wanted. I said I didn't want to be humiliated. But there's more. I want to work hard, very hard. I want to end up creating my own life. I need first and soon to see its drift, its current. I won't stop once there's a direction."

"John, what makes you think I've got ambitions like that? I'm not talented like you. I'm only admired."

Now he clasped her close, ignoring the clumsiness he caused, her hands trapped, her purse tipped, her hat falling. He kissed her eyes.

"Nancy, don't settle for less than yourself. Stay with me or don't stay, but give yourself all the chances. You're more than beautiful. You're a spectacular girl."

"You forgot to ask," she said, breaking away, "if I love you."

"I'm afraid to ask."

"Don't! It doesn't suit you. I love you. And now I need help. Aunt Jane's."

"What will you do?"

"Stay with you, sport. I decided five minutes ago. You just didn't notice, this being a serious talk and all."

When Jane put down the receiver after talking with Willa Ellen the fourth time in a single afternoon, she had finally admitted to her sister that she had suspected all along she was playing the duenna on the way to an assignation. Nancy had counted on her to get them out of Mobile with decorum, and as a result she was now returning in confusion. But as she sat inside the Pullman, alternately wondering and judging, she had to admit that ultimately she didn't hold any grudges against her niece, who was not one of those willful women who expected circumstances to remain unchanged at home while she went off adventuring. Nancy was deeply conscious that in leaving she had altered the relations in several lives—Willa Ellen's, Harold's, Blaine's, James's, her aunt's. In setting her own price, Nancy knew she would cost others. Jane finally came to regard her mission as uniquely necessary to *herself.* She had not been left on the sidelines consoling the Bowens out of an obligatory, if also genuinely loyal, kinship. She had been part of an extraordinary event that would become with time's passing explicable and acceptable—to Willa Ellen at least, if not to Harold. She had served not dishonorably but dutifully. She loved Nancy. Whether Nancy would gain or lose was not *now* the issue. All else could follow.

In the Midston House, without bothering to unpack Nancy's bags, they undressed as if hearing a starter's gun, one on each side of the bed; then they slipped under the sheet and coverlet. When John reached for her, Nancy drew back, pulling up the sheet to blot her tears and deny him a view of her body.

"You can't know! Nice girls don't come running. On the telephone Mother said at one point, 'Good luck.' My God! She's never said that to *anyone* before! And she asked me what she should tell James and Blaine, as if there were a catechism we could agree on."

When Nancy relented, they made love too fast and ended by clinging to one another, exhausted, as if they'd climbed out of a chasm. He whispered, "I know," as the light faded from the room, the dimming of universal energy at twilight, that hour of declination when people go home, telephones ring less and less, and in the hospitals, as interns soon learn to expect, the very sick and the very old begin to die in the lateness.

During the night, awake suddenly, Nancy chose to recall one occasion when John, in Mobile, had declared sententiously that sexual fidelity was a promise that never *need* be broken. A man could simply not have sex at any time or at any place. Whether it was practical, this bit of naïve wisdom, she didn't know, but it held a certain comfort. She believed him, especially him.

13

Their money, pooled, came to seven thousand, four of which Nancy originally brought from home in a banker's check. Jane had, on leaving, insisted on paying their hotel and other expenses, claiming falsely that the refund on Nancy's return ticket would reimburse her. In Nancy's stationery box was another check for a thousand—mad money that Willa Ellen had mailed to her the day of the four telephone calls. They couldn't afford to stay at the Midston for long, yet at war's end there were no apartments to be found except for cold-water flats on the Lower East Side. There were better, but much too distant, places in Queens and the Bronx. Their dilemma was solved by Cassie Newhardt. Cassie discovered where they were because Charles Hobson knew. A jungle drum had been beating somewhere.

When John met Cassie for the first time in the lobby of the Midston, he felt a shock of delight on seeing a woman of twenty-seven who fit the trite word *petite*. She was not more than five feet two, pinch-waisted, with shiny black hair and what some Southerners call "English skin," unblemished and quickly colored by fast-rising feelings. She reminded John of a personage he did not mention because she was long forgotten except by movie addicts like himself—Louise Brooks, a star in the "silents." Like her, Cassie wore her bobbed hair in a manner at once innocent and bold. Cassie seemed to him to be constantly in motion, exposing a view of her delicate neck or slender legs or her perfect teeth, which showed frequently because she burst into laughter while talking about almost anything. John wondered if there was some special humor so high-pitched that only Cassie heard it. Suddenly she kissed him.

"I want you if she gives you up," Cassie told John after inserting the tip of her tongue in his mouth.

Cassie returned the second afternoon to drive them to Greenwich Village in a white 1940 Olds convertible. She had found a place on Ninth Street that could be sublet for six months, until March the following year. Driving much too fast but expertly, she told Nancy that the car belonged to a man named Frank Johnstone, who was "going to help me get my kids back from Austin." The flat was almost unfurnished: a bed, bureaus, some kitchen chairs, and a sofa and armchair whose original stripes were barely discernible. The rent was not exorbitant: seventy-five dollars a month.

Once settled, Nancy found a job selling stationery at Hearns, the old department store on Sixth Avenue. She didn't tell John until she returned to the apartment after her first day at work. John was bent over *Webster's International*, as usual. When she announced she was to be paid six dollars a day and four-fifty on Saturdays, nine to one-thirty, John declared it to be no more than a deadend job but within seconds couldn't keep a straight face over the fact that the term exactly described his own. A week later this judgment was confirmed more knowledgeably by three old ladies—hardly anyone else was buying deckle-edged notepaper that far below midtown—who were so captivated by Nancy's accent and by her striking looks that they didn't feel too disloyal to warn her that Hearns might fail someday soon. It did fail, as a matter of fact, two years later.

One day at her counter Nancy heard her name called in an unmistakable voice. It was Carolyn Ellis, a classmate who had left the university a year earlier than Nancy and then remained in her hometown of Birmingham only briefly before heading for New York, where she got a job with the Office of Price Administration. Two weeks before Christmas of 1944 she had met an instructor at Columbia named Angus Farrand and married him six weeks later. A man of thirty-three who was not a veteran, Farrand was a graduate of the University of Michigan who had earned a Ph.D. in English at Columbia.

On discovering that Nancy was not at first blush inclined to discuss how and why she arrived in New York, in the Village, at Hearns, Carolyn quickly filled the conversation. She told Nancy they'd recently moved from a brownstone in the Bronx owned by a Danish mason who had built his house fifty years before while working on the Cathedral of St. John the Divine in Manhattan. It was so many years ago that he had been able to see the cathedral across the Harlem River from the Bronx and from its Gothic buttresses to observe the progress on his own house. Angus and Carolyn had rented a whole floor for thirty dollars a month, a consequence of the Danish couple's refusal to rent to Negroes—their half-empty house now stood like a rock in a sea of black people.

It was, Nancy told John excitedly on relating the encounter, altogether typical of Carolyn that she should be so precise: the mason, the amount of the rent, the views across the river. At Tuscaloosa, she'd been the brightest student in Nancy's sorority house, but no grind. John discovered Carolyn's quickness for himself when she invited them to dine at their new apartment on Riverside Drive. She had just quit the OPA and was working part-time at the Columbia library while waiting, she told Nancy, to be "made pregnant as soon as possible." At dinner she declared herself against moving into one of the ten thousand houses, all identical, going up on Long Island.

"One would be enough, don't you think? I mean, just to show what they were like."

But with her husband John failed with a small witticism when Angus asked about his fellowship at Yale. Was it not worth a lot of money, especially when one added GI Bill benefits? John replied that it wasn't money he worried would run out but rather his own patience.

"I might not, in a dissertation, wait on my own conclusions."

This led Angus to speak somewhat imperiously about the rewards of meticulous research. Yet John suspected that Angus was not himself going to be willing to plug along year after year, writing articles for academic journals and delivering papers at subsection panel discussions of the Modern Language Association annual meetings—all in aid of slowly accreting a professional reputation. Earlier that same day it happened that at New World Press he'd met a Princeton instructor of about thirty who said he was at the moment researching what the temperature read, and whence the wind blew, the day the tubercular poet William Ernest Henley entered the hospital in Edinburgh. Riding the subway after dinner John told Nancy that he'd lay odds that Farrand would within a few years seek an assistant dean's job in a lesser college with the aim of becoming its provost and, eventually, president.

"Come on, John!" Nancy was surprised. "You're prejudiced because he's so unruffled. Or maybe because he wears three-piece suits and serves wine." She didn't remind him that running things was one of his own goals.

It was typical that Cassie Newhardt should drive up to Riverside Drive, uninvited and without calling beforehand, to visit the Farrands. Surprised by her visit and not quite sure what her relation was to the "common-law Siroviches," as he called them in private to Carolyn, Angus asked if she worked. Cassie replied with a straight face that she had been laid off from the Third Avenue "El." Before he left the two women talking, Angus peered down at the street and asked who owned the "white slug," meaning the Olds convertible. Cassie at some length probed Carolyn's experiences in finding a job in New York. How much did the OPA pay? How long did it take to learn typewriting at Katherine Gibbs? Afterward she told Nancy that Angus was a "one-hundred-proof prick."

It seemed surprising that as brazenly candid as Cassie was about almost everything—except certain people in Mobile known to her and Nancy—she never intimated, let alone said, how she'd come to meet Frank Johnstone, the owner of the white slug as well as a spacious apartment on Greenwich Avenue in the Village where Cassie lived with him. Johnstone himself was no well of information. About all Nancy could tell John, before the two men met, was that Frank was a fancy dresser and in conversation wholly predictable. Within an hour he had told John of a tailor who fitted tall men, he himself being six feet four, an inch taller than Sirovich. He usually wore green gabardine suits with tailored white shirts and no necktie—this last omission enabled him to make a show of tipping the hatcheck girl at Longchamps on Madison Avenue five dollars for the loan of a tie when he took the four of them there. He carried flat packs of fifty-dollar bills in his front pants pockets, each a "roll" that didn't bulge the line of the cloth. Beyond clothes and money generally, he was routinely concerned with automobiles and specialty restaurants. He'd placed an order for the first postwar Cadillac, a 1947 model, with the big agency on Fifty-Seventh Street. Despite the chill of autumn, Frank took them, occasionally bringing along a short dark man called Taddio, on drives to Brooklyn and City Island in the Bronx to look for fish restaurants. The few occasions on which Taddio was heard to express an opinion was when Johnstone asked what he thought of the oysters or linguine or veal.

Cassie was delighted by the drives and likened parts of New York to Mobile quite without any basis in fact. Maybe, Nancy thought, it was a way of staying in touch with home—or making New York less foreign, however exotic. Cassie rarely spoke to Taddio and only once disputed him sharply. He had commented, the last time they were all together, that he imagined Sirovich must make four or five "bills" from his books. Even though John had gambled frequently in California in the old days, he didn't know the expression "bills." He had heard of a "C-note" for a hundred dollars but not this.

"He's not a bookie, you dummy! He *writes* books. He doesn't take bets."

"Tough shit," said Taddio, "and no dough."

In this bizarre company John and Nancy were uncomfortable as well as disquieted for Cassie's sake. After a few times out on the town, they begged off, but Nancy made a habit of stopping off at Greenwich Street when she finished work at Hearns, discovering that Frank was absent about that time. What he did with his time Cassie wouldn't say. John guessed that he ran a "bucket shop," a term he'd learned, not unusually, from copy editing *Crime as a Tax on Society*, another poor seller of New World Press. Somewhere in lower Manhattan, he surmised, Johnstone furnished a flat with telephones and fast-talking salesmen who foisted worthless "penny stocks" on widows and other pensioners. Taddio, who Cassie said carried a gun, might well provide security at such a locale.

Only once did Cassie come to Ninth Street while Nancy was at work. John was sitting with a manuscript on the unpainted plank laid across the arms of an old overstuffed armchair. He heard the door open and saw her standing against the light from a hall window. She wore a thin linen skirt under which, plainly, there was no slip or even panties. He looked at her wonderingly.

"You want to undress me?"

For a reason that had to do with his embarrassment, John

didn't pause in his reply. "Yes, Cassie. It would comfort me, but I doubt it would do much for you."

"Comfort? Comfort? John, I've scraped more than my knee the last year!"

"Would it help?"

"Screwing?"

"Yes."

"Help? No. It's like poetry—I mean, the way they taught you in high school. Screwing *is*. Just is. It doesn't mean anything. Goddamn it, we're talking. We're not going to do it, are we?"

"Sit down, Cassie. You really came over here to talk."

"Who are you, one of the Three Wise Men?"

"I'm your friend."

"You're stallin' me, ol' stick. You're so loyal to your girl you'd best not marry her."

"You could be right. All men are different, but all husbands are the same."

"Did you make that up just for me?"

"No, I'm not a Wise Man. I stole it. Cassie, tell me, if we leave New York for California, will you come with us?"

"I'm not a nanny, ol' stick. You're going there?"

"Where do you want to go?"

"If I knew that, I wouldn't be in New York. What's bothering you, John? You think I'm a whore? Are you trying to redeem me?"

"Good God, no!"

"Austin's mother, God sew shut her ugly mouth, says I'm Lilith. She's in the Bible, the original whore."

"Cassie, I've stopped asking people who they are. A girl I knew in California named Nita said I was like a G-man, always looking for someone's ID."

"Did you screw Nita?"

"No. We just talked, like you and me."

Cassie came across the room, picked up the plank, and dropped it to the floor, scattering the sheets of manuscript. As John rose and was still bent from the motion, she kissed his mouth with one hand around his neck. With her other hand she squeezed his balls so hard that he was forced to pick her up to disengage her grip. For a second he stared down at her wet lips and sharp white teeth and longed to carry her into the bedroom. Cassie sensed his hesitation and made herself entirely motionless. Then he reversed his hold and cradled her small body and walked into the hallway, down the staircase and the outside brownstone steps, onto the sidewalk. As he continued along the street still carrying Cassie, a few people paused to stare, wondering if there'd been an accident.

14

"Nobody wants to admit what the words are," Cassie told Nancy as they sat on a bench in Washington Square. The air was nippy, but mothers were airing their babies nearby and old men sat at stone tables playing chess or pinochle. "They say you get out of life what you put in. They all say that. You remember, mostly in grade school, the way the teacher told you it was a bargain: you put in a nickel of effort and got back five cents of success. It wasn't like the candy counter at the five-and-dime where you got a barrette or a Bakelite dish. Because in school you had to trade something real and hard and you only got back soft words—like hope or patience or prudence. You remember, Nancy, a long time ago they named girls with those words even before they were old enough to know what they'd owe. I figure us Christians won't work for nothing. It would surprise you, but I used to read the Bible a lot when I was ten or eleven. There's a lot of business in the Bible. Jesus is in the marketplace and everyone is counting sheep and talents. I told my daddy once that the Bible was a book of business. He made me stay in the outhouse a whole morning—on a hot day, for shit's sake!

"I never got loose from those soft, grand words, Nancy. I tried real hard to be hopeful and patient or whatever, and I didn't want to be paid back. My little girls weren't a reward, were they? That's making people into things, like slaves being bought and sold, really. Did you ever notice how people in families practice slavery? They can be mean to each other for free. The kids weren't part of any bargain I made, not me. My daddy used to talk about marriage like a business, too—about how it is a fifty-fifty proposition and all that. Austin's mother kept telling me you get out of marriage just what you put in—like a cake or a stuffed doll. I can't stand the woman. She's dumb and mean and she was like that before the Newhardts got ahold of her. I did try, Nancy, I really did. I learned to wear good clothes and dress the girls just right. I took a bath and put on makeup every day before Austin came home—even if it was noontime. I don't hate Austin. I just can't stand the notion he's allowed to be what he is. He's strange. I mean, weird. He really does know that ordinary people get up every morning to feed the chickens or hogs or to drive to an office or a mill. He knows that, but he thinks it has nothing to do with him. He's just not there, don't you see? It's like he thinks God gave him a permanent hall slip, like in school. He's rich, there's that, so he can pretty much think what he wants. The rich make bargains they don't talk about.

"There's no fifty-fifty for Austin. But how is it he's allowed to be every man's enemy? He can't have managed to make a deal with everybody, can he? If you study him, you have to ask what's the point of being good if all you get are those soft words, which don't protect you from the likes of Austin Newhardt, do you know? Does anyone keep score? I already know the answer, Nancy. You ought not to be bad just to get even with anyone else or even with God—because that's just more bargaining. If you feel like being bad, it's not so different from being good, because you find out too late there's no price list. Being good or bad is just a condition, I figure, like acne or rain.

"I suppose I can live with Frank because he never gives me

no mind. He believes in his cars and his money clips—not a fucking thing else. Frank doesn't believe in himself either—and that's kind of pure in a crazy way. It's about the only thing he's got going for him. I want my kids back, Nancy. That's all I want. Frank can help me. He's got lots of money and he knows people, even like that greaser Taddio, the kind of people who can help against Austin. They're crooks, Frank and Taddio. Taddio was in jail and he got Frank to 'pick up the drops,' as he calls it, while he was inside. And when he came out they were partners. People come to the apartment and leave money, and sometimes Taddio goes out and gets it. They blackmail somebody, maybe businessmen, and for them it's regular. But then, you know, Austin and his father and uncle are crooks, too. They make money off nigger houses. And they cream the cash off timber deals before they call in your uncle, Mr. Hobson, to write up the papers. You know the way Frank carries around those bills? The fifty-dollar bills? It's only because he hasn't got a big steel safe at home like Austin. Once, when Austin was drunk, he opened the safe and threw packs of hundreds at me. He knows money can hurt, yes he does. I'm going to steal my kids back. You can believe it, Nancy Tuck. I'm going to take them to California and let them grow up healthy without making bargains.

"I went to your apartment last week. I tried to get it going with John, yes I did, because I'm supposed to act like a whore. But you don't have to worry. He wouldn't do it. You won't believe this. He carried me all the way from Ninth Street over to Greenwich Avenue while I told him about my kids and how I was going to steal them. And John said he would help me and find a place for us in California. All I need is for Frank to bring me the kids. Did you know it's legal for a mother to take her kids away from a father if he hasn't filed a suit against her? It is. I need about five or six thousand dollars to get started. I can work, Nancy. I could chop cotton. I worked in Selma, you know—or maybe you didn't. I reckon people will say I made a bargain with Frank, whoring him in exchange for my kids and the money. I didn't really know what to do until I got to New York. This is the right place to make awful plans. Nobody gives a shit in New York. You could fall down crazy on Fifth Avenue or pee on the sidewalk or call yourself Jesus himself—and they'd keep right on walking by. I found Frank because he's willing to do anything. But he's not doing it for me. There's no bargain. I expect Frank is thinking to doublecross me once he gets the kids. With Frank, you see, I have to keep pretending. If I don't, nothing will ever get started. Still, Nancy, there's no deal. I'm not a whore. For God's sake, Nancy, I can tell *you*. I think Frank is probably queer but won't admit it. I don't know about Taddio. I don't think so. All Frank does is look at me when I'm plain naked and then he goes into the bathroom by himself.

"That day I took the train from Mobile, Nancy, it was the first time I did something for no reason at all. It was like dying. There wasn't anything needed when I left. For God's sake, I even put away the wash before I left. I just left because I had to. Afterward I felt free. Women aren't allowed to, though, are they? Men are afraid of women who are no-foolin' free. They call them sluts and ballbusters. Did you ever notice how, down home, the menfolk talk about women like they're niggers? They say women are patient and good-natured and willin'. That's what they want to believe. Did you ever notice, Nancy, how upset menfolk get whenever niggers in a crowd are just laughin' and cakewalkin' around? It's like that with women too. When did you ever see women together on their own except at a picnic or country club some afternoon or in the kitchen before supper? Men are afraid if women get together they might ask for things. They're afraid, that's all. And Austin is more afraid than most. He works hard at being a low son of a bitch. It's the only job he's got."

Nancy walked away from the park unaware that her cheeks were wet and that she was shaking. It had got cold in Washington

Square, and toward the end she recalled seeing Cassie's breath in spurts like sprayed mist. Cassie had been all together, not the least bit drunk, not chain-smoking as she did sometimes; and she didn't once laugh in that way that seemed to unnerve John so. When she was done talking, she stood and straightened Nancy's cloche hat. And Nancy felt it was like those times when Willa Ellen Bowen would adjust her bonnet or barrette just a bit while she stood waiting, shuffling her feet inside her patent leather shoes, as the family made ready for church.

To the owner it must have seemed inevitable that New World Press would soon sell out or close down. John had received more than mere intimations himself. His last two checks had been late in arriving; and after Thanksgiving the editor-in-chief, who was in fact the senior of but two editors, offered him a salary of sixty-five dollars a week—this after John had earned more than two hundred dollars over the four-day holiday by working at his desk board almost steadily. His regimen so oppressed Nancy that she left Ninth Street to take Thanksgiving dinner at the Farrands'.

From their apartment she called Mobile and informed Blaine, who had just returned from the Pacific, that she'd come home for Christmas. By giving this promise she forestalled her father's coming to New York, as he had suggested in a recent letter. It worried her that if her father came, whatever he said, however conciliatory or judiciously phrased, would result in her defending him to John. Some issues could never be resolved: each party could be reasonable to no conclusion and no avail.

Improbable though it would have sounded to Angus Farrand, had he known, Nancy left Riverside Drive wanting to talk over her *own* dilemma with Cassie and so stopped by Cassie's apartment. She hoped to avoid Frank Johnstone despite its being a holiday—why should a crook observe Thanksgiving when he was in the business of taking things! She found the apartment door open and the radio, which always was playing there, silent.

In the bathroom she found Cassie on the floor unconscious, and from her breath, which came slowly, there rose an acrid odor. When Nancy heard footsteps she was amazed to look up and see Carolyn. While they waited for the ambulance, Carolyn explained that she'd been called by Cassie about five o'clock, right after Nancy left, and had listened as Cassie talked without pause except to give out a few short laughs. Then she heard a crash as the receiver on Cassie's end fell and started tolling like a metronome—hitting against a table probably. Carolyn had rushed downtown on the subway.

At Saint Vincent's Hospital, in the emergency room, two interns inserted intravenous tubes. They searched the patient's arms and legs for signs of repeated use of needles and found none. They fitted her face with an oxygen mask, which proved to be too large, so they stuffed cotton batting around the edges. It made poor Cassie look like a First World War victim of a poison gas attack. The doctors reported to the three of them— John by now having arrived—that although Cassie was drunk, it would have taken more than alcohol to drop her so deeply into a coma. They must await test results, especially one for arterial gases, but in the meanwhile someone ought to discover what pills or tablets she might have ingested. John went off to Greenwich Avenue as Nancy and Carolyn spelled each other at the bedside.

John was admitted to the apartment by Taddio, who didn't speak but smiled slightly and followed him into the living room where Johnstone was seated in a swivel chair facing the window overlooking Greenwich Avenue. He didn't turn around when John entered, only said, "What does she want?"

"What? She can't talk! She's barely alive!"

"She's unlucky."

"I want to search through her things."

Johnstone swung around then on the tripod legs of the chair. John noticed, despite having seen the man a dozen times or more, that his middle was sunken in that manner of youngish men who seem never to become fat. His ankles were narrow and his shoes thin-soled.

"Search? Hell, no. You're not the DA. You can take her suitcases in the hall. We didn't bother to put in the lotions and stuff. She won't need those now."

"That's it? A suitcase in the hall?"

"Go see her husband if you want something."

"You son of a bitch. What kind of deal did you cut with him?"

"I see Cassie got ahold of your balls. Listen, you can't afford her. She spends in one day on clothes and presents for those kids what you make in a week. Get out, piker."

Vomit rose in Sirovich's throat. He strode toward Johnstone with his fists already made. He heard the movement of the swivel as Frank stood up. Then he recognized with a split-second objectivity that Frank must not have fought in playgrounds because his eyes were following the slow arc of John's left hand. John hit him short with the right. The blow knocked Johnstone backward into the chair, which unbalanced and threw his head into the plate glass. Shards formed in a sunburst, and when he rocked forward, Johnstone's face was streaked with blood. Turning around, John saw Taddio draw from his black coat pocket a small automatic pistol with his finger on the safety.

"Listen, Taddio, you're standing too close to get off a shot. You try and I'll kill you. I'd *like* to kill you."

Not until he was in his own apartment with his back against the closed door did he realize that he had run all the way from Greenwich Avenue, where a policeman had watched him long enough to confirm that he was wearing a suit and was not being chased. If Johnstone's carotid arteries had been cut by the glass, he might be lying dead downstairs in Saint Vincent's where Cassie lay upstairs. John called the hospital and reported he'd found nothing stronger than aspirin in the apartment. While he was in the bedrooms and bathroom searching, Taddio must have got Johnstone into a car. He didn't see either as he left.

John put down the telephone and stared into the unlit apartment. In the old days when his mother spoke of his father's only brother, who was drowned in the Adriatic while going home to war in 1915, she always repeated that Petar, as a habit, kept a revolver next to his plate whenever strangers sat at the table. He'd done so in the Sirović house at the coal camp in Sunnyside the night before he left. And John's Montenegrin godfather, who lay for three years in a Denver charity ward without speaking, cried out ten minutes before he died that he wanted his godson, then eight years old, to have his revolver. In the silence of Greenwich Village, John could hear his mother saying disgustedly that anger was always useless. But did she know that the Christians made anger necessary to righteousness?

Cassie's father arrived at LaGuardia airport still shaking from the fright of his first airplane ride. When he asked Carolyn, who met him, how far it was to the hospital, she assured him she'd pay the taxi fare. He kept asking if there were "good trains" to Mobile. She left him on the third floor of the hospital and felt sorry for the thin, worn-looking man whose skin was as dun as the country roads in Alabama.

"It's this town," he confided to her. "Cassie would have been all right in Mobile. She could have stayed, you see."

Nancy and Carolyn saw Cassie put aboard a Pullman car at Pennsylvania Station, and both felt a native shame as Cassie's father kept running ahead or, otherwise, lagging back, as if he were a minor official unconnected to the cortege. They had not given him Cassie's personal effects because it was too horrible to imagine the Newhardts pawing through her underclothes and the album of photographs. When they left the station, Carolyn apologized for Angus's not appearing. It was her first spoken criticism of her husband to Nancy, who thought it somewhat unfair inasmuch as John also was not on hand. John said he couldn't say good-bye to Cassie.

Aunt Jane described in a letter the scene at the LandN station when Cassie arrived on a stretcher "immobile except for her dark eyes." Austin had taken charge crisply without the least display of solicitousness. He placed his wife in the Mobile Infirmary under the care of private nurses around the clock, and at one o'clock each afternoon was seen to visit his wife for precisely fifteen minutes—just before she fell asleep from sedation. He would emerge from the infirmary, a nurse had told Jane Hobson, to stand at the top of its tall steps with a grave and knowing expression on his face. Cassie had returned home as the mute witness to her own defeat.

15

With Christmas only a few days away, John and Nancy went uptown to have dinner with the Farrands. On the way Nancy reported what Carolyn had confided to her at Penn Station. That time the Farrands lived in the Bronx in the mason's house amid the black neighbors, Angus had been terrified—despite there not once having incurred any slight or insult. He had demanded urgently that they move, and it was he who had found and put down the deposit on the expensive apartment on Riverside Drive. It was then that Carolyn discovered his parents were rich. They owned a car battery factory in Lansing and had been sending their son five hundred dollars each month that went straight into a bank account, unknown to her. That evening, having heard this, John looked at Carolyn with a renewed admiration—the reverse of the scorn he felt for Angus. She moved about the spacious rooms with no redundant gestures—serving a hot plate or removing a cold one, fetching an ashtray, refilling a drink. She was, he decided, blessed with great legs, although her figure was not as "deep" as Nancy's. The term occurred to him out of nowhere.

The Farrands of course knew that John Sirovich had only until the first week of February to take up his Yale fellowship. The wartime leave he'd been granted by the university would soon expire. Angus returned to the question of John's intentions, and his persistence irritated Nancy simply because it made her own role still more ambiguous, the girlfriend consigned to hang about until she was told what to do next—sign on, sign off, stay put, take off. Angus was unaware of her feelings and gave no thought to her position as he probed John's decision.

"Have you got a dissertation subject in mind?"

"Not now. Once I thought of writing on Ralph Waldo Emerson as a cryptofascist, but I can't remember why. Maybe I'll look for a subject in the newspaper one morning."

Angus laughed. "You won't find it there."

"I'm not so sure. I've got the notion that models for biography can be pieced together from headlines. Wingate would never have become a hero without first reading tabloids about T. E. Lawrence in Arabia. And maybe Eisenhower decided to become the Great Conciliator once Patton was skewered in the headlines."

"Wingate? Eisenhower? You seem to study power a lot, don't you?"

It was the yogi taunting the commissar.

"No, Angus. What I do is watch it. If you study power, you won't win it. You can't think and act at the same time. That last bit is Emmanuel Kant, not me."

Then, to everyone's surprise, including Nancy's, he spoke conclusively about the fellowship. Angus's taunt had somehow propelled him.

"No, I'm not choosing a subject for a dissertation. And Nancy and I aren't going to New Haven. I know I haven't the patience to take courses in Gothic or Icelandic. I admire all that, but I can't invest in it."

"Will you both stay in book publishing in New York then?"

Carolyn asked it with a note of relief. There wasn't going to be a fuss between the two men.

"Carolyn, I've been to enough houses to grasp that the way in, the way up, is through selling. We don't want to travel now."

In John's response Nancy recognized the basic stuff of his musing: how things worked, how authority, whether theorized about, or simply sought, was tracked.

"You're going to leave New York, aren't you, Nancy?" Carolyn asked with a tone of sad resignation. "Cassie said you were going to California."

"Carolyn, I'll call you. It's Christmas. There's time."

"What's in California?" Angus persisted.

"The movies," John replied and motioned to Nancy that they were ready to leave.

Goodnights said, kisses hastily exchanged by the women, and handshakes somehow avoided by the men, they rode down the elevator and began to walk to the subway without speaking, each chary of the other's interpretation of the events. Finally Nancy took his arm and made big strides.

"Be calm, sport. Everyone's upset about Cassie. Mother wrote again. She says folks think Austin is behaving like a gentleman. God!" She exhaled noisily. "It's so unfair to be a woman."

In the subway car, as the stations flitted by, John said, "Let's leave, then."

"Leave to where? You've got to say it again, John. You've got to say it to me."

"Los Angeles."

"Just like that? What about Christmas?"

"Of course. Let's stay in New York until a week after New Year's. You can't desert poor old Hearns during the Christmas rush—it may be their last. I'm working on three books at once right now."

"Blaine is home. What about my going to Mobile for a visit?"

"Please, Nancy. Let's finish here and then spend Orthodox Christmas with Tata."

"Don't I get a chance just once to make up our minds?"

"Nancy, what's happening tonight is that I'm paying attention to our lives, yours and mine."

"Angus was baiting you! That's not a reason for deciding now. My God, John, we're alone on this car except for a drunk down the way who's asleep. What a referee—in case we need one!"

"I don't give a damn about Angus. I do think about Carolyn. She's like you. She deserves better."

"Is that what I'm getting, better? Do they buy stationery in Los Angeles?"

"Of course," he replied, laughing. "They have to write home—nobody is a native out there. Let me tell you about chances. I was working on things before the war. Pearl Harbor came and I left. But there's Winterfield still there. He's interested in me. He knows a lot of people. He'll be interested in you. God, I hope he's alive."

"What's so magical about LA? Isn't New York the center of the earth?"

"Maybe. If all roads lead from home, then I suppose most of them end here. But it's a tough town. Not like California, where things are raw and most things are possible. It's vague, Nancy, all this, but it's true, vaguely."

"Then, too, John, you could be running away—or running home. You *are* a Westerner."

He leaned around and whispered into her lips, "Stick with me, Nancy Tuck. You can be rich or famous or happy, or all three at once. You just have to believe."

"I believe! I believe!" she cried and woke up the drunk who had lain snoring on his way to Times Square and glory.

Sitting opposite Nancy on Pullman seats on the *Twentieth Century*, John was reassuring himself of their decision. He was convinced they had made the move by agreement. If one was allied to John Sirovich, he was extremely generous: he shared his convictions as much as his possessions. He did so now. The Hudson River was a notional line, he was convinced, and important only if you crossed it, like the Rubicon. Nancy noticed that as they traversed Ohio and Indiana John was neither engrossed nor distracted by the landscape, but once aboard the *City of Denver* and speeding across the plains, he would now and then rest his head against the Pullman window and look out as if calmed by melancholy sights. What she observed was unremarkable: flat ground, high grass, little empty towns, single buildings like knots along the straight Union Pacific line.

But for John it was different. As the telegraph poles flicked past like film frames, John thought of the time when he was sixteen and his high school history teacher paid him to drive her car to visit relatives in the old Nebraska cattle town of Ogallala. Later he had published a short poem.

> Bearing true, Ogallala, along the Platte
> Half moons edged into the river's flat,
> Dry signs of the Long Trek, last tide.
> Routes unmanned. No Cheyennes ride.

One fall five years earlier, Jadwiga was perplexed by the appearance of a steadily accumulating fine dust on the windowsills. He told her it blew from Oklahoma and Kansas, as far away as four hundred miles. She was unconvinced until she saw Model Ts and pickup trucks on the highway bearing Okies westward. She had asked John if they were looking for their lost land.

As the train finally crossed into Colorado, Nancy awoke with a start and stared out at the desert, which poked stubbornly through the tilled gray fields. Passing railway junctions and small farms, she tried to liken these places to the up-country ancestral home of the Bowens, where they settled after what her father termed "a fourth remove," two generations spent in Virginia and one in Georgia. The Bowen place was several thousand acres of bottomland and pine forest between the Alabama and Tombigbee rivers. Her great-grandfather, Chandler Howard Bowen, built the house which to this day was the only very large dwelling in Manila—a name not considered exotic in a district that also held towns called Fatama, Burnt Corn, and Mexia. Nancy had spent six summers in this house, until she was eleven, always in the company of Blaine and James and their spinster aunt Bea and bachelor uncle Telford, both of whom were much older than their father and had never left Manila. Nancy had the run of the country and was pampered as the sole girl about the place—not counting Negro playmates. It was less fun for her when she turned ten and Aunt Bea decided it was unseemly for her to go barefoot and wear coveralls like James and their boy cousins. Her aunt declared the Chinese were not entirely wrong to bind a girl's feet. If Nancy Tuck didn't wear shoes, she warned, her feet would splay "just like a nigra's." Nancy couldn't appeal to Blaine. He was old enough to disdain games and to go shotgun hunting with the menfolk. She was also made to wear dresses, so that when she became a belle she'd learn not to show more of herself than was intended.

Nancy was still allowed to swim in the half-circle eddies and pools of the river, but only if Uncle Tennie stood guard on the bank. He was an old Negro whose house was raised up by her great-grandfather, who had—it pleased Nancy and Uncle Tennie to be reminded—freed all his slaves when he rode off in 1862 to join the Second Alabama Cavalry. Uncle Tennie knew just about everything that didn't require reading. He taught her how to command a hound, how to pick berries without pinking her fingers, how to keep close to her *known* needs, his example being those red cockade woodpeckers that drew sap from the pine bark with beaks sharp as needles and pecked out both a larder and workshop next door to their nests.

Uncle Tennie didn't talk much about the "old days." Nancy came to believe that this was an ultimate courtesy on his part, this not introducing a subject she couldn't intimately share. But she learned later that whenever Uncle Telford talked of Captain Quill, the friend of the Bowens who carried their cotton bales downriver to the Mobile docks where the LandN Station now stood, he was really borrowing the best recollections from Uncle Tennie. Every Mardi Gras, Captain Quill would invite guests to an all-night fete downriver to Mobile on the *Nettie Quill*, the riverboat named for his daughter, who was the hostess for her widowed father. It must have been Uncle Tennie who was aboard those nights, fetching and carrying beneath the iron stacks streaming black plumes into the spring air above the white wash of the paddle wheels. Listening to Telford, Nancy fancied how the ship bells and lighted decks brought onlookers to the landings through the whole night.

During her second year at the University of Alabama, she came down before Christmas to stay with Aunt Bea. The old woman lay dying of cancer. The house was as stark inside as outside, and the grounds were winter cold and winter bare. The rocks that lined the river looked dumped where they lay; and on the rise above the frosty fields the pines stuck into the ridge like Indian arrows. Nancy saw the house as it must have been always, perched on brick pillar foundations and with gray-faced, uneven clapboard. The holes in its underflooring were plugged with pitch. Cold air did not mask the odor from the nearby outhouses. And Uncle Tennie, for all of his being the favorite of the family, lived in a house really not better than the shacks of mill hands. The big house's central gallery was now a tunnel that drew the wet wind and whistled eerily. In her childhood it was a splendid scope to look through as she and James would race downhill at suppertime. In the bedrooms, lids formed on the chamber pots— and an ice pick was kept on the marble-topped dressing tables, part of a lady's toilette.

How was it possible that the Bowens, elsewhere affluent and publicly notable and, even in Manila, owners of huge tracts of land, could live so meagerly and meanly? On the urging of Aunt Bea, Nancy went visiting the cousins whom she'd seen only occasionally in Mobile through the years, mostly when they came down on business. Listening to their reminiscences, she wondered what strength of pride made them so self-assured that they repeated dull, factually untrue, pointless tales yet remained confident of her interest. The first day in Manila she was fatigued, the second disturbed, and by the third raging to escape. But it was not all that different from the plains of the West, now seen for the first time. Here, as there, the wind blew hot and cold and left the natives unmoved; and it seemed to Nancy that in both places life was punished beyond the ostensible needs of evolution—beyond what it took to test the strong and weary the weak. What was the point of fleeing home if most places proved to be alike? But you could not know that at first, or soon enough. Poor Cassie. She escaped because she had despised her prospects, but once driven from the hateful familiarity of home, she couldn't trust anyone but herself. And she couldn't solicit help without becoming Lilith. A woman, Nancy decided as she prepared to leave the train, could not persist long as a neutral observer.

16

In the early twilight, Ilija Sirović stood on the westbound plat-form of the Union Station. John strode toward his father and kissed him on the lips. Head to head they were the same height, both black-haired, although Tata's skin was darker both from inheritance and twenty-five years of outdoor work. A nervous silence followed when Nancy was introduced.

John said suddenly, "*Kako je kum pod mostom?* How is Godfather under the bridge?"

The tracks in Denver ran alongside the South Platte River that here was a mere trickle. Over its valley were six viaducts that led from downtown, and beneath these bridges were tar and tin shops, the old Tivoli Brewery, and a few houses wedged on the dark ground between Burlington and Union Pacific sidings.

Ilija was puzzled by his son's question—it had been years since they drove down the ramp from the Twentieth Street Viaduct to sit in a tiny arbor and drink wine which *kum* distilled from grapes so dusty they looked like raisins. Ilija explained to Nancy that he'd christened the man's child—by Serb custom the boy's father was also called *kum* by the Sirović family. Then he said that his godson stuttered because as he grew up he was interrupted by passing trains. Despite Ilija's heavily accented English, Nancy caught the joke and laughed.

" 'Tata'? It's the same as 'papa,' isn't it?" she asked as she stood on her toes to kiss his cheek.

Tata made her sit in the front seat of the 1933 Dodge so he could point out in the failing light the Capitol and the U.S. Mint; and before entering the alley to park next to the ashpit in the small backyard, he drove them past the front of the house. From the porch one could see across the street to the Bible Center and, separated by an empty lot as well as theological distance, Saint Barnabus, the Anglican church where John was briefly an altar boy, although at the time he was nineteen and twenty. Inside, Tata led Nancy to the best room, the first of a row of four upstairs that were once occupied by boarders—five men in all, because one would stay with Ilija in the basement, where he had framed out two additional rooms. Jadwiga and John had slept on opposite sides of the room next to the kitchen. Jadwiga died four years after they had moved to this house on Glenarm Place; and the house emptied as the roomers found lodgings where there was a woman to cook and wash. Ilija never moved from the basement.

They ate steaks in the kitchen, and when Tata had gone to bed, John sat in Nancy's room, she on the bed, he in the only chair. John started toward the bed but was interrupted by an exclamation of wonderment.

"You slept in the same room as your mother until you were seventeen—until you went off to college? It's a miracle you turned out to be a man!"

"We didn't read Freud in this house."

"Please don't be sore. Didn't you ever worry about taking Tata's place?"

"He didn't have a place. My parents were both Slavs and both immigrants and both poor, but they had nothing in common."

"They must have talked."

"Nancy, they argued."

She whispered, "I'll stay here. You sleep downstairs."

She came down to the kitchen early to find Tata seated at the kitchen table smoking. He had skipped work this Saturday but had awakened as usual at five o'clock. He offered her eggs and bacon and *kiełbasa* with what he called "Jewish rye bread"—the Star of David Bakery was under the Twentieth Street Viaduct.

"Will you marry Jovan?"

"When he asks me."

"We have brought shame to your mother and father."

"I can wait, Tata, even if my folks can't. John's got a clock in his head. He's waiting for the alarm to go off."

"You can trust him. He is honest." He pronounced it "hawnest." He leaned toward her. "Tell your father the judge not to worry." Then he added, unexpectedly, "Does your father swear in naturalized citizens? I tried to become one, but a judge turned me down because he thought I was a red. That was just before the First War when I was a striker in the mines."

Awakening, John heard this explanation through the open kitchen door that led to the basement rooms. He heard Nancy ask if his mother had been a citizen. Would Ilija risk admitting that his wife had been illiterate?

Tata said simply, "She was always too busy."

On Christmas morning Tata strode impatiently from the house to the car, waiting for Nancy, who on instructions from John was changing into a longer skirt and wiping off some makeup. They drove to the industrial suburb of Globeville where colonies of Slavs lived, Poles, Slovaks, Serbs, and Croats. On the way John told Nancy what to expect: no pews or chairs, no statues, no musical instruments. Inside, the nave was unlighted save for cheap green candles that gave off an acrid odor. Women in bulky coats stood on the left, the men opposite, their distance forming an aisle marked only by a series of standards from which hung tapestries that seemed to be woven with brass threads.

Unable to follow the Mass, Nancy became attentive to the choir's modulation of tone; and after a while she realized that a dialogue was being sung, declarative and plaintive, a bidding and a bringing. Across the three-portal iconostasis two priests moved, chanting Old Slavonic. She saw Tata and John standing straight as soldiers throughout the almost two-hour-long ceremony. During the responses they genuflected with their thumb, index finger, and middle finger fixed like the tip of a lance. After an hour Nancy's legs felt heavy and her eyes smarted from the incense and the compounding of human breath. She began edging backward, trying not to jostle other women, and escaped into the thin cold air on the tiny porch of the church. When Tata and John came out, neither asked if she was well.

Tata drove north toward Boulder, where they agreed to eat lunch near the university. About ten miles short of Boulder they turned onto a dirt road that soon petered out onto hard alkaline ground, mostly pebbly, here and there spotted with sage. In the distance a hawk planed. Westward, the land rose to a mesa and, beyond, to the Flatirons, great slabs of red sandstone thrust up like guardians at the gate of the higher Rockies.

"There's the slag," Tata said.

The huge mound, more than a hundred yards long and nearly as wide, was covered with weeds and ferns. Tata told Nancy it was "boney," the rock debris taken out with the coal and separated aboveground on gravity-roller chutes running down from the tipple. Of a sudden, hearing the name "Sunnyside," Nancy realized this was the sole remnant of John's birthplace. No building stood, not even a shed.

"Tata," John said in a scratchy voice, "in the Mississippi Valley there are piles like this, man-made. Nobody knows what they mean."

"I know what this means. And your mother knew."

He stood with his Stetson at his side, as he often stood at the open graves of his Serbian lodge brothers.

"Here the Big Six Company closed the mine because of the coal damp and flooding; they tore down the houses and the company store. I left and played poker for six straight days with some Croats and Bulgars in a shack in Louisville. When I came back, your mother was gone. She took you to Denver on the interurban"—he pronounced it "inter-ur-bona"—"and was working in a rooming house when I came down and caught pneumonia. She cleaned forty rooms and she tied you with a rope around the waist to the leg of my bed."

The wind rose, ruffling the ferns on the slag heap. Tata walked to the car. They drove directly to Denver and Tata let them out in front of the house before he parked the car and disappeared into the basement. Aimlessly John went to the back room upstairs to sort through his prewar civilian clothes—all hopelessly outdated—and he left them in a bureau dresser alongside his navy commission document and the pearl-handled gun bequeathed by his *kum*. He recalled telling RJ that he'd never owned anything. But now he was reminded that, even so, without property, he owed a lot.

The next morning at Union Station, Tata stalked the waiting room and never once sat down. Had they enough money—even though he had handed over to John five fifty-dollar bills? Had they checked the luggage straight through? Would they be sure to telephone a new address?

"Will he be all right?" Nancy asked John anxiously.

"Yes."

"You love him desperately."

"When I was little he made me feel safe."

The conductor called out. Tata took John aside and said something Nancy could not hear. Then he bent to kiss her, keeping his hat on so that his face was shadowed. She began to cry.

"It will be fine," he reassured her.

But he didn't wait for the train to pull out, despite their occupying Pullman seats on the platform side. John knew his father was fighting for breath.

Unless he had died during the three months past, John Winterfield would now be seventy-eight years old. When they met in 1941 he told Sirovich that when he was twenty-two—the year was 1889—his father gave him a large cash stake to start his own business. The father had made his fortune from the recurrent California land booms, not from buying and selling land but in registering deeds and insuring mining claims and, during the early days in Sacramento, from assaying gold and silver.

Following the final tense evening with the Farrands on Riverside Drive, Nancy had explained to Carolyn that one of John's hopes for California was made uncertain by his friend Winterfield's health—he and John had not been in touch during the war. Using the periodical index at Columbia's library, Carolyn had looked up Winterfield in the *Wall Street Journal*. The old man was certainly alive in October of 1945, when it was reported he had sold 40 percent of his company's shares in a "public offering." On hearing this, John dispatched a letter from Pennsylvania Station to tell Winterfield he was coming to Los Angeles to look for a job and, bragging, mentioned his companion was "the daughter of a United States district judge."

Nancy was introduced to California in perhaps the most evocatively typical place, the Union Station, where portals cut into ocher-colored walls showed views of huge palm trees and the oracle oaks whose acorns looked like tiny turbans. A person who came westward could find a deeper East, the smattery signs of that Orient sought by Cabot and Columbus, now marked by arabesques in public places and, elsewhere, bangles and bungalows.

John had stood in this station in 1941 with Lelia Dawson and watched her eight-year-old son Arthur drop his going-away presents as they waited on the train taking him to Chicago to spend Christmas with his father. Arthur was not anxious about traveling alone—he was already the experienced child of divorce—but he feared that in his absence they would change: his movie-actress mother, the cook and two maids in the house off Sunset, the gardener and chauffeur, and his tutor John Sirovich, who regularly took him on trips to the library on North Ivar Street or to play catch on the grounds of Hollywood High.

Now, four years later, a porter took up their bags to head for the taxi rank. John halted him and handed over a good-bye dollar bill. To Malibu by taxi was at least fifteen bucks, one way. When Nancy suggested he telephone, John grimaced and suggested they find a room first. This didn't prevent her from entering a booth and depositing change.

"Mr. Winterfield? I'm Nancy Tuck Bowen. Yes, John Sirovich is right here at Union Station with me. He's anxious to see you but is hesitating. Yes. Yes, sir. Thank you. That will be fine. Thank you."

She rocked back on her high heels. "He said that I must make you privileged. Isn't that neat?"

The Filipino chauffeur arrived in the 1941 Packard, which John recognized immediately. They traveled west on Sunset Boulevard, and he glimpsed branching off it the short street where Lelia Dawson's house stood and where he'd spent almost four months before Pearl Harbor. Soon they were through a canyon and winding up to the headland overlooking Malibu Beach.

As the car stopped on a bricked apron in front of the four-car garage, Winterfield stepped from the side porch. He was thinner than John had recalled but as stately as ever, his cashmere coat hanging evenly, his tie knotted in a vee that was a counterpoint to the wings of his vest. He held his usual bamboo cane but also wore a wide-brimmed hat, which became especially noticeable when he didn't take it off indoors.

"You are beautiful, my dear, very beautiful."

"Thank you, Mr. Winterfield. I admire that."

"John, do let Lucero take the bags. What kind of war was it for you? You never wrote."

"We won, of course—and very smartly did we win."

"Yes, you would want that."

He had first seen Winterfield in Lelia's living room, an old

man who had sat with a hand laid inertly on his knee, listening
with just enough attention to be polite to a voluble companion.
John had presumed him to be rich and idle but revised part of
that opinion once he began taking Arthur to Winterfield's place
in Malibu to ride the pony kept there with a one-time show
horse, a mare now retired to graze. He learned that Winterfield
was the owner of more than twenty movie houses in California
as well as being a sometime investor in United Artists. It was a
movie house company whose shares he'd sold to the public in
1945.

After luncheon John and Nancy went upstairs to a soundless
floor where half the rooms were closed off and the furniture was
shrouded in clean white sheets. Winterfield's wife had died almost
thirty years earlier. John knew from Lelia that neither his son,
who lived in nearby Santa Monica, nor his daughter, who lived
in the East, came to visit their father after their mother's death.
John and Nancy entered their spacious room and lay down. Soon
Nancy was asleep, her smooth leg across John's thigh as he sat
against the pillows smoking and wondering. Coming back to
California, he decided, was like tagging up at third base before
running in to score.

After a few days it struck Nancy that although they enjoyed
the gentle good manners of their host and the efficiency of his
four servants, nothing seemed to be happening. The old man
was obviously fond of John, yet when talking at mealtimes or
walking on the coarse grass around the rock gardens, he neither
imparted nor sought information that might be pertinent. Once
John told him how the Japanese had dropped phosphorus bombs
on his ship in the open sea during the Battle of Leyte Gulf, killing
and wounding forty of the crew. Winterfield repeated only that
he'd not heard from John during that time. Everyone seemed to
be waiting.

17

Then one morning Winterfield asked John if he'd been writing.

"I wrote a long essay on pan-Slavism, Win. I polished it so often it blinded the first reader. I put it away as a risk."

Win laughed and he offered to call an agent about a screenplay John mentioned he'd written during the war. It was agreed that John would send over a "treatment" of the script rather than the whole text. RKO's chief producer, a man named Jules Zernbach who hired John briefly in 1941, had once told him that "reading more than five hundred words ruptures any important producer."

A newspaperman named Connor lives in an Manhattan apartment next door to a young man, Jackson, who one day accidentally opens an envelope addressed to Connor containing sheets of mathematical equations. A week later a dark lady knocks on Jackson's door to ask his help for his neighbor; but it was not Connor, but a heavyset man with a knife in his liver; and when Jackson looks up, the dark lady has turned into three NYPD cops. Jackson breaks out of a police van and, returning to search Connor's place, finds a Havana address scratched on the silvered back of a mirror.

From the hallway a girl calls out, "I need a studio—not to speak of talent. If you're a thief, take your time." Jackson seizes a pert-looking girl named Cora and soon tells her all. Convinced by his garrulity that he's innocent, Cora joins Jackson to fly to Havana. They cruise the casinos and hotels in time to glimpse Dark Lady and follow her to a *finca*. Soon, in a shower of gunshots, Connor lies dead, the Dark Lady is dying, and their killers, two Japs, have just been shot from the windows by three guys in fedoras. In downtown Havana, the Fedoras say they're FBI, and Jackson relates how he was framed by Connor, who must be a traitor selling codes to Heavyset, a Russian agent, and the Japs killed Heavyset. "Makes sense," the chief Fedora says, smiling. Suddenly Cora groans, pleads cramps, and draws Jackson into an adjoining office where she hisses, "These guys are Russkies! Since when did American dentists install *steel* caps?" As they run for it, stealing a car along the way, Fedoras chasing, Cora explains, "Connor killed Heavyset, a real G-man; after setting you up, Connor and Dark Lady were followed by Japs, who were killed by the fedora-Russkies, who then suspected you have the real ciphers." At the harbor they leap from the car as it rolls off the dock into the Caribbean, Cora calls gaily to strangers, a yachtsman and his wife about to sail off, "We're the Baileys and were told to join you by the Pinchots in Miami!" Last shot: Cora and Jackson kiss outside FBI Headquarters in Washington as a Jap clicks a camera at an FBI agent upstairs who in turn is clicking at a Russkie across the street and the sound track ends, click, click, click, click.

On Vine Street John entered the office of an agent Winterfield said owed him a favor. He had half-expected to find some penitential private eye like Philip Marlowe inside, but before him sat an elderly man who was expensively dressed.

"Studios aren't much interested in spy stories now the war's over."

"Maybe. But then again, now we can criticize the Russians; and war secrets can be the stuff for a comedy."

"I'll do what I can. My connections are good at Warner's and Paramount and—unless *you* object—I can try RKO."

Christ! John had forgotten how small a town Hollywood was. He had returned there briefly in 1942, now a naval officer stationed at San Diego, to visit the RKO offices where he'd worked part-time as a scriptwriter while still tutoring Arthur; and he'd run into his former boss, Formayev, a short, thin man who worked for Zernbach. In Sirovich's absence Formayev had turned suddenly brave and now suggested that Sirovich had been Lelia's gigolo—else how could he have gotten a job from Jules Zernbach? Lelia Dawson was an RKO contract player after arriving in Hollywood from London. Hearing this, Sirovich scared the life out of Formayev. It was falsely rumored afterward that he had punched him and a studio guard. That was a long time ago.

"John?"

He recognized Lelia immediately. As he rose, his napkin fell to the floor, and in plucking it up he inadvertently appraised her legs; they were as shapely as ever. At sea the exec used to say, "With boxers the legs go first, with women, last."

Nancy and he sat in the Beverly Wilshire Hotel at the same table where Win and John had taken luncheon the day before Pearl Harbor. John had come to stay in Win's house after Arthur was put on the train for Chicago; and he never made it back to Lelia's house. From Win's he took a train to Denver to enlist in the navy. Now, four years later, they were sitting in the Beverly Wilshire in the course of returning one of Win's cars they'd borrowed to move into a room on Vermont Avenue.

"Are you from Colorado, Miss Bowen?"

"No, Alabama." She smiled. "It's where we met and where I got this accent."

"Where else did you spend the war, John?"

"In the Pacific, Lelia. Nancy and I have been staying with Win and just found a place near the USC campus." He paused. "Is Arthur okay now?"

"What an odd way to ask! Of course he's all right. He's thirteen and boarding at Andover and loves it."

John told Nancy, "In the old days Arthur and I talked of becoming hobos and running away."

"Arthur didn't run away but you did," Lelia said, her English accent reviving.

"Lelia? Are we talking Latvian? I need a translator."

"John, start again." It was Nancy who said this, more puzzled than alarmed.

"I apologize, Miss Bowen," Lelia said earnestly. "I'm afraid I've gotten off badly. John left Hollywood without telling Arthur good-bye, and we didn't even know if he was alive." She smiled at Nancy. "Will you and John come to stay with me one weekend? I'll call." She was away from the table now, having risen and collected her purse and cigarette lighter.

"Did you make love to her?"

"No, Nancy. I told you before. I lived next to the gardener in a cottage at the back, up the hill from the big house. Sometimes I spent nights in the house in Arthur's bedroom. I wasn't looking to ravish someone's mother. I wasn't Austin Newhardt."

"Come on, John! Aren't you even curious about it?"

"No."

"Well, she is."

The house on Vermont was old. Besides a gas ring for cooking, the rented room was distinguished by a Murphy bed—to Nancy a new device which caused her to wonder if the inventor, "ol' Murph," had been a constant satyr. She was beginning to accrue opinions on Los Angeles, one being that it was "footless" to make appointments in a city where you couldn't get *there* from *here*.

A week after they moved in, John heard a tooting and, from the window, saw Nancy seated behind the wheel of a 1940 Chevy convertible. She had spent her mad money. When John objected that they really had no place to go—even if they could get there—she argued he'd need the car if he accepted one of the two jobs he could accept straightaway if he was so inclined. He could teach English and Latin at a private high school for boys in Pasadena. Carolyn had urged John to write the headmaster, a former classmate of Angus Farrand. Despite its being the middle of the year, a position was open: the English master had broken his hip in an automobile accident. The other job—free-lance and piecework, as in New York—came about by means of the reconciliation with Lelia. When she telephoned to ask them to spend a weekend with her, she said a man named Bob Channing "might have something." Channing and Channing, Inc., occupied two rooms over a store on Santa Monica Boulevard far west of USC. John drove Nancy's convertible.

As Channing was only thirty-eight or so, John asked if the other Channing was his father or brother. Bob said that Aldous Huxley, who now lived in Hollywood, had told him that the English publishing house Faber and Faber had been founded by a single man who thought the name sounded weightier doubled up.

"I like the notion of the English pretending to lineage," John told him. "Everybody wants more of what he's supposed already to have."

Channing bought rights from New York magazine and book publishers to sell options on fiction or nonfiction stories to movie studios. In New York he hired readers to skim publications; and in Los Angeles he paid writers thirty dollars to create three-page script treatments to submit to studios. When he asked John to guess how many of the articles and books perused were finally optioned by a producer, John replied without hesitation, one in four hundred.

Impressed because the figure was close to the actual ratio, Bob asked, "What's your game? Poker? Gin?"

"I play everything except credit."

He had once asked R. J. Fredericks when was the best time to buy stocks or bonds, and RJ had replied, "When you have the money."

Channing told him his most recent sale was a new Graham Greene novel about an unfrocked Catholic English priest in Mexico and commented, "If MGM does produce it, they'll convert him to Anglican—there are fewer of *them*."

"Right," John concurred. "Ronald Colman. Unshaven. Soiled white shirt. Jaded, but excited by remorse."

What came of this talk was not John's writing script treatments but rather a comment by Channing on being told John had looked for a publishing job in New York.

"There's no publishing here, pal. Well, maybe penny-ante stuff. One of my old writers, a failed Ph.D. at Cal Tech, did start a tiny journal on particle physics, which nobody can define."

John Sirovich could define it. It wasn't his competitive pride-fulness that Channing had triggered but rather his curiosity. About journals he knew next to nothing, in fact only of two. The *PMLA* was for college instructors, heavy but obligatory professional reading. And his favorite history professor at Boulder had started from scratch *Renaissance and Reformation*, a scholarly journal printed in Denver in quantities of only four hundred copies per quarterly issue. Professor Harrison edited the journal and arranged for printing. His wife handled the subscriptions and mailing—all out of their dining room, where on a couple of occasions John gave her a hand.

Channing professed to be disappointed, as did the Pasadena headmaster, when John said he was "working on something else." Nancy was indifferent, quite uncharacteristically. She had got a taste of Hollywood during the third week of February when they stayed at Lelia's house overnight. At a Saturday-night cocktail party, she was introduced to a fast-talking short brisk man named Jacob Levinheimer. He immediately mentioned her accent.

"Tallulah Bankhead," he told her, "talks like you."

Nancy replied that Tallulah's drawl was authentic and mentioned that her family and the Bankheads were longtime friends.

"Well, regardless, Miriam Hopkins has a nice talk. But she's not big. She won't make it big now."

"Mr. Levinheimer, are you an agent or something?"

He was enchanted to tell her he was production chief at Paramount. Then his manner turned brisk and he moved away. Nancy was left with the impression he was bored with any conversation that was not also a transaction. Yet he returned in about ten minutes to ask if she had ever acted.

"Act?" She laughed. "Mr. Levinheimer, I've had to act all my life. It's what Southern belles do."

It was at this party that the Polish countess was introduced to John by Lelia, hoping that instant congeniality would result. Told of his heritage, she asked in Polish where his mother had been born. When he replied in a flat accent with limited diction, she sensibly switched to English.

"Of course," she said when he named the city of Nowy Targ, "it is not too far from Zakopane, a most pleasing resort. Your mother surely told you of it."

A resort! His mother on having her passage paid to America by the Botany Mills had mistaken Bremen for Danzig and Baltimore for New York City. Was there no inoculation against illusion for the titled or the moneyed? Oscar Levant, now in Hollywood, said it was tough sledding to do social work among the rich.

"Madame Modjeska came from Galicia, too. She founded a colony near here, a place called Anaheim, I believe. Her husband was well-meaning. He patronized radicals without agreeing with them—the only sensible way to be modern. You know, he and

Modjeska imported Poles here to live *la noblesse de la nature*. *Quelle folie!* They divided the work, and Modjeska herself was in charge of *la cuisine*. Can you imagine! The animals died of thirst. One cannot blame poor Sienkiewicz, who was a writer after all, but Snypiewski was supposed to be an expert on farming, yet he joined the others in playing Mozart while the crops rotted. *Quel désastre!*"

Could he imagine? Imagine a Polish Brook Farm or New Harmony? Of course he could! Centuries ago the Poles created the *liberum veto*, whereby a single gentleman in Parliament could stop a law from being passed—or could by himself dissolve the entire parliament—merely by saying, "*Nie pozwalam*, I don't allow it." Such a people could embrace the ideal in Anaheim.

"What a tremendous story!" John almost shouted it from a sudden joy. Other guests near them stopped talking. "Modjeska was quite right. Dreamers have to find places. Atlantis. Cibola. The Northwest Passage. America is the dream that was found."

"What can you mean?" She held her cigarette aside as if he'd risen from smoke. "It's unreal to me."

"Sure, it's unreal. It's why in America you can call things as you wish to see them. Poverty is an opportunity. Crime is a business. Education is an asset."

As the countess moved away, her face fixed in a smile, John looked about him, saw the others who had fallen silent; and then went outside through a side door onto a clay path that spiraled up the hillside to the gardener's house, winding past cockspurs and jacaranda and bottlebrush. The garden was overcrowded. In Los Angeles people tried to deny the underlying desert by attempts at floral extravagance. He remembered Lelia's English gardener complaining that the soil might be suited to olives but not to "flock and flax." He turned and reentered the house on the second floor, walked along the corridor to Arthur's old room, now empty of clothes, and sat on the window seat to look at the beads of light below on Sunset. Nancy found him there when it was time to go to bed.

18

Two weeks later at a small dinner party at John Winterfield's house, Nancy once more ran into Jacob Levinheimer. On being introduced by Win, who knew she'd met him at Lelia's, she was afraid he might not remember her. She was quite happily mistaken.

"Why, I know this lovely little girl," he said, "because we talked about who is the most Southern in the business already."

Nancy sat down quickly, because in high heels she was almost a foot taller than he. Win left them, and they sat alone on the glassed-in porch that commanded the Pacific.

"Mr. Winterfield says you have a sure instinct, like Louis B. Mayer," she ventured to remark. It wasn't exactly what Win had said, which was that Jake Levinheimer didn't take foolish chances.

"Ha! In that case I'm underpaid, however." He paused. "What kind of instinct was that?"

Nancy launched forth at once, improvising, as she declared that "movie presence" must be entirely different from "stage presence."

"Listen, your friend Lelia Dawson knows where she can make

it here regardless. She talks about going back to the stage, but she's smart she don't."

"I suppose one has nothing to do with the other. Did Irving Thalberg ever stage a play? He was the best producer of movies, wasn't he?"

"No, he wasn't. Thalberg was one of those things. He was a star, but he wasn't best. He was a nice, neat Jewish kid—and in Hollywood that's ten feet tall. But Mayer is better."

"Mr. Levinheimer, can I apologize?" She gulped air. "I really know nothing about movies—except for going to them. I'm out of my depth."

"I figured. Call me next week. I might give you a test. We'll see, regardless."

"Are you serious?"

"I'm always serious. You got a nice smile and a nice figure and you're a clean girl. Let me tell you, Nancy—it's Nancy, right?—old Louis B. used to tell those girls at MGM that what you need regardless is three things: big eyes, big smile, big tits."

On hearing her account as they drove through the canyon in the Hollywood Hills, John was amused and delighted. But he also noted with pleasure that while Nancy was exuberant, she was also alternately anxious, her hopefulness tempered by hesitancy. She had on her own learned that the movie business was always accompanied by talk, unremembered suggestions, broken "sure things," abandoned projects, talk, talk, talk. John was never at a loss for words, yet he wanted no part of theatrical parlance because it turned on *deals*. More and more he was unwilling to go out to meet strangers for no purpose other than meeting them. He told Nancy he wanted to earn the right to get away from people he would never see again or if he did would hardly remember him.

A small part of what was souring him was Lelia's averse manner. They had nothing to converse about except the absent

Arthur—and it seemed Lelia was keeping her son permanently away from John Sirovich. She said he had "just missed" Arthur on his midterm break, yet it occurred only the week before her party. And when John asked for Arthur's address she promised it without delivering it. John had never heard the boy's last name, that is, Lelia's ex-husband's name, and so was at a loss how to address a letter. In the old days, when tutoring Arthur and working at RKO and living up the hill in the gardener's cottage, it had been pleasant to be summoned when Lelia came home late from a party or from the studio when night shooting on the lot was under way. Lelia would sit listening over hot cocoa, her chin propped on an arm, the spit curl, her movie trademark, falling away from her forehead like a question mark.

That he was incapable of small talk without making an effort, therefore incapable, was no secret to Nancy or to Jane Hobson, who had suspected it in Mobile and seen it confirmed in New York. But people around John were often puzzled and captivated by his verbal antics, his rallies—as at the party with the countess. He would enter a subject as if trailblazing—which had led RJ to ask if everything happened to him for the first time. Win was aware of this too, of course. On the barest cue John would speak of how the City of Los Angeles stole water from the Kern River to the north and from the Owens to the east; or how the cavalry evolved into the tank corps; or how Bill Hart learned to speak a Sioux language.

Nancy was often surprised by his inability to take refuge in conventionality, his not knowing certain rules that enable casual conversation to proceed. If you knew how to deflect attention from yourself and avoid offending others, it made things easier. Nancy knew from experience that conventionality was learned. From the age of four she had been told never to touch her hair or nails or face in public, and when an adult not to rise when introduced to a stranger, and never to inquire or volunteer the fact of someone's age, or comment when introduced to a person that he or she looked or sounded like another person—it was no compliment to make someone seem common.

The editor Channing had called a "failed Ph.D." lived in a small blue-and-white bungalow smack against a one-time canal in Venice. His name was Larkin, a thin, balding man of only about forty whose big mustache made him look Italian. He wore Levi pants, which John had never seen before other than on workmen. Inside the house were stacks of books and journals and, similarly stored, hundreds of phonograph records. When John had telephoned, explaining that he was interested in the business of publishing journals but wasn't seeking secrets, Larkin had been cordial.

"Tell me," he began once they'd exchanged a few bits of autobiographical identification, "how did you come to know Channing?"

"I talked to him once about free-lance writing. Other than his dropping names and playing cards, I know nothing about him."

"Half of what he says never happened."

"And the other half?"

"Won't happen."

But Larkin was not cynical about his own affairs and was surprisingly candid. He told John that he'd started with several journals he did *not* publish. He had mailed out flyers to librarians and professors announcing a new journal, seeking subscriptions and soliciting payment; if not enough replies came in, he just didn't produce it, not even one issue.

"The librarians don't mind that?" John was amazed.

"Not if you write them and say it's postponed—and of course return any checks. It's done all the time in this business. They're used to it."

"How much do you charge for a scientific journal with, say, four issues?"

"About forty dollars a year. And the nice thing is that you are paid up front and don't pay taxes until later. Listen, I checked at Cal Tech while I was still working on the doctorate. Before the war, price was a factor. Now it's wide open. So much GI Bill money is coming into colleges and so many new state U's are being built that librarians pay the going price."

When he heard that Sirovich's own field had been English literature, he warned that "soft" disciplines were not a fertile ground for periodical publishing—nothing *crucial* was happening in literature or art history or musicology and the like. But in science and medicine and in engineering and mechanics, the specialist had a true urge to read about new developments.

As John left, thanking Larkin, he asked, "And how did you come to work for Channing?"

"Through my ex-wife. He was screwing her. She thought I ought to earn some money while I was going to Cal Tech."

"How did you find out?"

"He told me. Channing's got to win every move. Of course, he doesn't know chess—you don't play it that way. Now I'm free of her *and* him."

Sirovich had never before thought of librarians as *customers.* When he found out in the *Los Angeles Times Mirror* of a convention at a small resort hotel in Redondo Beach, he drove over and paid twenty-four dollars admission, writing "San Diego Public Schools" on the paper badge he was given to pin on his lapel. It was an annual meeting of college librarians from Los Angeles, Ventura, Riverside, and Orange counties. Unlike the trip to Venice, he thought this one a waste of time until by accident he found out about another product librarians would buy—the price be damned, probably. During a panel session a woman from Fullerton claimed that scholarly periodicals served not only the faculty but also those brighter students who, reading them, might be encouraged to go on to professional training. A man seated next to him muttered.

"Bullshit," he said and then turning to Sirovich whispered,

"Hell, I never saw a journal article *assigned*, let alone a kid read one."

During the coffee break John sought him out, shook hands.

"You mean that only graduate students would read issues of, say, *Studies in Entropy?*"

"Christ, I don't even know what *entropy* means. No, I doubt they would read it any more than junior college kids would."

"A publisher I know says there's a lot of money available to libraries—I mean, compared with before the war."

"There is. But let me tell you why the places like the new state U's and junior colleges will spend. They want prestige. They all want to be Stanford or Berkeley. Have you ever been to the Huntington?"

"Yes."

"Well, private libraries like the Huntington and the endowed collections in campus libraries hold manuscripts, rare books—firsthand sources, the real McCoy. These new places want sources. They want to say you can do true scholarship in *their* libraries. They'll pay for facsimiles."

The break was over. People gathered.

"Christ, I've been boring you! Why should the San Diego high schools give a damn, right?" he asked, looking at John's badge. "Being a navy town you must lose half your students every year, what with sailors being transferred. Great beaches though, right?"

John came away from Venice and Redondo Beach with two kinds of publishing in mind as possibilities: scholarly periodicals and facsimiles of famous works. These might just be the way to break in. He needed to know more; and he would need working capital. New money was harder to come by than new knowledge.

To Nancy, John's discoveries, inconclusive as his plans were, seemed further evidence that they had to move out of the Vermont Avenue room. In that one room, she complained, they had become "inseparable in the worst way." Moreover, what if Paramount did call? Could she go to a test rising from ol' Murph's bed and fortifying herself with a breakfast made on a gas ring? It was humiliating!

They dug into their capital and found an apartment for three hundred a month in Silverlake, that still somewhat bohemian section of Los Angeles below the Hollywood Hills. The four small rooms were bare, but Nancy set about buying secondhand furniture to keep busy and spoke of entering UCLA—it was closer to Silverlake than USC—and so earn the AB degree she'd abandoned at Tuscaloosa. Some of that speaking was conducted in telephone calls to Mobile and resulted in her father's sending a bank check for three thousand dollars with a note written from his chambers expressing a hope that it would cover her tuition and expenses.

On an invitation from Win, they drove to Malibu on a Saturday. Being the weekend, it was a perfectly natural time for an afternoon visit and dinner, yet Nancy wondered if Win was losing track of them—perhaps he thought John had taken a job and so was not available on weekdays. Certainly, with his movie connections, he couldn't have assumed she was already working at Paramount. She had taken the screen test, wonder of wonders, but there followed an enigmatic silence. She received no indication of whether she was being considered seriously for a role. John was indeed working but not at any paying job, and these days spent mornings in the periodical and rare-book rooms at the large library downtown and most afternoons in Nancy's car, calling on librarians in colleges nearby—not only USC, UCLA, and CIT, but also Whittier, Pomona, Occidental, and other colleges and libraries within a hundred miles of Silverlake.

To Nancy going through the white portal of Paramount's main gate had been thrilling in itself—like stepping into a movie credit or the opening take—and a little frightening. What if the guards didn't find her name in the log? All she'd received was a telephone call, no letter. But once she was inside the studio it struck her as obviously efficient, for all its size. The employees she met seemed expert, if also routinely curt.

Cursing was the local idiom with almost everyone, for makeup artists and wardrobe mistresses as well as for the boy who led her to the sound stage through the flat-sided alley. The stage stunned her, vast and silent and oddly unearthly, with air that seemed foreign, as if not to be breathed by human beings. After the boy left, she stood alone next to a single fixed camera, and within a quarter hour—presumably no overhead was to be wasted on an untried actress—there appeared the first of eight people to conduct the test. Within the hour they were ready and the test was under way.

The script was a short scene from a 1939 movie that starred Priscilla Lane and consisted of her talking into a telephone. Nancy was to react variously to a man on the other end of the line who was telling her slowly, but no less definitely, that they would not be seeing each other again. She was at first gay, then did her best to sound hopeful although agitated, then became gradually suspicious and fearful, until she ended bravely, in tears. Win told her that Levinheimer's hand was to be found in this choice of scripts. Everyone, after all, has experience talking on the telephone. And she had no need, appearing alone, to harmonize her voice or gestures with those of another actor. Luise Rainer had won an Oscar for no more than four minutes on the telephone in *The Great Ziegfeld*.

Shortly after their arrival at Win's place in Malibu, as they were sitting on the terrace on the lee side of the big house, a woman drove up in one of Win's cars. She stepped out carrying shopping bags, each with the logo of a Beverly Hills shop. After being introduced by Win as Patricia Lindley, she excused herself and went upstairs, quite clearly at home. Nancy was attentive. From that first day in Los Angeles, she had wondered about the implications of a closet full of expensive and currently fashionable clothes—a closet just outside the master bedroom—and now she was certain.

"I knew he had a mistress!" she said in a hoarse whisper as Win went inside.

"A mistress? He's seventy-eight, Nancy. She could be just a friend."

"Mistresses *are* friends, dummy!"

At luncheon Patricia Lindley became "Pat," and the talk became animated. She was a pretty woman, not beautiful but quite winning, about thirty-five years old, plump, a true blond. Her neck and waist and legs were shapely but her fingers and wrists were thick. Nancy noted that she cleverly wore no rings or bracelets, not even a wristwatch. Nancy appraised her cloisonné necklace at no less than five thousand dollars, judging from the stores on Wilshire Boulevard and North Rodeo Drive she had looked into one day with Lelia Dawson. For John it was hard to guess where Pat came from originally. Her diction was now and then off center. Pat spoke of New York and Sydney and Toronto and Key West. Of the last she commented wryly, "It's an outpost; only, the Apaches are inside."

After Win declared himself in need of sleep and Nancy confessed she still succumbed to Alabama siestas, the remaining two strolled, Pat chatting mostly about LA, along the paths to the stable and back around the water tower that fed the rock pools and the wind-dried lawns. Outside the paddock she asked if he remembered the mare that years ago was stabled there.

"I used to ride her. You brought Lelia Dawson's boy to ride the pony. Win told me each time you came."

"He didn't tell me about you."

"No. You are Win's friend. Now you've found he had another friend—one who perhaps doesn't fit your recollection of how things were. It happens that way, John. Don't worry about it."

"I was rude. I'm sorry, Pat. I wish I'd seen you in 1941."

"I was here. Win probably didn't want to shock you."

"Was I that young?"

"You were that strict."

"Pat, how sick *is* Win?"

"Very. He needs your kind of friendship now more than ever. John, he feels manly in your company."

"I don't know how I can help. I never seem to know how to help intangibly."

She laughed. "You're no do-gooder. You should be glad of that. Listen, I know people who call you up on behalf of worthy causes and can ruin your life!"

She steered him back to the house by taking his arm. He could feel the fullness of her breast. When he asked how long she'd known Lelia, her grip tightened slightly.

"We don't get on. She finds me wanting. I've never worked, or created anything, not even a child. I find her wanting, too."

She drew away and hugged herself against the rising westerly wind. Then she moved a step toward him, placing her palm to the side of his neck, for him a surprisingly erotic gesture.

"Talk with Win often, won't you?" As he turned to open the French doors into the house, she stopped him, put her hands loosely on his hips and looked up. "One more thing. Lelia takes a different view of you than you suppose."

19

Paramount telephoned with a request: Could Miss Bowen take another test? Levinheimer was present on the second occasion, as was his assistant, a man named Philips. When the takes for lighting and positioning were tested and approved, a telephone call was made, and within half an hour Levinheimer and Philips appeared on the sound stage.

Nancy stood stock still, untouched by all the noise, by the bustling of studio hands, and the rudely unfunny commentary that passed mouth to mouth. She did not comb her hair or straighten her seams or otherwise indicate her readiness. Her composure made Philips look at her seriously. And several people between her and the camera began to behave as if she were waiting on *them*. In the center of her awareness she was convinced at that moment she had movie presence—whatever it was, however Jacob Levinheimer defined it. After the fourth take, Levinheimer left. Philips said he would call her "within the next few days or a week." Then, pausing as if to remind himself, he said that Paramount was casting a movie already set for production.

Her elation was not wholly released until she was back in Silverlake. Her heels tattooed the steps of the apartment house as she ran to the third floor. She was breathless and tearful as she told John it was going to work—it was really going to work! He looked at her proudly, laughed, and gravely stood to shake her hand. The days after the second test passed as if dragged through the calendar. Nancy began to look for houses on Hollywood Hills. And she gave up the notion of taking courses at UCLA. Then she decided nothing would come of it: if Paramount was so efficient she would have heard, surely. She had told Levinheimer she was out of her depth and now the studio had proved it so. One morning she declared in a mock brazen tone, "Aren't you lucky I can't act?" and whipped off her nightgown as she stood over him at the secondhand desk where he kept his notes and copies of various journals.

That John Sirovich had never talked about marriage or a common future was the greatest secret of her life. No one could suspect this was possible, not her family or Tata, or Carolyn and Angus, Win and Lelia, or anyone who observed the obvious evidence of their living together and how intricately each showed the other both trust and affection. Her mother, like Tata, had by now come to believe they were bound by intense love, so that each was the trigger to the other. They assumed that when Nancy was ready, she could in minutes make John memorialize their intimacy. It was not so. No one but Nancy could know that John was incapable of making the statement "Let's marry" unless he could invest it with the whole of his life. This extremism had at the beginning, in Mobile, struck her as a sign of awful egotism— as if his sentiments were the sole issue left to be resolved between them. One morning, about five-thirty, she awoke to the odor of cigarette smoke and heard John say to himself, "The past runs out, just like the future." She mumbled acquiescently in the hope he would go back to sleep. Instead, he reached over to cup her breasts and she knew they'd make love. It was a wonderful way to enter the morning, slowly at first, then sensationally.

When Nancy was finally summoned to Paramount, she was un-prepared to talk terms. The elation she felt was so great that it did not occur to her that she'd need an agent or a lawyer. Money had not entered into her fears and hopes as she'd waited; nor did it now, as she anticipated acceptance. When John urged her to call Win about hiring someone, she asked *him* to come along—she regarded it as too late to deal with a stranger.

Levinheimer's office was typical of the real Hollywood—not an immense stage with gleaming floors, lighted logs in fireplaces, and sparkling crystal on cocktail bars. Nor was Levinheimer Edward Arnold or Lionel Atwell. After some desultory talk that required no responses, he asked how long John and Nancy ex-pected to stay in Hollywood.

Nancy, suddenly agitated, ready with emotion, asked, "Mr. Levinheimer, if I failed the tests, why did you ask me here?"

"Now, now," he said, "don't you be upset by a busy man already."

He explained he was prepared to cast Nancy in a featured part in a B comedy in which a nurse played opposite two leading men, a doctor and a war veteran patient.

She was at once contrite and turned to John. "Say it's what I heard!"

Levinheimer now poised an ivory letter opener between his thumbs. His eyeglasses barely glinted in the morning sun show-ing through two big windows. He was practicing his game as a negotiator. When John asked what terms were proposed for Miss Bowen, he was quick to retort.

"What? Terms? Standard, regardless. Standard."

"Mr. Levinheimer, I suppose this is the only moment a be-ginning actress can ask questions about money."

"Listen, friend, this is a feature role I'm talking."

It exploded from him as he rose, but the impression he meant to convey—one of commanding presence—was dispelled by his being only five feet two, so that his coat fell below the edge of the desk and he looked like Balzac in the monk's robe writing while standing.

"You got to be meshuga. This girl ain't even kicked a shoe, nevertheless. It's a contrak, a regula contrak."

"May we read it and get back to you?"

Nancy blanched and put her fist to her mouth, her fear suddenly renewed. She knew, sickeningly, that John would persist. When she had asked him to accompany her, he had explained that a producer at Paramount would not have ordered two screen tests—and appeared himself to monitor the second—unless he had a good hunch about her. John had even listed to Nancy her own assets, borrowing from Levinheimer himself: she was very good-looking, spirited, authentically upper class, a Southerner, cheap to hire—and, yes, a clean girl. Paramount gained nothing if the transaction were to fail at this point. He was convinced that Levinheimer would not turn her down—even if she was a mere girl who had never kicked a shoe in a chorus line. He put his hand to Nancy's forearm, motioning her to her feet. She resisted, fearful to leave, like a woman pausing over her jewelry in a burning house.

"Okay, then. Okay," the producer said with a knowing and tolerant expression that barely covered his displeasure. "Okay. The contrak you can pick up Tuesday."

On the sidewalk outside the studio, Nancy's hands were still trembling. What they said was true. What they said was that in Hollywood, as on Wall Street, it all shows and it all plays. She didn't ask John what had set him off to argue in this way. Had she done so, he would have said that Jacob Levinheimer had made a mistake: he had put fear into Nancy too early with his question about how long she'd be in town. The off-putting blow should have come later. Plainly the man was no scriptwriter.

The next day Nancy was invited to a sneak preview of a Paramount picture at a small movie house in Gardena. Levinheimer's deputy, Philips, a neat man who wore a white shirt and a lightweight suit with silk threads showing, introduced John and Nancy to a long-legged and deeply tanned girl who he said was under contract to the studio. Her companion turned out to be Bob Channing. Nancy, who had not met him, saw a big, strong man who worked his fists while talking—had he just given up smoking? His curly blond hair was brushed straight back without a part.

Bob drew John away from the others as they all waited under the marquee for the regular feature to end. "Are you married to that terrific girl?"

"No. Is that your wife?"

"No, my wife is pissed off permanently. We're arguing over the property. Is she going to sign with Paramount?"

"I'm sure she is. Her lawyer is working on it."

"Philips says his boss doesn't fancy you, but he's not a sorehead. I've got a tip for you. It's a job writing dialogue, a lot of money in short order because the script chief at Paramount needs it in a hell of a hurry."

The next day John sat for an hour outside the man's office, doodling on a copy of *Fortune*, converting the bar graphs into windows and cornices. When he was invited in, the chief told him Paramount was filming Van Meergeren's remarkable story. Expecting an immediate positive reply, he asked John impatiently if he knew who Van Meergeren was.

"Sure. He sold Göring a Vermeer he'd faked and then, recently, he painted another Vermeer just to prove he was not a Nazi collaborationist, only an artist who hated critics."

"Well, we'll make him into a patriot. You want to write extra dialogue? Three weeks. Three thousand."

"Thanks, no. I don't know enough about art. Your staff writers can do it better."

Three thousand was more money than he'd ever seen on a check except for Nancy's banker's check in New York. But he had no intention of owing Paramount and thus affecting Nancy's negotiation. John was now sure that Channing was pimping for

Paramount. The leggy girl had been invited to the sneak preview to give Bob a chance to put an offer to Nancy's boyfriend.

As soon as Nancy picked up the contract, she brought it to the apartment in a great rush, slamming the car door and again tattooing the stairs. She nudged John impatiently as he scanned the twelve pages—as if to spur him to a faster reading. He ignored the boilerplate clauses because he assumed Frank Hopkins—Winterfield's lawyer who had already offered to act for Nancy—would protect her against rapacious small print. Finally, he said the contract wouldn't do.

"*Won't do?* What does that mean?"

"It's a contract for a girl who ordinarily would be expected to take acting instruction, attend publicity parties, and maybe take more tests. It's not a contract for a girl Paramount wants to put in a picture right now."

"John, it is *my* contract. It gets me started. It puts me inside. You always said that just getting inside was half the battle!"

"Yes, I suppose I did. But, then, the same holds for a prison sentence. Nancy, this makes you work for Paramount for *seven years*. The salary is too small. There's no provision for raises depending on pictures you make and no provisions for your being lent out to other studios. Lelia's deal with RKO always made her money because of being lent out."

"You're not a lawyer! Win got me a lawyer. I need your support. Why look for complications? Don't be clever, please. Please! I love you. Now you love *me*."

"Tell Hopkins to try for better terms."

Nancy was sobbing as she ran from the room. John heard the wheels of the car crimp, whining.

Two hours later the telephone rang. "John?" It was Harold Bowen. "I hope you and Nancy will make it this Christmas." A pause. "It's hard to believe that she's got in hand a real contract to make a movie. I rejoice in her skill. I'm sure you do, too."

"Judge, the contract is not just to 'make a movie.' It's a contract for seven years."

"Yes, of course, but surely it's not worth arguing the points now. Afterward, no doubt, there'll be room for adjustments. Mr. Winterfield suggested as much when Nancy called from his house."

"Did he say it should be signed as is?"

"Well, no. He spoke of his lawyer, a Mr. Hopkins. Nancy feels Mr. Hopkins is neutral."

"I'm not neutral, Judge. I'm on Nancy Tuck's side."

"So am I. We are not in any event comparing ourselves. I'm much too old for that. I'm a father and a husband. I believe you are neither."

John Winterfield waited out front, on the bricked driveway of his four-car garage, to convey his sense of urgency, to signal that he could be of aid. He came out when he heard the car shift gears as it wound up the last hill. Earlier he'd asked Pat to call John Sirovich at Silverlake to urge him to come to Malibu. Nancy had driven on to Lelia's and would not await John's arrival. Especially frail, Winterfield stood with his face pinched from the cold, his eyes hooded against pain.

Once they were inside the house, he said, "I sent Lucero for you, John, because we need to talk. Frank Hopkins was here. He gave Nancy a good proposal, one I think Jake Levinheimer can accept without losing face. It's for four pictures."

"Win, it went wrong somehow. All I tried to do was to give her advice, that's all."

"Ah, that *is* all. That is the risk. I never could give advice to my children. I didn't know how."

"Surely, you must have. You gave me advice."

"But that was easy. You were interested in my life—and not worried about your own. One's children seem not like that."

"Win, I never seem to know what people want."

"Marriage may suit you then. You can trust Nancy to know, I think."

Pat came downstairs and after greeting John told him Nancy was spending the night with Lelia—she'd just called to make sure John was with Win. Would he spend the night with them? He agreed.

"I'll make sure your old room is ready," she replied and left them with drinks, soda for Win, coffee for John.

"I was an uncertain father," he said suddenly.

Winterfield had never spoken to John of his long-dead wife, nor of his son or the daughter who lived in the East and who, after she left a prep school at Dobbs Ferry in New York thirty-five years earlier, had returned to California but twice.

"I was uncertain probably because I was an indifferent husband. It never occurred to me that I could just not marry."

"I don't understand."

"It didn't occur to me that not everything *has* to be done in the long run, so to speak. A man ought to be able to seek companionship that is not formally a demand on him forever, but of course as a husband, as a father, that's not the case. All my life I've found it hard to make serious comments without the risk of their being taken as my pledges to the future. It's especially so here—in the movie business, which is changeable and unsettled. Triviality is the safest tone in Hollywood, not the most profitable, only safest." Winterfield paused as if in pain, as if constrained. "John, Patricia suits me because she knows the difference between men and women. You can owe a man and pay or not pay as a matter of character. It's hard to owe a woman." A man went through life paying ransoms. Shakespeare said it first. Winterfield was sure Shakespeare meant married men.

At dinner Win said, needing to stop the course of his thoughts, "What will you do then? Nancy says you have started two journals on money you had left from the navy. Was it much, may I ask?"

"Three thousand dollars, Win. Nancy has been paying our keep in Silverlake so I can get started."

"I don't know your business. Will two of these periodicals carry you very far?"

"No. I need to publish ten or twenty. But it will come along."

"What are the names of these magazines?" Pat asked.

"*Soil Mechanics* and *Power Grid Design.*"

"Oh, Lord," she exclaimed, laughing, "just the thing to read under a hair dryer."

Later, after John went upstairs, Pat sat in the kitchen sharing with Win a good night drink of hot milk and honey. The servants were in their quarters over the garage. The house was silent.

"You reached Frank Hopkins, Win. I heard. Nancy will listen to him. She's not really so headstrong. She's suddenly found herself where she wanted to be. She's being sought. It's heady."

"Yes. But she's got to learn that John can't leave matters alone, even if he's uninterested in large questions of contention. I remember before the war we managed, one day when Arthur was busy riding the pony, to convince each other that political parties exist because of arithmetic—you need two in order to count—to count supporters, enemies, votes."

"That sounds like him. He puts labels on things so he can put them away. Is he really so cynical? I can't tell. Nancy I know like a book."

"No, he's just careless about people, generous but careless."

"That can hurt."

"It can."

The next morning Win asked John to drive him down the coastal highway to Santa Monica to a storage warehouse where he intended to sort through medallions and seals left by his father—remnants of the gold rush days when everything in California was immediately commemorated. But when they reached Idaho Street, he protested he was not up to the "long walk and all the dust." They drove back to the house. Outside the garage, on the smooth bricks, the ignition off, neither moved. Win held his cane like a plumb line, pinching the silver top with white fingers.

"Please don't tell Nancy until you must. I'm suffering from melanoma, a cancer of the skin that made me bald and my scalp scabrous. Now I've perhaps six weeks left at home before I must go to the hospital for a long treatment."

"I'm so very sorry!" John swallowed. His mouth hurt. "What can I do for you?"

"Nothing. Nothing at all, I'm afraid." He smiled as he turned toward him. "When I was young I determined not to miss anything. Then about eight years ago I was badly enfeebled and thought about suicide until it occurred to me that even old age is in itself a *new* experience." He turned away. "I do complain at times. Pat is a good listener to complaints. But I don't want you to listen. You've always talked and that's a comfort. I knew the world was still turning when you talked."

John wanted to touch his shoulder, but Win seemed so frail that he hesitated. And in any event John never considered this stately man someone whose arm you could take, even as you laughed together. They sat silently.

"Let's not have a final meeting, John. In the best of all possible worlds, there would be only penultimate meetings, don't you think?"

Inside the house, Pat watched as they sat in the car, two figures motionless, unreal for their lack of animation. She had not said to Win last night how much the bluster over Nancy's contract had irritated her. Nancy wanted it all—a career, John's success, love and laughter and children. And it was too much. People who wanted it all were reliant, relentlessly so, on gifts or sacrifices.

20

Paramount bought the deal but not before Frank Hopkins, who had begun talking with Philips, was asked to see the boss himself and asked, moreover, to bring Miss Bowen with him. Hopkins's proposal was for four pictures, twenty thousand for the first, forty for the second, sixty for the third, and one hundred and twenty thousand for the fourth. And, following John's suggestion, Hopkins said that at the end of the fourth picture, or at the end of the fourth year following signature of the contract, RKO held no option but this: it could "top" by 10 percent any offer Nancy Tuck Bowen obtained from another studio. Somehow, Paramount had learned it was Sirovich's idea.

When they arrived at his office, Levinheimer shouted almost before the door was closing behind them, "What kind of chickenshit is this 'topping'? You mean I got to *buy* the privilege to offer more? You mean that regardless? Listen, Frank, a thousand shiksas would lie down right here for this part!"

Hopkins kept silent and Nancy stared as Levinheimer paced the room, keeping to the perimeter as if it gave safer passage. In Silverlake that night Nancy reenacted his movement in the nude, to John's intense pleasure, likening it to the two-dimensional figures on Egyptian pottery who moved along surfaces with arms outspread and palms flat.

Laughing, she had exclaimed, "You don't suppose ol' Jake is an Egyptian at hand? At foot? At bottom?"

When Levinheimer returned to his desk, Balzac once more, he was calmer but bitter. "I don't like bidding for what I already found. It's bad business to pay twice for the same article. I won't argue, regardless. I'll take this lousy 'topping' your boyfriend is so horny for."

He sat down and looked at Nancy seriously for a moment before telling her in a calm voice, "Miss Bowen, you are a good clean girl. Win says so. I say so. I don't want to see your boyfriend around with you in public. You're not married. I don't need bad publicity. No matter half my actors are drunks or drug fiends. I don't need noise. I take your word for it, nevertheless. It don't need to go into a contrak. Frank, tell Philips you got a deal."

Nurse on Duty began shooting the second week of November and was in the can by mid-March and showing in theaters as a second feature by April. It was produced and cast as a B movie, with Dan Duryea and Nancy billed as leads. Some shots of the navy hospital in San Diego were taken without the three leads; the rest was shot on the studio lot. The picture was on schedule and on budget—the last scene was filmed five days before the Christmas holiday.

It was plain to studio insiders that Nancy would succeed with audiences, even if she was not skilled enough to handle short dialogue, interjections, epithets, and queries: "Of course" or "Please tell me" or, simply, "Why?" She was rescued by a film editor, a middle-aged woman who regularly burnt holes like rosettes in her peasant blouse from chain-smoking as she spun film back and forth on a Movieola. Splicing, she put in shots of the heroine listening when, to be fair, the camera ought to be on the speaker. She also restored footage in which Nancy sparkled just standing still, her cap more a bride's than a nurse's, the high heels hardly standard hospital issue under a too-short uniform. From the cutting room she emerged in the picture as the girl the hero was astonished to discover was still unmarried. She represented what many men seek, the thrill of first possession.

John's ban from the screening rooms, sneak previews, publicity parties, and other studio functions not only suited his temperament and relieved him of small talk with strangers but also gave him more time to proliferate his first ventures in journal publishing. He had founded and incorporated Past and Present, Inc. It seemed natural to suppose—not just John, but also many academicians did so—that the release of the atom bomb over two Japanese cities and the emergence of the story of its creation at the University of Chicago, at Oak Ridge, at White Sands, would have led to the creation of a vast array of new publications in physics and mathematics. It had not. John's first thought was to publish two physics journals entitled *Particles* and *Studies in Entropy* and a journal called *Algebreica,* but his months of reading in libraries and interviewing of twenty or more librarians during that initial research revealed that the secrecy cloaking the development of nuclear physics had persisted long after its terrible dawn at Hiroshima. The atom bomb had shocked and excited students and scholars, launching searches in science that made old disciplines seem almost new. One of Sirovich's general editors said that the postwar period was going to be like the 1870s and 1880s in Oxford and Cambridge and some German universities, or like 1900 to 1914, when radical theories were advanced and some proven, Einstein's relativity being the foremost. But U.S. government control over nuclear research attendant to the atom and hydrogen bombs was now so complete that it was as if a blanket had fallen over physics and mathematics—no new journals *could* be started. John began with engineering and launched two journals at once, then a third within three months. In the "catalogs" these periodicals were listed as:

JOURNAL OF ENGINEERING LUBRICATION

The journal will provide new information on controlling friction in mechanics, materials, modes of delivery, and endurance testing.

JOURNAL OF SOIL MECHANICS

Physicists, agronomists, and chemists study ways to exploit soils. Reports erosion control, irrigation, reinforcement, and transportation and mixing of soils.

JOURNAL OF POWER GRID DESIGN

Reports on actual grid design as well as theoretical models. Issues are: conductors, insulators, transformers, structural materials.

The timing was right for profits. The swell in college enrollments in the fall of 1946 was astonishing. Quonset huts were used as classrooms and dormitory buildings. Matriculation at the University of Minnesota took three days rather than the usual one. Construction was begun in Lansing, Fort Collins, and other places where "Aggies" or even teachers' state colleges were being converted into State Universities. In Lansing, for instance, Michigan State was hoping to compete with the well-established University of Michigan at Ann Arbor. John persuaded a chemical engineer at CIT and a mathematician at USC to act as general editors. They in turn helped him build a list of readers to perform the so-called peer review of articles solicited. Learning from Larkin, the "failed Ph.D." in Venice, he had mailed announcements for his two journals, but unlike Larkin, his odds were very favorable—he had hit on eight of his first ten attempts.

It was in the third week of December, just as *Nurse on Duty* was closing, that John got the telephone call. Nancy had by now got used to the drill of going to bed by ten, sometimes nine, so that she could rise at five o'clock and report to the set for makeup by six. It was about seven o'clock when the telephone awakened him. It was Hopkins. Mr. Winterfield was dead.

John interrupted quietly: "He killed himself."

"You knew? Did the police call you, John?"

"No. Win told me. Not literally. Not that I could have done anything about it."

"There's a letter he left for you. I'll drop it off later today."

Yesterday it struck me that all deaths are untimely except suicide. I couldn't wait for a bad ending, as you probably guessed from our penultimate talk. John, I thank you for your company; and if I complained about your not staying in touch, it was only because my father was like that, too. I'm leaving my library to you. I took pleasure in collecting it and I hope will bring you capital when you sell it. Might you expand your publishing business and stay in Los Angeles? Nancy would like that. Patricia, too. I don't know what my life was meant to be. It seems allowable to confess this when it is irrelevant. Good-bye. Win.

Lelia stood before the Unitarian altar, really a dais, a place sacerdotally bare. She read: "John Jackson Winterfield was born in Sacramento and died in the house on Malibu he built fifty years ago. He was a gentleman, for which role he had no need to study, so natural was his demeanor. He respected privacy and despised intrigue. He did not count his friends; and if he suffered enemies it was unknown to them. He left this life as he entered it, in his own time. He did not fear his journey. Let us rejoice in his memory."

John wrote this eulogy while Lelia drove him back from Malibu the day after Winterfield's death. They had been summoned to join Win's son Thomas at the house by Hopkins, who said that the old man's will left no instructions for his interment. Thomas, a short man with a closed expression owing to a slight squint, declared his father, who was baptized an Episcopalian, was never a practicing Christian. The others vetoed Frank's suggestion that they hire the hall of the Ethical Cultural Society in Culver City. Lelia proposed the small chapel behind the Episcopal cathedral, implying that its size would not call into question Win's religious indifference. In the end they agreed that the Unitarians, with their mere liturgical setting, could best accommodate a nominal disbeliever.

On the church walk, as the mourners left or lingered, Nancy saw Jacob Levinheimer standing with another man who waved and started toward them. It was Jules Zernbach, now heavier and balder than when John knew him in 1941.

"A long time between wars. You stayed with Win back then, didn't you?" he said as he appraised Nancy.

John introduced Jules. "Afterward too. Miss Bowen and I were his guests when we came to LA."

"No wonder Jake crows about you," he told Nancy. "You are a stunner. John, I hear you are in the publishing business. What a way to go broke. I also read your Havana story treatment. Not bad. If Miss Bowen will take the lead, I might produce it."

John laughed. "We're not two of a kind in blackjack, Jules. You can't split, losing on me, winning on Nancy."

Nancy liked Jules Zernbach at first glance. What could have gone wrong between John and this man's assistant—"Formayev," was it? She'd asked Lelia, who said she knew nothing of it. But she did say John had a reputation for hitting people and recounted an occasion when he hit a man who had asked, maliciously, what else he did for Miss Dawson besides tutoring her son.

Realizing that probate would be slow, John telephoned Thomas Winterfield to ask his approval to stay in the house several days to take an inventory of the books and maps. Thomas was prompt, cheerful, and helpful. He drove over from Santa Monica to give John the keys because the servants had left. He knew nothing of his father's collection and asked only that if some books weren't wanted by Sirovich he might give them to a Catholic charity of which he was chairman. He added, "My father didn't approve of my conversion." Thomas also asked if Sirovich would be willing to return to Mrs. Lindley some few items of clothes, makeup, and costume jewelry she'd forgotten or mislaid in the house. He said it without irony.

CHAPTER

21

John became quickly accustomed to the terms of book collecting by perusing bookseller catalogs: Gilt edges (g.e.), manuscript (ms), facsimile (facs), various dates (v.d.), lithograph (lith.). The gaining of this meager knowledge confirmed that he was not competent to judge the value of most items. He needed an expert. Pat Lindley steered him to Henry Shaikin. His shop off Pershing Square bore no sign and its front was bare except for a window holding only pennies—thousands of pennies spilling into the bottom corners of a cube, one side of which was visible to the street.

Shaikin was a short man given to brief bursts of action, like a mongoose. John liked him immediately except for his habit of leafing through books as he talked, which John found irritating because he conceived reading to be private, not unlike hygiene.

"Are there incunabula in the collection?"

John recognized that he was being given a ten-second IQ test and replied, "No books printed before A.D. 1500. Why are the pennies in the window?"

"I don't mind telling. I'm no cabalist. Listen, a passenger with a broken watch once got off a train in Minsk and found a shop with watches in the window and when he asked the old Jew inside to fix his watch with no result, three times, he complained, 'If you're not a jeweler, why are watches in the window?' The old man says he's a *mohel*. He cuts the foreskins of Jewish boys. He asks the traveler, 'So what should I put in my window?' There it is. My books are too expensive to be bought by street trade. Pennies don't bring in coin collectors—or robbers."

"I think, Mr. Shaikin, you keep the pennies to tell the story. I think, too, we can do a little business—a little buying and selling."

Shaikin jumped up to shake his hand and exclaimed, "Ha! Smart! You know that business is buying and selling."

Pat had told John about Shaikin when they had lunch together at the Beverly Wilshire, after he'd delivered her things to an apartment on South Rodeo Drive. "I'm sorry about the funeral service," he said abruptly, knowing no one had mentioned inviting her.

"Your eulogy was just right."

"You were there? I didn't see you. Pat, I'm sorry about the staff from the house."

"That's the second time you said you're sorry. John, don't turn polite. Being nice to older women is pretty awful—the next thing to last rites." She leaned over to kiss his lips.

"When did you first meet Win?"

"John, that's last rites, too." She put her hand to the side of his neck, as she'd done that afternoon on Malibu. "If we see each other, don't let it be a memorial."

The collection was valuable for its Californiana. Shaikin bought for himself a number of books; and when he acted for Sirovich as broker, he took the regular commission of 25 percent of the first five thousand dollars, 20 percent of the next four, 10 percent thereafter. He bought for four hundred dollars a signed letter from Father Tomás de la Peña dated 1787 on the sea otter trade in Upper California. As a broker he sold to a collector in San Diego for two thousand Guzmán's 1833 *Breve Noticia del Estado del Territoro de Alta California*, which was in excellent condition, its pages neither faded nor "foxed." Altogether, John netted twenty-seven thousand dollars, a third of which came from a single work, a prize so great that Shaikin at first could not believe it to be the original. It was a letter from Father Junípero Serra dated July 20, 1776, addressed to the California captain commandant, urging him to place more missions between the two presidios, Monterey and San Diego, so couriers could sleep safely after a hard day's ride of twenty-five leagues.

"Nancy?" It was Carolyn, crying, calling at eight o'clock New York time, five o'clock in Silverlake.

"What's wrong? Carolyn!"

"You didn't get my letter, then. Angus has had a stroke. It was four days ago. He can't move his whole left side. And he can't speak."

A stroke! It seemed implausible, although Nancy knew that high blood pressure had kept Angus out of the armed services.

"There's really little chance. Angus won't live. I know it but can't tell his parents. They're here. Why is it I know for certain such a terrible thing?"

"Because you care."

"It's something else. I'm pregnant."

Nancy wanted to go to New York immediately, convinced that Carolyn's family, whom she'd never met, would not now come to her side. The Farrands, she felt, shouldn't hold the field uncontested. But she'd begun a second movie and couldn't leave. She settled for sending a check for two thousand dollars and calling Carolyn frequently, oftentimes missing connections because by the time she was free of Paramount, Carolyn was at Columbia Presbyterian in New York. It was again five o'clock in the morning when she got the second call.

"Angus died at midnight. He never spoke. Nancy? He was dissatisfied with me. I saw it in his eyes."

"Carolyn, right now it's hard on you. Don't think about that."

"He didn't get tenure at Columbia. He didn't think this was a good time to have a baby. He had asked his mother to talk to me about it."

A week later she wrote: "Angus's folks took his body to Lansing. Mr. Farrand was very generous. They set up a trust for the baby, who will get two thousand a year until he's eighteen, then more to age twenty-five, then the principal. I'm grateful, but I couldn't promise the Farrands that I'd keep their name for the baby if I remarried. *They* brought marriage up! It wasn't a trade, was it?"

And weeks later: "I found an apartment near Doctors Hospital with the rent only a fifth of Riverside Drive. I'm big as a camel, just waiting, just munching. I found a job cataloging papers for a prominent family in New York. The hours are good, but the pay is low. *Nurse on Duty* is showing on upper Broadway. I'll see you in the movies! Isn't it a relief you kept your real name? Nobody in Tuscaloosa or Mobile can now say, 'Dint ya usta be Nancy Tuck Bowwin?' I take it back. They will ask anyway. Say hello to John."

When Robert Allen Ellis was born—he bore his mother's maiden surname—Nancy received with the announcement of his christening a check for two thousand dollars. Sometime later, awakening as Nancy rose at five, John heard Nancy mutter, half-asleep, "Damn that Angus. He left her."

They had to move, Nancy was convinced. John's books in the apartment had spread glacially, sliding off stacks to rest under furniture and against doors. A turned ankle was inevitable—the sort of minor accident that can be catastrophic to an actress or a ballplayer. And the routine whereby she went to bed early while John, working full tilt at his business—Past and Present now had a staff—stayed up long past midnight, had caused him to begin sleeping on a sofa so as not to wake her on coming to bed. It was a bad omen when lovers were solicitous over each other's getting enough sleep—there wasn't the least practical thing about desire.

With a poke of twenty-five thousand, some given by John, some from *Nurse on Duty* and an advance on her *Lady on the Range*, Nancy made forays with real-estate agents in tow. She settled finally on a house on the slope of Hollywood Hills, taking a mortgage at 4 percent from the owner. The agent showing the house to John once the deal was done proudly named it "genuine Franciscan terra-cotta," pointing to iron balustrades and glazed tiles. John commented afterward it was more Bengali than Franciscan, but Nancy warned, "Don't tell him, please. He's happy with his ignorance—and his commission."

Their first dinner guest in the house was Lelia, who had become a chum of Nancy's and was reported in the daily edition of *Variety* to appear at tennis parties with her. In Hollywood two people made a party. What Nancy in fact attended were singles matches between her and Lelia on a court newly built behind Lelia's house, the hillside having been leveled, with full-grown pepper trees planted to soften the effect of the Cyclone fencing. Not once did John accompany her.

Shaikin stopped by at the house one evening in August to invite John to go partners in buying one of the five extant copies of the earliest California laws. John declined. Nowadays he had branched out from the journal business, which was up to twenty-seven periodicals, to publishing facsimiles of rare books. He had bought from Shaikin Thomas à Kempis's *The Imitation of Christ*, published in 1498. It was the first facsimile produced by Past and Present, an edition limited to 495 hand-numbered copies, printed by lithography on all-rag paper, and bound in Nigerian goatskin—this last obtained from a binder in San Francisco who had stored it through the war for a now-defunct limited-editions book club. John priced the work at five hundred dollars a copy and within three months had sold it out. He followed it with Harvey's *Exercitationes de Generatione Animalium*, dated 1651, the first book on obstetrics. It sold out before publication. Now he was on the scoreboard—he had scored after tagging up.

By the time Shaikin stopped by the house, Sirovich had no time, let alone inclination, for partnerships. He was nowadays employing copy editors, salesmen, order-and-billing clerks, and warehouse packers and pickers. P and P occupied an office on the lower end of Sunset and a warehouse in Inglewood. Usually working late, he now had a further, and legitimate, reason not to accompany Nancy to parties that were part of her Paramount career. The only exception to his seeming misanthropy was Pat Lindley, with whom he had lunch every ten days or two weeks. It was Pat he told that Past and Present would no doubt grow by mitosis, with one job splitting into two, then four, then eight, on and on. She began to call it "The Blob" and found a kind of horror in John's predictions that it was inevitable that disappointment awaited some of the pioneers in the business who had fetched and carried and stayed late to pack and mail, the people who quite rightly would come to think themselves indispensable. A few of them, John knew, would in the years ahead become managers but be adjudged by newcomers as no more than clerks, seen then to be too light in ability and too heavy as overhead. They would be retired or fired, always generously and with genuine regret, yet dismissed without doubt.

Pat objected, "If you can see that coming, why not prevent it? It's just too awful."

"I'm not talking about good intentions. Listen, Pat, think of guerrillas who win in the mountains and have to come down to the capital. Those brave partisans who blew bridges and pushed cannon through the snows are now faced with repairing the waterworks and making the buses run on time. Their honor lies behind them and their failures can no longer be looked upon as brave missteps on the road to victory."

"Win was wrong about your not caring about politics. You *are* talking about Mr. Tito, right?"

"I'm not interested in politics, not in ordinary terms. Politics and gambling and business are forms of warfare. The spoils of war and politics are just that, spoils."

"John, you're wound up like a ball of string. Take time out, won't you?"

"Where from, Pat? The past or the future?"

22

Blaine Bowen came to Los Angeles a week before Nancy was to leave for the mountains on the western border of Yosemite Park at Placerville. *Lady on the Range* was a Western, whether an A or B picture Paramount had not decided—that would be settled after the last rushes were viewed and the picture subjected to criticism at a few sneak previews. Nancy was playing opposite John Hodiak and Charles Bickford, herself a Southern gentlewoman who comes west to inherit a ranch for which Bickford lusts. At first a hardbitten cowboy, later in love, Hodiak is Bickford's foreman, who becomes disenchanted with his boss's schemes and enlists as Nancy's defender—the final chase occurring near the grand heights of Yosemite.

Nancy was steadily excited by the prospect of Blaine's coming. It was the first solace to her hurt at the fact none of her close relations had come to stay with her in LA, even after she bought a house with a guest room. Jane had heard this complaint and wrote her niece just as Blaine prepared to go west.

You don't suspect, Nancy Tuck, that your family loves you less because they haven't come to Los Angeles? Your father, truly, for all his devotion to you, isn't up to staying in a house bought by his daughter and shared by her roommate. I know it sounds cruel, Nancy dear, but the trouble is it's hard to describe John right now. Harold is still upset over the argument with John on your movie business. Willa Ellen is concentrating on your getting married and she won't consider other things until it happens—it reminds me of when we were children playing jacks and she wouldn't look up! See what you can do about Blaine, won't you? He says he'll attend law school, but he won't. He's making money trading in stocks and bonds "on his own account," as your Uncle Charles calls it, but mostly he squires foolish girls to the Fredericks place on Dauphin Island or, a little more innocently, to the Bienville Club. Talk with him, Nancy Tuck.

To John, Blaine appeared a powerful figure, tall and bulky, a man who chain-smoked and in the evenings drank heavily without ever seeming the worse for it. During the four days he stayed in Hollywood Hills he took Nancy to parties on her circuit of "events" good for an actress's image. Other times he and John spoke mostly of the war and the navy. On the occasion of seeing P and P's offices, he asked John laconically how he'd come to make "so much money so fast."

John described P and P's procedures perfunctorily but was soon agreeably surprised that Blaine asked pertinent, even detailed questions: why catalogs were so singularly important in marketing; why discounting was uniform without variable deals for certain buyers; how governments abroad, despite the cost of reconstruction from the war, found funds to subvent both scholarly journals and reprints of noted works of scholarship. This mood of professional interest persisted until Blaine left for Mobile. But on his last evening, Blaine got a lot settled that was, so to speak, domestic.

"How come you don't drink, ol' John?"

"My father's people are gamblers. Winning, or for that matter losing, is as big a kick as alcohol—or so they claim."

"Austin Newhardt would argue that. I just remembered, you met Cassie in New York."

He had not just remembered. A keynote was sounded. "Yes. I saw her thrown away like a burnt match. Is she still in the infirmary?"

"Rosemary—she's Brownell now, not Roberts—and some others see her a little. Cassie still can't talk. The nurses walk her around some. What became of the guy in New York?"

"I don't know. The last time I saw him I knocked him through a windowpane."

"What made *you* all that sore—that they were living in sin?"

"Blaine," John replied curtly, "let's talk about it. Your sister could have married any man, any day, in Mobile or New York or here. But she didn't, did she? She fell in love with me and while that's a fact, it's not the entire story. She wanted to get away from Mobile—and she came out under my protection. I didn't use her and she didn't use me. We're still together."

"You took her to bed quick enough. And you're pretty slow taking her to the altar."

John stood, flushed, his forearms strained at his sides, and said with disgust, "Christ! It's just not possible to talk to a man about having sex with his sister. If you're nervous, or just curious, let me say it: I haven't as much as shaken hands with another girl since I met Nancy."

"Hell, John," Blaine said, laughing, "you can sleep with a girl without first shaking hands! It's not a prizefight. You are closer to being married than you know. You'll get an engraved invitation one day. Nancy has proved your point, and you've proved hers. I'd say there isn't any issue left between you. But then, who am I to know? I'm not married. But I'm not prejudiced either. Why, some of my best friends are black, Catholic, and married."

Two days before Nancy departed for Placerville, an unexpected call came from Lelia Dawson. Lelia had avoided John quite simply. She saw Nancy on occasions that did not call for John's presence: shopping on Wilshire, playing tennis at Lelia's house or at her club in Bel Air, meeting with women who were raising funds for an actors' retirement home in San Bernardino. What prompted her present invitation to John, she told herself, was guilt over not letting him see Arthur on at least one occasion when it could conveniently have been arranged. As a matter of fact, it was more impelling that Jules Zernbach had asked her to reacquaint herself with Sirovich: he had in mind asking Levinheimer to lend Nancy to RKO for a picture on New Orleans—a dark story of a girl lost in the Marseilles of the South—one in which Nancy might well fit with small cost to RKO.

But there was a further reason. Lelia needed his help as a writer. *Redbook* couldn't get Vivien Leigh or Madeline Carroll to write a one-page piece on the "bright young things"—that consciously carefree generation of the post–World War I period who were depicted in Evelyn Waugh's *Brideshead Revisited*, a novel that had become a best-seller in America. Lelia knew too well she couldn't write; indeed, she didn't know where to begin, even if a one-page article seemed too small to have a beginning, middle, and end.

He agreed to come. She thought it expedient, given the estrangement both felt, to see him in a familial setting; so it was that they once more sat in her kitchen one late afternoon. The cook had brought tea and English butter biscuits made in east Los Angeles but sold only in Beverly Hills. Once together and seated, Lelia became afraid the very intimacy of this mise-en-scène might lead John to dwell on his not seeing Arthur. She was quite right.

"How is he?"

"Growing, maturing, very keen. You'd be proud of him—as his former tutor."

"Is he going out with girls?"

"I certainly hope so!"

"I wouldn't bet that I'll ever see him again." It was direct. It was a challenge.

He was, she felt with a sudden bitterness, incapable of regarding her apart from Arthur. It was unnatural. After all, Arthur had outgrown him, but she herself was unchanged and he could, if he were not so stubbornly remote, pick up the brightly colored threads of their past, short as that history had been. She leaned forward, the famous curl falling free from her forehead.

"You don't bet against yourself, John. Even if you *are* confident. Mostly you are careful."

"Lelia, is this going to be like that time at the Beverly Wilshire? Should I find a translator?"

"It's quite proper English."

"Okay. Then tell me what the topic sentence is."

"Don't be condescending, John. I can think even if I can't write."

"Lelia, nobody ever accused you of not being 'versed,' as they say. Why would I accuse you? That would be unfair. You taught me a lot. And I'm grateful."

"Yes, I believe you are. But you don't recognize *other* feelings. Feelings frighten you. You never once kissed me."

It was said so circumstantially that she could have been a customer in a store complaining of poor service. John, she saw, was astounded and now so perplexed or abashed that he elaborately extracted a cigarette from a Lucky Strike pack and lit it with a match from a paper folder advertising Chicago's American School: by mail become a butcher.

"No. And aren't we *both* glad. I hate the fooling around, Lelia, the snatch and grab. Jesus! It turns the language into bad puns, even your own proper English."

Lelia brought her hands together silently, holding her fingers fixed like a steeple. Now she made this gesture of joyful surprise to mock him. Once earlier she did so genuinely, on the occasion of their first meeting at the Hotel del Coronado, when she tipped him forty dollars—twenty of which he immediately returned—in gratitude for his looking after an obese eight-year-old in the children's dining room. She had laughed when John said he was "trying not to have a future." John had been especially solicitous when Arthur's English nanny became disgusted with his daily habit of overeating, which caused his pants to fall after he loosened his belt to accommodate double orders of roast beef. The nanny would summon John to shinny up his pants and refasten his belt.

Still mocking him, she asked, "Is that the last word in the last hour, John? Are you suddenly wise? No, you're not—you are always playing it safe."

He realized her feeling of injury was so great that, to save pride, she was making this conversation as impersonal as possible, as if she were a member of an audience confronting a lecturer with a sharp question.

"If it takes bravery or careless disregard to start an affair, it takes cowardice to end it. You're divorced, Lelia. You know better than I do what lies must be told to make the break—and afterward."

Lelia thought it meanly clever that John would introduce at this point a circumstance and a setting over which she had had the least possible control—her divorce, with court proceedings, arguing through attorneys with an angry husband over the custody of her child. John knew nothing about her husband except that he had never been involved in the theater or movie-making and now lived in Chicago. She looked down into her cup, waiting a moment to say it, say it with the least theatricality.

"You're a prig. You won't give up that secret part of yourself. Is it so precious? When we met at the hotel in Coronado, I'd have gone to bed on a mere nod. What would it have cost? You hoard your pride, but it makes you poor. When you lived here, you made such a point of being young, being Arthur's teacher and my defender, I could have screamed. I did. Several times. It is bloody awful what you do. I don't want to pay for intimacy. I don't want Arthur to pay."

She watched him rise, move to the door, leaving it ajar. Whatever else she expected, it was not silence.

It was at such moments one reached for axioms, John reflected ironically, but he found few of much solace. There was Plato's "The life which is unexamined is not worth living." Lelia had examined John's life and found it wanting, but that was not relevant. Who appoints the examiner and for how long a term? The episode confirmed to John that he did not know what people wanted. He had said as much to Winterfield. But how did you find out? Perhaps, had they sat as travelers far from home on a veranda in the Pacific, in the dark, their presence visible only in the lighted ends of those Dutch cigars Win kept in an oval brass box, each might have told of his secret self. There lay in the echoing chambers of a man's heart the unsaid, the shame of not admitting what he really wanted. No, maxims would not serve, not where there was a deep pain, nor a stirring wonderment.

It was never clear to Willa Ellen why it happened as it did. She knew John to be eccentric and she had small notion of what moved him. Nancy told her it happened at a cocktail party, an occasion of the sort John in principle did not normally attend. They went because he had felt an obligation. They left because she was shocked.

It was the sixtieth birthday of Jules Zernbach, the producer who had before the war given John scriptwriting work at RKO. The first time, looking for a job, John had arrived at Zernbach's poolside in the bright sunlight after emerging from a trellised passageway thick with the white blossoms of mock orange. Now he stood again under the same trellis with Nancy. Jacob Levinheimer approached, nodding to John and saluting Nancy with a kiss on the cheek as she timed perfectly a curtsy to bring her cheek within his reach. An hour later, as they left, Zernbach accompanied them down the grass mall leading through iron gates fifty or so feet from North Rodeo Drive. Saying good-bye, Jules revived the banter of their first meeting. He asked if Nancy was now willing to bet on her half of the "pair of aces."

"Jules, maybe when I come back from Yosemite, you can ask Jake to lend me to RKO," she said, pleased.

John added, as if she'd not replied, "You can't split this pair, Jules. We're getting married as soon as Nancy finishes this picture. Maybe we'll do it on the way to Yosemite. At Reno."

"Reno? Why not Caliente? In case you've already had your honeymoon—or several, like me—you can at least have a good time on the horses."

Nancy hadn't heard this riposte because, like a woman slapped, she stood stunned. A moment later she was running. By the time John intercepted her down the block, she was sobbing so hard she had to stop to catch her breath. She felt his big hands and was immediately lifted and cradled against his body as he carried her past the Zernbach house to the car. She felt the stares of guests like pinpricks.

She turned her head against his shoulder and whispered hoarsely, "Damn you, John. Just damn you."

"Nancy. Please, Nancy. Will you marry me? Nancy? I love you forever. Nancy?"

Now she could laugh. "What wuz yo doing all that time?"

At Placerville the assistant to the director of the "second unit" informed Nancy on their arrival in a rented car that she was to stay in a nearby tourist lodge. Without hesitation she objected and prevented John from reentering the car. She demanded a trailer holding a dressing room, saying that no doubt Charles Bickford and John Hodiak occupied such accommodations. Clearly alarmed by Nancy's stand, the assistant backed down. The dispute was won.

As they were putting down their bags inside the trailer, Nancy angrily proved her point. In a squared-off space serving as a closet were hung two shirts bearing the assistant's name on the collar.

"You think I'm mean, don't you?" She challenged him as they lay on the narrow bed.

"No, I think you're psychic. How did you know he was lying?"

"Lelia says you have to guard against anyone trying to make a reputation for the first time on your picture. He was just the type."

"Is that really a profound saying, Nancy? Where else could you use such advice? Buying a used car? Getting a job in the mailroom?"

"You want to stay in this bed, sport? Then love me forever. Tonight."

The second night, before John returned to Los Angeles to give instructions to his staff prior to flying to Mobile, he was glad of the chance to play poker with Bickford and the key grip and three other hands working on *Lady on the Range*. It was a low-stake game, but a fast one because two of the players were careless bettors. He got back to the trailer after midnight, undressed in the dark, and inserted himself between the sheets as quietly as he could.

Nancy stirred and murmured, "Did you win?"

He avoided wakening her with a reply but risked lighting a small night-light so he could smoke. During blackouts on ships, smoking could seem as innocent as breathing unless you concurrently saw the smoke exhaled. He lit a second cigarette from the first. How do you win? You let circumstance work. You let things run to their end. He had not accepted this article of his present faith as early as had Jean Fancher at the Hotel del Coronado in San Diego, where they both worked, when she gave herself to him without doubt. She was joyous for the first time in her life and naïvely so, expecting no advantage from her generosity. Afterward a guilty knowledge had oppressed him.

He had merely sought the thrill of possession. Yet he was now convinced that his declaration of love had diminished Jean's youth. Those few years when a girl is truly young, when her body and mind are open, without fear or guile, those years could have already become in her memory and reminiscence altogether final and unrecoverable. John lay now in the dark next to a woman who had given to him the care of her love, and he could confirm out of experience that love proffered, if memorialized, was a gift of time.

23

In Mobile a terrible swiftness of events awaited Nancy. Had someone told her that Rome did not fall in a single day or that the High Renaissance didn't begin on the Tuesday afternoon scholars arrived in Florence and Rome after the fall of Constantinople, she would have argued that such events were possible. Over the period of a few days, Pat revealed an intimate intention, Blaine took the first step on a long journey, and Nancy heard her husband foretell a mismatch in their lives.

Once Pat Lindley heard that Lelia Dawson had sent her "regrets" to an invitation to stay at the Bowens', she retracted her own and accepted. She was the sole guest from the West. Tata, having extracted from Nancy by telephone the promise to christen her children in the Orthodox church, thought it unnecessary to attend the wedding—in this he was echoed by Blaine, who told his brother that the Siroviches had already consummated their marriage "a thousand times." Frank Hopkins begged off from Beaulieu Street, saying to Mrs. Bowen that a Hollywood lawyer must make telephone calls day and night. He booked into the Battle House along with two Paramount publicists, a *Silver Screen* writer and photographer, and a UP reporter. When Willa

Ellen objected to the nuisance of flashes by photographers, Judge Bowen was pressed into service and awarded the church to the local newspaper, the house to the screen magazine, with venue to all at the reception on the Bowen grounds. In the eye of the camera, Nancy looked gloriously commanding in her grandmother's wedding gown. It emphasized her narrow waist and high large breasts; and the lace capped her thick auburn hair regally. She confided to her Aunt Jane that it was too bad John could not be wearing a white uniform with brass buttons. Jane said that she was married late, true, but more important, married finally.

Frank Hopkins described to Judge Bowen how the publicity of the wedding had been encouraged in the hope of persuading Levinheimer to renegotiate Nancy's contract now that *Lady on the Range* was completed, the second of four pictures. How Levinheimer reacted to Hopkins personally the latter never knew. Frank's three-piece suits, like his accent, were of an Eastern cut; and the Phi Beta Kappa pin on his gold watch chain showed whenever he looked at the pocket watch kept in his vest—he used both hands. He'd gone to see Jake on the assurance that *Silver Screen* was running a long feature on Nancy's wedding in Mobile. He counted, moreover, on another bargaining chip, Jake's egotism. *Lady on the Range* had been expensively produced. In Hollywood a producer's success was gauged not only by how much he earned, but also by how much he spent. But Jake held firm, Hopkins was sorry to recount.

Judge Bowen had by the second day found a ground on which to reestablish relations with John. "It is astonishing, your now having almost two hundred employees."

"I'm myself astonished," John replied. "P and P now publishes forty journals. Our overseas business alone is already past two million dollars a year. I've just rented two other offices on month-to-month leases in Los Angeles. I keep resisting the temptation, Judge, to build a headquarters."

"Why resist? Property in Los Angeles must be valuable, once developed."

"I'm afraid I'll end up in the real-estate business, not publishing."

"John, you sound to me like a man who has already made up his mind. You've read Henry Adams's autobiography? Of course. He speaks of the principle of acceleration: everything happens faster than either the perpetrator or witnesses believe it can."

"I like 'perpetrator,' Judge." John laughed. "It fits business."

R. J. Fredericks was a little off-key meeting John Sirovich again. He had of course heard of his business successes, which did not surprise him, and of Nancy's Hollywood breakthrough, which did. And he had become friends with Blaine Bowen, which, for some reason he couldn't define, kept him from resuming the old bantering with John Sirovich. RJ resolved his social obligation to serve as a host during the period of the wedding by inviting only the ladies to his house for Sunday luncheon afterward. It did not occur to him that John might be further disappointed. He had never been invited to RJ's home in Mobile.

RJ's luncheon left the Bowen brothers together with their father and John on Sunday. After lunch they went into the library and there watched Lucas, the butler, pour café au lait by holding the oppositely placed handles of matching silver pots and letting streams of coffee and cream merge into liquid twists. John observed James Bowen and saw him as more acquiescent to the Judge than his brother. He was lithe but smaller than John expected from his photographs. Obviously he was intelligent, adept, but John guessed he was less gifted than Blaine or Nancy. He'd spoken of his regret at not having had the chance to fly in the navy. Even if called up for Korea, which had opened up suddenly, another adventure of war, he could not pass the physical, having recently developed a loss of vision in one eye. At present he was in the third year of law school.

Blaine was expansive as usual and urged his father to describe his visit to Washington, where he had attended a meeting addressed by the President. Specifically he wanted Harold to comment on Truman's intentions in Korea.

"Blaine, if I was told, I missed it. I don't have a feel for the Pacific. I still think of 'abroad' as England and the Lowlands, France, and Germany. It's political of course. Senator Vandenberg was right when he said the Atlantic is a Democratic ocean, the Pacific a Republican one."

That night John and Blaine returned to the subject when they met by chance in the study, almost at dawn, both having surrendered to insomnia.

Without warning, John said, "You'd give anything to get back to Tokyo, wouldn't you?"

"I would. I wish I could watch MacArthur turn the Japanese into a better class of Americans."

As Blaine sipped milk, he shifted direction seemingly by asking if *Captain Cook's Three Voyages Around the World?* would be a good work for Past and Present to make expensive facsimiles of.

"It's eight volumes, as you know, Blaine, with probably two hundred maps. I doubt anyone would pay for it."

"Well, I don't know much about your business, but I'd bet *Cook* could sell in Japan now. MacArthur's cultural attaché told me that tens of millions of dollars will be spent on libraries each year, almost all subsidized by our own government."

"There may be bigger game there—scientific books and journals."

"Aren't they too low-priced?"

"Singly, yes, but they're big revenue in sets. Once a library subscribes to a journal, it wants all the back issues."

That encounter was the seeding of Past and Present, Tokyo. Blaine left for Japan within a month and soon became managing director of one of the few American companies—IBM being notable—that escaped the law limiting foreigners to minority ownership in Japanese businesses. In this, Blaine's influence with the American Headquarters staff was of aid, as it was later when he obtained grants to republish literary and historical documents in Japanese. Years afterward, whenever Willa Ellen spoke of Blaine's successes, her pride was edged by puzzlement. John Sirovich had managed to lure away two of her three children.

At the rehearsal the Friday before the wedding ceremony at Saint Emmanuel's, the Reverend Mr. Wilkins sought to create some affinity with Nancy's "young man."

"I'm told by Mrs. Bowen that you were once an Anglican altar boy. So was I, in fact. The parish here is not, of course, High Church."

"Yes. I'm Orthodox. Anglicans and Orthodox share communion. If you want a priest in a hurry—say, to marry or bury you—you can call either one."

Mr. Wilkins adjusted his metal-rimmed eyeglasses slightly and said, "I do hope we can talk again—some less hectic time, perhaps."

Once he'd moved away, James said, laughing, "Jesus, go to church, John. He thinks you're a religious bargain hunter!"

That evening John drank glass after glass of champagne and, aware of the excess, went out into the Bowen garden to find the stone bench where he and Nancy, each not confiding in the other, had first begun to think of their lives as a couple. Jane, watching, followed him out. He glanced up, surprised, as she took a seat beside him.

"I've had too much to drink, Jane."

"I noticed."

"Funny, I was just remembering having dinner in the house of a professor in Boulder. He was almost sixty and his mother was very old and wore a choker of pearls. She lit a kind of *Mikado* fan of newspaper that set off white birch logs in the fireplace— an expensive fire. She said her father had taught her to make such a fire before the Civil War. That long ago! Why am I telling this?"

"Because you're a little sad."

"But I feel fine."

"Drunks should feel fine."

"Jane, Ralph Waldo Emerson said that in a hundred years all will be one."

"He was quite right. Everything is the same. Children know it."

The afternoon before John left for New York, Pat asked him to walk in the Bowen garden. She hugged herself, a familiar gesture, as they proceeded on the path along the azalea beds. It had turned chilly and wet. She was talking randomly when she surprised herself by asking, too starkly she realized, if he "liked these people." Misunderstanding, he stiffened and replied that it hardly required a special tolerance to get along with the friends of the Bowens. Alarmed, she took his arm to hold him still.

"Give me a break, John! I don't mean the Bowens. I walked downtown yesterday. The poor people seem to stare, and sometimes they look dangerous."

"They're like poor people everywhere, Pat. They're sent to work, sent to war, and between they wait." He smiled down at her then. "You didn't come out here in this clammy weather to listen to sociology, did you?"

"No. Your friend RJ wants me to stay in Mobile."

"And you won't stay unless he proposes?"

She was pained by his clever assessment and routine acceptance of something so drastic, but she went on. "He'll have to do more than that. I need money settled on me. That doesn't sound right, does it? Win left me a trust that pays six thousand a year—he got to be too old to realize how little that would be in the 1950s. Except for some paintings, he left the rest to his son and daughter. People do try to make up for it before they die."

"Pat, why are you being hard on yourself?"

"I'm blue. I'm nearly forty. I'm really thirty-nine—but that's a Jack Benny joke. RJ will propose, of course. And I *will* stay."

"I'm glad, Pat." He put his hands on her waist and kissed her. She could tell he was surprised to feel the wetness of her open mouth.

"I'm in love with you. Don't say anything. You can't help me, John. This has happened before—my falling in love to no good end. That day when Win and Nancy were upset over the contract and you came to the house, I realized I didn't think Nancy deserved all your attention. I would settle for a lot less."

She tried to smile bravely and failed. "I'm not talking about money now."

For Nancy it got worse the afternoon John left. She had already been told by Blaine of his interest in working for him; and it seemed possible that she might never again see this brother who always had declared her too fine for the likes of his own friends. Then Aunt Jane told her that Patricia Lindley would marry RJ. Nancy assumed it was Pat who told her, but in fact Jane had heard from John. It struck Nancy as oddly unfair that Pat could enter both her past and her future by the mere act of staying in Mobile, a choice she herself had rejected. And now John behaved badly before the girl from Condé Nast who had missed the wedding but gained an interview nonetheless.

The girl looked a bit of a mess and couldn't keep her legs together while sitting on a kind of slipper chair in the living room. Her long hair kept catching on the rims of her eyeglasses.

When John brought his bags down for Lucas and entered the room, the reporter inquired of him how it felt to be the husband of a movie star. Nancy dreaded John's reply as she watched it form contentiously in his eyes.

"I feel like Charles Francis Adams."

"I don't understand."

"Adams said he used to go home from the bank on State Street in Boston and kneel by his bedside, put his face in his hands, and laugh and laugh and laugh."

The reporter was ready for him. "How do you spell his name?"

In the hallway Nancy was shaking with fury. She reminded John of the occasion in a Los Angeles restaurant when she'd turned away from a woman who asked if she was Nancy Tuck Bowen of the movies. John had accused her of being unfair, because if she depended on a movie audience that was really a collection of strangers, how could she claim privacy? Now she asked him how she could conduct a public life if he made private jokes.

He kissed her. She held back. He didn't persist.

"Nancy, you're right. I'm sorry. But I want you to pay attention to our being together—publicly and privately. You know I'm off to New York to rent space for a headquarters, not a branch office, but a headquarters. Are we going to live on opposite coasts? Or commute? Nancy, I don't like our choices."

From the living room she heard Lucas say, "Thank you, Mr. John."

24

It is the conventional boast of almost any American city businessman to tell the returning visitor, "It's grown so you won't
recognize the place!" John Sirovich recognized New York; and
riding the subway downtown to the Hudson American Bank on
Pine Street, he felt accustomed. He was back.

Chase Bank had offered him a line of credit of two hundred
thousand dollars, but he was seeking other arrangements. Inside
Hudson American he sat before the desk of a vice president about
his own age, thirty-one, a slim man who tapped his thumb with
a Ticonderoga No. 1 pencil. On hearing Sirovich's explanation
that he intended to rent space in midtown, he suggested he
contact their branch on Forty-Fourth Street. When John told him
that he had already sent a letter to the bank president, Mr. Stratton, the man raised his eyebrows. John reached over to palm the
pencil like a relay baton.

"Tell Mr. Stratton that like Calvin Coolidge I hate to see
Americans turning away business. It's unpatriotic."

Returning, the vice president was preceded by a man who
didn't disappoint. He was a Paul McNutt figure, tall, heavy,

smiling, tanned, white hair. When he'd ushered Sirovich into his large office, he asked him if he'd really said "unpatriotic."

"I did, yes. We owe it to Calvin Coolidge."

The president laughed. "Tell me why you don't want Chase's line of credit." Then he caught himself. "What can Hudson American do for you?"

"You can take deposits, charge interest on short-term loans, handle foreign drafts—and one day set up a pension trust for still-unhired, and even unborn, employees of my company."

"Ouch! Let me admit it: we can't find your letter."

"It's at your branch on Forty-Fourth Street."

"We'd be honored to lend you money. Are you free for lunch?"

"Not today, thanks. And, Mr. Stratton, I want to deal directly with you."

"Certainly. It's the reason you're not going to Chase."

Inside a ten-story building on Forty-Seventh and Madison, John met a Mr. Abrams, the head of a large real-estate company who was a sometime customer of Henry Shaikin. Behind Abrams's desk, two shelves held old-fashioned papier-mâché file boxes with leather spines bearing lettering stamped in gold. They looked like sacred texts.

"Ten thousand square feet?"

He took down a box marked "410 Madison Avenue." It was this building.

"A three-year lease, four-fifty a square foot. On the Coast you use monthly rates. Here it's annual."

"Mr. Abrams, three-fifty for the first two years, five-fifty for the next three—five years in all. How about that?"

Abrams closed the box.

"Too bad," John continued. "We're a classy client for your own headquarters building. Professors will be coming in and out. I don't need the freight elevator."

Abrams reopened the box and peered inside as if searching for a *pilpul*, that Talmudic scholastic device for finding some minor point that legitimizes a doubtful venture.

"I can give you a whole floor, fourteen thousand square feet, all private, with your own elevator lobby."

"Okay, three-fifty for the first three years, then six-fifty for the next two."

"You're asking me to bet on your success?"

"Mr. Abrams, don't you want your neighbor to prosper? Think of the neighborhood."

"It's my nickel."

"It's my *pilpul*."

"You're not Jewish. How do you know that?"

"Henry Shaikin."

"I should deal with him. God save me from Gentiles. I want ten thousand on signing."

"You got it. Can I sublet with your approval?"

"Mr. Sirovich, the suit is made. No more alterations."

At the hotel on Central Park West, at too great a cost, John rented a suite for a month, hoping to lure Nancy from Los Angeles. He succeeded by chance. Now thinking it an A picture, Paramount wanted retakes of *Lady on the Range* but couldn't get Bickford and Hodiak back within three weeks, which allowed Nancy to fly to New York. She realized that in the 1930s no studios would have spent money on retakes to "better" a Western. In Hollywood money was readily available—along with uncertainty. She passed her days shopping and museum-going; and in the evenings, when John couldn't leave his work, she persuaded Carolyn Farrand to go to the theater. But on weekends she forced John out of the city to stay in hotels and inns as far away as Connecticut and Pennsylvania. Bereft of his paperwork, John tended to concentrate on whatever was at hand, in this instance his wife. They talked four or five hours at a time and afterward could not recall a word, a good sometime prescription in a marriage.

Before Nancy left for Los Angeles she adjured John to "help out" Carolyn, then asked him outright to give her a good job in P and P. To make him feel the urgency, she told him more of Carolyn's early travail. They had roomed together in the Kappa Delta house their sophomore year until Carolyn departed in the middle of the second term because she was informed by the university bursar that her father had failed to pay her tuition. Nancy and other sisters watched Carolyn walk away from the house carrying a suitcase, headed for the bus depot. She had later taken a train to New York looking for a job with but thirty dollars in her purse.

John went one day to Carolyn's apartment but was denied entrance by a shiny black Jamaican woman who said across the chain of the door latch, "I never heard of you." He waited outside on Lexington Avenue, leaning against a wall as he read *The Seven Storey Mountain.*

"John! I'm late. I'm sorry! I bet Marcie wouldn't let you in. She's not sure of white men, but then neither are white women. I just can't wait for you to see Bobby Allen—he's darlin'. I see you're reading Thomas Merton. Angus knew him at Columbia. I mean before Merton became a monk. Here we are, Marcie, meet Bobby's godfather, Mr. Sirovich."

Deftly made a *kum,* John saw the boy standing with his large blond head raised expectantly, a round face with round blue eyes. His hands were balled at his cheeks in glee at seeing his mother. Carolyn deposited the grocery bags and picked up Bobby to carry him to John's lap after first running a practiced finger around the edges of his blue cotton pants. Once she saw Marcie off, she fed the boy as they talked, using a silver christening spoon— like many Southerners, she was not afraid to use her "good things" day to day.

The next day Carolyn led him to a grand house on Fifth Avenue where she had for almost eighteen months worked on index cards, helping to create a register of papers and artifacts owned by the Younger family, which had came to Connecticut in the seventeenth century and which, Carolyn told John enigmatically, might come to an end in the twentieth. He went along with Carolyn because Nancy, by telephone, spoke of her worry that Carolyn might remain "too loyal" and allow herself to be talked out of an opportunity.

Mr. Younger was about sixty years old, slight of stature, with high coloring. He avoided shaking hands. Carolyn was as nervous as a girl introducing a date to her father. Younger restated Carolyn's duties by saying he had commissioned Professor Dixon Wecter to write the family history, noting that Wecter was the author of the best-selling book on New York's "Four Hundred." John remarked that Wecter had been one of his English professors at the University of Colorado and that he'd often wondered if the professor had some presentiment about his health because Boulder, while a mecca for the ailing, was hardly cosmopolitan.

"I don't ask of infirmities," Younger replied, turning his head to catch John's eyes straying to a large niche in the teak wall of the library where there stood a vermeil statuette, a nude with her right hand raised to the right shoulder, her left knee bent so the foot rested on a celestial globe. Her hair was wreathed twice to effect both a laurel and a crown. For John the tension in the pose was sensual beyond admitting.

"You think it's a Cellini?"

"I don't think so. The sculptor loved women."

"Ah. And do you?"

"Well," John said, smiling, "I love my wife."

"Admirable. Admirable."

Younger was predictably displeased and worse, petulant, when told Carolyn was leaving. He complained he should be given more than two weeks' notice. This irritated John so much he responded that he was making Mrs. Farrand an officer of his company and couldn't himself wait. Younger left without saying more. They let themselves out.

On the street Carolyn was overwhelmed by tears. John insisted they walk to the Ritz-Carlton to eat lunch in the Oriental Garden there. Carolyn felt much better as she watched ducks paddling in a tiny stream flowing at the side of the table. She said she wished Bobby Allen could see them. Over dessert she reported that Shelley Younger, who was the family's sole child and a woman over thirty-five, had once told her, "If you find secrets, only the recent ones will interest me."

"And did you find any?"

"You did. You said you loved your wife."

"It's the least a married man can say."

"Shelley says she's for certain only her mother's child." Carolyn paused, put down the dessert fork, bit her lower lip. "When Nancy met Shelley one day in my apartment, she said she's afraid Shelley makes up for her father's lack of interest in women."

He exclaimed, "Nancy said that?"

"I suppose such things are obvious in Hollywood."

"Not for me, Carolyn. I never seem to know anything personal."

"What do you mean? You *help* people!"

"I'm not sure what I mean. Yes. I do. In *The Great Gatsby*, Gatsby presses Daisy, the girl he lost once, to admit she never loved her husband, not even initially. When she won't admit it, he concedes by saying, well, it's only personal. That's perfect, isn't it? An ambitious man would explain intimacy that way. Or a generous one. What's wrong, Carolyn? Carolyn?"

She stared at him, tears dropping to the overlapped lapels of her trim jacket, and said, "I don't miss Angus. That day you and Nancy left, I hid and cried. How I wanted to go with you! It's crazy, isn't it? I mean both Cassie and I wanted to go. Poor Cassie!" She wiped her eyes with the napkin, failing in her anguish to find a handkerchief. "Thank God for Nancy. I've never known if someone would be good for me. Now, it's different. I have Bobby Allen and now the job at Past and Present." She smiled brokenly. "I won't hold you to promoting me to an officer the day I am hired, really I won't! You said it because you dislike Mr. Younger."

From the beginning she was adept, handling the production of journals, learning the eccentricities of scholars who contributed articles and those of the librarians who were P and P's largest customers. By the time she was sent to set up an office in London, in 1952, she was earning thirty thousand dollars a year. She stayed six months: she rented a flat and found a school for Bobby Allen in Saint John's Wood, leased space off Berkeley Square, hired a staff, and lured a senior editor from Oxford University Press. It was one, two, three. After John fired a man in the New York headquarters who'd been unable to keep his promise to quit drinking, Carolyn Farrand became a senior vice president of Past and Present, which by then had offices in New York, Los Angeles, London, and Tokyo. She was earning forty-five thousand and could afford not only an apartment overlooking the Fifty-Ninth Street Bridge but also the cost of enrolling Bobby Allen in a private school. She stayed single.

With the Western finished and released, Paramount hesitated over the third picture of Nancy's contract. Hopkins assured her this pause had nothing to do with her capability or popularity. He cited current uncertainties which made it seem that studio bosses had left the well-traveled roads and were headed into new staging areas where the visibility was poor for all the construction dust. Grim movies appeared in imitation of *Open City* and *The Bicycle Thief*. Philips at Paramount told Nancy that it was a bad sign that black-and-white pictures were "darker" than before the war, with less lighting, more shadows. He quoted Levinheimer as saying this was no mere style but an attempt to hide the picture from the audience. Then wide screens were installed in drive-ins and 3-D glasses installed on audiences. Musicals became so expensive that overseas business, always considered "gravy" by studios, became vital to recouping costs.

Nancy didn't wait on universal solutions. She took off for New York, glad to resolve temporarily the nagging question of where she and John would live when each was working on a different coast. On Madison Avenue and Eightieth Street she found six

rooms plus maid's room and bath. She hired plasterers and paint-
ers and masons. Tiles were installed on bathroom and foyer
floors, new hardware on doors. Several times she pulled John
from his office to make raids on showrooms to buy mahogany
commodes, chinoiserie cabinets, and bright blue and orange Por-
tuguese rugs. It was for her an adventure, for him a nuisance.
He never went out in New York except for business luncheons
and dinners. He had not once introduced her to anyone.

It all came to seventy-eight thousand dollars. Frank Hopkins
planned to charge part of this total to Bonan, Inc., the company
he had formed in anticipation of negotiating a new contract with
Paramount. And Hopkins asked if John Sirovich would bear part
of the cost in P and P, perhaps designating the apartment a
"showcase" for his high-priced books. Sirovich was indignant
and told Hopkins to practice tax evasion somewhere else. Nancy
had to wave Frank off.

Nancy's staying in New York eliminated some of her husband's trips, which, because they were solitary, he came to regard
as a parole—much as he felt when a business visitor at the last
moment canceled an appointment. He tore from his calendar the
weeks as they lost currency; and when finally he began to save
calendars, it was on the advice of a tax attorney, just in case.

John had seen his father sporadically by stopping over in
Denver every third trip or so to and from California. Nancy had
seen Tata on but one trip. Typically, Tata would refuse to visit
them in Los Angeles. He'd taken a vacation from the gas company
only once, in 1928. All other years he'd taken cash in place of
time off. It was a joke at the gasworks that he feared his gang
might go berserk in his absence and pierce a water main while
digging, or fray a lady's lawn while laying feeder pipes to her
furnace. His reputation for meticulously repaving streets and
resodding lawns was such that it was repeated, "You can't tell
where Eli's gang's been."

Ilija maintained that if once he took up his suitcase he would
not stop before reaching Belgrade, but his threat was not given

much credence by Blažo Nikitić, a Serb from Lika, or the Montenegrin Danilo Vujović, or Zoran Čucović, who owned a bar and pool parlor on Champa Street. They knew Ilija suffered staying at home; they knew inaction is the revenge visited on pridefulness. As a boy John had witnessed his father's prideful thrust to act. When he was twelve he had been insulted for not having the right change by a neighborhood grocer who accused, "You're like the rest." At home Jadwiga attempted to soothe her son by saying this taunt meant nothing, but Ilija arose, took his revolver from a dresser drawer, and motioned to Jovan, "*Prekini. Dosta priče. Ajdemo sada.* Stop. It's enough talk. Let's go now." His wife and son, pleading, had seized his arms, and he relented only because Jovan was at age twelve deemed a man and able to defend himself. Later Jadwiga argued that a few cents in change wasn't worth a shooting, yet in Ilija's native science revenge was exacted not by the weight of an insult but by who gave it and who took it.

Regret for his own inaction was constantly in Ilija's thoughts, for in his mind's eye were images of postwar Yugoslavia: two million deaths, barren fields, empty huts. Ilija did not speak of such scenes, not because they were unspeakable but because it was cheap bravado to savage the communist leaders of Yugoslavia from the safe haven of America. Nevertheless Ilija and his friends knew the details of the internecine killing—the Ustaša, fascist Catholic Croatians murdering four or five hundred thousand Orthodox Serbs along with numerous Gypsies, Jews, and Muslims. In Serbian-language newspapers in Pittsburgh and Cleveland and Chicago there appeared stories of such atrocities. There were also articles on the rise of the millionaire Jovan Sirović. *That* news started a pilgrimage.

The receptionist on Madison Avenue one day whispered over the telephone to Miriam, John's secretary, "A man out here says he wants to kiss Mr. Sirovich's hands. Miriam, what do I do? Should we call the police?"

This Serb was like other Yugoslav petitioners—usually Serbs

either from Montenegro or from Serbia, seldom Croatians and never Slovenes—who sought jobs, loans, gifts, character references, or simply the momentary celebration of a common ancestry. Secretaries found it impossible to distinguish between the mendicants and the scholars with a worthy manuscript; but in any event those who submitted manuscripts in Serbian were no different from many other authors who proceed on the incongruity that while a writer must trust an anonymous book-buyer to judge his work by the text alone, he must convince the publisher in person. Did you see Shelley plain?

In such manuscripts John found fantastical accounts of the Orthodox stabbed, shot, and clubbed to death by the Ustaša in 1943 and of Croats, victims of Serbs, stuck like pigs with thin blades entering the hollows of their necks—above tied hands. The killing, compounded by murders committed by Germans and Italians in occupying the country, was so vast that after the war it seemed categorically inhuman—like Krakatoa, a monumental calamity of nature. There arose among the survivors the fear that the dead were not murdered for any cause at all; and so a contention between sects and nationalities developed, each seeking a retroactive pity and some ironclad remembrance. Who counted the internecine dead? Not Tito. Ilija Sirović knew with an enormous pain that Tito had cheated not only the innocent—that was easy—but also the guilty.

At Stapleton Field in the fall of 1951, when John had landed from New York, Ilija drove him directly to Ćucović's place to eat goat cheese and black bread and scathing peppers quenched by refills of beer. John was suddenly gripped under the shoulders, lifted clear of the plywood booth, and, incredibly, carried sideways.

"You weigh less than a lamb! Tell me, Ilija, shouldn't a rich man show a little fat? Your son looks like a beggar in a Turkish town."

Bogdan was formidable still and even more fierce-looking now that he was gray and wore mustachios. Asked about Ten Sleep, Bogdan said the mill was shut down and the forest cut over, with no pines left "big enough to hide a boy." He had mined coal steadily during the war and, once allowed to travel to Alaska, prospected for gold. John asked him to come to New York, explaining the need to deal with all the Slav petitioners, but Bogdan dismissed such a job: "*To je ženski posao.* That's women's work." Then John mentioned he'd bought a Cadillac but couldn't drive it himself because parking was a nuisance in Manhattan. Bogdan looked at Ilija, who nodded, and it was done.

In New York they went immediately to the garage to pick up the sedan and drove across town with John seated in the rear on Bogdan's insistence. Bogdan dropped his suitcase off at a place on Forty-Eighth and Ninth Avenue, a district where the few Serbs in Manhattan congregated. When Perović had rented this apartment John didn't know; nor did he ask if anyone else lived there. Such discretion served John but not Nancy, who was puzzled that Bogdan could be unfailingly courteous yet remain evasive about John's childhood.

"*Gospodjo*, I knew the gardener of Doctor Michael Pupin, our famous scientist. He and Nikola Tesla were Serb geniuses. The gardener told me the doctor lived only in the mind. Jovan is like that. I don't know much about him."

On hearing of this dialogue, John asked Bogdan if he'd really known Pupin's *băstovan*—he had had to look up the word for gardener, a term hardly common in coal camps. Bogdan looked at him steadily and said, "He didn't have one." For John, Bogdan was a great straight man, but Nancy too often found reason in such jokes to resent her husband—and, for that matter, his father and brothers and their friends—to resent that male consanguinity that collects men to kivis, caves, huts, and glades, while women are ritually denied a long youth.

Toward the end of 1951 there occurred on the set of Nancy's new picture, *Boss Lady*, an accident every studio head dreads. The picture centered on a young woman in a corporation who is promoted over her husband and in the comedic climax gives birth at a board-of-directors meeting. Whether the picture was really clever, or merely cute, was never adjudged, because one morning on the sound stage the male lead, a man no older than forty, dropped dead of a massive coronary. Because he had appeared in almost every take thus far, thousands of feet of film would have to be discarded. Levinheimer and Philips were reported by Hopkins to be "noodling" the tragedy. Nancy also was forced to assess her choices. Being paid even if the picture was abandoned might enrich her financially but hardly professionally. An actress needed to be *seen*. Typically, the "topping" clause in her contract was far from being effective. As of the moment she had starred in and completed but two pictures, *Nurse on Duty* and *Lady on the Range*.

There was still more suspense for Nancy. Her menstrual flow, always a bit irregular, had now skipped twice. Each time, she picked up the telephone to call her husband and her mother, then decided against it. It would be too awful to disappoint them. She would wait for the third miss. Nor did she tell Blaine when he came through from Mobile on his way to rejoining his ship, USS *Rochester*, which was at sea off Japan, being readied to bombard the coast held by North Korea. He was back on active duty, leaner in body and face and quite dashing in a full commander's uniform, three stripes on the sleeve and scrambled eggs on the cap visor.

At Hollywood Hills she had few friends to visit. Lelia Dawson was accessible, but she too obviously avoided mentioning John Sirovich. Nancy knew of John's quarrel with her but presumed it had to do with Winterfield, because Lelia had been so openly protective of Win while critical of Pat. Moreover, Nancy's absences in New York kept her from attracting the usual studio camp followers—beginning actresses who eagerly attended the established ones, the sort who, Nancy once complained, sought to make their reputations on *your* picture. Oftentimes alone, she went on reading binges, working her way through volume after volume of an Oscar Wilde edition both printed and bound in vellum—she called it "luxuriating in literature." Then she decided to buy an Exercycle to tauten her calf muscles, but her gynecologist halted that. Finally, she picked up the telephone.

"John, did you just get into the apartment? I've been ringing. Come home. I want to talk."

"Nancy, are you all right? Talk. *Boss Lady* again? Am I fired?"

"Hardly so. You're promoted. You're going to be a father."

He arrived the next afternoon and took her straight to bed as if fearing the baby would claim her too early. He became so expansive that he called her father—although the Judge talked almost daily with Nancy—to assure the Judge that she was in the best of care. The same day Hopkins telephoned to express his concern over the double delay—the probable scrapping of *Boss Lady* and the incapacitating effect of Nancy's pregnancy. On Nancy's insistence they went together to Hopkins's house in Bel Air. There John met Cynthia Hopkins for the first time, a woman of forty-five who was, like her husband, originally from the East and who at one point commented on California's being "still the *frawn-tear*."

"Do you publish anything I would read?" she asked.

John did not reply, only looked at her. Her husband became flustered. In Hollywood even Easterners knew who were the heavy hitters, the ones whose commonplace remarks were sought eagerly: "Mel, tell Nathan here how you bought the whole damned island."

On this occasion in Bel Air, Hopkins said, "John, do tell Cynthia about your having met Dr. Einstein."

After it was agreed that *Boss Lady* would never be reshot, Nancy asked if Frank had got anywhere in searching for a "television movie." He reported there really was no such thing. He was right. It was commonly known that when General Sarnoff, the head of RCA, came to see Louis B. Mayer about the co-production of movies by MGM and RCA, he was turned down. Within months, wonder of wonders, Mayer was fired—but not for turning down RCA. Television, Frank concluded, simply wasn't comprehended by Hollywood as a source of income. Cynthia Hopkins underlined the point by declaring she had not seen a single TV set, let alone owned one. It caused John to comment that in his New York apartment he often watched broadcasts of women's softball from Chicago. She stared at him as if he'd admitted to masturbation.

Frank said quickly, "I'm afraid you'll just have to sit it out, Nancy."

She felt disabled, like a runner whose legs were suddenly mismatched, and replied, rising to her feet, "You can sit it out, Frank, because you live here. I'm going home."

They packed eight suitcases, paying the extra fare, and flew to New Orleans to be met by James. As they drove through Pass

Christian and other old Mississippi coastal towns, James talked of working at Uncle Charles Hobson's law firm. As he held the wheel, Nancy stroked his hair and smiled at him frequently. She had met his fiancée on earlier visits to Mobile and now said several times to John, "She's darlin', the prettiest thing," reverting more and more to her native accent as they closed on her hometown. She asked James if he had talked with Blaine, causing him to look disquietly at his brother-in-law. They both knew that Blaine had twice called his sister by radio telephone from Japan, and she had in turn conveyed his messages to her parents, who otherwise received only a short letter now and then. When they pulled up under the portico of the house, she rushed in tears from the car to be clasped in her father's arms.

After a few days Patricia Fredericks reported to John that people in town were saying that Nancy Tuck had arrived home "not quite herself." How was it possible that such impressions could be assayed and conveyed so quickly? The Frederickses lived in a large suite in the Battle House, where they had converted half a floor at great cost, RJ having sold his father's house. For his part, RJ still held back from exchanging his former finely tuned banter with John Sirovich. John's wife, whom RJ had known since she was an infant, had become a stranger by dint of being a public figure; and his own wife had known Sirovich before she met him—to what degree of intimacy he could not estimate and did not care to consider. Fredericks was content just to look upon his pretty wife. He trusted her fidelity and was assured that little other than the assaults of old age could now disturb him. RJ had come to feel almost content toward God and his fellowmen.

On Beaulieu Street Willa Ellen hired a carpenter to cut a door between Nancy's old bedroom and Blaine's. She furnished one as a sitting room, papering both a flocked blue and repainting the woodwork white. Downstairs she welcomed the steady company of her sister, who had taken charge of her niece's wardrobe, although only four months were left for the wearing of the maternity dresses. These were turned out on Jane's sewing machine like Chinese boxes, each larger than the last. Nancy had bought no maternity clothes in Los Angeles, and this worried Jane, who wondered if her niece was overconcerned about her figure. No doubt a pregnancy was disfigurement, however temporary, for an actress. But even if you did not glory in your enlarged and greater body—as Jane herself had longed to do over two decades—there was no disguising the plain condition.

Willa Ellen had an answer of her own: "Nancy Tuck has not been living with girls her own age who've had babies. For her, Jane, it's rare. After all, even her friend Carolyn gave birth without a husband alive, long distance, so to speak."

It showed through his armor that John Sirovich was no longer operatively a Westerner. He would no longer care to recall that he'd ridden the rails to California as a college student. Nowadays he didn't bother even to correct the misapprehension of most New Yorkers that Colorado was in the Midwest. On the other hand, except for the Pacific islands and not counting short trips to Mexico before the war and to Canada afterward, he had not traveled to foreign lands. Carolyn became aware, after the fact, that John went to a lot of bother to avoid traveling abroad—perversely, she thought, given that he was the son of Europeans and himself a lifelong student of English literature. She complained about the cost of bringing four employees from London to discuss setting up offices in Brussels and Frankfurt rather than John's going there himself.

Bogdan did not find it unusual that Jovan should avoid traveling to his home countries, Poland and Yugoslavia. One evening they sat in the empty office after the cleaners had left and as the radiators cooled. They drank coffee while seated next to typewriters that were shrouded, silent, between engagements, like cannon on the horizon. Bogdan reported that he'd taken a bottle of Vat 69 from a man named Tick Johnson, one of P and P's editors, the night before, on the grounds that Slavs didn't allow drinking in offices. Johnson had cried out that Sirovich was the only Slav he'd ever seen in an office, and Bogdan replied, "One is enough." It reminded him, he told Jovan, of the current anecdote about the television announcer in Zagreb who defended himself against the charge of ass-kissing because he closed his broadcast every evening by saluting the chief of the Croatian Communist Party: "*Laku noć, druže Bakariću. Good night, Comrade Bakarić.*" The announcer pointed out that, after all, the chief was the only person in Zagreb with a TV set. One was enough.

"I've been in the office too long, Bogdan. I've never had a vacation since that time in the Big Horns."

"There are worse memories."

"Maybe I'll go to *Stari Kraj*, the Old Country."

"Talk with Ilija. See your father."

Before leaving Los Angeles, he called Tata to say he'd spend a weekend in Denver on his way back. He had already informed his vice president in Los Angeles that the P and P staff there would be reduced to four or five persons, adding that the officer himself could transfer to the New York headquarters. When the manager offered to assemble the whole staff to hear the bad news, John quickly demurred. No, he would see them one by one, each alone. If he was going to face the discontented, let him not help them organize themselves. Moreover, he wished to give out extra, and therefore uneven, amounts of severance pay, an act better performed in private.

Bob Channing managed to run him down in the office, on what information John didn't know, to invite him to a poker game at his house. He'd seen Channing only twice since that time he had acted as a shill for Paramount, and they'd been cordial enough. Each time Channing had invited him to play cards, each time saying that the other players were "loaded but not skilled." John didn't trust Bob but, illogically, he had not been uncomfortable in his presence. This time he decided to go, as a relief from his grim mission in LA. Bob greeted him at the door after John told the hired driver to return at midnight. He was unchanged, strong and trim, his grin in place, his handshake more a contest than a salute. Next to him stood, barefoot, a tall blond girl whom Channing didn't introduce. At first John thought she was wearing a negligée, then realized it was simply an unusually revealing long white evening gown that showed her breasts to be large and round and free.

The other players at the table were all middle-aged. John got the impression that, except for two movie producers, they had nothing in common but their acquaintance with Channing. There was a man who owned a string of auto shops in the San Fernando Valley, a highway contractor named TJ, and a real estate dealer from West Los Angeles. When Bob offered John his chair, the real estate man said he was leaving after the present hand; and then when the girl asked if he wanted a drink, John asked for coffee and followed her into the kitchen. Her name was Joyce Melville, and she said she knew "all about" John. She said she was "living-in" but protested laughingly, "I don't do windows."

Then she added, "Your buddy Bob is still talking about divorcing his wife. Don't look like that! I know how often he plays that tune."

"Then what's in it for you?" John asked, immediately sorry he had.

She frowned and said, "If you aren't going to be nice, why did you follow me?"

"I apologize, Joyce. I've just spent two days firing a lot of people and feel sorry for myself. Can you imagine how *they* felt?"

"What did they do?"

"They were pioneers." She frowned, so he continued, "Joyce, you're a beautiful girl. Can't one of those producers out there help you get a part?"

"One said he would—the bastard. He called me Joan when

he came in tonight. He doesn't know me from ten thousand other blonds."

"Maybe I can help. Maybe with TV."

When they heard Channing call "Ho!" she kissed him lightly on the lips. It felt like cotton candy.

The game was stud poker. Sirovich had expected as much, guessing that Bob Channing was a card counter. In stud the first card was served facedown, the second faceup, and then the betting began. For a player who was quick at keeping track of the cards cumulatively—both the cards in "live" hands and those showing in hands discarded by players who'd quit betting. Speculating on the opponents' hole cards was the entire strategy.

John bought five hundred dollars in chips and lost them within forty minutes. He bought another five hundred; and soon he added a thousand more. Joyce didn't show up until, coming downstairs, she answered the door when it chimed at midnight. It was John's driver. John asked her to tell him to wait. He'd just won four hands in a row, three of them large. It was getting noisy, although the players seemed to drink little. "Valley" won a fair-sized hand and laughed too hard, probably because he'd bluffed. One of the producers left the game, and as he went out the door John's driver started his engine mistakenly. The remaining producer, a man named Manell, complained of his lack of high cards and was told by TJ not to argue his hand but play it. Channing was the big winner so far, and he seemed a little hectic, grinning and stroking a hand upward on his cheek, as if rubbing a hunchback for luck.

Manell was dealing. Channing cut the deck. After the first face card, a seven, Manell quit, but of course kept dealing. TJ and "Valley" stayed, as did Channing and Sirovich. On the fourth card, the third one showing, TJ drew a king. Channing drew a heart seven. Sirovich also drew a king. Now TJ, with a pair of fives and a king, wisely folded—he was already beaten on the board because John showed two kings and a seven. "Valley" had one jack and two queens. Channing was not higher but stayed with three hearts in a sequence: ten, nine, eight.

After the bets were made and met, Manell dealt the fourth and last "up" card. John knew "Valley" would drop if the bet was high and so bet five hundred dollars. He dropped. So Channing and Sirovich were left face to face. It figured. Channing showed hearts in a row: ten, nine, eight, and now, a seven. If he held either a heart jack or a heart six, he would win with a straight flush. Sirovich, staring at the cards, was going to play to the end no matter what. But by the rules of good stud, he *should* keep on simply by betting against Channing's competence: a good stud player like Bob wouldn't stay on past the second or third round if he hadn't at least an ace in the hole. Sirovich would be justified in figuring him for an ace heart in the hole—which would make an ordinary flush that could be beaten by a full house.

For Channing it was presumably harder. If Sirovich held in the hole either a king or a seven, he'd have a full house. But the odds were seriously against his holding either one. Channing himself held a seven. In TJ's dead hand was a king, in Manell's a seven. What were the odds Sirovich held the last seven in the deck or the last king? Long odds.

"Table stakes, gentlemen. I've got four thousand here." Channing moved all his chips and a fan of fifty- and twenty-dollar bills to the center of the baize; and when Sirovich reached for his wallet, he said generously, "Just be light, old buddy. How much are you light? Two thousand? Okay. Too bad, old buddy."

He turned over his hole card. A heart ace. A flush.

"Not bad," John replied, turning over a king, making three kings and two sevens, a winning full house.

John hadn't noticed that Manell and "Valley" had gone out the front door until he heard an engine start up and immediately shut off—it was his driver again.

"Bob," he said hoarsely, "you cut Manell's deck deep. You saw a king and figured your Valley friend got it in the hole. But you figured wrong." He turned over the dead hand's hole card. It was a jack.

"So? Shit, you won all the money."

"You've been cheating all night."

TJ stubbed a cigar out and declared to no one in particular, "I wish I knew if that was true. I'd *take* my money back."

"Why don't you say good night?" John asked him. He complied and passed through the foyer, pinched Joyce on the fanny, and caused John's driver once more to start his engine briefly.

"You bastard, Bob!" It was Joyce. Her eyes were wide with affront. "You said you asked him here only to beat him."

A rush of blood brought John to his feet, and his arms shot out as he reached for Bob's shirt. Bob broke away, righting himself, and as he lunged forward he was struck by John's right fist. Channing fell heavily, blood spilling from his nostril. When he sat up he held a front tooth in his hand and seemed to regard it marvelously.

Outside the house the driver watched uncertainly as Sirovich walked toward him holding his right forearm with his left hand. Then he saw a blond girl, barefoot but carrying shoes and a man's coat, hopping across the bluestones of the driveway. Before they drove off he saw her extract several items from the coat—a wallet, a spray of big bills, and chips. He wondered if those chips were redeemable anywhere, like the ones at Las Vegas.

At the hospital emergency room a resident with sleep in his face peered at the first X rays, then filled a syringe. "Your heart's okay? This dope has Adrenalin in it." He plunged a local anesthetic, set two fingers and a fractured knuckle, plunged the needle four times more, and finished up with more X rays, plaster of Paris, splints, gauze, tape, and an arm sling.

In the waiting room the driver sat bent over, his hat on the floor upside down like a cuspidor. Joyce's bare feet were tucked up under her evening gown. After they all left, and stopped in front of his house in Hollywood Hills, Sirovich told Joyce to give the driver two hundred dollars; and when she whispered she'd already paid him fifty to fetch her suitcase from Channing's, John whispered back to take a thousand for herself. It startled her. She said he didn't owe her, but thanks.

Then she had a question: "Can I ask you, wasn't it enough to catch him cheating? You wanted to beat him fair and square?"

John stared at her. Was Channing like Johnstone in New York, merely an excuse for his violent righteousness—for purging the mistaken and the disbelievers?

"I owe, Joyce. I'll get you a TV job. Catch the Tuesday flight to LaGuardia. Here's the office number. Ask for Carolyn Ellis. She'll arrange things."

The next afternoon John was sitting in Tata's basement room hearing, "Did you break your hand signing papers?"

"Please, Tata. I hit a man in LA. He was cheating all night at stud poker."

"All night? Why did you wait then?"

"Tata, let up. He hated me and I didn't know why."

"So it wasn't money. That explains it. Bogdan says you *give* money away."

"I gave a few thousand dollars to Saint Sava's in New York to bring three seminarians from Belgrade and Niš."

"What for?"

"I felt sorry for them. What else, Tata? Tito killed their past."

"Communists," Ilija said, "sell the future like priests. They both promise heaven."

To gauge Ilija Sirović's aging year to year was not simple for his son, who knew no relatives to liken him to. Ilija had no relatives in the U.S. John had never seen Jadwiga's two older brothers, who had left a coal camp in Portage, Pennsylvania, to return to Poland before the war and had not been heard from again. Nor did he meet her sister, who died childless in Hamtramck, Michigan. Jadwiga's youngest brother, only a year older than she, had come to stay with them for a few months during the Depression. Tadeusz Choparski was a small and amiable man who left for Alberta in 1933, there to take up farming with some Old Believers who much earlier had emigrated from Russia. After Jadwiga died in 1938, he stopped writing. Even to a stranger Ilija's physical appearance was misleading. As he turned sixty, his hair remained coal black and his voice neither dropped from fatigue nor rose from bad hearing. John was aware that Tata didn't make actuarial decisions. He still bought new Sunday clothes.

Indeed, Ilija looked no different from the picture on the wall in which he sat with his hands loosely clasped on his knees, a gold cruciform lodge key hanging from a heavily braided chain across his vest. Jadwiga always hated this picture, in which she stood with her hand held conventionally to his shoulder. John was there too, on the other side, standing in a three-piece suit bought at the Golden Eagle department store for seven dollars. For Jadwiga the occasion for this picture-taking was one of profligacy. As soon as its prints were available and his visa confirmed, Ilija took all their savings to travel to his birthplace in a show of worthiness attested by his wearing a business suit and thin-soled shoes. His mission was in part undertaken to convince a certain Radovan Simić to marry his ungainly sister, who at the age of thirty-two was still a spinster.

Ilija had left on a late May morning, kissing the hair of his sleeping son who was home on vacation from school. His hope was to celebrate Vidovdan, "the day we shall see," the day first glorified on June 28 of 1389 when the Serbs were defeated at Kosovo and again, the same day in 1914 when the Serb Gavrilo Princip killed the archduke and his wife, Sophia. It was June 28 when the marriage banns were said in the little stone church in Prokuplje, the Sirović village. When Ilija emerged from the church, an old man ran up to him crying, "It is Vidovdan, but what shall we see? We fought the Turks, the Bulgars, the Austrians. I lost my brothers and sons, as your brother was lost at sea before he could join them in death. What shall we see? You are from America. Do you know? It is too much! We do not need peace. We need victory. What will happen to our king?"

Six years later the king was killed by the Black Hand far from home, in Marseilles. The old man was no more crazy than Ilija's own brother.

Was he never to be amnestied for not having fought a war? In 1907 there was no war when Ilija and his mother walked along the Toplica, his shoes hung around his neck to save the soles, until they reached the point where the river merged with the mighty Morava at Niš. There he took a train for Trieste and boarded a ship for America along with other Serbs, Croats, Italians, Greeks, and Bulgars who sat and slept in the hold, staring or playing cards in the gloom until allowed topside, like prisoners. As the ship neared Ellis Island, all rushed to the rail to gaze at the Statue of Liberty. And Ilija remembered that a Bosnian had expressed the fervent hope that she would prove to be the only unassailable woman in the New World. Then they disappeared into the huge interior of America like trickles into the karst of Montenegro, so that over the years Ilija could not tell for sure who had lived and thrived and who had quit or died, except for Vuk Černović, who accompanied him to the steel mills in Pittsburgh, to the navy pier under construction in Chicago, and to the mines in Carbondale, where Vuk began to suffer the blackdamp that turns a man's lungs lacy. Another threat at Carbondale was aboveground. Vuk used to tell how the Ku Klux Klan raided the immigrants in their boardinghouses.

He used to say, "They ran out of people to hate—you see, they should have started with a longer list."

As John sat with his father in the basement that night, nursing his bandaged hand, he asked suddenly about who was shooting and who got hit in those night raids in Carbondale.

"How the hell should I know?" Ilija answered. "With a pistol you can't hit a man unless you see his bad teeth. It was dark. The Croats laughed at Vuk, saying it was too bad the Klan hadn't heard of the Orthodox. They thought we were all Catholics. Poor Vuk! At least he didn't live to see Serbs and Croats murder each other in the face of their common enemy."

They were back to the question, the only question that night. John said, "Tito is a Croat himself."

"That is not his crime. He's harder on his own people than on others. He probably speaks with a Russian accent. What did Tito do? He won. Draža Mihailović was as brave. He fought the Germans and the Italians and the Ustaši. He saved the American fliers. But Draža's fault was simple. Too simple—he lost."

Huge tears filled Ilija's brown eyes. He rose to his feet.

"Jovan, Tito's Partisans killed my sister and her husband, Simić, and my two uncles. We were Chetniks, following Draža. My mother froze to death in the winter of forty-four. They were killed by *naši*, our own."

"You waited this long to tell me! Tata, I can't stand that! You didn't trust me!"

"I trust you and I know you. You are strict. I did not want you to think you could do anything about it. Not then. Not now. Bogdan told me you want to go to *Stari Kraj* to spend the *dinari* your company has there in the banks from selling books."

John had his answer. Serbia was to be seen only in the dimming distance. A man who went back to Prokuplje carrying a secondhand lust for retribution would appear an impostor. And he could become a dangerous conceit to the people who lived there. He leaned forward to kiss his father on the lips.

"*Tata, pusti, molim*, let go, please. Nobody is going back."

Ilija held his son by the shoulders and felt that his hands were too deft for this awful moment as he said, "Your mother understood that we came here forever. No one can be a guerrilla on a visa. *Laku noć, sinac.* Good night, Sonny."

Nancy was oppressed by moods that alternated suddenly: one moment excitedly hopeful, the next becalmed, distracted. She did not wish to think herself eccentric and so decided her sentiments were in a natural process of righting themselves, like a pendulum. This suggested she could respond to herself even if, as was the case, she didn't want to respond to others, not even to expressions of polite interest. The fact was, she didn't wish to see anyone, didn't wish to make herself ready, nor even to rise and sleep by the clock. Nothing seemed as it had been, for the feeling of change was larger than herself. A war was on, Blaine attending, yet people on the street were strolling or smoking or driving idly by as if men were not once again dying. She was a private person in her old bedroom in the old house, yet hundreds of thousands of strangers knew her name and face. In her bedroom, in the long afternoons, she was shamed by an insistent desire to be touched and penetrated, her skin outside and inside tormented— this at a time when desire was conventionally deemed unseemly if not dangerous.

Nancy was inept at avoiding old friends, at turning down invitations to lunch at the Country Club, or deflecting Rosemary's proposal to invite "the old gang" from Tuscaloosa for dinner. John was in general much better at maintaining privacy. When in doubt he was generous. Quite typically he made old friends and acquaintances into employees and became, somehow, less familiar with them. It was so with Bogdan and Carolyn Ellis. He got Joyce Manning, the blond, a job on TV through P and P's advertising agency. There was nothing between them—although Nancy could guess what rumors circulated at the agency—yet he had involved Joyce in an ugly dispute and immediately committed himself to her welfare. In LA people came to accept that he did not appear with his wife publicly yet didn't make sinister judgments about their marriage. It was known, all too simply, that "Nancy's husband works all the time." She could fabricate nothing similar to explain her wanting to get away from Mobile within two days of returning. She awaited John eagerly. They had told each other, "I love you forever," but that did not settle tomorrow or next week or next month. They didn't test their love, only their passing needs.

When he arrived, she was ready: *"I heroji su od majke rodjeni."*

"That sounds Montenegrin: 'Even heroes are born of women.' Did Bogdan teach it to you?"

"I made it up. Tata translated."

"How do you feel?"

"I'm impatient."

"What can I buy you? What do mothers want?"

"They want children to live near home. Ask Willa Ellen Tuck."

John spent the next six days noticeably subdued. Nancy was certain it had little to do with his having punched Bob Channing. Were her oddities contagious? John seemed to be on guard without anger, as if warned by a friend, not an enemy. James took him one afternoon to an AA baseball game but couldn't persuade him to go hunting up-country at Manila. One evening Jane came over to play bridge. Like James she asked how he came to wear a cast and a sling. When John was about to explain he had caught a man cheating at cards, he decided it was unworthy and went on to say, deflecting the question, that he had been obliged to let people go at the Los Angeles office. *That* bothered him more than crooked cards.

"I'm sure, nevertheless, that you are easier on your employees than you'd ever be on your superiors." He was caught on the blind side and looked at her suspiciously. "Don't be offended, John. My husband said it. Of course, you don't have any superiors."

John had not been offended by Jane. Indeed, worried as he was, she was the sole person he could approach. The night before he was to leave for New York, he drew her aside and asked about Nancy's condition. Some nights, he told her, Nancy woke crying. Her skin and hair did not seem oily and smooth, as everyone expected of a pregnant woman. Jane was reassuring but said nothing specific. In bed John tried to hold Nancy without pressing against her belly and kissed her eyes to avoid the sensuality of her mouth. She wept and soon after slept. Had Willa Ellen heard her crying? Mothers always hear.

He spoke again to Jane late on the morning of his last day. "Should I call in another doctor?"

"Oh! Do talk with Nancy's mother, John. Please do that."

As he left the house for the airport, he told Willa Ellen of his decision to seek another opinion on Nancy's pregnancy.

"John, dear, Nancy's father has already spoken to the chief of medicine at the infirmary. He's looked in on Nancy."

John was rattled by this. The Bowens had never before acted covertly. It was precisely their dependable good manners that now made him agitated and resentful. Their calling in another doctor was averse, perhaps a way of making Nancy their own responsibility. She had of course remained their daughter all the while that he was so late in claiming her as a wife.

"You should have told me. It affects my child."

"John, be kind. You were traveling. Harold felt we shouldn't wait."

"I can always be reached. I *pay* people to keep track of me. It is Nancy who is hard to reach." Then he asked, "What did the other doctor say?"

"Everything is normal."

"You called him in because you didn't think so."

"Do you want to talk with Dr. Thurman? Or Dr. Weathering?" Her voice wavered on the brim of tears. "Nancy needed this spell at home, John. I know it. But I'm not sure how I know it."

He left it at that. He could not argue with instinct.

On his desk John's secretary Miriam had left a note, along with dozens of letters and memoranda. A Mr. Earlson had invited Mr. Sirovich to lunch at his downtown office "opposite the old Custom House on the Battery." Mr. Earlson's occupation or title was not stated on the stationery or in the text. The next morning, John asked Miriam to "do your thing," which was to flush out the likes of bond and stock salesmen while not, in the process, insulting a potential author or customer. She reported that Mr. Earlson was no piker, in fact no less than the chairman of Paine & Westville, a public company whose shares traded on the New York Stock Exchange. As he was seated behind Bogdan in the Cadillac, John read P&W's financial results in *Moody's* and the history of its incorporation and its acquisitions in *Dun and Bradstreet*. He'd already read five of its annual reports, published as required of a public company on the Exchange.

The Paine & Westville offices were capacious but showed no taste, neither good nor bad. Opposite the elevator doors sat a gray-haired man in a cheap blue business suit and policeman's nobby shoes. He sent John's last name, mangled, through a telephone to a middle-aged woman, who in turn arrived to lead John to Earlson's office. James Earlson arose, shook hands, and waved him to a wingback chair across from his desk. He was sandy-haired, balding, with blue-gray eyes, his own teeth, and a clear skin that showed only the natural laxity of a man nearly sixty years old. He picked up the latest Past and Present catalog and, without glasses, read the preface to John's first list of fac-similes, which John reprinted in each new edition of the catalog.

William Hazlitt said, despite all his reverses and contentions, "Well, I've had a happy life." Good authors seem to be born unabashed. In time, good readers might become so. Past and Present, Inc., reprints old books at a low price when value is found wholly in the text, at a higher price when the edition itself is as rare as old silver.

Earlson lowered the ninety-six-page pamphlet and said, "That's a pretty fancy beginning. I'm not sure how it applies." Then he said, "How come you have a Euclid, an original, priced at two thousand dollars? You didn't reprint it?"

John was pleased by this unfussy beginning and was not put off by the slight criticism. He replied vigorously, "Once in a while we buy a rare book but find it's too risky to reprint it. Then we sell the original just because we can't afford to keep our mistakes—rare as they are."

It was overclever and self-serving, but this time Earlson passed over it to ask another question, "You don't have that problem with journals, do you?"

"No, not really. In that other catalog on your desk are listed, for example, issues of the *Journal of the German Society of Genetics*, with issues from 1889 to 1938. The issues aren't worth much singly, but the set is priced at eight hundred dollars. Come to think of it, *one* issue might be rare, the last one—by 1938 the Germans had taken a novel view of human genetics."

Earlson was not entirely surprised by these embellished replies. He'd earlier spoken to a professor at Rutgers who knew Sirovich well enough to describe him: "He's learned but quick, sound but showy. I trust him. I'm not sure he trusts himself."

Earlson was determined to follow the line of questioning he'd laid out. "How come the librarians pay so much, eight hundred dollars and more?"

"The need for completeness. The *Index Medicus* consists of fifty years of issues from the Royal Society of London. It's priced at eight thousand, five hundred. A good medical library must have the whole set."

For his part, John Sirovich had already grasped that the host was not interested in buying books but in buying a business.

"Let's eat, Mr. Sirovich."

In a small dining room a white-jacketed man brought them melon, then steaks on luncheon plates that had not been separately warmed. Finally coffee was poured, and Earlson began.

"Roy Westville was a job printer in Troy, New York, and once he offered to help someone find a part for his letterpress. Soon, he was knee-deep in the business of supplying parts. A press is like a mine pony. Feed it and it runs forever. Roy had a nice trade going when he met Clarence Paine of Dayton—Paine was originally a bicycle maker, like the Wright brothers. He was turning out automobile cams and rods in his forge and mill. They liked each other and merged their companies in 1911. In the First World War, Paine & Westville won cost-plus contracts to make artillery sights and machine-gun belts. Then, in the depression of 1921–1922, it bought carloads of army and navy surplus and sold items through mail-order catalogs. In the early 1930s we bought newspapers and radio stations in Ohio and Indiana. The founders died in the same year, 1937. Despite the new depression starting before the war, P&W had a good year in 1937—sixteen million in sales and over three million in net profits. The founding families went public in 1938. At the time, neither had control. I owned sixteen percent myself.

"As for me, I went to Rutgers and afterward sold wire for the Olmstead works in Trenton. In 1922 I joined P&W as chief buyer for the goods sold by mail order. Roy and Clarence offered me bonuses in stock or cash, and always I took stock. In time, the families needed cash to pay death duties. The Paines held thirty-eight percent, the Westvilles thirty-five. Besides my sixteen, about eleven percent was held by other employees in small lots. We went public at sixteen fifty a share in 1938. Today the market of 'outside' shareholders owns sixty-nine percent, and of the remaining thirty-one, the families together own twenty-three percent—although they're hardly together these days. I sold some shares when we went public and now hold eight percent. The other employees sold out altogether. We get along, the families and I, although they'd like a higher dividend rate—even though we already pay out about twenty percent of our earnings each year.

"Mr. Sirovich, P&W last year, in 1951, reached one hundred ten million in sales and made eleven million in net profits. Seventy percent of those revenues come from mail order and newspapers, eighteen percent from radio advertising, and about twelve percent from machining. That brings us to my point. I'd find it quite interesting to talk about the possibility of P&W's acquiring your business in a swap of shares—but only if you would stay on to run your company."

Earlson had throughout looked steadily at his guest, his eyes flitting away only when John lighted a cigarette. He hadn't pushed back his chair, crossed his legs, or scratched an ear. He was a man in charge of himself—and of the presentation. For John it was an impressive recital and heady stuff.

"Mr. Earlson, I doubt you'd want to pay what Past and Present is really worth."

"Try me."

"I figure at the end of 1952, this year, we'll attain sixteen million in revenues and about two million in net profits."

"That's this year. I gave you last year's P&W figures. What kind of borrowing do you do?"

"A million dollars short-term—into the banks in April, out in November."

"Your contracts with the Japanese and German governmental agencies and with the British academic societies, how solid are those?"

"This is a little one-sided, isn't it? How much is the Dayton factory worth—the one that turns out only an eighth of your revenues?"

Earlson's face was slightly pinched as he pointed out dryly, "We're a diversified company. No single part hurts or helps enough to change the whole."

"Well, P and P's contracts for unpublished works are worth a lot more than they're carried on the balance sheet for—which is zero. About six million dollars of inventory sits in our New Jersey warehouse, although it's carried at about a million and a half because we write down fast, one third, one third, one third."

"Mr. Sirovich, let's talk valuation. I figure P and P is worth ten times earnings, about what a P&W share is selling for on the New York Stock Exchange for—fifty-five dollars. We have two million shares outstanding."

"How does that work? Oh yes, I see. Two million shares times fifty-five is eleven million in earnings. And ten times fifty-five is also eleven million." John paused. Now it was not arithmetic but barter. "I'd say my stock is worth twelve times. We're growing at about thirty percent a year—and that's a lot faster than P&W."

"Twelve? Too much. Your company hasn't much of a track record. How old is it? Five or six years? P&W is forty years old."

"I might be willing to take part of the payment down and the remainder paid on the basis of future years' performance."

"No, you wouldn't. That way, you'd pay a huge tax because it would be a contingency deal and therefore not tax-free to you."

"What if I was willing to pay the tax?" John replied without fear of exhibiting his ignorance. After all, Earlson must know he had never bought or sold a company.

"Then Paine & Westville wouldn't be willing because, you

see, we don't want to amortize all that goodwill, which is the difference between the book value of your company and the price someone pays for it. In a stock deal we would pool your financial statements with our own, just as if P&W and P and P had been founded together, and that way *not* recognize the goodwill."

"Are you saying that goodwill is *never* accounted for?"

"Well, I suppose you could argue that someday it must be reckoned with." He frowned. "But that's ridiculous. That day would have to be, literally, the last day of all accounting for all the companies in existence!"

John was elated. "What a great delusion! There's a heaven, after all, Mr. Earlson. It's the place where all the goodwill awaits!"

"The valuation, Mr. Sirovich," Earlson said wearily, bringing him away from the brimstone of unreal speculation.

"If P and P is figured at ten times 1952 earnings, that's twenty million dollars."

"It's right arithmetic, but wrong transacting. Let's talk apples and apples. 1951 figures."

"One way or another, P and P's faster growth rate has to be recognized. Mr. Earlson, before today I never once thought of selling P and P. I'm not playing hardball. I'm just not in the market. For the right price, we can talk. I do appreciate your listening."

Earlson smiled for the first time.

"You're doing just fine for a rookie. You will surely have second and third and fourth thoughts, as will I. Shall we talk again in a week or ten days?"

In midtown Carolyn said, "My curiosity is killing a hundred cats!"

John laughed and steered her into his office. She listened without interruption. Her eyes, throughout, were alight with rising notions.

"You can't mean it!" she cried out. It was so loud she covered her mouth as if not to frighten the neighbors. "You mean you sat down with a stranger and, one, two, three—just like that—you almost sold the company? John! It's obvious he knew all about us. You'd never heard of his company before he asked you to lunch. Why did you talk terms so fast? Isn't there some sort of sequence in merging companies? Isn't there a formality?"

"You don't post banns, Carolyn."

"But it's an enormous decision!"

"All decisions come down to yes and no. IBM found that out making computers."

"Your maxims don't help, John. This concerns a lot of people."

"I know."

"Are you positive you do?" She squinted as she said it, as if he sat in the middle distance.

"Carolyn, now listen to me. I created all those jobs for our people from scratch. It wasn't a town meeting at the start, and it isn't one now." He paused and said in a low tone, "I *know* the temptation. When the risk is big, so big that you may be talking about the whole of your life, there's the temptation to lay it down."

"That's awful, John."

"No, it isn't. Hope and temptation are born of the same mother. But Carolyn, let's pretend this afternoon didn't take place. I may never hear from Mr. Earlson again."

Carolyn sat coping with images of the future, all the quickening complexities induced by possibility and ambiguity, each summoning the other. She stood, and in her fist a knotted handkerchief was tight from twisting and sweat. It had been like a stick held between a soldier's teeth while undergoing field surgery.

27

One night Sirovich stood before the refrigerator, the door open, and downed a quart of milk without stopping except to breathe. Bloated, he went to sleep without his usual dose of Nembutal. The omission was a mistake. He awoke at two o'clock, too late to administer a whole night's worth of pills and too early to go downtown to work. He went into the living room, a little-used space where the chair cushions stayed fluffed and a sweeper kept the nap of the rug evenly bent, like Bermuda grass. Something impelled him, and he could not identify it, to take from a shelf Joseph Conrad's *Victory*. He hadn't read it since high school, but he remembered Heyst, the man who died of resigned virtue; and he recalled that Conrad showed how a blade can be slipped between a man's early promptings and his late doings, severing the connection that holds him erect.

He awoke with the book on his lap. It was five-thirty. He bathed and shaved and in the dawn walked down Madison to order breakfast at the all-night Child's on Forty-Seventh Street. It was Thursday. Miriam had booked him on a three o'clock flight to Atlanta, where he was to spend the night so he could catch an early morning flight to Mobile. In the office, as will happen, most of the persons he dealt with regularly managed to wait until his last two hours to bring to his desk all sorts of problems, like cats proudly depositing unpalatable prizes on the house doorstep. He wasn't able to get away until just an hour before his plane was to depart LaGuardia. Bogdan had been circling the block, and seeing John hesitate at the curb over a yard-wide stream of spring slush, he stopped the car and stepped out to pick up his boss and hoist him across. John's dispatch case hung from his hand like a school lunchbox. On reaching his apartment house, he tore through the lobby and raced upstairs to grab his travel bag. A few minutes later he was in the hall locking the door as the uniformed elevator operator waited. Inside, the telephone began to ring. He paused. The elevator man looked at him speculatively.

"John? It's you?" It was Jane Hobson.

"Yes, I'm running for the plane now. Nancy knows when I land. I'll call from Atlanta."

"I know. Your office told me. John. The baby died. Nancy delivered a premature child—six weeks early. Stillborn. My god, John! I'm so sorry. She's out of danger, thank heavens. She's quite all right herself, I assure you."

"When?"

"A half hour ago." Her voice was strained, hesitant, whispery.

"John? Do you want the child blessed? There's a Greek Orthodox priest over at Fairhope, I know."

"No. No blessing. Was it a boy?"

"Yes. A boy."

By the time he reached Atlanta, there was no night flight leaving for Mobile, although one was headed for New Orleans, stopping at Birmingham. He decided to take the one to New Orleans and rent a car. Calling the house in Mobile, he reached James and told him of the probable schedule. But then the flight was canceled owing to heavy rain and he didn't bother to call again. Through the night he sat in the airport waiting room.

First the coffee counter closed, then the ticket counter; then a black janitor sloshed the floor with a ragged string mop. Finally he was alone. How old would his own brother have been, had he lived? Thirty-seven? Bobby Allen was almost six and could say "conflagration" and "palpitation," words John had taught him on trips to the Central Park Zoo and to the ice cream parlor down the street from the Plaza. But then again, Thomas Babington Macaulay was only four when a hostess spilled hot tea on his legs and he assured her, "Fear not, madame, the pain has abated." When John was five he had discovered finality. A nickel was lost forever when he pressed it into the slot of a door latch. His mother had consoled him by giving him another nickel, but it wasn't the same. Had his own son had blue eyes or were they emerald?

She was being scolded, yet it wasn't at all clear what she'd failed to do. She must not have failed—the tone was not one of urgency, but of harsh instruction. She awoke to the urging of a man and two women. He wore green, they white. They stared down at her, their bodies partially blocked by rails. Was she in a crib? They kept saying, Wake up now! It's time for you to wake up! Had she delayed them? Soon, more and more was added to the scope of her wakening senses: the bed with the side rails, the tan walls and white ceiling with tiny cracks like old people's skin, the doctor's mask under his chin like a bib, the nurses' hats held in place by hairpins underneath.

She was immediately alert. "How is he? Is he a boy?"

"You are still under, Nancy Tuck."

It was Dr. Thurman speaking. She had known him since she was ten.

"No, I feel fine."

She raised her head and was stabbed back and front above her thighs.

"Well, at least I feel better. How is he?"

"Nancy, I would have preferred your father told you. The baby was premature. Stillborn. He was dead at birth."

It couldn't be true because it took so little time to say it. If so terrible a thing had happened, then it would have required a just and proper amount of time to describe and explain—to make it seem sensible, however awful. It wasn't true because if true it must be a confidence and it wasn't right for those strangers present to hear the same information as she. She was ill. Then she was not. There were tricks, as in a parlor game, fast moves, yes and no, no and yes. Someone ought to slow it, slow it enough so that you could see what was happening.

"Nancy Tuck, there is nothing to be done, my dear. Here's your mother."

They all came then. Mother and Daddy and Aunt Jane and Uncle Charles and Jamey and Catherine Ellen and Rosemary and Auntie Cora and Lucas. Afterward more came, RJ and Patricia, girls who'd enrolled the same year as she in the Junior League, girls from college, three cousins from Manila. What they said, any and all of them, was of no avail. Was that a quality—something being of no avail? She had the unpleasant sense she was thinking like John, making an occurrence less important by means of inquiry and generalization. But even John, his eye always on the future, could not dismiss her present pain. It was hers, entirely hers. People said that when you gave birth, it was like taking off a heavy wet coat in a hot room. But it wasn't like that at all. The last six weeks, she had in fact felt lighter. She had bled a little bit, but not so that it hurt, just losing a little fluid, not substance. She'd not told anyone, not her mother or father or the doctors, because once the bleeding passed it seemed no more than a shudder.

She heard voices outside the door. John had arrived and she heard Jane say, "John, dear, you will understand, won't you? You can help Nancy. Only you can help her now."

"What can I do? This has been your family affair."

She couldn't hear her mother speak. Had Willa Ellen turned away, as if struck by an open hand? After a long time, her mother said, "We can comfort each other, at least that, John. We are Christians and do not suffer alone."

Jane said, "John, you're angry. That will pass, but the passing doesn't excuse us. We thought we knew just what was needed for Nancy, probably because our families have lasted so long a time in home places. Everybody else becomes a stranger to us. Maybe you should have taken Nancy away—even for this."

Nancy's back was to the door. Her head lay on her hands, clasped as in prayer, against a wet pillow. She looked out the window at the tropical rain, calming because it was steady.

"I waited all night," she said when she heard his coat dropped onto a nearby chair. "I didn't commit a crime. A stillborn child is closer to his mother than to anyone else."

She felt John drying his hand on the coverlet before laying it lightly on her hair, which had been combed but was still limp. Then she turned to lie on her back and felt his lips on her forehead. She couldn't read his eyes.

"I should have been here to help you, Nancy. I love you."

"It wouldn't have saved a life."

A nurse entered carrying a basin and cloth but left immediately. John had moved a chair to the bedside and sat kneading the palm of Nancy's left hand.

"I don't remember my baby." She heard her voice break into a higher pitch. "Do you hear? I can't remember my child!" When he didn't reply, she said, "Dr. Thurman says I took care of myself. Dr. Weathering came to the house every other day."

"It's all right, Nancy. You had the best of help. Things went against us." He kissed her lips and the sheet above her breasts. To Nancy her own lips felt thin. More than earlier, her body hurt.

"You weren't here, John."

"Nancy, the baby came too fast."

"It wasn't his fault."

"Please, Nancy. I don't live here. I had to come from a distance."

Tears appeared on her cheeks and seemed to gain heat when they fell to her neck. From the beginning, from the middle of the night, she had known this would be said.

"A place is still home after you grow up. You said it that night at Daddy's club. You said all roads lead away. I believed you. I came with you. I loved you first, John. I came back here to be myself."

"We'll have another child."

"People like us ought not to have children. I don't want to remember. I want to sleep now. I'm very tired of being myself."

She didn't hear the door close.

Down the corridor John saw the nurse who earlier had carried the basin into Nancy's room. "Is Mrs. Austin Newhardt still in the infirmary?"

"Why, yes."

"Which is her room? I'd like to say hello."

"Mr. Sirovich, you do know, don't you—she's not all that ready?"

"Yes, I know. We are old friends. Thank you."

He approached Cassie's room circumspectly. The lighting was bad because of the heavy rainfall outside. The door hung ajar. Who said that a half-open door was one of the most ominous of ordinary sights? It was the short-story writer W. W. Jacobs. It did not distract him, this.

Her bed stood in the center of the large room. Two windows opposite the door looked onto the long lawn below. A wardrobe faced the bed with its doors open, showing frocks; on a bottom shelf, shoes were lined neatly; and above, hat boxes. Cassie must be allowed up and about. Perhaps she was even permitted furloughs from the infirmary. This encouraged hope in him, as did the yellow flowers in vases and bowls on seemingly every surface: jonquils, freesia mixed with white, daffodils, and snap-dragons.

"Cassie? It's John Sirovich. John from California."

She turned her head and the motion brought him hopefully to her side. Her hair was arranged, her skin a little heightened by rouge and eye shadow. The negligée showed the pale curves of the top of her breasts. Blue bows were tied into the French lace of the neckline.

"Nancy is here, too. In the same building. Cassie? Nancy's here, downstairs."

A frown appeared on Cassie's face and seemed to require considerable effort, this merest of expression. Should he tell her? It seemed only fair. "She was pregnant, but it went wrong."

The effect was immediate and calamitous. Cassie's eyelids parted wider, the pupils darkened. She raised a hand no more than an inch off the line sheet. Her nails, he noticed, were freshly manicured but not colored.

"Cassie, I'm sorry. I brought you pain. I didn't come to do that. I just wanted to see how beautiful you are." He leaned closer. "You are a girl I dream about, Cassie."

The fingers bowed on the sheet. It was a motion minutely genteel, a response to homage. He could leave now without giving offense—further offense.

"They ask about you, Cassie." He kissed her cheek and then her lips, which were surprisingly full. "All the young men ask."

In her eyes he conceived he saw a sentence, some whole expression. He read it as gratitude. But then he recognized she'd merely given him agreement. She strained forward unsuccess-fully. He put his ear to her lips and felt a word like a feather.

"Nobody."

When he looked up, her eyes were closed. She had released him. He backed out from the room, leaving the door as he'd found it. The nurse didn't seem to notice he had passed. In front there was no taxi, so he walked down the driveway carrying his raincoat and soon felt his shirt turn wholly wet under his suit jacket. When he reached Old Shell Road he turned north and finally came to French Court. He didn't enter but remained outside. He couldn't formulate any reason for being there. He caught the bus headed downtown and got off at the Federal Building. In front of the First National Bank he found a cab to take him to the airport, where he waited for the rain to stop and the fog to lift. He boarded the first plane going anywhere at all, which happened to be Chicago. In Birmingham, there was an hour to wait and he paid for a shave and shoeshine. In Saint Louis he bought a newspaper. It was April 11. President Truman had fired General MacArthur. A million Chinese infantrymen had run across the frozen Yalu River, driving the Americans into humiliation. Truman had not let MacArthur bomb the river, not even his own half of the river. It was madness.

28

On the telephone Ilija cleared his throat each time he started to speak. He did not say he was shocked. Why was it necessary? Of course it was shocking, as was all finality. Nor did he speak of another time, another child. His son was a man who did not care for trivial talk, unless perhaps it was historical. But there were his own reasons. Ilija could not countenance an "unnatural death," which by his accounting was unworthy. A man ought to die in league with others, or from old age. But to die from accident was an event belonging to witnesses, mostly strangers.

Those nights when John was eighteen and his mother lay in Saint Luke's hospital, he would come home late and hear, from the basement, the dreary sound of the *gusle*. This instrument was Ilija's sole prize brought from Prokuplje after his return in 1928, wholly wooden in the making and meant to be held lightly on the lap. A single cord stretched across a shallow bowl covered with lambskin. It was stroked, sawed really, by a crudely carved wooden bow holding twenty or so strands of horsehair. On Ilija's *gusle* a dove perched on a ring through which a knot tightened the cord. Below the ring was a horse's head and a long neck scored with geometrical designs that ran to the sounding board. One time his son told him that the *gusle* probably descended from the horse cults of Central Asia. This Ilija had angrily rebutted: What had a dove to do with horses or, indeed, the snake carved on the bottom of the bowl that grasped the string in its fangs?

"Mama has only a few days left."

Ilija lifted the bow to play and said, "Help her then." He inclined his head and asked, "You think it is wrong I don't come with you?"

"Yes."

"She doesn't want to see me. She needs you. Maybe that's the same thing. Now you know the truth about hate."

"You despise death," John hissed, trembling. "Tata, you go to funerals but not to sickbeds. Are you afraid?"

Ilija stood and put aside the *gusle*, resting it on his desk chair. He came over to place a hand on Jovan's shoulder. The light bulb hanging in the center of the room almost touched his head.

"I cannot allow anyone to call me afraid."

"I know you can't—I'm sorry! But, Tata, look at me. Can't you see how angry I am?"

Ilija felt his son's fingers clench behind his back and John's head press hard against his chest as he sobbed, struggling for air but not consciously seeking it.

"Don't be sorry. It's right to be angry. Try to understand. Something is cheating Jadwiga. I am not religious, but I believe we are born for a reason, else why are there so many nationalities and so much left to be invented? It is a terrible thing not to see a sensible end. Jadwiga won't live to see your children."

He stepped back and sat down, taking up the instrument again, pausing with the bow held suspended.

"Is she remembering before we were married?"

"Yes. In Passaic. You won't come?"

"It's better this way. She thinks I ruined her life and she may be right. We came from different countries. She wanted you to work hard and make money. I wanted you to know yourself and know your enemies."

"Tata! Oh, Tata! This isn't *Stari Kraj!* There aren't many Magyars or Turks or Bulgars in the streets! I don't have enemies."

"You do. You will. They will come looking for you like drunks in the night. Jovan, you make enemies but you must learn to recognize them. Don't forget yourself. If you dream, keep your back to the wall. The Montenegrins say that."

Several nights later Jadwiga spoke steadily, despite her voice being sodden from the morphine that stoppered the pain from her cancerous stomach. She told her son that in Passaic the landlord beat his wife, yet it was because of her own intervention that she'd become godmother to his two little girls.

"I was godmother seven times when I was working at the Botany Mills. It's a lot, isn't it, Sonny? It was the style that the godmother before the christening should bring a piece of food every second day—chicken, say, or butter. You could buy a pound of meat for eight cents—and they gave you liver free because nobody knew it was good for you.

"We went to Mass at five o'clock before work. You sucked wool to thread the machine. One of my friends turned yellow and died. In Passaic three of us girls slept sideways on the bed and we paid two dollars a month each. A Jewish man and his secretary came to collect the rent every two months. He took the money and the secretary wrote it down. They had the business, the Jews, because they paid attention. Poles! They drink too much to run a business. I had four brothers, Sonny, but you saw only one of them. Stefan died eating wild berries as a boy. Wojtek almost died in the 1918 flu. Jędrek cheated our father out of the last of his land. Your uncle Tadeusz told me. You remember Tadeusz when he stayed with us, Sonny?"

That night John said, "She has nothing left but her story."

They sat down on Tata's bed to listen to his song, which the *gusle* underscored. The pentameters told how Miloš Obilić killed the sultan in 1389 at Kosovo. John thought: Who was Miloš to Jadwiga Choparska? Did Miloš work for a living? Was he kind to his children? It was ridiculous. Mama had counted her life by days and weeks, not centuries.

She said, "I was herding sheep for my uncle. I slept in his barn. Some people came from the city and one said, 'Let us have one of the sheep.' Were they serious or just cruel? Their black clothes frightened the lambs and they ran into the woods. I cried.

"When you were born in Sunnyside, we lived in a two-room shack with no water. When you were one year old I showed a woman my baby was ruptured. She told me to go to Louisville for a doctor to operate on you. A man took us in a hay wagon. But coming back I carried you, walking the six miles. Then you got pneumonia and you almost died. But I covered you with wool and you lived. Sunnyside was a bad mine. It was flooded. Your father and the other Serbs and Croats lost their tools. It was like the Big Four mine at La Veta, no good at all if you wanted to live.

"I never went to school even one day. I don't know why I was not allowed. My father came to America after my mother ran away to Budapest. You know about that. And then Tadeusz got lost from the railway station and I stayed two days by the cold stove. I mean, that was when we came here on the ship. I stayed in the station until my father sent money to the official. When I got to Lilly, Pennsylvania, a Polish family gave me hot milk and bread until my father came. His shack was nothing but a bed and stove. The family told him to buy me a ticket to New Jersey.

"Every morning you went to the iron gates to stand. That was at Botany Worsted. If the men inside the gate pointed at you, you got a job. After a week outside the gates I couldn't help crying. I hadn't eaten in three days. A clerk who spoke Polish gave me a yellow paper and opened the gates. But nobody would teach me the machine. They said the machines were made in England—they were big. I was so short they put boards down for me to stand on. After a month, I ran two machines together, one across from the other one. It was for wool suits. Lots of weeks I made four dollars. When you finished a hundred yards, and I learned the numbers, you pulled it all out and tied it up and a clerk gave you a slip. They paid you on the slip. I could read the numbers, Sonny.

"At the Botany in Passaic I was happy. I bought a dress and a brooch. I went to the *Dom Polski* with other girls and danced. I wanted to rent a house and keep roomers. I could have run the house and still worked in the mill. But then the Bulgars in the IWW—that's a union, Sonny—told us to strike for more money. So we went outside the gates and we lost our jobs. I have never trusted Bulgars. Then I took the train to Colorado when my mother came to America and asked me to help her in the boardinghouse.

"I couldn't save enough, Sonny, to get started. Nobody. Nobody gives people anything. You have to work. Your father was ashamed we were poor. But we didn't choose to be poor, did we? I am glad we came to America, you and me. There is no future in the Old Country. I wish I could see your children, but you are only eighteen. I know that you will educate them. There is no good reason to be ignorant. *Bądź zawsze uczciwy, synu, ale unikaj kłamstw ludzi. Jesteś odpowiedzialny tylko za samego siebie.* Always be honest, Sonny, but stay away from people's lies. You owe only yourself.

"Sonny, remember me. Tell your children how I came to this country and how I worked and all the strange times. You will never be ashamed like I was at the Big Four mine when it shut down and your father went crazy and carried an ax around with him. I was alone for four days without food and went over to some people named Bielecki and asked for bread. I was so hungry I had to! I turned my back because I ate so fast Bielecka told me I'd get sick and to sit down. You won't be ashamed, Sonny. You were always the best in school."

"Mama? Mama?" She was almost asleep. For a moment, he feared she had died. He said into her ear, "Mama? Mama? I remember the Polish prayer."

"No, Sonny." She didn't open her eyes but her voice was clear. "We won't beg."

CHAPTER

29

It was Pat Fredericks who told him that the child had been registered in death as John Sirovich, Junior. After the Episcopalian requiem was said, the infant was buried in the Christ Church graveyard. And it was Pat who called—within an hour of running into Jane Hobson at the Battle House—to report that Nancy was at last safe at home. Earlier, when Harold Bowen telephoned John in New York to exchange carefully perfunctory remarks, Harold sensed a lassitude in him quite unlike the man. He seemed disinterested, so detached that he might not be able to muster anger. Harold suggested that John call Nancy the minute she was home from the infirmary. This came hard for Harold because it was a plea, no matter how natural it seemed.

It was the judge's reluctance to ask for help that caused Pat to become an interlocutor. RJ sensed Bowen's mood and informed his wife. That Harold would assent to a stranger's speaking for his family was an indication that between him and John there was not enmity so much as confoundedness, a disturbing willingness on both sides to be misheard.

Pat told John, "Please don't you or Nancy, either one, leave any stones around to throw at each other later on. Call it show business, call it anything but your own marriage."

It wasn't much as advice, she confessed to RJ, but then *he* had been of no help. Throughout the crisis in the Bowen family RJ had remained grave of expression but had made no pertinent or useful remarks. When Pat asked him to call John Sirovich, he refused. No longer was he obliged to pretend to good fellowship. RJ stayed at his wife's side or waited for her return on those afternoons when she played bridge or attended charity functions. Jane Hobson, especially, admired Pat's marital regimen. Pat regularly declined invitations that might keep her away from RJ in the evening or on Sundays.

Despite his rigorous remoteness, RJ couldn't avoid listening to his wife's opinions. Pat said it was beyond fathoming that Judge Bowen would not go to New York to talk with his son-in-law. After all, she argued, hadn't he spent most of his life trying to find elements of reason amid the disorder of people's lives? He was a just man, everybody said—just to his friends as he was just to litigants in his courtroom. But the fact was that Harold Bowen had failed to offer to John Sirovich anything tangible, anything that could be accepted or else rejected for good reason. RJ told Pat that Harold was reluctant to intrude. In reply she asked hotly, What else did judges do but intrude? As a twice-divorced woman Pat was qualified to ask that question. What she didn't comprehend was that Harold Bowen was here not in his robes but in his slippers. He was bewildered by a favorite child who had with unprecedented audacity left home with a man whom she did not first marry, who had become a public figure by means unfamiliar to him, and who had come home to bear her child with a seeming high-spiritedness that almost immediately turned clamant. Such a father, given such circumstances, would not risk exploring her motives and could not, from inexperience, define all their probable causes.

Pat had once heard John tell Win that what happens to you

is pretty much like yourself. Pat hadn't liked hearing the axiom because too many uncomfortable things in her own life might be ascribed to her own subtle urging. In any event, she thought such generalities helped little in getting through the day. Someone, anyone, must begin by talking. Talk was like running water in disputes between men and women: it obliterated deadly silence with a neutral noise. *That* was her axiom. And it proved itself.

Pat had called John in New York and was talking aimlessly according to her own principle when she said she'd been invited to spend an afternoon with Nancy. Earlier John had told her he'd been discussing with an executive of Dumont television the possibility of Nancy's acting in a TV series.

Sirovich had earlier come to know of Dumont through P and P's advertising agency, but he'd never been to its offices on Madison Avenue. Now he came under the impulse of a defined personal need. The account executive introduced him to the agency president, a Mr. Harvey, who was about forty, lean, tanned, custom-tailored. At first John misjudged the man because of his solicitous mannerisms, sudden acts of gentility that distracted rather than aided: moving an ashtray closer, rising to adjust the blinds to let in the early summer sun, smiling in the midst of a prepositional phrase for no dictional purpose. But he quickly revised his opinion. Harvey was not the sort of man who tried to sell when no one was buying, and he proved to be generous.

"How do I talk with someone at ABC or Dumont about financing a show for a star, or perhaps a series of shows?"

"Do we handle TV for you?"

"No, our account is too small for TV. You handle direct-mail ads mostly. Mr. Harvey, this has nothing to do with Past and Present. I'm interested in the leading lady."

Harvey's expression of polite puzzlement soon turned to one of understanding: he had just connected John Sirovich to Nancy Tuck Bowen.

"But why ABC or Dumont? They are third—and a bad fourth—to NBC and CBS."

Bill Harvey was searching for more connections. It wasn't every day that someone came in to see him about financing a television show without worrying over how the cost could be recouped from advertising.

"Maybe your wife knows Goldenson through Paramount. He bought out United Paramount Theaters when the government made the studios sell their theater chains, didn't he?"

"Mr. Harvey, it isn't that complicated. I doubt that NBC or CBS would make a single show on spec, even with all the costs covered, don't you?"

"You're right about that. Maybe we can join forces in this?"

Even as he said it, Harvey was reminded how typical the remark was. In show business, everything began with talk, most of it desperate.

Through Harvey, Sirovich had met a senior officer of Dumont, a Peter O. White, and explained he was the investor and that Miss Bowen and he would put together one show on film and perhaps prepare scripts for two or three as sequels.

"She's on holiday right now. How much do you figure production costs would be for a half-hour show, not counting actors' and writers' fees?"

"Don't hold me to the penny. Forty thousand."

"When I give the word, we'll pay twenty up front."

"Fine. We can use the business. Let's drink on it."

John had recognized, even that first time they met, that White was overly prompt as a drinker, already seated at the table John had reserved at André's on Fifty-Fourth Street. He was one of those Manhattan executives who arrive early to down a double martini before the colloquy begins over still more drinks.

The separate meetings with Harvey and White had taken place while Nancy was still in Los Angeles, still uncertain that she was pregnant. Now that she was in Mobile, suffering her inactivity, he met White again at the restaurant. Between the two occasions, he'd sent Joyce Melville to White for a job. On John's orders from Los Angeles the morning after his fight with Channing, Carolyn Ellis had called White—whom the P and P account executive at the agency had recommended. She had told him, hating every second of it, that John Sirovich would "stand good" for Joyce's salary up to three hundred dollars a week for at least six months—until she either made it on TV or didn't.

This time both were wary. Carolyn had warned that White had sounded cynical about Joyce, presuming immediately she was Sirovich's girlfriend. Even the fact that Joyce had, on her own, gained a supporting role in an afternoon game show on Channel 5 might not have dispelled the impression of idle patronage.

"I didn't drop the plan, Mr. White. I just disappeared. Are you still game to produce a half hour? You don't have to agree to run it except in a screening room. It's all my nickel."

"Sure. Why not? The costs have gone up since we met, of course. Not much, but some—say, sixty thousand. I've got to admit that I thought I was being had after we first met. I mean, when your woman Ellis—does she eat nails for breakfast?—sent Joyce Melville to me. But Joyce straightened me out in a hurry. So did our treasurer. He says your credit is damn good. Joyce goes further still. She thinks you're God."

"I've not seen her on TV. How is she?"

"Let's not be telling her you don't watch Channel 5. Even I'm hurt."

Sirovich concluded the luncheon by handing over a check for twenty-five thousand dollars, this despite White's insistence that they draft and sign an agreement at a later date—the sensible way to do business. What White could not have guessed was that Sirovich was forcing his own hand, pushing circumstance to work.

One of the times they talked on the telephone, John described to Nancy the television series—or rather, its probable outlines—and spoke for at least twenty minutes without interruption. She understood what he was up to. He had waited until he had hold of something both real and elaborate. The lengthy description of the Dumont deal was intricately sequential. But why should she, on this sticky June afternoon walking in the spacious garden, examine precisely what methods led to precisely what ends? That was tiring because probably unalterable. Over the years since she left Mobile she had, almost as a deliberate reversal of her upbringing, refused to dwell on why people said or did things. For her, subtlety did not lurk.

But was she entirely deserving of self-congratulation? As a person near famous, Nancy Tuck Bowen had learned to carry about a defensive doubtfulness and to mind the motives of fellow workers—all those scribes and armorers and courtiers within a studio's realm. She had found out that in Hollywood the agents and lawyers and publicists were altogether too familiar with fame: they saw in every rising star a dying meteor. That day when the girl from Condé Nast sat in the living room while husband and wife harried each other in the hallway, Nancy had returned to reply to one more question. It now and then still rose to the surface of her musings. Do you sometimes, the girl had asked, find it unpleasant to *owe* people you haven't even met—I mean, your fans? Nancy couldn't find a credible answer at the time. But it was hardly a trivial question. Since returning home from the infirmary, she had spent nights wondering why it could be hateful to owe people for their kindness. Help *had* come—from that dear old fool the Reverend Mr. Wilkins. He appeared at her bedside in the infirmary and within moments he seemed to her quite unlike his usual self.

"My dear, you are in a state of grace."

"I don't know what it means."

"You have only forgotten. The sacraments are the sure witnesses to your state. You earned your grace, Nancy Tuck. God gives it to you gladly because you are worthy."

"How can you know?" She had been distressed by this extravagant compliment. "No one has ever seen or touched or heard grace."

"No, it's not like a tree or even a cloud, Nancy. But love or, let's say, mere common sense, is also not to be seen or weighed or stored, is it? Surely it would be a stupid faith that blamed a woman for having tried to create life. No, that's not our faith, yours and mine. Because we seek and preserve life, we must honor your intentions and your effort."

"Does it make a difference? I wonder."

"Does grace? Nancy, I'm not going to bother either of us with the difference between gaining and regaining a state of grace. That's for theologians to explain, or dispute. What I can say without contention is that you are worthy before God and you are loved by man. If in your pain you forget, that's allowable by God, who causes all things."

Nothing was ever so fine as his leaving then, with no gesture, without another word.

When John called to say that Dumont had sent him an agreement to produce one program and, amazingly, had promised to run the show on the air with or without advertising, Nancy felt a keen curiosity but was immediately suspicious.

"You're fixing, aren't you? You've written off my movie contract, haven't you? And killed off Levinheimer, poor ol' Jake?"

"Nancy, please let's not have this conversation go on without us." He waited for a reply, but she could tell he didn't expect one. "When can I come to get you?"

"Soon." Then she was assailed by doubt again. "Where would we go? We're people on the road, any road."

"You decide."

"Come for me."

She could hear his breath held back before he said, "I'll catch the noon flight to New Orleans and drive over."

"No. I'll meet you in New Orleans. You're not Mr. Bowen."

"Where do you want to go from there?"

"New York."

"Lord, I love you!"

Hanging up, she'd heard his sob. It was the first time he'd cried within her hearing except for the time when he described his parents' marriage.

But in New York things didn't change; nothing remarkable occurred. Nancy was disappointed that she remained listless, quite unwilling to anticipate what might happen next. In the apartment they went to bed together but didn't touch. Moving about the rooms they stood aside to let one another pass and smiled carefully. It was a movable purgatory.

Nancy took to playing Broadway show tunes on a big Capehart phonograph, but when John suggested they buy tickets for musicals, she declined. Then she took to reading Dickens in a Chapman and Hall edition which the rare book dealers Bartfield's sent over by messenger. John commented that as bed reading rare editions was epicurean, "like jotting telephone numbers on vellum." A further elegance was lent to her seclusion by Aunt Jane, who sent three huge silk bolsters—white, blue, and pink. At times, Nancy would leave the bed to lie on the sofa in the living room, wearing only a shirt top and brief panties. She felt slatternly. She was dressed so one night when their talk became suddenly direct.

John came home to the unlighted room about nine o'clock. A yellow light from the street lamps and buildings opposite highlighted the stray filaments of Nancy's hair as she sat with her back to the windows. Dropping his dispatch case, shedding it, he sat opposite.

"I don't believe . . ." She stopped. "I don't believe our boy died for any purpose."

"No, he didn't."

"It was for nothing."

She cleared her throat, fighting her involuntary reactions.

"Reverend Wilkins came to see me in the hospital. He said I was in a state of grace. He didn't say how the boy stood."

"No, he wouldn't. Even old people find it hard to guess why they themselves live while others of their generation die. No one says of an ordinary person, 'He died in vain.'"

"What does it mean? Are you saying a person is not responsible for the beginning of his life? Of course he's not. His mother is."

"Nancy, I want you to listen to me. I've had too many months to think it over. Please. You owe me ten minutes. I told you once that my mother and I didn't read Freud. But I've read him. He says it takes a lot of sophistication to believe in chance. But somehow he doesn't bother to explain that chance is not randomness. Look at me, Nancy, please! If you toss a coin a million times, it doesn't come up heads half the time for several reasons—the most obvious being that the last throw can itself change the whole series. Don't stare at me. Let me finish. Listen, randomness is statistical. It can be computed. But chance is very different. It touches on luck because it speaks to character. We all know people who are generally lucky—and those who are generally unlucky."

Anger rose in her throat like vomit.

"Are you telling me that our boy was unlucky?" She laughed, and it hurt to say, "And that I'm lucky?"

"You are. Our son was not."

"It's just too awful for you to lecture this way! God, John, fatalism! Next, you'll tell me that when the pilot of a plane is unlucky, it kills all the passengers!"

"No, I won't tell you that. No, Nancy. The passengers are unlucky to a man. Lucky people miss or cancel flights on which the pilot dies. They are in the right place at the right time. Can't you see that? Chance is characteristic."

"And you spent all that time making this up?"

"Nancy, our son came into the world on his own, as human beings must, and he didn't make it on his own. I can live with that conclusion. Can't you?"

"And where does that leave us lucky people, you and me?"

The question was sour with complaint. She was weary from a long disbelief: Hurry, John, hurry!

"It leaves us with another try. Our next son will be lucky. I feel it. I know it. My mother lost a boy to the cold and hunger, but under almost the same conditions I was born and I lived. God, Nancy, we have to give our new child a chance!"

When Nancy didn't reply, she saw in his eyes a shadowing. Had he run out of his own luck? Had he capitulated? Then something broke in her—it was like the water before the birth. She came over to sit on his lap. But a millimeter or two of cotton separated her flesh from his hands.

"I'm tuckered, John," she said into his ear, "but I'm not afraid now. You're a terrible stick, ol' John. I love you. But remind me never to ask you the time of day because you'd tell me just when the world will end. I don't want to know that. I want to go to bed and wake up and start again; and I want to live forever even if I never find out why I have and others haven't. Don't explain. Just come to bed."

30

Earlson called twice. He didn't suggest a meeting in an office or club, or a luncheon. Rather, over the phone he came to the point each time. Was Sirovich still interested in talking? Was he sticking by his insistence on two million as the stated net profit that was to be multiplied by ten, hence twenty million in P&W shares for all of P and P? John didn't alter his stance at first.

"We both have companies to run, Mr. Earlson. There's time enough."

Then, one morning three weeks after their luncheon downtown, Earlson called to say that if Sirovich could agree to eighteen million as the valuation—more or less halfway between their initial positions—they could begin to allow each other's auditors to examine and confirm inventories, contracts, licenses, payables, tax returns, and any pending litigation. Sirovich agreed. He then proposed a final stipulation.

"I've never sold or bought a company before, as you know, but it occurs to me that neither of us ought to be looking at the *Wall Street Journal* every morning to calculate how many shares you'll pay and I'll receive, dividing eighteen million by the share price. The stock stood at fifty-five when we talked in your office.

It's dropped a bit since then. If it goes to forty, I get more shares—and you may get nervous. If it goes to eighty, I get fewer and will start to fret. Can we agree on a number of shares paid to P and P regardless of the price at closing?"

Earlson decided then that Sirovich had been coached by an investment banker. He was wrong, but his presumption that a professional had devised this request in part led him to agree. He said that three hundred and forty-six thousand shares met Sirovich's request, about eighteen million at present prices, and just under fifteen percent of the *total* shares since the Sirovich shares were now added to the original two million. It was done.

"He could have at least taken you to dinner," Carolyn complained.

"No, I like his style. It wasn't a romance. It was a message. More words would have cost one of us money—like a telegram."

Over the next three weeks John Sirovich felt like a mayor who, sick abed, cannot escort visitors to the best sights in town or explain works in progress. Paine & Westville attorneys and auditors, like those of Past and Present, were examining records and inspecting offices and warehouses. During the three weeks of this tour, John and James Earlson spoke several times—now over luncheon or dinner—and circumspectly agreed that the merger would increase prospects for both companies. And Earlson avoided using the term "synergism," a word then emerging in Wall Street. P and P's banker, Mr. Stratton of Hudson American, had already warned John of this newfangled illusion: "If they tell you synergism will result—that combining one and one will make three—just remember that it's bad arithmetic. Go for a good deal, good for both sides. A *great* deal is an unequal equation."

It came time to set the concrete finally. In the P&W office downtown Earlson, for the third time since they had begun negotiations, asked if Sirovich wanted an employment contract.

"No thanks, James. I'll come to work as always. And I'll like sitting on your board, I must say. Perhaps I can suggest other acquisitions."

Earlson paused and asked slowly, "How specifically, all things taken into account, would you suggest, given enough money, that we proceed?"

This fussy syntax was quite unlike the man. He was slowing the pace, telling Sirovich he would listen only to impeccable—not impetuous—recommendations from a lieutenant. But the response seemed discrepant to John because, after all, Earlson had just bought out Past and Present, which had little in common with the functions and products of his own company.

"You've looked over the field, I'm sure," John said, backing off.

"Yes, but I would like to know. It will be of aid to others, to us all, to have the present benefit of your thinking."

More fustian. John could retreat no more. He had underestimated the other man's capacity to shift gears, to slow or speed away.

"If I were pressed, which of course I'm not, I might look into textbook publishing or publishing regional directories of addresses—not everyone owns a telephone."

Where on earth had he dredged up the latter suggestion? He had never seen a purple cow.

"Well, it's quite a bit," Earlson replied, changing tone, laughing. "Tell me, what caused you to make up your mind so fast? To sell P and P?"

"I learned that big decisions are best made flat out, fast. On small ones you can linger—probably because there isn't so much at stake."

"And when did you learn that?"

"The day we first talked."

Going up Broadway seated behind Bogdan Perović, John said, "I made the deal. That president of the big company wants to buy our company. I just said yes."

"What for?"

"He wants to make his company bigger and richer."

"Piss on his reasons. What are yours? I thought you are your own boss."

"Bogdan, why did Miloš Obilić get so far into the camp of the sultan at Kosovo?"

"That's too simple a question. You can't cut a head farther away than an arm's length."

"*Bogami, Bogdane, možda ću i ja nekako da se pridružim tom taboru.* My God, I might just get into that camp."

It was not until Nancy invited Fred Stewart and his Swiss-born wife to luncheon at Robert's off Fifth Avenue that she realized she was back—willing again to meet and talk simply for the pleasure of it. Fred had been the director of *Boss Lady*. He looked older now and a bit haggard, but Michele was unchanged, thin and bony, her eyes rimmed by kohl or some such substance to match—if indeed that was the word—the purple-black hats she always wore. She was unchanged, moreover, in her constant mobility—searching a huge bag for a lighter never found, fluffing a scarf that covered wrinkles like Bantu necklaces, seizing some-one's wrist to italicize a remark or bum a light.

"Can you believe," she cried, "that he was only forty years old and still managed to die on the set?" She was of course speaking of the unfortunate leading man. "That tart of a wife of his probably got the whole fee. Fred got only half!"

Nancy consoled her by saying, "I'm sure Jake Levinheimer will team Fred and me up again."

"Oh, my dear," Michele said, her voice becoming tremulous, "There's nothing you can do with Jake."

John said quickly, "You aren't *non grata*, are you, Fred?"

"No, but just barely not. Since Hiss was convicted and Fuchs made a run for it, Hollywood has been hell. CBS out here, for God's sake, is requiring performers to sign loyalty oaths!"

His wife broke in urgently. "Fred was never involved with the Ten."

"Of course he wasn't," John replied reassuringly and, Nancy thought, condescendingly. "Fred, it will pass. Ideological wars don't last long in Congress. Americans are not equipped for ideology. In the end, it's embarrassing."

"Even the Ten didn't subvert anything," Fred declared, revived somewhat. "They didn't commit any *act*. They were just believers."

"There's no harm in that, surely," Michele added.

"There is," John said firmly. "Believers make martyrs of people who can't read the small print on their flags. Anyway, Hollywood is the worst place to argue politics. Consider how lousy movies are as propaganda."

Those remarks left Fred glum and Michele looking lost. Nancy regretted John's impetuous attempt to keep Michele from speaking of her career and wasn't as afraid as John seemed to assume. She asked Michele what she had been about to say.

"Dear Nancy, it's simply that I heard that Jake told Philips, who told Fred, that he's not scheduling a picture for you until you 'present' yourself to the studio."

"Jake may have heard that we're selling our house on the Coast and settling for sure in New York because of a television show."

She saw John look at her with an admiring curiosity. She had decided to sell the house that very moment.

"John's arranged a show. It's a series, really."

Since irony plays against the known but not the obvious, it was quite natural that Carolyn Ellis's life should become the raw material of the show, with Nancy playing a recently widowed young mother who lives in Manhattan. In the apartment next door was her confidante, a pert girl named Peggy; and as friendly nuisances, the script summoned men who tried to date both the heroine and her friend—among them the landlord and a brash delivery boy. The first script included a few sight gags. Peggy lay in a fake faint speaking into the bell of a young physician's stethoscope, "Are you married, engaged, or free as a bird? Press here one, two, or three times." It was a comedy that depended on one-liners.

The director Nancy and John hired, Mulvaney, was twenty-seven years old and his brief experience was wholly in live television. Although he had inflated his credentials somewhat—not unlike listing summer jobs on a résumé—he proved to be bold and ingenious on the set. But he was plainly no editor. When Nancy saw the first cut, she cried out, "It's too damned slow! You've lost the good parts!" And she ran from the screening room, to the amazement of her husband and Peter White and Mulvaney.

There soon arrived in New York, stunned by more than nine hours of flying, the reliable editor from Paramount who wore cigarette burns on her blouses. She had agreed to moonlight over the weekend and immediately set to work at the Movieola with Nancy at her side. By the time she caught the eight A.M. flight back to LA on Monday, bearing a check for five thousand dollars, she had left with Dumont a trim and funny show of twenty-six minutes.

It had been this editor's idea to use sixty seconds of the opening for a montage that could be repeated in later episodes should the show be continued. It consisted of still shots: a pregnant Nancy walking in Central Park with a young husband; Nancy dressed in black, shaking her head gently to older women, obviously her mother and mother-in-law; Nancy paying a middle-aged black baby-sitter before going out the apartment door carrying a briefcase; then the working woman at the end of the day, picking at her food in the apartment kitchen, wearily wearing hair curlers and fluffy slippers as she watched reruns of a program about a young working widow. This montage helped to sell the series because Dumont executives clearly saw the framework for additional situations. On his own John sent the editor another five thousand dollars when Dumont signed for thirteen shows. When White asked about the title, Nancy didn't hesitate: "Nancy's Baby."

The "closing" took place at the downtown headquarters of the lawyers for Paine & Westville. In attendance were eight lawyers, the P&W executive vice president, a man named Thorgersen, and the company's treasurer and secretary. From P and P there were only John Sirovich and Carolyn Ellis. Earlson had not come. This Carolyn interpreted as rudeness. But John was impressed by the man's reticence—James Earlson wasn't going to be seen to gloat as John Sirovich surrendered his independence. After contracts were signed and stock certificates handed over, John vetted the text of the press release P&W would send out that day. He made certain it contained the statement that "Mr. Sirovich will be elected to the Board of Directors and to the Board's Executive Committee at the next directors' meeting of Paine & Westville, Inc." This statement was the sole guarantee of the promise made to John. He recognized that, after all, no one can contract to become a director—you can only be elected by a vote of shareholders or, as in this instance, by a standing board between annual shareholders' meetings. The press release forced their hand.

P and P's three lawyers and John and Carolyn stood in the late afternoon sun that slanted into Battery Park but could not reach into the glades of Pine and Wall. Carolyn was misty-eyed, as if they'd all been dismissed out of hand. Bogdan sat nearby in the parked Cadillac, observing, as they shuffled about aimlessly in their momentary reluctance to part. The ceremony had been spare and had lacked a climax, partly because Sirovich's lawyers, while they might in the future write a will for him or review an apartment lease, were no longer players, no longer the counsel for Past and Present. P&W's lawyers would take over. As a denouement John handed his dispatch case to the senior attorney and asked him to sort out those documents that he might later need personally. Carolyn objected, taking the case and remarking she'd hold it "in the event of the divorce."

Inside the car Bogdan asked for directions brusquely, "*Je?*" And on the East River Drive he said curtly in Serbian, "You cannot salute and take aim at the same moment." John laughed but refused to translate for Carolyn. In the Palm Court of the Plaza, she frowned over iced tea, started to speak, stopped, and finally got it out.

"What if Mr. Earlson decides to reorganize our company? You might have to quit."

"Too late to think of that, Carolyn."

"He'd find it hard to run P and P without you!"

"He's running a much bigger company without the aid of the redoubtable Mr. Paine and Mr. Westville."

As she fell silent, he surmised how it might go. At first everyone would get along to beat the band. A small difference might appear but would be dismissed immediately as no more than a mere problem of "communication"—that omnibus explanation that was being heard more and more in the halls of American commerce. Next a P&W vice president might light on the word "liaison" like an errant bee on a dry flower and would suggest that he participate in the acquired company's production or marketing meetings. The suggestion would no doubt die of inattention rather than opposition. So far, so good. But the day would arrive when the two initial negotiators, the chairman of the "surviving corporation" and the president of the subsidiary, would have to talk. They would begin gingerly, seeking to make inquiries out of statements and preferences out of criticisms.

31

In ordinary conversation James Earlson rarely dwelt on politics, not even on the era of good feeling that was the Eisenhower administration. At a board luncheon John overheard him tell one of the "outside" directors that it was a very odd businessman who was also a dedicated political partisan.

"Mostly," he'd said, "politics is relevant to business only in taxes and war."

Beyond this John knew little of James's views in general, or of his earlier days, or even of his wife and family—it seemed somehow unworthy to seek such confidences when the two of them would never be intimates or even friends. But even so, between the parent company and the subsidiary, no disaffection took root from envy or scorn, and none arose from misunderstandings. They proceeded through the winter, Earlson and Sirovich, meeting day to day as congenial superior and subordinate, nominally equals on the board of directors.

Past and Present kept its headquarters on Madison Avenue and soon rented additional floors. It gave Mr. Abrams the landlord the opportunity to commend both himself and his client on having won the bet on the future. He came up the elevator from his own offices bearing a magnum of champagne and—just right!—a papier-mâché box with John's name lettered in gold on the black spine. Sirovich in turn presented Abrams with a copy of the notorious "fake Bible," causing the old man, who remained a collector and indeed John's sole link to Henry Shaikin, to remark that the book was valuable in the way a misprinted stamp can become.

A comptroller was sent uptown by Paine & Westville and proved to be expert and helpful without evoking suspicion that he was acting as a Paine & Westville secret agent. The only large request P and P made of its parent was approved, this being the purchase of a monotype plant in Rahway, New Jersey, which was needed for setting text—including foreign languages, signs, symbols, chemotaxonomy, and the like. At no point was John worried about the threat of editorial interference that was feared by some of the P and P employees. Himself an editor, he knew the risk in allowing editors to consider themselves a priesthood, keepers of formal knowledge. When the investment banker for the company, a director named Carter, asked if his editors were chary of the parent, John replied with a flourish—one that was not, it turned out, appreciated by James Earlson—that editors were in truth safer if directors knew what they did in normal times. That way, directors would be familiar with editorial risks should trouble occur. This sententious declaration soon came in handy.

The blanket that fell over scientific journals because of secrecy at Alamogordo, where the government was working on atomic, then hydrogen, bombs, was lifted about 1951. P and P was ready when physics, mathematics, and biophysics articles were written for immediate publication in universities in the U.S. and in the U.K. and its commonwealth. A flood of information burst upon universities, laboratories, and corporations, much of it confirmed or conveyed by machines of the new science of computers. P and P originated fifteen new journals in 1950, twenty-two in

1951, and thirty-six in 1952; and its hardcover books in physics, math, and biochemistry reached four hundred by 1952, most of them priced above fifteen dollars per volume at a time when hardcover novels sold at three-fifty and four dollars. As for the Sirovich fondness for facsimiles of rare books, these were no longer essential to the financial well-being of P and P, and their large prices were more remarkable as publishing gossip than as accounting facts. The *Journal of Colloidal Suspension*, dealing with the properties of substances suspended in gaseous, liquid, or solid mediums, had earned in a few years more than any book P and P had published. A fact.

Tick Johnson, the same man whose whiskey had been confiscated by Bogdan one night, persuaded his boss to publish a facsimile of a Bible printed by the great printer John Baskerville in 1763. Tick was an old-time figure on the edges of New York literary life. He had worked with Marianne Moore on the *Dial* in the 1920s and had known Carl Van Vechten and Lewis Mumford. He told Sirovich once that he'd decided not to write his memoirs for the good reason that "Mark Twain told us how American lives begin and Melville how they end." As for the Baskerville Bible, Tick had explained that although original copies of the Bible itself could be bought for six hundred dollars, there existed but one copy of an illustrated edition, for the reason that the drawings (by no less a personage than Canaletto) were never engraved—the originals had been interleaved into a copy of the Bible. The year Baskerville published his Bible, Canaletto became president of the Venetian Academy, and among his subscribers was George III's great friend Lord Bute, who then found out that Richard Dalton, surveyor and keeper of the Royal Collection, and Joseph Smith, the English consul to Venice, had commissioned the artist.

"Imagine!" Tick exclaimed. "They got Canaletto to draw *capricci* in pen and ink."

"Tick, what in the hell is that?"

"*Capricci* put contemporary buildings and objects in imaginary settings. You see Whitehall and Picadilly through the pillars and tent poles of Jericho and Jerusalem!"

The fact was that Tick never saw the drawings at the start, only as they were engraved once the work was under way. He saw photographs and they were enough for him. They were not enough for his boss, however, who instinctively guessed he was making a mistake even as he made it—out of boredom, out of willful endangerment. Past and Present printed a facsimile edition of 250 copies at a price of one thousand dollars. When it transpired that the drawings were fake, the newspapers and *Newsweek* told the story in full, with the incredible result that P and P received more than sixty orders for the work "as is." The Paine and Westville directors rather liked the notoriety, having learned of its inception as well as its conclusion. And Tick kept his job.

The publicity over the "fake Bible" hastened a summons from Mrs. Paine to John Sirovich to take tea at her apartment on Eighty-fourth and Park Avenue. He was ushered into her presence by a Negro maid. She sat with her head held erect by a six-strand choker of pearls. A slight jerkiness centered on her chin.

"I'm a chain-smoker, Mrs. Paine. May I?"

"Clarence Paine smoked all his life. It may have killed him."

They sat on Empire chairs with lute-shaped backs that were pitted from long use. John recalled that when an antique dealer on Thirty-eighth Street had asked Nancy if she wanted a chair "distressed," the term for artificial aging, she told him, "Just make it anxious." In Mrs. Paine's apartment the furnishings were not distressed and few were machined: Persian rugs, gold leaf lamp stands, coin-silver salvers, crystal braced by silver tracery.

"Mr. Sirovich, I'll invite Mr. Robert Westville to join us. He is in the next room. You don't mind?"

"No, of course not, Mrs. Paine, but I think that Mr. Earlson also ought to be present."

"He knows we are meeting. I informed him but didn't invite him."

Westville soon followed Mrs. Paine into the room, short but

strong, a brown man, his hair and eyes and mustache seemingly matched for color. The mustache was not currently fashionable, but when John heard him speak, he realized it covered a harelip scar. Mrs. Paine had imperiously waved them both to be seated. She was ready to begin.

"Our two families have differed in the past, Mr. Sirovich, as you've heard. But we now agree that James Earlson is denying our reasonable wishes."

"Is it the dividend rate?"

He had heard at several board meetings the family attorneys— no Paine or Westville sat on the board—seek a larger payout of earnings to shareholders. It was a long-standing issue.

"James keeps more cash on hand than the business requires." This came from Robert Westville. "There's two million in the company's portfolio of stocks, and more than that in cash."

"It's a lot," Sirovich replied with an insipid neutrality.

"Clarence Paine spent his life building this company"—Robert gave no sign of distress on hearing this—"and he did so by spending money on sound ventures. We're not asking that the company distribute funds as extra dividends to shareholders."

"I'm afraid I've lost track."

Robert explained, "We think that money should go toward buying companies like yours. That way both the dividends and the stock price will go up—all boats rising."

"But James Earlson was quick to buy Past and Present!"

"You didn't know?" Robert leaned forward. "James didn't find your company. Carter, that old investment banker, did that. Even so, our attorneys had to press Earlson not to let you get away."

"Mr. Westville, I don't doubt it. But may I remind you, I wanted P&W stock, not cash."

"And I'm sure James didn't press cash on you—but no matter. Some owners *do* want cash."

"*I believe*," Mrs. Paine said, the two words striking a note of finality, "that you will be willing to hear our views seriously one day. It is our privilege and your responsibility. My lawyer and Mr. Westville's represent all shareholders, including you, just as you as a director represent all, including me."

It was neat, the legally correct definition of the director as fiduciary. The families after all the years were taking refuge and probably revenge in the tribal laws of corporations.

John said, "Mrs. Paine, I'm the newest director and the youngest officer."

"Mr. Sirovich, I don't think either condition is disabling or permanent."

When they sat the next day in Earlson's office putting final touches on the 1953 budget—it was March of 1953, and the financial statements for the year past were at hand—James asked about Mrs. Paine.

"She thinks you're Silas Marner."

It was the sole time John heard James laugh without constraint, from the belly up.

"Honey," John told Nancy as they lay together, "get rid of Frank for television, won't you? You really ought to form a new company just for TV because the tax treatment of income and expenses is different. Bill Harvey told me about a lawyer. Also an agent named Timothy Martin, who's said to be Italian, although he must have handled his own passage without pausing at Ellis Island."

"I know him." She positioned herself on top of John, making conversation of short term. "He's a scream. He talks like this: 'Big.' 'Special.' 'No way.'"

"Bill told me, Nance, that Martin has the ear of Bobby Sarnoff. Is that really a credential in the TV business? It's like a surgeon saying he knows a good tailor."

"Sport, will you shut up?"

It was not uncommon to see Bill Harvey in the P and P offices. He had signed Toni as well as Kraft to sponsor the first thirteen weeks of "Nancy's Baby," a considerable feat. The second series of thirteen weeks was being shown currently on Channel 5 in New York and a third series was in production. Nancy was especially impressed that Harvey had not once, according to her husband, sought to represent those parts of Paine & Westville in which, unlike in Past and Present, advertising was "big bucks." It put John more at ease, this; and they didn't talk business when Bill enticed him on several afternoons to watch the Giants. Each time John emerged from one of the tunnels under the grandstand at the Polo Grounds, he caught his breath on seeing the greensward and the powdery white bases. It was like turning a corner and seeing paradise.

Nancy worried that except for Bill, John didn't see anyone outside the office, and soon it was apparent he was isolated inside as well. This was partly because Earlson didn't encourage socializing among his subordinates and didn't himself invite them to dinners or luncheons, although he did keep in touch with Haskins, the Dayton plant man. Earlson's mechanism for what little corporate camaraderie did exist was the Planning Committee, which met the first Wednesday of each month. James was of course chairman; the members were Sirovich, Haskins, Thorgersen, the executive vice president of P&W who ran newspapers, the comptroller, and the two vice presidents for radio and direct mail. There was no agenda. Discussions proceeded more or less in the manner of James's asking, "How are things going with you, Chuck? Fred? Bennett?" Thorgersen's secretary kept notes and later mailed to each the typewritten transcriptions, which were topical, unconnected, and trivial—almost like conversations overheard on a bus. The talks held on "new projects" were in fact a series of prefaces with no text. Whenever John raised the issue of P&W's making acquisitions of smaller companies, he ran into James's adept manner of urging his subordinates to keep their eyes on immediate needs, with the result that a long-term plan was easily subsumed by events.

The board meetings were hardly better as a forum. Among the directors were five employees—Earlson, Thorgersen, Haskins, Sirovich, and the corporate treasurer. Two directors received income from P&W for their professional services: the corporate attorney, and a commercial banker. The only directors who were paid fees for being on the board were six "outsiders": the investment banker Carter, the Paine attorney, the Westville attorney, and three men who headed companies unconnected to Paine & Westville. Earlson did not, as would be the case in most corporations, use Carter as an "insider." He didn't nowadays buy any public companies. He ran the P&W portfolio himself. Further, a curious hazard was created by Earlson that all the directors witnessed. It was not that Haskins reported directly to James instead of the executive vice president—that was understandable because Haskins was James's oldest colleague, in age and in tenure both. Rather, it was that the chairman himself ran the company's portfolio of bonds and stocks with the aid of the comptroller, who was not a director and was by corporate custom—not to speak of P&W's own bylaws—the subordinate of the company treasurer. John wondered if James hadn't deliberately pushed circumstance, created this hazard—himself like Sirovich at times another Daedalus. He was sixty years old and had seen and heard it all—perhaps too many times.

It occurred in August while they sat alone in Earlson's office revising the 1953 budget with midyear figures at hand. After waiting for the right cue John complained that the Planning Committee meetings were not a place to discuss long-term issues. He said, for example, that he wouldn't want to take to the committee the particulars of a five-million-dollar company that might be bought through careful negotiations.

"No doubt," James said with niggardly amusement showing in his eyes, "you just happen to know of such a company."

"I do. It's a textbook publishing house owned by its founder, who was once a vice president at Ginn. He's put everything he owns into his business—including loans on his house and cars."

"We don't need a house and cars, John. He sounds broke."

"He's doing well. Only he hasn't enough working capital to expand in a fast-growing market."

"Lord! The usual story! I get people in here repeatedly claiming that all they need is 'capital and distribution facilities,' because, you see, they already have great ideas. Business *is* mostly working capital and distribution. We all have ideas."

"No. This man has good product, not just good ideas. He's selling a lot of books but has to use too many commission salesmen rather than his own employees."

"And he wants cash?"

"For working capital, yes, but not for his stock. He might sell his company in an exchange for our stock."

"No doubt he's asking something crazy like ten times next year's earnings."

"That's what I asked—and was paid. What if he does, James? Look at our revised budget. P and P is streaking ahead of the rest of Paine & Westville—at almost double the rate than when you and I shook hands on the deal."

"All that success doesn't hurt your P&W shares, does it? The stock has gone up."

"Let's talk about the textbook publisher."

"Let's. What if we charged him three or four points above prime rate as interest on intercompany loans? That would put a dent into his earnings, wouldn't it? Taking money from a parent isn't free—it is still borrowing."

John stared at him. Earlson was clutching the bird of cash, preventing it from flight, from venturing. The moment Evelyn Paine and Robert Westville had primed John for, that moment had arrived. Now he must make the speech he'd rehearsed since the especially dilatory committee meeting the week before.

"James, I want to say this as fairly as I can. P and P has not been borrowing from the parent, *but what if it did?* The parent has money to lend; and if it didn't, we could go to our banks. P&W's portfolio makes no sense to me. Why do we invest in *other* companies? If every corporation did that, baking and candlestick making would stop and we'd all be huddled, hungry, at the curb of the stock exchange in the dark."

"You do have a way with words," Earlson replied sarcastically. Yet he kept the argument going. "Let me tell you about textbook companies. Old-line ones like Ginn or McGraw-Hill took years to become profitable. Your man is too small. It would take twenty years for him to compete evenly with the others."

Paine & Westville itself owned some newspapers in small towns, in Lima and Hamilton in Ohio, in New Castle and Brazil and Lafayette in Indiana; and although several of its radio stations were located in large cities, none was at the top of its market.

"We've got small ventures, too. Looking at this budget, it wouldn't be hard to say that P&W is stalled."

"Stalled?" Earlson was incredulous. "You wouldn't say that to our directors. They know better."

It was a mistake, a bad one. He was inviting Sirovich to continue their dispute in the only setting where they were presumably equals, one man, one vote.

"Perhaps I will."

"You have a list of particulars, do you now?"

"The Dayton plant is a relic. It loses money. The format of our radio stations needs changing. Radio soap operas are losing advertising to TV."

"You've never mentioned that at the committee meetings. Were you saving it for some reason?"

"It proves the meetings are no place to talk seriously."

"But at least its members are polite. I've heard you say rather ignorantly that we ought to use mail order to sell across the board, selling your books together with P&W's products, I suppose. And you've asked for free space on our stations and in our newspapers when your product would in fact worry our present advertisers about what market we thought we were reaching."

"I never said I couldn't learn."

"I've not embarrassed you in front of the others. I didn't tell you cross-marketing is an amateur notion. It doesn't work because companies are like families—nicer to strangers than to relatives." Earlson rose and buttoned his coat. "John, I've not used my experience or my record against you. You might think about that. You might spare me your own inexperience."

Losing his argument on points, John was not to be deterred by James's conciliatory epitaph. He must finish what he started with an incriminating question.

"I'm told that other directors had to push their chairman to keep negotiating to buy Past and Present. Is that true?"

"I'm head of this corporation. You're not. Between us is a distance you can't jump and I won't close. You're convinced you are talking principle. It could be. But we both know your motive. It's ambition, nothing less."

"Maybe. What's your ambition? Are you waiting for anything at all? Is business that grand?"

Earlson surprised Sirovich by smiling. "You're good. You are damned good. But it's bullshit—very fancy, but bullshit."

32

Carolyn peeked around the jamb of the open door and raised her eyebrows: should she remain or leave? With the telephone receiver cradled on his shoulder John waved her in. She tried not to listen—unsuccessfully. He was telling the textbook publisher in Cincinnati, a man named Marvin Toland, that P&W might well make an offer for his company if Toland's attorney would agree to send pertinent financial statements directly to Sirovich in New York. She couldn't hear Toland's end but inferred from John's responses that Toland was reminding him that no third party could claim to have been the matchmaker here, no "finder" who brought them together. John had told her about this negotiation but had kept it in confidence because of the confrontation with James Earlson. Apparently John had met Toland at an educational exhibit in Detroit.

"Big things are happening."

She could see he wanted her to press him for details, but she had something else to say.

"John, I know this is not a good time to talk about outside matters. But then when is it ever a good time?" She smiled but realized smiling shows nervousness more than goodwill. "Big things are happening to me too."

"You've gotten Bobby Allen into Norton School?"

"No."

"You're not moving again?"

"Will you listen? Bill Harvey is moving in with me and Bobby."

"What? Bill? He's married!"

"Of course he is. I know that."

"He's got a wife and kids in Scarsdale."

"Please don't be difficult, John. He has a wife, yes; what he doesn't have is a divorce—not yet."

"You can't do this! It's wrong for Bobby Allen. He's too young. Why can't you wait?"

"John, please don't shout. I came to you because until now you were the only man who's ever protected me and Bobby."

He came around the desk to sit next to her on the sofa.

"How long will it take? I mean, the divorce? Is Bill pressing you? Let me talk with him."

"You shouldn't do this, John. Really you shouldn't. You and Nancy lived together a long time before marrying."

"That was different. Neither of us was married. We didn't have a child."

"It's *always* different, isn't it? I'm not going to be mean to Bill. We love each other not next year but now, and we ought to live together now. It can hardly corrupt Bobby Allen, if that's what you are thinking. He needs a grown man around. You ought to realize that better than anyone else! You spent several nights at our apartment, John."

"*That* was different, too. Jesus, Carolyn! This sounds like one of those dumb soap operas I told James Earlson were dying out on radio. Are people beginning to live inside them? You spared me a bed for a couple of nights and it gave me the chance to play with Bobby." He stood up angrily. "Don't liken me to Bill Harvey."

"How could I do that—even if I wanted to? How? I don't know you. You never were curious about me, about myself alone. You never wondered if I was seeing anyone, if I needed company. Am I just a widow who needed a job, or a mother supporting a boy you're crazy about? Joyce Melville still tells people you're noble. She actually says that! It's too awful. Your being generous is too often the same as your being unconcerned, John."

She fled, sobbing. For a moment John wondered if people in the outside office would find it strange, his shouting and Carolyn's running and weeping. But he'd lost track of time—it was past six o'clock and everyone had gone home. He imagined he heard Carolyn crying at a great distance, but of course that couldn't be so. She must have taken the elevator.

One night a week later, after dinner with an executive from Dumont, he and Nancy had gone back to the apartment quite late. Nancy fell on the bed still wrapped inside her coat, which was pay in kind for modeling it in a *McCall's* ad.

He stood over her, frowning, and decided he'd waited long enough.

"Nancy, a few days ago Carolyn told me she's going to let Bill Harvey live in the apartment with her and Bobby."

"I know. We talked. About two weeks ago."

"Damn it. You didn't tell me."

"She didn't want me to. She was going to ask you about some legal things, I think. But she never had the chance."

"I told her to make Bill get a divorce first. Then she ran off crying. No doubt you discussed that too."

"We did."

She reached up and seized his coat lapels to pull him down on top of her, her heels and his toes touching the white rug at the edge of the bed.

"Carolyn is my wisest and best friend. Yet she made the mistake of thinking you can talk to one man about another man."

"Why does sex have to stain everything?" He tried to pull away, but she held him tightly as he continued, "Why can't people deal with each other without the memory or threat of passionate love? Jesus! Sex just can't be the condition of getting through an ordinary day."

"John?"

She kissed him with her mouth open, her breathing shallow under the weight of his chest.

"I'm pregnant. I want you to kiss me and I want you to thank God and Chance. We can talk, if you want, but not about another woman."

Mrs. Paine looked at him with justifiable satisfaction. "We seem to meet in bad weather, Mr. Sirovich."

It was the same tableau as before, the three of them seated in the Empire chairs. Now, however, Bob Westville was more outspoken.

"You want to buy a company and James doesn't? That's right, isn't it? No doubt he will resent your going behind his back to meet with me and Mrs. Paine?"

Here, precisely, John must choose his ground. It would suit the families well to regard the two executives, Earlson and Sirovich, as two bull elks locked in a struggle for primacy. Then they could choose to support Mr. Sirovich and, by so choosing, indenture him for years to come. John had now to avoid becoming *their* candidate, just as James had. In earlier days James Earlson had himself been at pains to prevent the deadly nepotism of the Paines and Westvilles—as employers or as directors—from continuing on and on, *per stirpes*.

"James is not being petty. He's not being ruthless either. I hardly think he's much concerned over his authority. What he's doing in this instance is arguing policy. I disagree with his policy in an important way, as do you, Bob, and Mrs. Paine. The last time we met, both of you said the company needed to expand and not harbor its cash. You said, correctly I think, that we might then command a higher stock price in the market as well as pay higher dividends. I don't know if James will look with favor on this Cincinnati textbook company. He might when he sees all the figures. There's a policy difference here, true, but it could be resolved."

Neither of them spoke. Mrs. Paine decided of a sudden that if John Sirovich was going to narrow the issue, he ought to withstand such narrowing himself.

"You told James that we ought to sell the Dayton plant. You're not acquainted with manufacturing as James is. If we renovated the plant as my husband did, it would come around."

John did not reply, nor did Bob Westville, both for the same reason. The case for revivifying the Dayton plant was no more, at bottom, than a longing for the past. As the moments passed, Mrs. Paine's look grew forlorn as she stared at the two of them, like an old lady who has misread an address and stands waiting on the sidewalk for assistance from a stranger. Bob Westville sat still, his hands closed lightly on his knees. On his face were little tics of triumph. Dayton was Evelyn Paine's hometown, not his.

"What's to be done then, John?" he asked.

"I'll make a proposal to the board next month, probably. It could go to a vote right away. But I won't call for a vote unless I think the motion will be carried."

"I don't understand," Mrs. Paine complained.

"There are a couple of rules." John lit a cigarette as they waited. "Don't ask for a vote unless you are pretty sure how it will turn out."

"What's the other one?" Bob asked.

"Never leave a boardroom while the directors are in session."

"What if they are voting on your own salary?"

"Stay and give them a hand."

Westville laughed, looked at Evelyn, and nodded his head in no special agreement with her. Her own expression was one of toleration, as if observing boys at play.

"What do you expect of me, Mr. Sirovich?" she asked.

He turned toward her and spoke slowly. "It would help if your attorney supported the motion when and if it's made."

"And will James resign if the directors vote for it?"

"I don't know. I suppose so." John paused.

They sat waiting to hear the rest. There had to be more, both of them thought independently. There had to be something in it for themselves.

"If James does resign," he went on, "I will propose that the slate of directors for the proxy statement mailed to shareholders include you, Mrs. Paine; Bob; your attorneys; James Earlson if he wishes; Thorgersen; myself; a new commercial banker, Mr. Stratton of Hudson American; Mr. Carter—and then, I think, Dr. Edwards of Princeton, one of our authors and general editors at P and P; and also Mrs. Carolyn Ellis, whom you know about."

Mrs. Paine was not entirely mollified by the inclusion of her name. She sought now to broaden the discussion, so as not to leave everything in John Sirovich's control.

"Have you forgotten the three gentlemen on the board who are presidents of their own companies? They represent all of us shareholders, of course."

"If they vote against this kind of motion *and James Earlson does so too*, then I'd guess one or more of them will not want to continue. That's entirely up to them. They are elected by shareholders and can't be fired by other directors willy-nilly."

Before she could reply to this, if indeed it called for a reply, Bob asked how many votes on the board would give Sirovich enough authority to run P&W should Earlson resign. He actually had been drumming fingers on his knees, counting, as John had named directors.

"Enough, Bob. You can't run a corporation day by day without assuming the normal support of the directors. Otherwise it would be like holding a town meeting weekly in New York City—literally democratic but pragmatically impossible. Being a director is not a full-time job unless you're also an employee."

Mrs. Paine in the end rescued Westville from a further lecture by saying, "Mr. Sirovich, I shall give you an answer when you inform me exactly what the motion is and if it will be posed."

As they left the apartment on Eighty-fourth Street, John offered Westville a ride downtown. In front of the Barclay Hotel, they stood under the canopy.

"Well, it may happen your way. I doubt if Evelyn Paine realizes how much you're like James, far more like him than her husband—or my father. I'll like becoming a director again. You know of course that James got Evelyn and me off the board about eight years ago. That's how our attorneys came to represent us as directors. I've got no illusions left, but I don't mind just watching." He smiled. "Where did you get the idea of never leaving a boardroom?"

"A director of a giant company told me once his board was worried over an inept president. I asked why they didn't remove him. He said, 'He's such a nice feller.' Then one day the president was fired and I congratulated my friend for the directors' courage. He said the president had asked for a vote of confidence and left the room—the way we all did in grade school while electing head boy—and in his absence they realized they could do without him."

Bob Westville gathered himself in, clapping his sides and laughing until tears formed.

"You son of a bitch! It's going to be fun watching you. Don't be put off, by the way. In the Dakotas where I live, everyone is a son of a bitch, which makes it easy."

Riding up Third Avenue behind the silent bulk of Bogdan Perović, John tried to detach himself from the complexity and celerity of what was happening. He couldn't make himself disinterested of course: he was a player. To get started, Hamlet should have killed the king.

33

Three old-timers not connected with Paine & Westville were enlisted: the banker Stratton was one; a senior partner of P and P's old law firm was the second; and its former auditor, now working in a two-man accounting firm. Each knew, on being summoned by John Sirovich, that he was acting on his own. None asked about reimbursement. From Toland in Cincinnati came voluminous records describing both the history and current condition of Learning for Life, Inc. Sirovich traveled there to meet alone with Toland in a hotel on Second Street. Over a period of eight hours, amid the ruins of two meals ordered from room service, they finally arrived at what Stratton termed "min-max." It was a range between the highest and lowest prices considered tolerable by the two sides. If the Paine & Westville board agreed, the negotiators would settle on a dollar amount which then would be divided by the New York Stock Exchange price of P&W stock as averaged ten days before the closing. Marvin Toland would own shares in a public company with the same tax advantages that John had himself gained in selling P and P; and Paine & Westville would not have to charge off the goodwill—not on earth, at least. For the board meeting on January 8, Sirovich prepared much like a candidate for a Ph.D., ready to defend his dissertation in the presence of specialists.

Thirteen were at the oval table. They sat on heavy chairs upholstered in a light brown leather with high backs and no arms, reminding John of lobbies in old hotels like the Claymore in Indianapolis, the U. S. Grant in San Diego. The meeting began as any other: minutes were read; the auditor's report for the fiscal year just ended was said to be ready within a month; the current budget was presented as "tentative" because not all the financial trends of the preceding year were yet known. As usual James Earlson ran a calm and routine meeting, neither exciting nor discouraging discussion. He was tactful too, as when he withheld information until he could frame it as a reply to some director's inquiry, making the question more important by virtue of its answer.

Then Earlson asked for "new business." It was a term he never used and one which was straight out of *Robert's Rules of Order*—more fitting for a gardening club than for a large corporation. Said now, it had an ironic ring. Taking Earlson's cue despite the tone, Sirovich noted he'd mailed to each director a description and financial summaries of Learning for Life. He offered to answer any questions. Nothing. After ten seconds had passed, John deduced that James would himself have broken this interstitial silence had it not suited his purposes. Silence was present ex officio. John began to speak briskly and sought to make a climax out of a challenge: if Paine & Westville missed this opportunity, another like it might not appear for several years.

His hyperbole was cleverly tempered by the Paine attorney, who said, "I don't know it's all that fateful, John, but I'm impressed by what I've read. We've not had much time to study the data, but if we assume that Mr. Toland has suitors other than us, then it's best to make a start. I move that the proper officers enter into negotiations for the acquisition of this company in an exchange of common stock, the terms to be presented to the directors at their March meeting."

The Westville attorney seconded. Now, under *Robert's* or any other rules, the chairman had his chance to slow the train and throw off any dangerous baggage. John sat tensely, aware that he would have no defense if Earlson simply said that P&W would of course begin negotiating, and of course prudently and with deliberation. With such a statement, by decelerating, Earlson could effectively derail events. Yet, characteristically, because he disliked ambiguity, he didn't wait and called for a vote on the motion. John looked at Michael O. Underwood, one of the three "outside" directors, and saw his eyebrows rise quizzically.

To Earlson's right, Thorgersen voted no. Next, Haskins, no. Sirovich, yes. Carter, the investment banker whose pickings had been nil over the years from not being asked to raise capital by the sale of shares, voted yes. The tally stood even, two to two.

The commercial banker, who handled day-to-day transactions, was harder to read. Naturally he always wanted P&W to borrow more money so that his bank could earn larger amounts of interest, but this was not decisive for him. Everyone on the board knew how he disliked Earlson's not using his bank to handle the assets in the P&W pension fund. James had made this his personal preserve, paying no fees to an outside financial institution other than stockbrokers' commissions. The banker voted yes, making it three to two in favor.

The treasurer voted yes more out of desperation than bravery. John had counted on him because his position was so insecure. Earlson's circumventing him by dealing directly with his subordinate, the comptroller, was an affront. Indeed, just before the meeting commenced, he had told Sirovich that the chairman hadn't bothered to ask him to analyze the Learning for Life financial statements—"not even," he said, "to torpedo them." It was now four to two.

A "no" vote was cast by the corporate attorney, who in any

event could hardly go against the chief executive officer who authorized the fees he collected quarterly. Even had he favored the motion, there was no way he could be freed—unlike a delegate to a political convention who can be "released" when his state's governor or senator, a "favorite son," admits he can't himself win the national nomination. Now the vote stood at four to three in favor.

When the family attorneys voted yes—and presuming the chairman would vote no—the predictable but incomplete result would be six yes, four no. If the three outside directors supported the chairman, the motion would fail, six to seven. In a public corporation such directors were nominally considered disinterested, neutral, because they had no personal financial stake in the board's decisions. But a fine point of corporate etiquette made these three heads of companies, at least initially, the guests of the chairman of the board, who hardly would have proposed them for election had he personally distrusted any of them. John knew them only superficially. At board meetings and at the luncheons following, they'd conversed in that cocktail party manner in which no one raises questions that can't be replied to in under a minute. However, the day before this meeting, Sirovich had telephoned one of them.

He had asked Michael O. Underwood if he could visit him in Scranton, where his company's plant made compasses and meters and gauges. Underwood testily remarked he would not be "privately" persuaded on any issue as important and complex as an acquisition. But he didn't deny the interview. Within twenty minutes of hanging up the telephone, John was on the road with Bogdan. They arrived in Scranton just after four in the afternoon; John noticed the power was still on in the factory, machines humming. Obviously, the plant ran a second, maybe even a third, shift. Underwood himself sat behind a laminated-wood desk under whose clear glass covering was Kipling's "If" printed on simulated parchment. He wore a gray suit, eyeglasses with mother-of-pearl specks on the earpieces, and a Masonic sword in his lapel. The part in his full white hair was like a scar.

Without rising or offering John a chair, he straightaway stated his mistrust of Sirovich, who, he said, was showing himself to be "insubordinate." When John admitted he opposed some of Earlson's policies, Underwood was not mollified by the use of "some." Then, searching for an opening, John declared that if the motion was defeated he would himself leave the board for the good of comity, but should Earlson be willing to look into buying the textbook company, no one need be embittered, none need resign.

Underwood was a little calmed by this and remarked, "That's honest enough, I guess, but it doesn't change your stripes."

"I earned my stripes in the war, Mr. Underwood, but here we are talking money and numbers. About a third of the P&W stock is held by persons who worry over our not making more acquisitions."

"You still report to James Earlson."

"Of course I do. He's not at issue. Neither am I. If he favors negotiating for the company, there is no personal issue."

"I won't vote to put James's job on the line."

"You know more about running a company than I do. He doesn't have to gamble his job. He's performed his job well enough in the past. He's handled the founding families correctly—in fact, saved their company for them."

"What's in it for you, then?" His tone was no longer discordant. "What do you want?"

Sirovich smiled. "I want to vote yes. It's not un-American."
And he left.

At the table, the other two outsiders voted no, making the tally six in favor, five against. It was Underwood's turn, on the chairman's left, and now he made the speech he had prepared after Sirovich's visit.

"James, I'm really sorry to see a board—any board, for that

matter—come to a vote like this one. It's just not good, by my lights. Hell, James, we all have confidence in your fine leadership. You don't need me to tell you that! About this textbook company, why don't we sign a 'Swiss-cheese' letter, one full of loopholes? We can back off if we don't like what we discover in detail. James, I'm going to abstain. You settle it."

He leaned back, pleased by his apparent resolution of the chairman's problem. If James voted yes, the motion would pass bearing his stamp directly; and if he voted no, he'd surely give his friend a supportable reason to change his vote from "abstain" to "no," thereby defeating the motion.

"No, Mike, I've got to go against. This proposal would scatter our effort and dilute our stock. This publisher is saying, in effect, 'Give me a bundle of your shares, then lend me working capital, and later, much later, I may contribute to your earnings.' No. There are better companies than his to look after."

"Which ones?"

It was the right response and it came from the right person: Underwood. What the chairman had done, leaving his friend Mike adrift, was to alter the object under scrutiny. Then he weakened his own rebuttal by not offering a specific case.

"Well, I haven't got one right in the palm of my hand, but I know we can buy TV stations cheaply. Some in the 'Second Hundred' market nowadays are counting on a favorable depreciation to throw off a lot of cash, but they're trapped because they lack current income. I know stations in Michigan, for example, selling local advertising spots for as little as five dollars a half minute! In our hands, don't you see, the depreciation schedules of such stations would be gold?"

At that moment John felt wholly exonerated. How could anyone doubt, listening to this exposition, that James Earlson went to the market each day half-expecting it to be closed? He *was* Silas Marner.

"It would only have to be a Swiss-cheese letter."

"I know, Mike, but we have a business to run day by day. Learning how the other fellow runs his can be wasteful of our time."

"I'm sorry, then, James. I have to vote yes," Underwood replied. Then he concluded in a low tone, "We're friends."

Earlson smiled quickly. He closed his board notebooks and looked about. His voice was even as he said, "The motion is carried seven to six. I owe it to you all to say I'll resign as chairman and chief executive officer by tomorrow morning. I hope to continue as a director. I do still own a lot of shares of this company."

He paused, smiled conventionally, and concluded, "This may be one of those times when it's best not to say more. I'll be seeing some of you over the next few days."

There ensued the gestures of those who, being embarrassed, became too-pointedly busy, clicking binders and scraping chairs backward to a position where they could either stay or leave unobtrusively. Earlson remained seated, fending off invitations to lunch and politely turning away two or three directors who asked, obtusely, if he had "a minute."

Soon he and Sirovich were alone. Between them lay a litter of pads and pencils under the yellowed pall of the overhead fluorescent lights.

"What will you do?" the younger man asked.

"I would hardly know, ten minutes after losing my job, would I? Once you quit, you're through. The elevator man might not offer to take me, though God knows he only goes up and down."

Earlson's secretary came to the doorway, but he waved her off. "I own a warehouse on five acres near Trenton. An engineering professor I know at Princeton wants to start an electronics business. I just might go partners with him."

John was startled. "You'd take the risk?"

"It was a risk to vote no."

Sirovich looked slowly about the room. Why did he sit here?

What remained to be told? Nothing portentous need be said. James Howard Earlson was not a man to allow his former subordinates to memorialize his thirty-five years with an office party or a dinner—to let his career be summated by graceless words inscribed on a bric-a-brac mantel clock.

"You went to see Mike Underwood. Did he give you any assurances?"

"No. He didn't even offer me a chair."

"But he gave you some notion."

"I saw him because I'd read about his company. He took over from a family in 1934 when the business was almost bankrupt; then he merged into a larger company in Pittsburgh but by some bold stroke ended up as chairman—what our bankers call an 'upstream merger.' But you know all about that, I'm certain. That plant of his in Scranton works two shifts, at least. I'd guess he thinks we should shut down Dayton. None of that matters, does it? If you'd given him a good reason, he'd have voted with you."

"You think I threw it away?"

"Yes."

"Well, I'm not so sure. Without the Paine stock and Westville's and your own, you don't really believe that Carter and that ass of a treasurer would have joined you?"

"Yes, I counted. So did you, once."

"Fair is fair, is that it? Lord, you could ruin this company just for the hell of it."

"I didn't give anything away. I'll be P&W's first professional manager."

"Is this more fancy bullshit? You are a shareholder, a fairly large one, so what's so 'professional' about you?"

"I'm not interested in stock as a weapon, in settling old scores and starting new ones. I see stock as capital, something to be invested, spread around to create jobs and new works. Anyway, as we make more and more acquisitions the present large family blocks will be greatly diluted. It will happen. Is there any other good choice?"

"How can I tell? I don't read the unknown, like you. I'm not even religious."

He rose and walked out. It was the last Sirovich saw of him. James Earlson did not stay the week; and in March he asked that his name not be put forth as a director for the coming year. He had the wit to resign and the grace to depart instantly, not allowing others to celebrate his tenure at the most inappropriate time, on the loss of it.

In the apartment, through the morning and through the luncheon hour, Nancy waited. She'd received no bulletins. John had not promised to send any signal, nor would he have done if asked. She heard the door close, jumped up, and ran to him, searching his eyes for a sign. He looked strained but not dejected.

"He'll resign tomorrow. I'll be elected chairman and chief executive at a special meeting later tomorrow."

John sat heavily, lighting a cigarette, blowing smoke like an exhaust. He looked to her surfeited, even overweight. She came to stand over him directly, in front of the chair, her legs braced apart. He was stirred, and despite his fatigue, or because of it. He recalled a story by Faulkner, or maybe it was Floyd Dell, in which a man stands at the edge of a lynching mob and sees a man hanged and afterward at home looks into the bathroom mirror to find the leer of someone who's just had a woman.

"You look like all get out, John! You feel sorry for him?"

"I'm glad I won. I'm sorry he lost."

"So that's the profound conclusion? Is that the final awful word?"

"Take it easy, Nancy. I'm about to have to run a hundred-and-sixty-million-dollar company."

"A man just can't be a bystander, can he? Even an ordinary man like your Mr. Earlson. Even he is given medals for losing, I suppose."

She was stalking the floor before him. It was hard-heeled turns on an empty stage, Pirandello and cane-bottom chairs.

"Nancy, because it happened fast doesn't make it easy."

"Running a big company is a cinch for you. Why are you so impressed, John? You have the talent to do a lot more than that! I don't have your nice problem."

Why did she choose this moment to make the distinction? Was it significant, this timing, this issue? That first evening in Mobile years and years ago, when he stood sweating in his white uniform, he had told Nancy's father that he'd not read Blackstone, not the law, but he had read history. Judge Bowen had comforted him by saying, "It all helps." But now he wondered. Nancy said he could do more. It seemed perverse, indeed irrelevant. If a man looked upon the uneven advance of persons in the same generation, and if he looked upon the finely graded sophistication of human misery, he might also say, "It all hurts."

By the time he looked up, Nancy was gone. He had not heard the door close. For the first time in months he fell asleep without pills—just as he sat.

He dreamed he heard a girl child sobbing. The sounds were diminishing and that worried him. At Twenty-Fourth Street Elementary School some Gypsy kids would wait for him at day's end behind piles of telephone poles across from the school yard. Usually he lost the fistfights. One time he waited them out by standing inside the alcove under the keystone bearing the chiseled letters BOYS. That was when he had heard the crying on the far side of the playground. He had stepped out and walked around the corner of the building, but no one was on the playground, no one near the slides and swings. Had she run away? He wanted very much to touch her, to tell her there would be other times, other endings. That was when he was about seven or eight years old, a time when people still lived downtown next to banks and hardware stores.

One Saturday he stood outside the rooming house on Arapahoe Street as his mother swept the public sidewalk. Then she placed her palm on the thick black burls of his hair and gave him a nickel to carry to the public bathhouse on Broadway to buy a tiny square of yellow soap and rent a small towel with no nap. On the way he saw an arrow drawn in white chalk on the sidewalk, then another and another. He followed the arrows across Curtis and Champa and Stout and California and Welton. At each street crossing, a long chalk line led to the opposite curbstone, still visible under the treadmarks of passing cars, placed there undoubtedly so that he would not lose heart. But the arrows stopped without punctuation on Glenarm Place, on the sidewalk across from the house where his family came later to live, where the coal miners sat on the porch when laid off in the summertime and the packing-house workers waited the season while sheep fattened on the foothills of the Rockies. Who had drawn the arrows so finely? An intent child, a girl, he was sure. It was no coincidence that she had stopped opposite the place where he grew to manhood, where his mother died and his father still lived. Coincidence was not at all remarkable. It was fated statistically. Numerals must be related so that their addition and subtraction and integration come out right in the end. Of course this must be so, else nothing would be attempted in the world save for the uncalculated courage of the ill-born and ignorant. And in his dream he saw himself standing beyond the last arrow and it became clear how far he'd come from home and how, by coincidence, what he remembered favored him.

Nancy had left him nodding, falling away into sleep. In the evening she would make it right. They would talk when he was ready—ready to restart himself, as it were. Now she headed for Carolyn's apartment, having earlier in the day telephoned her at the office to ask if Bill Harvey would mind a visitor in late afternoon. As it turned out, he was away on a business trip. Carolyn was ecstatic at the news of John's triumph.

"How does he feel?"

"He's tired and more than a little sad—and a little sorry. You'd think he would let himself enjoy it. John refuses to let a single emotion reign unopposed. Those are his words. I don't recall who it was he accused of that."

"He loves you, Nancy. That's a single emotion."

"It's not!" She laughed. "You've found that out already, Carolyn—with Bill."

"Did you tell John about Cassie?"

"No."

"Whenever he learns about it, he'll feel cheated. He's helped a lot of people, but he couldn't help her."

"Mother said Cassie smothered herself with a pillow. I still can't believe it. Surely there's some sort of mechanism in the body that prevents you from stopping your own breathing?"

Carolyn unclasped a handkerchief she'd squeezed tightly in a ball. She smoothed it out. Then she said, "Cassie found it. She finally found a way to shut out all the ugliness."

"Do suicides hate themselves? They must."

"They must hate others. You can't survive your own death."

Two weeks later Nancy heard more from Patricia Fredericks, who appeared in New York to buy clothes for a trip to Europe she was making alone—RJ had declared he would not be "deported." Pat's decision to stay with Nancy was in part at the urging of the Bowens. They regarded Pat as an intrinsic connection to John, this despite the many telephone calls between New York and Mobile. Harold and Willa Ellen began calling daily once told of Nancy's pregnancy, and their elation at its healthy progress was obvious. There remained nonetheless an incomplete agenda between Mobile and New York; and questions trailed the principals like childhood hurts. Blaine had no part in all this, for he was away in a greater sense than the distance measured by land and water. When Nancy heard news of James and the others from Pat, she conceived the melancholy notion that Blaine was not to return to the States until he was an old man; and that long after the death of their parents, he would show up in Mobile a white-haired, attenuated figure with a worn ivory face and minute gestures—the legacy of his long life in Japan.

Could nothing obliterate the standing grievance the older Bowens felt toward John Sirovich? Their stewardship of Nancy when she came home to give birth was now, as she grew large with a new child, less conversable than ever. A phrase here or there would inevitably let slip a darker meaning, and Jane Hobson hinted to Pat that her sister would never forget the "unnatural thing" that had brought Nancy Tuck to the damp bed in the infirmary to stare in the face of incompetent circumstance. Pat thought it extravagant, this stubborn brooding, but to herself explained it as the result of Nancy's being the heroine of a too-privileged and tenured upbringing.

On the morning when John was to drive Pat to LaGuardia, where she would take a flight to New Orleans to meet RJ before sailing to Genoa, Nancy asked about her husband.

"He goes to the office for a couple of hours a day, Nancy, but it's mostly to take naps. He's a lot richer than the hometown folks can guess. RJ's so rich he's glad *not* to make new money."

"I think John wishes he heard from him. He talks of RJ. And Win, of course. Do you miss Win?"

"I miss all the men I loved. About Win: his son and daughter are suing the estate after all these years, over the trust. Can you believe that Win left *trusts* to middle-aged children? I hated hearing that."

At LaGuardia Nancy waited in the car while John and Pat stood on the pavement waiting for the porter to put tags on her luggage. Pat stood on the luggage platform and neatly brought her face up to John's while holding her pillbox hat perilously over one ear. She winked. He picked her up by the waist to lower her and kissed her lips. He was surprised to feel the trembling in her body.

"Save yourself, John."

34

At Paine & Westville all was awhirl. It seemed to observers that nothing would stop the motion of the company once it had been released like a top with a sharp twist. Marvin Toland was ready for almost everything once his company was merged into P&W, so ready that John Sirovich had been obliged to prevent him from combining Cincinnati's order and billing and accounting functions with those in New York. P&W couldn't improve on Learning for Life's own performance, the chairman figured, and he didn't want to give managers in both cities a cause to criticize—to lay off their faults, like professional bettors. He had heard quite enough from Haskins about New York, which the old boy conceived of as a mythical lair. Those comments ceased when the Dayton plant was sold to Bendix through the efforts of Carter, who was now at last earning investment-banking fees from Paine & Westville.

Toland took a genuine interest in John's speculations on the management of companies, which Sirovich termed "working secondhand." Marvin felt free to criticize the parent now that he sat on the board and once asked why P&W's accounting division so clumsily handled cash requests and ledgering. John treated him to a disquisition.

"All companies, Marv, inherit certain tendencies. It's genealogy, really."

"Inherit?" Toland was dumbfounded.

"Listen to this, Marv. I think Mr. Paine hired a clerk, let's say in 1918, a middle-aged woman who then trained three or four younger women who in turn indoctrinated still others, the very ones who sit on the sixth floor of this building doing the same jobs in the inherited pattern, making the same mistakes of course. I think evolution can be carried even further. We call them 'clerks' and they call us 'bosses,' but the truth is that we're really their instruments of evolution—they need us only so they can get on with their jobs."

Toland was incredulous. "That's depressing."

"Take heart, Marv. None of it may be true."

Not that Toland needed a measure of courage. Within six months he proposed acquiring a company specializing in college textbooks in the physical sciences and another that published books for nurses. Thorgersen caught on, too, finding a Minneapolis firm that was the country's third-largest publisher of stenography and typewriting course materials—a poor third to Gregg and Southwestern but a contender in an enormous and long-lived market.

Pursuing their leads and his own, John found himself hour after hour sitting with directors and shareholders, talking, as it were, from zero. Always he assumed an air of rapt attention, even while knowing that of a hundred companies he might hear of, only thirty or so would come to be examined, and of these only about eight would engage in negotiation, with five coming down to the wire and only two crossing. Talking with single owners or partners who had founded or inherited a business and now considered selling to Paine & Westville was for Sirovich an effort requiring a great reserve of patience. Speaking of money, of profits and capital gains, was not enough for such sellers. Sooner or later John found himself explaining why they should sell their stock, how the sale could be good for their employees, and how in the long run it could actually better carry out the goals of the founders of the business. It helped that John generally believed what he declared in these sessions, despite now and then recognizing flaws in his discourse—like a conductor who admires the score even as performers miss a beat, or cheat on a high note.

He was away from New York eight times in April and May. His secretary booked him frequently on night flights so he could be certain of a full day to talk at both ends of his journey. He sat in nearly empty DC-6s writing notes and reading reports until, without realizing he'd stopped doing so, he shook himself awake. Once, on a flight from LaGuardia caught just an hour after leaving a dentist's chair on Fifty-Third Street, he heard a whisper in his ear, "Sir, you are bleeding from the mouth. Are you all right?"

35

The flight from Denver had twice been delayed by rain and mid-July electrical storms over the high plains, and it landed finally not at LaGuardia but Newark. Sirovich entered the apartment just before six A.M. and, as quietly as he could manage, entered one of the two spare bedrooms to avoid waking Nancy, who was suffering insomnia during the seventh month of her pregnancy. The room was musty, little used, closed against the city dust. He opened the windows and took off all his clothes except his shorts. Then he stripped the bed. The pillows looked like hot dough, but he threw himself down. He was lying sweating on the bottom sheet when the sensation came. He took note. It came again. He waited, hoping wanly it was no more than a muscle spasm, the involuntary consequence of letting go, only that. But the assault was uncompromising, neither transient nor self-correcting—no mere scolding reminder of a too-crowded day and accidentally long night. It hit again, a deep ache at the top of his spine, and now he named it.

He called out to Nancy but she could not hear—too many closed doors between them. He reached for the telephone to dial the "business number," which rang only in the kitchen and living room. Thirty seconds—at least that many—passed before she answered in a sleepy voice. He was conscious of his own patience and regarded it as a good sign.

"Nancy! I'm home. In the blue bedroom. Call a doctor. Do it now! Nancy, fast! I'm having a heart attack."

She screamed, and he heard the receiver on her end drop, followed by the scraping sound of her slippers as she ran along the parquet floor in the corridor. She was losing time coming to him, because his own telephone was not available. Its receiver was gripped tightly in his fist, which lay against the rug next to the bed. Sweat poured out of his body and he confused its trickles with the blood in his arteries, which seemed to be draining away.

Nancy returned, this time to wait. Her eyes were wide with fright, the fingers of one hand bunched against her mouth as if to warm them. Under her blue nightgown could be discerned the oval-shaped distention. The baby was carried low. She did not ask useless questions, nor did the doctor when he arrived and drew morphine into a hypodermic needle to plunge it first into the left arm and next into the right, each time asking John to make a fist. It was disappointing to comply so weakly—it was like failing to make an A on a test.

Now, with a fine deliberation, John observed minutely how one motion succeeded another, how the light changed in hue and intensity as he was moved from bed to stretcher, into an ambulance, and next onto a caisson—no, a trolley—and at last to a bed. His body was raised by four pairs of hands as a fifth slipped a hard cold plate directly beneath his back. Overhead a machine whirred and blinked through the hairs of a gunsight. There were diverse penetrations: light from the overhead lamps narrowing his pupils; liquid pulsing into his arms; oxygen cooling his nostrils.

Nancy sat in an armchair next to the bed and soon was asleep, her breath coming huskily through her half-open mouth. She was present but not sentient, and that was good but also not good. She needed the sleep for herself and for the boy. The child was certainly a boy—he must be so. But then she might not awaken in time.

She stood on the railway platform. She wore a dark suit with a round hat pinned to her auburn hair. In one arm she cradled a black fur coat. Her other hand dropped to grasp the hand of a blond-haired boy whose shoes shone with white polish—even the shoestrings had been washed. She had just stepped down from the Pullman car to a metal stool and, laughing, had watched as the boy was caught in the arms of the Negro porter.

But now she was looking down the platform expectantly. The boy was restless and kept peering up at her. Now and then she smiled at John distractedly in what seemed an unnecessary mood of resignation. Then they saw Dobrica Suknović, a huge man bent from digging rooms at the Big Six mine. He held his cap in both hands. John recalled he had himself stood that way when he was five or six or seven, when he posed with others before the casket of a fellow Serb inside the dim nave of the Serbian Orthodox church in Globeville. It had happened many times, the miners dying, and always he blinked when the photographer's flash was triggered.

Dobrica approached at an angle to avoid confronting the boy and Nancy. Oddly, as he had standing with Nancy, John saw himself on the platform, yet he had no recollection of riding on the train with the boy.

"Jovane, tvoj otac je pao na ulici pre jedan sat, baš pošto smo zaokrenuli iz Arapahoe ulice u Sedamnaestu." The boy left his mother to encircle John's knees with his arms. He stared upward with wonderment and fright. Didn't he comprehend? Dobrica had spoken factually. "John," he had said, "your father fell to the pavement an hour ago, just as we turned the corner from Arapahoe Street into Seventeenth."

Dobrica patted the boy's fine yellow hair with a heavy hand. "John," he said finally, turning, "Ilija stayed up all night. He was anxious because it was the first time you brought your wife and son here, all together. Ilija drank almost a quart of whiskey, but it was no more than drinking water from the Toplica before setting out on a long walk. Then it happened. A man in an expensive suit kneeled and felt Ilija's neck. He told the policeman that Ilija was struck by a heart attack, a very big heart attack. He said your father was dead before he reached the street pavement—like a man beheaded.

"It was bad, John, very bad, his dying like that. He did not see death approaching—at least so he could have made a fight. Why is it that a man does not witness his birth and his death? How is that God sees the miraculous beginning as well as the final settlement, while a man is left only in between with his suffering? Even the great poet Njegoš did not claim that a man is able to remember his first hopes and last wishes. Your father was excited, don't you see, because you were coming home with your son. What is the boy's name? Does your wife understand our language? You will tell her in your own way. I will wait with the others."

Later John stood on the porch at Glenarm Place. Nancy and the boy were inside. He was among the old men he'd known always, the Montenegrins, Bosnians, Dalmatians, Herzegovinians, Serbians. They had come to ask him to hold their money as Ilija had always done. They didn't trust banks, or else they refused to concede they were unable to read or write English.

John spoke using *ti*, the familiar form. He said he lived too far away, almost an ocean's length away, and could not hold tens of thousands of dollars. Be practical, please, he asked them. Consider that he might not be available when a man needed part of his savings to travel to Butte or Rock Springs or Raton, or if a man wished to send a thousand dollars to relatives in *Stari Kraj*.

They were not deterred. *"Ti si mlad. Živećeš duže nego mi. Neko mora da vodi računa."* That was what they argued. "You are young and will live longer than we. Somebody has to take account."

And they waited, their gaunt heads held still, their hollow

cheeks made deeper by their thick mustaches. John looked closely at them as though a scene were being reenacted. That was entirely probable. After all, they had been with him on many occasions: in the church, at Serbian lodge outings on Bear Creek, on train platforms in Trinidad or Thermopolis. And of course they used to stand, smoking and laughing at century-old Montenegrin jokes in front of the house in the summertime. Then he remembered.

In Tata's room in the basement was a photograph of the royal occasion in the year 1910, the year that Nikola elevated himself from Prince to King of Montenegro. The King entertained foreign royalty and he reviewed his troops. Every Serb knew who these men were, born combatants though there was but a small standing army and no conscripted soldiers. When shots were heard, they left their houses in the night to form brigades on the karst slopes and on the ridges, each bringing his rifle and powder; and after a day's fighting, their wives and sisters came with food and carried back the wounded and dead out of reach of the Turks.

In the photograph in Tata's room gaunt figures with gray hair and mustaches, the veterans of 1878 strode on the parade ground dragging rifle butts in the dust, the barrels gripped in no recognized military form. On their heads were the pillbox caps colored in memory of Kosovo, black for mourning, red for courage, gold for glory. Tata said one night: "Look at them. They only endure the King. Nikola serves them, not they him. They will die for themselves, not for the government, not for the King. He serves their purpose, which is to celebrate their names before both friends and enemies. Do not forget, John, that enemies remember you. It is a particular way of honoring people."

Then, once more on the porch of the house on Glenarm Place, the old men came up one by one and kissed him on the lips. He wanted to speak to them, to form placating and memorable words. But after all the years of talking, of his talking without doubt even when unsure of his listeners—after all that, it now happened that he could hear but could not speak.

CHAPTER

36

The wind is silent except when it contends, when it is not permitted passage. Then it is heard in rumbles and buffets, as on a shore. The back buildings at the hospital stand on a bluff overlooking the Hudson River, and you can see the notches cut into the Palisades where the upper and lower roadways enter New Jersey. The wind blows from the west, and impeded by the tall buildings it lessens, then swirls against the half-open windows. At the bottom are glass shields canted inward that become baffles and hold the swift air long enough to release it as sound without movement, like a far cannonading.

The nurse says routinely, "It isn't cold but the wind sounds cold." She doesn't bother to examine the windows and notice that the metal framing will not give, not like wood. It makes a difference.

The intern says, "One fifty-eight over ninety-seven—not bad, not bad at all." The interns sometimes remind patients they are doctors despite their still being schooled and despite having to perform routine tasks like inserting needles. Not all of them are expert. The veins inside the elbows wear out, the fluid infiltrating, and one must look elsewhere, on the backs of hands, even on fingers.

"For Christ's sake," the cardiologist complains, "I don't want the portable EKG with only five leads. Get another machine."

"Yes," he admits, "there are extra systoles, one in three or four beats, and the T-waves are not anything to write home about. Still, it's pretty good."

His own doctor will not be satisfied. He wants his patient put in the intensive-care unit where the nurses can watch the screens day and night. Do they agree, the cardiologist and his doctor? As they move out of the room, it seems important that they should agree.

A nurse comes to turn on the tole lamp with the pierced chimney and a shade painted with gold fleurs-de-lis. Routine sounds console because they are unsurprising. In the rooms the telephone bells ring and on the corridor linoleum the wheels of food carts squeak. At five o'clock, the second shift of private nurses moves off to eat dinner. What is not routine is to hear the loudspeaker suddenly call out, "Hear this, Nine East, hear this, Nine East."

After ten o'clock is the declension. Guests depart. Corridor lights dim. The nurses are slower to answer the signals. The night supervisor with blue eyes and a copper cap of hair is a mother superior with keys at her waist, so stealthy is her glide. Ice water dropped into the plastic pitcher makes it milk-white like American china. When the door shuts, the stopper sighs and its tongue latch is hushed by a leather strap stretched from knob to knob.

Morning begins with a dialectic. Arms are bound and unbound, systolic and diastolic. The EKG shows the heart is dichotomous like ovaries and gonads, but it is also singular. In the paired chambers, dark venous blood draws into the auricle and is released bright red from the ventricle, but neither half of the heart can proceed without the other and neither can inherit the whole.

Across the corridor a nurse scolds an old voice, "Why do you complain so about the food? You didn't come here to eat, did you?" That's a point. There are others. A Slovene and a Montenegrin fall into a deep dry well. The Slovene piles stones and says he is working to get out, but the Serb is scornful: this is not a time to work but to die. That's a point, too.

The floor secretary delivers the *Times* and soon is followed by the barber, a small sallow man with bright black eyes who holds the straight razor like a violin bow over the pillows of foam. But the razor is not quite authentic. Its frame grips a Gem blade. Some women in San Juan, the nurse says, carry Gem blades in their hair to cut unfaithful lovers. The barber talks of famous people he has shaved—Mr. Mackay of Postal Telegraph, Henry Luce, Ambassador Douglas with but one eye.

"Mon, you are taller on the floor." The Jamaican orderly confirms that being wounded diminishes a man. He walks alongside into the bathroom where the wind shoots the baffle in the window. White tiles are grouted to fit neatly around the fixtures; a nickeled discus backs the shower handle; porcelain domes with ivory centers can summon help to the toilet or the tub. "Mon, I leave you here. You see the rack? It holds your tube bottles. Now don't you be trying to push it back to bed. Mon, you ring."

The young intern's hair is fragrant from shampoo. "Look at the ceiling." Searching for broken capillaries, she peers into the eyeballs, the sole site where without surgery you can watch the flow of the arteries. It figures. Eyes are two-way mirrors. Someone is said to be waiting in the solarium. Do they still say "solarium"? People leave for Radiology in the basement, the lower depths, and wait in rows, wheelchairs and stretchers lining the hallways. Now and then, names must be lost and some are left abandoned, like consumption patients on porches in Colorado's cold, thin air. People will wait out of fear, or politeness, or out of embarrassment, and will queue up even on the way to labor camps.

"It is ridiculous, don't you know, that they keep alive that three-hundred-pound woman over in Nine East. She's black. She's really dead. They have three tubes going in and three drains coming out. It must cost two hundred dollars a day to keep her, don't you know? More, I bet. Well, I wonder who pays?"

"I don't understand when you say the signs are too good. That is a contradiction, surely?"

"No, I've seen this before. The whole scan is better, the enzyme tests are better, there's a dramatic improvement—and then the patient dies."

"I don't know how to respond to that. What do you want me to do? I could change the dosage in his IVs."

"Put him in intensive care. You've got a spare room. A man died, I heard, this morning."

The fat Puerto Rican nurse says she has twenty-five years in and will return to Ponce, where the nuns taught her as a girl. She says the cathode-ray screen over the bed has a link to the nurses' station, where there are ten screens, two for the private rooms and eight for the ward. She warns the barber to be delicate. Offended, he recounts he has shaved a man with eight leads to the chest, not counting intravenous tubes, and never has cut a wire or a throat.

"You know that radio guy, Long John, the one who talks after midnight to those weird people who telephone in? Well, he was in Harkness, right next door to this man. Late at night, he would walk the halls two or three hours without changing his pace. He wore this terrific cashmere robe all the way to the floor."

"Is this going to take long?"

"No, listen. He scared the hell out of an old woman with high blood pressure and bad kidneys. She thought he was death coming for her."

"So, what happened?"

"Miss Quinn mentions this to Long John, see, and he goes right in to see the old lady. He tells her that death is a handsome young man. He says heaven begins right away, like love at first sight. She kept saying, 'God bless you, Long John, God bless you.' "

"So, what happened?"

"She died the night he left Harkness, that's what."

Everyone is told when visiting hours begin and end, but in intensive care, you can stay all day and all night, although you can't go into the rooms or the ward except with a resident. Relatives sit in a little foyer opposite the two rooms.

CHAPTER

37

"He's been here four days. Nothing. Nothing at all. I've really got to send him back to Harkness. We need the space in here."

"I still don't like it. His body is jumpy and the signs are still too good."

"That's hardly a scientific term, is it, that 'jumpy'? One more night, but then he goes back to Harkness."

"Lord! God! Oh God! I went downstairs to the cafeteria with Carolyn when the loudspeaker went off. It kept announcing, 'Hear this, Nine East, hear this, Nine East.' A nearby intern or resident ran for the elevator. Oh! I just knew it was you. I knew it! I thought my legs wouldn't carry me down the hall. There were so many people around your doorway, I couldn't get in. I was crying and pushing to get in when suddenly they all clapped their hands. Thank God! They all smiled. Your doctor arrived, but it was over. That big Jewish resident with the black beard was still standing over you. A surfboard was on the floor and two things like Ping-Pong paddles with wires attached. And huge needles, like horse syringes, four or five inches. Horrible! But I have to tell you this. You said, 'Father Abraham?' to that resident, and he laughed and told you that you weren't in heaven, and you said you were glad to see him, either way. I told him you try to make everything interesting. I had to tell you because it's a good sign, isn't it? Your doctor said the screen saved you. There were all of a sudden hundreds of beats, wild beats, the blood pumping only to the heart itself, nowhere else. I wanted you to know it's over with. You'll be just fine now. I'm across the hall in the foyer. Ask for me. Ask the resident. I've been here since last night. Can you hear me? I love you. God, I love you. I have to leave now."

The original Zapotecs did not speak of progress. They had their reasons. For them time was a pool, all about and around, rather than a stream, rather than a line from past to future. For them, memories and hopes must have looked alike. Somebody said this about the ancient Zapotecs, but the ones who today live way south in Mexico near the Gulf of Tehuantepec don't seem to recall it.

From the hallway the light throws a weak beam across the bottom rails of the bed, and it falls on the high-topped shoes and cuffs of the corduroy pants. On the corduroy knees, two hands rest ready, hands big as the shanks of a lamb. A young nurse blocks the light, raises the arm too quickly, winds the band, squeezes the bulb to force the mercury up, and lets the heavy liquid ease downward. Then she strips away the band like a blindfold and, piccolo, turns heel on the waxed floor.

"Is that man in there his father? I can't see his face. How is he allowed while you can't go in?"

"He's our driver. They couldn't keep him out. If you saw him, you'd know."

"Why isn't his father here, Nancy? Is he in New York? Surely, you've talked to him about how serious it is."

"His father won't come. He says he won't wait on murder."

"That sounds terrible! There has to be more to it. I think I shouldn't be here either. Are your parents at the hotel?"

"Carolyn went to see them. Please stay, Pat. Stay until we know more."

"Know more? He's already been gone once—and come back.

He must have a notion in that room, sending signals like an SOS at sea. Down the hall the nurses are watching the screen. And that man is in there on guard."

"Stay for my sake, please."

"You belong here, Nancy. I don't. I watched once before, in California. I'll stay in the hotel and you can call me if you want."

Waiting once again. Is waiting inordinate, the thief of time? No, it's not. It can be an occasion of sorts. Pausing, you can confirm the color of the sky; you can give someone a chance to catch up. At Twenty-Fourth Street School they would wait, standing in alphabetical order, until Miss Meriweather gave the signal to march to the cafeteria where they served a brown sauce holding granules of meat poured over unheated white bread. At the junior high, Cole, the boys sat waiting on the gym floor against the wall, their legs spread and ankles grasped in both hands to show soles of feet and naked crotches, where ringworm hides like lichen in stone crevices, while the gym teacher, Mr. Hill, would move, crouching and squinting, along the line. In the Field House at Boulder, the graduates snaked below the platform so that one by one they could, on hearing their names, climb the steps to receive the fake scroll. Only later, well into the summertime, were the real diplomas mailed. By then, the graduates were scattered, gone home to La Junta or Longmont or Durango, others gone so far east their absence wasn't notable.

On the way to Panama from the South Pacific islands, the ship followed the Mexican coastline. A storm blew up off Puerto Angel and the ship ran for shelter into the Gulf of Tehuantepec. There, a whirlwind had pushed waves onto the rocks in great heaves, leaving cold edgy water in the narrow defiles of the shore. Through the wet heavy air they saw the skiffs and trawlers of fishermen drawn around a stricken British cargo ship with its keel caught on an underwater shelf. It was a tableau of the written law of the sea: once the captain gives up his command, those waiting can plunder at will. On *Zenith,* they saw the cargo ship's blinker lights. It was like peering through bars at a dim and desperate message. As the fishermen waited on the captain's resignation to the rule of the deep, a shuttered light requested rations and medicines. The supply officer and the medical officer from *Zenith* went down the Jacob's ladder, each minding to hold the side ropes in alternation, handgrips and footfalls opposite, else a man might twist in the wind.

After they had moved on, no one later found out whether the cargo ship was saved, whether the jackals had been outwaited by their prey. No one said. It was dangerous, that bay. Any place you seek, if it has use of you, can become your captor. It's how holy cities are founded and martyrs made. But the Muslims don't mind because for them whatever happens is destiny, so none can be eternally wronged. It is not that easy for us. We are not tolerant of death and will not oblige. Yet you have to recognize there are times when it is just right, when doubt is overtaken by purpose. Alongside the steel bulkhead you line up on the main deck as the ship treads the shallow water, the screws turning slowly and holding the hull in place. Behind, the gun batteries on the battle line stop firing, but as the planes crossweave, the black blossoms still burst on shore. And on the deck you wait, sure at last that you are going in.